THE COVERT-ONE SERIES

THE JANSON SERIES

ALSO BY ROBERT LUDLUM

ROBERT LUDLUM'S

THE

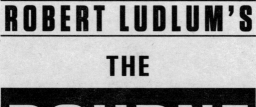

BRIAN FREEMAN

G. P. PUTNAM'S SONS
NEW YORK

PUTNAM
— EST. 1838 —

G. P. PUTNAM'S SONS
Publishers Since 1838
An imprint of Penguin Random House LLC
penguinrandomhouse.com

The Library of Congress has catalogued the G. P. Putnam's Sons
hardcover edition, as follows:

Names: Freeman, Brian, author.
Title: Robert Ludlum's The Bourne Evolution / Brian Freeman.
Description: U.S. edition. | New York: G. P. Putnam's Sons, 2020. |
Identifiers: LCCN 2020018114 (print) | LCCN 2020018115 (ebook) |
ISBN 9780525542599 (hardcover) | ISBN 9780525542605 (ebook)
Subjects: GSAFD: Mystery fiction. | Suspense fiction.
Classification: LCC PS3606.R4454 R63 2020 (print) |
LCC PS3606.R4454 (ebook) | DDC 813/.6—dc23
LC record available at https://lccn.loc.gov/2020018114
LC ebook record available at https://lccn.loc.gov/2020018115

First G. P. Putnam's Sons hardcover edition / July 2020
First G. P. Putnam's Sons premium edition / May 2021
First G. P. Putnam's Sons international mass-market edition / May 2021
G. P. Putnam's Sons international mass-market edition ISBN: 9780593332665

Printed in the United States of America
1 3 5 7 9 10 8 6 4 2

ROBERT LUDLUM'S
THE BOURNE EVOLUTION

MYSTERY HANGS OVER LAS VEGAS SHOOTING

October 9, 2019
WASHINGTON (AP)

Nearly one year after sixty-six people were killed in the nation's worst mass shooting incident, the FBI announced last week that it had concluded its investigation into the tragedy. However, the agency's report, which offers no clues about the motive of the killer, seems to leave the public with more questions than answers.

On November 3, 2018, Charles Hackman opened fire from a room on the nineteenth floor of the Lucky Nickel hotel in downtown Las Vegas. Targeting a crowd of more than five thousand men, women, and children gathered for an antique car show, Hackman killed or wounded dozens of people during an eighteen-minute shooting spree before being shot and killed by police.

Hackman, a fifty-four-year-old actuary from Summerlin, Nevada, had no prior criminal record and no history of mental illness or substance abuse. Despite what the FBI called an exhaustive investigation of Hackman's personal background and behavior, the agency was unable to identify any political, ethnic, or religious motive behind the shooting. The agency said it found no evidence that Hackman had been a member of any extremist organization and concluded that he acted alone.

But with no explanation for what caused a seemingly unremarkable man to commit the nation's worst act of mass murder, the FBI's report has prompted a flood of online conspiracy theories and accusations that the agency is covering up what really happened. Despite attempts by social media platforms to limit the spread of "fake news," millions of people have now read and shared articles suggesting without evidence that Hackman was either a jihadist recruit or the victim of a government frame-up.

Even the number of victims in the tragedy has become a subject of controversy. While the official death toll was set at sixty-six in the days following the incident, the hashtag #66or67 has begun trending this week, reflecting allegations from anonymous sources in the government that a missing victim was not counted in the final total and may have been the first person targeted in the shooting. . . .

@abbeylaurent_ 4/9/20 4:12pm

Live-tweeting: Ready for Congresswoman Sofia Ortiz to speak on tech privacy abuse in New York's Washington Square Park. Huge crowd, lots of chanting, lots of signs. Intersections blocked, traffic at a standstill.

@abbeylaurent_ 4/9/20 4:28pm

Still waiting. No sign of her yet.

@abbeylaurent_ 4/9/20 4:29pm

Want more on Ortiz? Check out my full profile of the first-term New York congresswoman in the online magazine The Fort. tinyurl.com /yxl8mpdo

@abbeylaurent_ 4/9/20 4:39pm

Here she is. Cheers are deafening. Ortiz wasting no time working up the crowd. "We're here to tell Big Tech that WE own our personal data, not them, and we're taking it back!"

@abbeylaurent_ 4/9/20 4:43pm

Ortiz confirming what my source told me last week. She's accusing tech companies of covering up a massive data hack. Source unknown, could be foreign. "Affecting nearly every American."

@abbeylaurent_ 4/9/20 4:46pm

Ortiz now calling for expansive new federal regulations and oversight. "Biggest change to privacy laws in a generation." Says tech giants have proven they can't be trusted.

@abbeylaurent_ 4/9/20 4:47pm

Crowd really getting riled up. People spilling into the street, some confrontations with cops. Ortiz is asking for peaceful protest—WAIT—OMG!!!!!!!

@abbeylaurent_ 4/9/20 4:48pm

ORTIZ SHOT!!!!!! CONGRESSWOMAN ORTIZ HAS BEEN SHOT!!!!!

@abbeylaurent_ 4/9/20 4:50pm

Ortiz is down twenty feet away from me. Blood everywhere. It's pandemonium. Crowd charging the stage. MORE GUNFIRE! GUNFIRE IN THE CROWD!

@abbeylaurent_ 4/9/20 4:52pm

Have to move. Not safe here.

@abbeylaurent_ 4/9/20 5:21pm

Riot!! Guns, bottles, knives being used as weapons. I can see two bodies in the street and eight cars on fire. Looting, too, numerous store windows broken.

@abbeylaurent_ 4/9/20 5:32pm

STAY AWAY from the Washington Square area.

@abbeylaurent_ 4/9/20 5:41pm

Anarchists leading the violence, masks over their faces. Not sure where they came from. Police nowhere close to getting this under control. Have to move again.

@abbeylaurent_ 4/9/20 5:56pm

Police rounding up everyone on the street. Mass arrests, including yours truly. Anyone got bail?

@abbeylaurent_ 4/10/20 7:05am

Okay, I'm out. Got my phone back. Update: Five confirmed dead from last night's riot, area still locked down. Congresswoman Sofia Ortiz killed from a shot to the throat by a sniper. FBI calling it an assassination.

@abbeylaurent_ 4/10/20 8:35am
My source telling me there is a suspect in the Ortiz assassination. NOT in custody, location unknown, armed and dangerous.

@abbeylaurent_ 4/10/20 8:37am
Suspect is ex-government operative gone rogue, believed to be part of a radical anarchist group. No identity yet, just the code name Cain.

@abbeylaurent_ 4/10/20 8:38am
Who is Cain?

PART ONE

ONE

THE man in black lifted his binoculars and studied the rain-swept boardwalk. The benches that stretched along Dufferin Terrace, on the cliffside looming over the lower town and the St. Lawrence River, were empty. His contact hadn't arrived yet, but that was to be expected. It was only nine-fifteen, and he'd told her to be on the boardwalk at ten o'clock. He wanted the extra time to survey the meeting ground and see if he was walking into a trap.

He'd left a car behind near the port and then taken the funicular to the Haute-Ville. Now he stood like an invisible man in the darkness, behind a stone wall on the hill of the Citadel. Cold rain sheeted from the sky, blurring the nighttime lights of Quebec City. A fierce wind rattled the winter skeletons of the trees, drowning out the other sounds with its moan. In front of him, the Château Frontenac hotel rose like a medieval castle. At the base of the cliff, the lower town's ribbon of lights glittered beside the great dark stain of the river. Along the boardwalk, a row of antique cannons aimed their muzzles out over the water, as if anticipating the return of American invaders.

The cannons weren't wrong.

The Americans were here somewhere. Looking for him. *Where are you hiding?*

He waited, patient and motionless, not reacting to the cold or the wetness of his clothes or the bite of the wind. He'd trained himself to be immune to such things. He used the binoculars to examine every window, every doorway, every shadow or corner where someone could hide. Even the best operatives usually made mistakes. The flicker of a match as a cigarette was lit. The swish of a curtain. A footprint in the mud. When he'd completed his survey, he repeated it two more times, and he still saw nothing to alarm him.

He was starting to feel safe.

Then someone screamed.

He tensed, but this was a happy scream, mixed with laughter. A young couple, drenched by the downpour, ran hand in hand along the glistening boardwalk below him. They took shelter under one of the canopies next to the cliff, where they began kissing passionately. He zoomed in on their faces under the gazebo lights. Both were in their twenties, both attractive. The woman had pink-and-blond hair that was pasted over her face, and she had the lean, strong build of a runner, wearing skintight leggings. The man with her was several inches taller and had black hair and a long, deep scar on his cheek.

He tried to decide who they were.

Two harmless tourists.

Or two killers.

The truth was usually in the eyes. He watched carefully to see if either of them broke cover long enough to throw a surreptitious glance at their surroundings, but if this was a performance for his benefit, they stayed in character. When they'd kissed for a while, they walked back into the rain. Each looked at the other with a hungry grin, the way lovers would. They headed north toward the grand hotel.

That was when he saw his contact arrive on the boardwalk. She was early. She walked down the steps from Governor's Park, seemingly not bothered by the rain that pummeled her. A large leather satchel purse hung from her shoulder. She reached the walkway just as the young couple passed in front of her, and he worried that the timing was too perfect. He could picture it all happening. A pistol in the hand of the man with the scar. One shot, no chance to run, his contact collapsing with a bullet in her throat. He yanked his own gun into his hand and prepared to dive down the Citadel slope, even though he was too far away to stop what was about to happen.

Except he was wrong.

The young couple waved at the woman. She smiled back. They were simply three strangers enjoying the romance of the rain. There was no ambush, no gunfire. He watched the couple continue on their way to the Château Frontenac, and his contact crossed the boardwalk to the gazebo, where he'd told her to wait. She grabbed her phone from her purse and checked the time. Then she stared at the hillside in his direction with her hands on her hips. He knew she couldn't see him, but she had the look of someone who could feel that she was being watched.

He examined her closely through the binoculars.

The journalist named Abbey Laurent was a couple of years past thirty, medium height and a little skinny. She wore a waist-length jean jacket over a white T-shirt, forest-green cargo pants, and black calf boots. Her hair was colored to a deep dark red, falling in wet strands to her shoulders and across her forehead in spiky bangs. She wore lipstick that was as dark red as her hair, and her mouth was folded into a curious smirk, as if she were enjoying the excitement of what she was doing. Her eyes were dark, and they were smart eyes that didn't miss a thing.

She pushed some of the buttons on her phone. A second later, his own phone buzzed. She'd sent him a text.

I'm here, mystery man.

He allowed himself a tight smile. He liked this woman. But liking and trusting were two different things.

He let her wait without replying to her message, and meanwhile, he did another thorough check of the area through the binoculars. They were alone. The young couple on the boardwalk had long since disappeared. He saw no sign that the woman was being watched, but even so, he let their meeting time come and go. Ten o'clock. Ten-fifteen. Ten-thirty. She sent more texts, which grew annoyed and impatient as time wore on.

> Hey, where are you?
> You're late.
> I'm here getting soaked and you don't show up?
> Seriously? I'm not going to wait forever.

And she didn't. At ten-forty, he watched her lips form a loud swear word. She stamped out of the gazebo into the rain, past the old cannons and into the wet grass of the park beside the Château Frontenac. When she disappeared from view, he sprang into action. He slipped his gun into his jacket pocket and hurried to the base of the Citadel hill, where Quebec City's old stone buildings faced each other across narrow, hilly streets. He jogged down Rue des Grisons for one block and waited in the doorway of a small guest hotel, where he couldn't be seen.

At the end of the street, the redheaded journalist crossed the intersection. She walked with purpose, not looking back, not concerned with being followed. He ran to the next corner and saw her hike past the art conservatory into the cobblestoned paths of the Parc du Cavalier-du-Moulin. He accelerated, falling in behind her, closing the distance between them. She was half a block away, unaware of his presence.

This was how he'd been trained. Always let the first meeting go by. Let anyone who is watching assume it's a bust, and then intercept the contact afterward for the real meeting.

But the ones who had trained him were also the ones who were looking for him now.

They knew his every move.

As he climbed toward the park where Abbey Laurent had disappeared, he saw that the streetlight ahead of him was broken. His instincts screamed a warning, but he was too late to retreat. A man appeared from the shadows in front of him. It was the tall man with the scar from the boardwalk, and the man held a Beretta with a suppressor on the barrel, aimed across the twenty feet between them.

He didn't have time to pull his own gun. With a grunt of exertion, he shunted sideways and dove to the wet ground, rolling until he slammed against the brick wall of the nearest building. The low pop of the Beretta and the splash of bullets on the asphalt chased him. He pushed off his knees and ran, bent over, then threw himself behind a blue panel van parked on the sidewalk.

The van provided cover as he drew his pistol. The rain poured over his face and drained loudly through the gutters, making a flood down the street. There was no light. He couldn't hear or see. Slowly, cautiously, he crept around the rear of the van. As he spun into the street, he pulled the trigger three times in quick succession. The man with the scar was there. One of the bullets tore into the man's gun arm, causing him to fire back wildly.

Bleeding, the would-be assassin lurched away behind the other side of the van.

He only had a few seconds, and he knew what he had to do.

Get away! Get to the car!

Quebec had been a mistake. The meeting with Abbey Laurent had been a trap from the beginning.

He backed away with his gun trained on the van. There was an alley behind him where he could run. He blinked, trying to clear rain from his eyes. The wind tunneling between the buildings roared in his head. His senses were focused on the van as he waited for the man with the scar to unleash another round of gunfire. Only at the last second did a breath of motion alert him to a deadly new threat behind him.

The young woman with the pink-and-blond hair pounced from the alley. She swung a long-bladed knife toward his neck, and he jerked back in time to avoid having his carotid artery cut open. He lashed out with one leg, kicking her in the stomach, driving her backward. She shook off the blow, bared her teeth, and charged again, leading with the knife aimed at his throat. He had a split second to grab her wrist and twist hard. The bone broke; the knife fell to the street. Before he could bring his gun around and fire, she uncoiled like a spring, driving her skull into the base of his chin with a loud crack. His head snapped back, and he tasted blood in his mouth. He let go of her, momentarily dizzy.

More pops, like muffled fireworks, exploded around him as the man with the scar leaped from cover and fired again with his injured arm. One shot shattered a window in the stone building on the other side of the street; another ricocheted off the sidewalk. He grabbed the young woman by her broken wrist and yanked her in front of him. She screamed in pain, but the scream cut off as the next bullet, which otherwise would have landed in the middle of his chest, burned into the back of the woman's head.

The man who'd been kissing her on the boardwalk a few minutes ago had just killed her.

Still holding on to the woman, who was deadweight, he raised his own gun and fired a precise shot that struck the man with the scar under his chin. A kill shot directly through the throat.

Just like Sofia Ortiz.

He stood there, the pungent smell of smoke filling his nose. The dead woman dangled at the end of his arm like a grotesque doll, and he lowered her body to the wet street. Her eyes were open and fixed, staring at him. Blood pooled behind her head, but the rain quickly washed it away into the rivers that flowed along the curb.

Get away! Get to the car!

The jaws of the trap were springing shut.

He saw the shimmer of the boardwalk lights at the east end of the street. He headed that way, staying close to the stone walls. At the next corner, he surveyed the cross street and assessed the trees scattered like soldiers through Governor's Park. He wasn't alone. He felt it. But he couldn't see where the threat was. He measured out his breaths one by one, then burst from cover, sprinted across the street, and dove into the muddy grass of the park.

Bullets spat at him from two directions. As he slithered through the grass, he spotted one man on the steps of a guest hotel behind him, another in the darkness of a parking tunnel under the Château Frontenac. He got up, zigzagged as the cross fire zeroed in on him, then swiveled and fired four shots into the blackness of the tunnel. The assassin in the parking garage collapsed, but the man on the hotel steps continued to fire. When a hot spike burned in his upper chest, he knew he'd been hit. He dragged himself to the shelter of an ash tree and ripped open the flap of his shirt to see the bloody ring of the bullet hole.

More fire rained down from the man on the steps. He waited until there was a pause as the man emptied his magazine, and at that moment, he broke from cover and fired back, six more shots.

The other shooter rolled down the hotel steps to the street.

There was no time to tend to his wound. More men would be here soon. He swapped his gun to his left hand and applied pressure to his chest. He was numb, but that wouldn't last long. Marching through the park, head down, he passed the Château Frontenac and hurried down the steps to the boardwalk. Lights gleamed on the far shore of the river. The rain and wind assaulted the cliffside. He limped to the far side of the boardwalk and clung to the metal railing to steady himself. The rock of the cliff face went down more than one hundred and fifty feet below him, with a nest of bare trees climbing toward him from the old town. He closed his eyes, feeling faint, knowing he was losing blood quickly.

"*Jason Bourne.*"

The words hissed at him from a few feet away.

And then another word. "*Traitor.*"

His eyes shot open. He lifted his gun with a jolt of pain. He wasn't alone; he'd missed someone hiding in the shadows. A man in a gray trench coat and fedora stood near the gazebo, and he had a gun, too, pointed at him through the downpour. The other man was older by fifteen years, shorter than Bourne but as tough and weathered as a husk dried in the sun. He knew Nash Rollins well. In another life, he would have called him a friend, but not anymore.

Not since Las Vegas.

And now this man was here to kill him. Or be killed. Those were the only two options.

Bourne had kept count. There was one cartridge left in the magazine of his gun, but one was all he needed to kill an old friend. Pull the trigger. Watch him die. His brain weighed his options and assessed his strategy. His heart debated whether he could really kill the man in front of him.

Rollins had obviously wanted to be here personally for the takedown. That was a mistake. He hadn't been in the field in years. Showdowns were about concentration, about not being distracted, and that was hard to do when your skills were rusty. As the staredown continued between them, Bourne waited for the older man to give him an opening, because he knew it would come. A surge of wind whipped into the man's body and made him flinch. The lapse in his attention lasted barely longer than a blink, but that was enough.

Bourne fired. He shot into the flesh of Rollins's thigh, causing the man's leg to collapse under him. His friend toppled, unleashing a bitter wail of pain, but in another second, the old man would realize he was still alive, and he wouldn't bother to wonder why he'd been spared. He would simply raise his own gun and fire back.

With nowhere to run, Bourne dropped his empty gun, took hold of the boardwalk railing with both hands, and threw himself over the cliff's edge. The agony of his chest coursed through his body. Gravity grabbed hold of him, but he hovered in the air for a microsecond like a skeet target. His old friend, writhing on the ground, found enough strength to bring up his gun and fire. One shot.

One shot that grazed a burning, bloody path across his skull.

Jason Bourne fell into darkness. He was a meteor streaking through a cold universe, a tiny fragment lost in empty space. The ground far below him was like an alien planet, new and unexplored, roaring toward him at what felt like light speed. At the moment of impact, everything went black.

THE Canadian ambulance crew wanted to take Nash Rollins to the hospital, but he refused to leave the boardwalk. He wasn't going anywhere until they'd found the man on the cliff. He leaned on a cane that one of the paramedics had given him and bit his tongue to try to take his mind off the pain that pulsed through his leg.

Below him, the lights of searchers bobbed in the cobblestoned streets of the Basse-Ville, hunting for the wounded American killer. Rollins knew he'd hit him as he fell. He'd seen the red cloud spray from his head. It seemed impossible to think the man had survived the gunshot and the fall, but so far they'd found no body, only a blood trail that came to a sudden stop on the Rue du Petit-Champlain. The man had simply disappeared.

Bourne was a ghost. Impossible to kill.

But then, that was what they'd trained him to be.

Rollins felt no guilt about what he'd done. He'd brought his team to do a job, and the job wasn't finished. His prior relationship with the man didn't matter at all. The fact that the man had spared his life by shooting him in the leg, not the head or the chest, also didn't matter. The only thing that was important was to *stop him!*

He took his phone out of his pocket. When he dialed, a woman answered on the other end with a single word.

"Treadstone."

"Go secure," Rollins requested.

"You're secure," she replied after a moment of dead air on the line. "What's the situation in Quebec? Were you correct? Is it Cain?"

"Yes, it's him. Just like I told you."

"Has he been neutralized?"

"No, it seems that he's still alive."

"That's unfortunate," the woman lectured him coldly.

"You assured us that you'd deal with this. Director Shaw is concerned. If Bourne is linked to the assassination in New York, it puts the whole Treadstone resurrection in jeopardy."

Rollins grimaced as pain stabbed through his leg again. The pain was going to make him collapse soon, but he didn't care. "Don't worry, tell Shaw that I'll find Bourne. He's wounded, and he can't go far. I'll find him, and I'll kill him myself."

TWO

ATE-NIGHT drinkers packed the pub on Rue Sainte-Angèle at one in the morning. Abbey Laurent sat at the bar in the semidarkness, under a low ceiling studded with rough-hewn beams. Her clothes and her mahogany-colored hair were still damp, making her shiver. Her fingers tapped on the keyboard of her laptop, in a tempo greased by the rhythm of the jazz quartet playing a few feet away. She owed her editor, Jacques, three thousand words for the next online edition of *The Fort*. The article was due first thing in the morning, but she'd waited until now to write it, hoping that the mystery man would give her a story.

Instead, he'd left her standing alone in the rain.

Every few sentences, she took a swig from the bottle of beer in front of her. She found it hard to concentrate on her work. Her problem wasn't the noise or the crowd; she thrived on those things. She could bang out a story in the middle of the World Cup final. No, she kept thinking about the man who'd stood her up.

Who was he? *Where* was he?

Why had he gone through an elaborate series of secret contacts to meet with her, only to not show up?

Abbey grabbed her phone and did what she'd already done half a dozen times since she got to the bar. She scrolled back to the very first contact he'd made with her, one week ago, three days after the murder of Sofia Ortiz in New York. It was a text message sent from an unknown phone number.

> We need to meet. I can help you get the answers
> you want.

As a journalist, she received cold calls like that all the time. Most were hoaxes, sent by conspiracy nuts or men who wanted to meet the woman they'd seen in the photograph next to her byline. But something about this man was different. Intriguing. He knew things. He provided her with details about the shooting that the police and FBI had never released. When she checked it out, she discovered that everything he'd said was true.

Her reporter's radar was pinging.

But Jacques had told her that the meeting was too dangerous. Her editor was nervous by nature, and he was still hyperventilating about the Ortiz assassination and the Washington Square riot. However, Abbey had never been one to let fear stop her from doing anything.

Okay, she'd written back to the mystery man. *Your place or mine?*

They'd agreed on her place. Quebec City in three days.

She didn't know his name, or what he looked like, or anything about who he was. He was obsessive about protecting his anonymity and cautious to the point of paranoia. He'd sent her elaborate instructions for making sure she wasn't followed, and he'd given her an exchange of code phrases so they would know each other in person, like they were spies in some Cold War rendezvous.

She'd say: *What do you like most about Quebec?*

He'd reply: *Those wonderful little maple candies.*

And after all that, he'd been a no-show. It didn't make sense. She checked her messages again, hoping he'd sent her a text to explain, but all she saw were the unanswered texts she'd sent him from the boardwalk.

Abbey sighed with defeat, because she wasn't getting anything done tonight. Jacques would have to wait for the story. She shut down her laptop and turned around at the bar to finish her beer and listen to the music. The boys in the band all waved to her. This was her place, her neighborhood. Her office at *The Fort* was four blocks away, and her studio apartment was six blocks away. She traveled constantly, but when she was home, she typically wrote her stories here at the bar until closing time. As a writer, she made almost no money, but the bartender slipped her the occasional drink for free, and in return, she threw a mention of the bar into the magazine whenever she could.

The bar door opened, letting in cold damp air. A few

people left; a few others pushed their way inside. She examined the faces of the new arrivals. As comfortable as she always felt here, tonight she had an odd sense of unease. It was the same sensation she'd had on the boardwalk, that multiple sets of eyes were watching her. This was more than the usual attention she got from guys looking for a hookup. No one in the bar looked suspicious, but the feeling didn't go away, and her lips pushed into a frown.

She felt paranoid. Just like the mystery man.

Where are you?

Even the mellow jazz music didn't calm her nerves. The bassist was a slinky Spanish woman named Emilia who had magic fingers. On most nights, Abbey loved listening to her play. The trouble was, when she saw her face now, it wasn't Emilia she saw. It was Sofia Ortiz in Washington Square Park. Her memory replayed that awful moment over and over, when the woman's neck exploded in a shower of blood, when she pitched backward to the stage, when the screaming began, when the crowd surged out of control. An assassin had *murdered* a congresswoman right in front of her.

Her source said the killer was a former U.S. intelligence agent code-named Cain.

Who was Cain?

She hadn't told Jacques the truth about how bad the night had been. There was blood on her shirt after it happened; that was how close she'd been to Ortiz. Then, in the riot that followed, she'd nearly been killed herself. There was gunfire everywhere, craziness, madness! She'd seen one of the anarchists aiming a pistol *at her*, and she'd only survived because someone in the crowd had run into her at that exact moment and they'd both tumbled to the ground. By the time she got up, the shooter had disappeared, but she could still remember his black hood and the gun pointed at her head.

With her hand trembling slightly, Abbey finished her beer. She got up from the bar, but at that moment, over the noise of the band and the crowd, she picked out two words from someone's conversation.

"*Château Frontenac.*"

And then two other words. "*Dead. Shot.*"

Abbey tried to isolate the conversation. *Who was it?* She grabbed her laptop and shoved it in her bag. As she waded into the crowd, her ears pricked up to eavesdrop on what everyone was saying. She picked up snippets of talk about sports and drugs and drinks and sex, but nothing about the hotel castle on the cliff. Nothing about murder. And yet she knew, *she knew*, that something had happened.

And she knew that in some way it was connected to her.

"*Police everywhere.*"

There! Two burly young men, one black, one white, both in Nordiques jerseys, were squeezed into a corner booth behind the band. Their voices carried over the crowd. She shoved her way through the bar and bent over their table. A dim sconce light cast shadows on their faces.

"Excuse me."

The two men stopped their conversation and sized her

up from behind their beers. They liked what they saw. "What's up, baby doll?" one of them said.

"Did I hear you say that something happened at Château Frontenac?"

"Oh, yeah," the white Nordiques fan replied. "I was just up there. Whole area's shut down."

"What's going on?"

"Dunno. I heard people saying there were bodies in the street. Some kind of shooting. Hey, why don't you sit down, and we can—"

But Abbey was already gone.

She threaded through the mass of people toward the bar door. She needed to get back to Château Frontenac *right now* and find out what had happened.

When she got outside, the chill hit her wet clothes, and she shivered again. The rain had stopped, but the pavement was still damp. Rue Sainte-Angèle climbed sharply in the darkness, and she began to head up the street. As she did, a man crossed the road to intercept her. He'd obviously been waiting for her.

"Mademoiselle Laurent?"

She glanced nervously both ways. She was conscious of the fact that the two of them were alone on the empty street. Her hand covered the latch on her bag, in case she needed to reach for the Taser she kept inside. Her reporting often took her to uncomfortable places, and she'd learned to be prepared for anything.

The man gave her a bland smile and repeated his question. "You *are* Abbey Laurent, aren't you? The reporter?"

"What's this about? Who are you?"

"We had a meeting. I apologize for being late."

"*You?*" She reacted with surprise. "You're the mystery man?"

"That's right."

"Well, where the hell were you?"

"I'm sorry. I was detained. It was unavoidable."

Abbey relaxed a little, but she studied him with a faint disappointment. He wasn't what she'd expected. He was tall and solidly built, with thinning blond hair and gold-rimmed glasses that pinched the bridge of his nose. He wore a brown raincoat over a neat, expensive beige suit and tie. He looked like a middle-aged accountant, not a spy, and she'd pictured her intriguing mystery man as more Chris Pine than Jonah Hill.

"I'm glad I was able to find you," he added in a voice that was almost sugary in its politeness. "Obviously, I went through a lot of trouble to meet you."

"How *did* you find me?"

"Everyone leaves a footprint online, Ms. Laurent. Routines are easy to track. We know a lot about you. We've followed your reporting for some time."

"We?"

"I'm a member of an influential group. You said you wanted a story, didn't you? They're part of the story." He gave her another of his bland smiles and waved toward the end of the street. "Shall we take a walk?"

"Yes, okay."

The two of them headed side by side to the intersection where Rue Sainte-Angèle met Rue Saint-Jean. They walked down the middle of the cobblestoned street past trendy shops and restaurants that were closed for the night. There was no traffic and no other pedestrians. Her mystery man kept his hands in the pockets of his raincoat, and Abbey noticed that he never looked directly at her. However, his eyes moved constantly, examining the shadows around them.

"Looking for someone?" she asked.

"Just being careful."

"Are you expecting trouble?"

"I always expect trouble."

"I heard there was an incident near Château Frontenac," she said. "People were killed."

"Yes."

"Is that why you were late?"

"Yes."

"Was this because of our meeting? Was I in danger?"

"There were dangerous men near the hotel," the man replied, "but they were looking for me, not you. They were hoping you would lead them to me."

"And did you kill them?"

This time he stopped and looked at her. She saw that he had icy blue eyes behind his gold-rimmed glasses. "Is that what you think I am? A killer?"

"I don't know what you are. I don't even know your name."

"Names are unimportant."

"Except you know my name," Abbey said.

"True enough, Ms. Laurent."

They reached the old stone wall at Artillery Park, part

of the city's fortifications that had been built three hundred years earlier when the British and French were battling for the land. Without asking, the man led her down the stairs into the park, and then he stopped near the grassy hill under the wall. He lit a cigarette and blew smoke into the air. He smiled at her again, and she decided that she didn't like his smile. The location where they'd stopped was hidden from the view of other buildings in the area. Alarm bells went off in her head.

"What does this have to do with the murder of Congresswoman Ortiz?" she demanded impatiently. "You said you'd help me get answers. I want to know why she was killed. And who shot her."

He held his cigarette delicately between two fingers. "That was a terrible night."

"Yes, it was."

"You were near the congresswoman when she was shot, weren't you?"

"That's right. I was. Do you know who did it?

"The American government thinks it was Cain," he replied.

"Who is Cain?" Abbey asked. Then she added with an undercurrent of horror, "Is it you? Did you kill Sofia Ortiz?"

The question seemed to amuse him. "Me? Hardly. I'm not in his league. Cain is a ghost. A legend. I'm simply flesh and blood."

She realized he was playing with her. Toying with her, the way a cat plays with a mouse before it bares its claws. This whole meeting felt *off*. He'd promised her a story, and now he was dancing around all of her questions. The way he looked, the way he talked, the way he acted, none of it felt like the same man who'd texted her.

And then she remembered.

She hadn't used the code phrase the mystery man had given her. She'd never confirmed that *he* was the man she was supposed to meet.

Abbey summoned a casual smile to her face. "So what do you like most about Quebec?"

He stared at her, his brow creased with puzzlement. "I'm sorry?"

"We ask that of all the tourists. Canadians are very polite, you know. What do you like most about Quebec? I mean, I know there's so much."

She needed to hear him say the words. *Those wonderful little maple candies.* She held her breath, waiting.

Say it!

He threw his cigarette to the ground and crushed it under his foot. He took off his gold-rimmed glasses, wiped them carefully with a handkerchief from his suit pocket, and repositioned them on his face. His hands returned to the deep pockets of his raincoat. "I guess the lower town," he said. "So picturesque."

She tried to stay calm and not give anything away. She reminded herself to keep smiling and to keep the terror she felt off her face. *It wasn't him.* This wasn't her mystery man. He was a stranger, and more than that, she knew he was a killer.

He was here to kill *her.*

"I could use a cigarette, too," Abbey said, unlatching her satchel purse so she could reach inside.

But he wasn't fooled at all.

Her hand dove inside her purse, her fingers clawing for the plastic grip of the Taser. As she drew it out, the man with the gold-rimmed glasses slipped his own hand out of his raincoat pocket. He held a black pistol with a long barrel, and his blue eyes had the sharp gaze of a hawk. Abbey squeezed her eyes shut and yanked the trigger, and the wires of the Taser ejected, filling the man's body with fifty thousand volts. His arm lurched; he fired his gun into the air, making her scream. She pulled the trigger again, delivering more electric shocks. He collapsed to the ground, wriggling and jerking in fits, the gun spilling from his hand.

Abbey threw the Taser down.

She ran blindly from the park, making a zigzag path around dark corners to get away, losing herself in the deserted old streets of the city.

THREE

JASON didn't know if he was remembering or dreaming.

Bits and pieces of a life buzzed through his head like the clickety-clack of film in an old projector. He saw children lined up in formation, a dozen boys in gray uniforms being scolded by a stern old man who marked all of their demerits on a clipboard. He saw a gravestone at his feet, blue marble, with two names that were blurred by a kind of fog. He could only read the year of their deaths: 2001. He heard explosions that made him cover his ears. Gunfire. He heard words coming out of his mouth in foreign languages. He saw places that were unfamiliar to him, and yet he knew he'd been to all of them. Cities around the world. Streets and monuments at night. Churches, not to pray, but to meet people in secret. Boats on the water, borders, checkpoints. Walls to be climbed and buildings to be infiltrated.

The hazy images raced in and out of his brain. Through it all, he saw one face. A woman. She kept reappearing, kept interrupting the movie to whisper in his ear. *Stay with me, my love, stay alive.* She had flowing black hair, a nose hooked like an eagle, dark passionate eyes, a wicked laugh, olive skin. He could feel her body wrapped up hungrily in his own. Her mouth, teasing him. The fullness of her lips, the softness of her skin.

She was in his arms, and they were happy.

Then she was in the arms of someone else, being carried away. Her eyes were closed, her face lifeless, her blood spilling to the ground. He heard himself screaming.

No!

His eyes snapped open from unconsciousness. He was awake, but lost in a cloud of confusion. Everything that had been in his head scurried away, like cockroaches afraid of the light, leaving behind an empty place.

Bourne lay in a twin bed. The sheet under him was damp from his sweat. He must have thrown off the blanket sometime during the night, because his body was uncovered. He was naked, on his back. The room was small and unlit, but he could see a crack of light around the blinds that covered the double window, which let him examine his surroundings. There was a single door that led to the outside; a small bathroom, barely larger than a phone booth; an empty closet. Two watercolor paintings hung on peeling burgundy wallpaper, showing sailboats on the water. A lamp sat on a desk near the window.

He felt disoriented, trapped in the middle of a strange dream.

He tried to get up, but pain knifed through his body like a flaming arrow. He collapsed back to the mattress, breathing hard. His head pounded, and his vision made a cartwheel, turning upside down before righting itself. When he looked at his torso, he saw a bright white bandage below his left shoulder, with a large circle of red where blood had seeped through the gauze.

He needed to think, to *remember*. He pushed his fists against his head, ignoring the pain. His breath thundered in his chest, and a whole new sheen of sweat formed on his skin.

The sweat of panic.

The sweat of fear.

Jason tried to get up again, gritting his teeth against the agony in his muscles. When he swung his legs off the bed, he managed to push himself to a sitting position, with his feet on the hardwood floor. He waited until the next wave of vertigo passed. The pain he felt wasn't just in his chest. It was in his head, too. He put his hand to the base of his skull, and the barest touch felt like a lightning bolt. He felt a gauze bandage there.

His senses fed him information that his brain tried to process. Outside, he heard the trill of songbirds, along with a whistle of air squeezing through the door frame. It made the room cold. He smelled the dankness of his own body, but he also smelled brine, as if from the sea. He stood up, propping a hand against the wall near the bed to keep himself from falling. He went to the window and separated the aluminum blinds. He was in a vacation cottage, looking out on a wooden porch. The pale blue water of a small bay lapped against a rocky beach only steps from where he was. Evergreens dotted the green grass near him, and he could see a heavily wooded promontory on the far shore of the inlet. The tide was out, leaving much of the basin exposed, with seagulls picking at the mud. The bay opened into a much larger body of water, where no land was visible.

He knew this place. The St. Lawrence estuary.

He remembered now. He was at a beachside inn in Saint-Jean-sur-Mer, two hours northeast of Quebec City. *Les chalets sur la rivière*. A hideaway with access to marine traffic in the Seaway, where he'd slipped aboard ships to break apart smuggling rings. Contraband. Drugs. Human trafficking. But there was more to remember in this room, so much more. He'd been here with Nova. They'd made love in that twin bed, her voracious appetite leaving him sated and exhausted.

Yes, he knew where he was.

The events of the recent past crept back slowly, sluggishly, like escaping from quicksand. The violence in Quebec City. The confrontation with Nash Rollins.

And prior to that, New York. The assassination. The riot.

It happened that way to Bourne sometimes, those paralyzing moments of forgetting. He'd learned to live with it. He was a man with a fractured history, a man without identity. Only a few years earlier, he'd lost his memory to a bullet in his head, which left him with no past, just fragments of who he once was and another name from another life that meant nothing to him. That life belonged to a stranger. He'd had to start over in his early thirties. Make new memories. And to this day, he still occasionally woke up in a fog, with no idea where he was, terrified that he'd lost everything again.

Barely able to walk upright, Jason staggered to the bathroom. He yanked on the string that turned on the bulb overhead. Under the dim yellow light, he propped himself with both hands on the porcelain sink and stared at the face in the mirror.

It was a square, handsome face, but pale and drawn now, lacking color. His hair was dark, so deep brown as to be almost black, and it was cut short and swept back on a high forehead. He had intense blue-gray eyes, and the bags under his eyes reflected a chronic lack of sleep. He hadn't shaved in days; his stubble was forming a beard. He was more than six feet tall and athletically built, but he saw a web of fresh cuts and multicolored bruises all over his skin, the product of his fall from the boardwalk. This wasn't the first time. His body was riddled with the scars of previous injuries, including one over his right eye and another below his ear.

When he peeled back the bandage on his chest, he saw fresh stitches closing up the small, tight hole of a bullet wound. Stitches. A doctor. He remembered that part, too. He'd staggered from the cliff in the old town and nearly bled to death while he drove half an hour outside the city to find a discreet man whose steady hands he'd used in the past. And then he'd paid the doctor's daughter an exorbitant amount of money to take him here while he slept in the back seat. He needed rest, time to recover, but he couldn't stay long. There were only so many doctors in a radius around Quebec City, and soon enough they would find a retired surgeon named Valoix and his daughter. They would trace Bourne here. Hunt him down. Kill him.

For God's sake, why?

But he knew why. They thought he'd become Cain again. A name from the past, a name from *his* past. An assassin.

In the other room, a loud bell jangled, startling him. His hand twitched, his fist opening and closing. His first instinct when surprised was to reach for a gun, but he'd lost his gun on the boardwalk. He glanced at the night-stand and saw a hotel phone. He limped across the room and picked up the receiver, but said nothing. He waited to hear who it was.

"*Bonjour, monsieur,*" said an old man's voice. "*Comment ça va ce matin?*"

He understood the language, but he let the silence stretch out. Then he replied quietly in a gravelly voice: "Who is this?"

"*C'est moi, Monsieur Bernard, bien sûr. Avez-vous faim? Voulez-vous le petit dejeuner?*"

"I'll eat later."

"*D'accord. Avez-vous besoin de quelque chose?*"

He thought: *Yes, I need something. I need to know how I was set up in New York. I need to know who framed me for murder.*

"I'm fine," Jason replied. "What time is it?"

"Nearly eleven o'clock," the hotel owner told him,

switching to accented English. "You told me to wake you earlier, but the young woman who brought you here said *le médecin* was very insistent. You needed sleep. I hope that is all right."

"Yes. Thank you."

"Your clothes are clean and ready for you. Shall I bring them over?"

"Please."

"If I may ask, will your beautiful wife be joining you on this trip?" the man asked.

"My wife," Bourne murmured.

The hotel owner heard his hesitation. "Oh, I hope I didn't speak out of turn. That lovely creature with the black hair and the eyes that always dance. You are a lucky man. Even an old man can feel his heart race seeing a woman like that."

That lovely creature.

Nova.

No, they weren't married. That had been their cover when they first came here. But cover stories had a way of blurring with reality, and at some point, they'd realized there was a genuine attraction between them. They made an unlikely pair, the half-Greek, UK-based intelligence agent and the Treadstone operative with no past. For two years, they'd enjoyed stolen moments in places around the world, whenever they could get away from their other lives. They'd even dreamed about a time when they could be together for good, but making plans was a foolish game for people like them.

"It's just me this trip," Bourne replied.

"Ah. *Quel dommage.*"

"Has anyone asked about me?" Jason inquired. "Does anyone know I'm here?"

"Of course not. Your presence here is confidential, per your standard instructions. You can always count on my discretion."

"I appreciate it."

"Well, you are always most generous, monsieur. I will see you shortly."

Bourne hung up the phone.

He stood in the darkness of the hotel bedroom, momentarily paralyzed with inaction. He was still thinking about Nova, still remembering her, but he couldn't afford that luxury. Nova was gone. She was dead.

Treadstone had killed her in Las Vegas.

Jason had a new employer now, and he needed to make contact with them. They'd be wondering where he was and what had gone wrong. He went to the small table by the window that overlooked the bay. His phone was there, a pay-as-you-go phone he'd purchased with cash in Albany as he made his way north out of New York. He reinserted the battery, which he'd removed to make sure the phone couldn't be tracked or remotely accessed, and he powered it on and waited for the phone to acquire a signal.

The contact number was supposed to connect him with a woman named Nelly Lessard. She would answer with the words "Carillon Technology. How may I direct your call?" The extension Bourne asked for would send one of several messages: *Call me back. I'm being followed. Requesting a meeting. Everything is fine.*

There was one extension that was like a 911 call. Human Resources, seventh floor.

It meant: *Emergency, need immediate extraction.*

He dialed the phone and waited, expecting to hear Nelly Lessard's voice. Instead, a whistle whined in his ear, and he heard an electronic recording. "*Your call cannot be completed as dialed.*"

Jason heard a roaring in his head. The wound in his shoulder throbbed.

Had he misdialed? No.

He tried again and got the same message. And again. And again. The number was supposed to be monitored 24/7. Nelly was *always* supposed to be there to take his call. Instead, the number had been shut down. Taken away from him, taken out of service. He knew what that meant.

The operation had been terminated. He'd been burned.

There was only one other way to get in touch with Carillon. He still had one other person he could reach. Scott DeRay had given him a special private cell phone number that he answered himself day or night. Jason had never used it before, but he dialed the number now.

A man's voice answered on the first ring, but it wasn't the voice he expected. The voice belonged to a stranger, not a friend.

"Who is this?" the man asked.

Jason tried to make sense of it. Why was someone else answering this phone?

"I need to talk to Scott," Jason said.

"You have the wrong number."

"I know that's not true!" Bourne insisted. "I know you can reach him. This is his phone. It's urgent we talk."

"I can't help you. You have the wrong number."

Liar! Jason wanted to shout into the phone. He squeezed his eyes shut and debated how much to say. "Look, I need to talk to Scott right now. Or to Miles Priest. Tell them it's about . . . it's about *Medusa*."

There was a long stretch of dead air on the phone.

Then the voice said, "Don't call this number again."

The next long silence told Jason that the man had hung up.

The setup that had started in New York was complete. They hadn't missed a single detail. Jason was a wanted man, cut off from rescue, cut off from his lifelines. Even a friend who went back to his forgotten childhood had set him adrift.

Bourne was on his own.

FOUR

THE screams of the gulls kept Jason company as he hiked along a rocky beach toward the streets of Saint-Jean-sur-Mer. The April air was crisp and cool. He wore a blue wool hat pulled down over his forehead and a pair of sunglasses supplied by Monsieur Bernard. His clothes were clean now, no evidence of bloodstains, and he'd showered, shaved, and replaced the dressings on his wounds. He looked like any other early-season visitor taking a holiday in the small tourist village.

People came to Saint-Jean-sur-Mer because of the river. They sailed, they fished, they ate lobster rolls in the seaside cafés. Art galleries and bakeries hugged the north-south highway that followed the water. The houses all had the same peaked roofs, white siding, and cherry-red trim. Without the French signs, he could have pictured himself in Cape Cod. Only a few hundred people lived here, and most of them could trace their family roots to this same place for generations.

Jason dug in his pocket to check how much money he had left. He'd paid the doctor and his daughter and Monsieur Bernard, and now he only had a couple hundred Canadian dollars in cash. Somewhere he'd need to get more. He was certain that the bank account that Scott DeRay and Miles Priest had set up for him was shut down, with special instructions to delay the man who came to the bank looking to withdraw funds.

A message would be sent. Killers would be dispatched.

He felt something else in his pocket. When he pulled it out, he saw a plastic, electronic hotel key for his room in New York, overlooking Washington Square Park. That was the room where the shooter had set up a rifle while Jason was in the crowd below. That was the room where the fatal shot on Sofia Ortiz had been taken from an open window.

A bullet in the throat. The signature of Cain.

He broke the key in half and divided the pieces among two separate waste bins he found outside the sidewalk shops.

Jason realized he was hungry. It had been more than twenty-four hours since he'd eaten anything at all. He chose a brasserie that served fish and chips and fish soup, with windows that looked out on the bay. It was a one-room restaurant, and all the tables had plastic tablecloths decorated with pictures of vegetables and flowers. Ropes, fishnets, and life preservers hung on the walls as decorations. He sat at an empty table in the corner, near a door that led to the beach. He took off the sunglasses he was wearing, but left the wool cap on his head.

"*Oui, monsieur?*" a waitress asked him sullenly, as if his arrival in the half-empty café was an imposition on her time.

He ordered a plate of fried shrimp and coffee.

There was a small television over the restaurant's bar, tuned to the international version of CNN. A week later, the assassination of Congresswoman Sofia Ortiz was still the top of the news. He saw footage from the riot that had erupted after the shooting, but he didn't need a reminder. He'd been there. *Riot* was the wrong word for what had happened. Riots were organic, unpredictable, uncontrolled affairs. The violence in New York had spread neatly, like a controlled burn, as if someone, somewhere, were writing a script for it and sending out actors to play their parts. This was a riot with a plan, and part of the plan had been to make sure that Abbey Laurent was one of the victims.

Jason had followed her out of the park after the shooting. So had someone else. She'd been tracked by a man in a hood, but not a random thug, not part of the anarchist chaos sweeping the streets. This man never took his eyes off her. When Jason saw him aim a gun across the rioters at Abbey, he'd staged a collision to rescue her, and then he'd doubled back to take the man out with a choke hold around his neck.

The man had no ID, nothing to explain his presence in the riot. He was a pawn.

He was Medusa.

The waitress put Bourne's lunch in front of him. He devoured it hungrily, not sure when he'd have time to eat again. He gulped down the coffee, too. He found himself staring out the window at the beach, where a few children hung out near the river, throwing stones. In the distance, he could see a ship gliding eastward toward the open waters of the Atlantic. If he couldn't break apart the conspiracy, that might be his future, escaping overseas in the cargo hold of one of those ships.

On the other side of the café, the front door opened and closed.

Bourne shot a glance at the door and swore under his breath. It was a policeman. He was a local cop, dressed in a zippered olive-green police jacket and a black brimmed cap. He had a holstered sidearm at his waist. He was a tall beanpole, young, probably not even twenty-five, and he knew everyone in the café. The sullen waitress came alive and flirted with him. The chef made jokes.

It might be a coincidence that the cop had arrived here now, but Bourne didn't think so. The word had already gone out. The police were looking for him. He watched the cop out of the corner of his eye, and the policeman made a careful survey of the restaurant as he chatted with the waitress. He spotted Bourne at the corner table, and his stare fixed on him for an extra beat. That was all. Then the cop looked away, too quickly.

Jason knew he'd been spotted.

He unfolded two bills from his pocket and put the cash on the table to pay for his meal. Casually, he finished his coffee and popped the last fried shrimp into his mouth. He put his sunglasses back on, got up, and used the rear door to exit the café. A handful of wooden steps led to the beach, where the children were playing. He joined them at the water and threw a couple of stones, the way they were doing. Then he stole a glance over his shoulder.

The policeman was watching him from the patio. He had a radio in his hand, calling for backup.

Jason strolled eastward along the beach. Not far ahead of him, a wooded section of land encroached on the river. He could see the peaks of several houses tucked among the trees. When he stopped to tie his shoe, he shot another look behind him and saw the policeman following, maybe fifty yards away. The young cop had his right hand close to the holster on his belt. He wasn't even hiding his pursuit, but Jason could tell from the man's jerky motions that he was nervous.

When a pursuer is nervous, make them more nervous. Do the unexpected. Keep them off balance.

Treadstone.

Where the trees grew close to the river, Bourne saw steps leading to a waterfront house. As he neared the stairs, he suddenly bolted into the woods, making no effort to hide his escape. The sudden movement sent pain knifing through his shoulder, and his brain swirled through a tornado of dizziness that almost drove him to his knees. He thundered up the steps and stopped, waiting for his mind to right itself. The house in front of him looked like a summer cottage, with a large porch and picture windows overlooking the river. When he crept to the rear windows and looked inside, he saw patio furniture stored near the door and covered with a plastic sheet. No one was home.

Jason looked back toward the trees. The policeman came after him, slowly, uncertainly. A smart cop would keep him pinned down and wait for backup to arrive. A nervous cop would try to be a hero. Bourne crouched and waited for the man to get closer, and he could see that the cop had his gun in his hand.

Do the unexpected.

Bourne stood up, in plain view, his hands over his head. "I surrender! I surrender, and I need your help!"

The cop aimed his gun at Bourne. "Don't move!"

Jason moved anyway. *Keep them off balance.* He came off the porch, hands still in the air. He invented a limp as he walked toward the cop, locking eyes with him, feeling the man's fear. "I'm unarmed. I need your help. They're going to kill me!"

"I said, *Don't move!* Stay where you are!"

"You can't let them take me. *You* have to bring me in. If the Americans get hold of me, I'll disappear."

"One more step, and I'll shoot!" the cop insisted.

Jason stopped. They were ten feet apart across a muddy trail. "Yeah, sure, whatever you say. I told you, I'm unarmed. Look, I know how this goes. I turn around, I get on my knees. You put on the cuffs. I don't want any trouble. I want everybody to know about this. I'm telling you, that's what's keeping me alive. Hell, call the TV news and get them out here. Get your picture in the paper."

"*Shut up!* Do it just like you said. Turn around and get on your knees. Do it!"

"Sure. Absolutely. Thank you. You're saving my life!"

Bourne turned around and sank to his knees. He laced his hands behind his head. He closed his eyes and held his breath, focusing all of his senses on *listening* to the movements of the cop behind him. He heard the splash of boots in the mud and heavy, anxious breathing. The cop got closer. He was right there behind him, squatting, inches away. Then Jason heard the noise he was waiting for, the smooth slide of metal against leather as the cop holstered his weapon in order to reach for his cuffs.

Instantly, Bourne twisted and drove his elbow into the cop's kidney. As he spun, he fished out the cop's gun with his other hand. Bourne shot an elbow upward and cracked the man's chin, snapping his head backward. At the same time, he backhanded the man's ear and knocked him sideways. He swung the heavy gun into the cop's forehead, drawing blood and dizzying him. Bourne hit him again, harder, and this time the cop crumpled onto his back with his eyes closed.

Jason scrambled to his feet. He felt wetness on his skin and glanced at his shoulder, where blood seeped through his shirt. His stitches had opened. He stumbled down the steps toward the beach, but as he neared the water, he stopped. They were already coming for him, but not the police. He didn't hear sirens. Instead, overhead, he heard the fierce throb of an engine getting louder.

A helicopter.

He looked up and saw a black helicopter descending toward the beach like a giant insect. Before it even landed, half a dozen operatives in paramilitary gear leaped from the open door and landed in the shallow water not even a hundred yards from the trees. They all had automatic rifles in their hands. From where they were, he was invisible, but his location had already made its way from a nervous cop's radio to the men who were hunting him. They knew where he was. Half of them moved down the beach, heading straight for the woods, and the other half crept toward the street to cut him off.

Before Bourne could move, he heard another engine. A second helicopter soared into view over the trees and descended toward the other end of the beach like a pincer, squeezing him from both directions.

Jason backed up the steps, then turned and ran toward the house. He ignored the pain. He ignored the dizziness. The young cop was still unconscious in the mud, and he jumped over him on his way toward the highway. He had to get away *now!* In less than a minute, the road would be shut down in both directions by men with guns. He ran past the house and down the dirt driveway to Route 132, where he put up a hand to stop an Audi sedan that was barreling toward him in the southbound lane.

The Audi's brakes squealed as the car jammed to a stop. There were two people in the front seat, a man and a woman. He heard the driver swearing at him.

Bourne ran to the car's back door and threw it open and pointed the cop's gun at the man's head.

"Drive."

The man behind the wheel was a bearded fifty-something businessman in a navy sport coat and open-collared dress shirt. He had a blond woman in the seat next to him who was less than half his age. The anger in the man's face bled away as he saw the gun, and his eyes widened with terror. "Oh shit, oh shit, just take the car. Take the car!"

"*Drive*," Bourne repeated, pulling the back door shut and stretching along the floor of the car. "I've got a gun pointed at your spine through the seat. You stop for anything, I fire, and you're paralyzed. Got it? Now go."

"Yeah, yeah, whatever you say."

Jason heard the wheels screeching as the car accelerated.

"*Don't* speed!" he directed the man. "Don't draw any attention to yourself. There may be men with rifles heading toward the highway from the beach. Ignore them. If you do anything to signal them, you're both dead."

"Okay! I'm driving! Don't hurt us! Where do you want to go?"

"Just keep heading south," Bourne said, closing his eyes and applying pressure to the bloody wound on his shoulder. "As soon as I figure out where I'm going, I'll tell you."

FIVE

ABBEY knew that the policeman didn't believe her story. There was no evidence left in Artillery Park of her encounter with the man in the gold-rimmed glasses. He was gone. Her Taser was gone. There were no witnesses.

The police officer had the look of a butler at a royal palace. He was in his thirties but oozed the kind of pompous condescension that most men take at least fifty years to perfect. He was slim and tall, with brown hair parted in the middle and greased down, and he sported a pencil mustache that he kept combing with the tip of his finger. He had prominent cheekbones and ears that jutted from the side of his head.

"You didn't know this man?" the cop said with obvious skepticism. "You'd never seen him before?"

"No, but he knew me. He was waiting outside the bar. He called me by name."

"Could he have seen you while you were inside?"

"I suppose. I didn't see him, but it's possible."

"Did you have a lot to drink last night?" the police officer asked, staring down his nose at her.

"I had one beer. What does that have to do with anything?"

"Hmm," the cop said, working his mouth as if he were chewing something unpleasant. "And you say this man pulled a *gun* on you?"

"That's right. He was going to kill me."

"How do you know that?"

"Well, the gun was my first clue," Abbey snapped.

She shifted impatiently on her feet and looked around the park to see if anyone was watching her. It crossed her mind that maybe she was being followed; maybe she'd been followed for days, ever since New York. She felt tired, angry, and paranoid. It had been a bad night. She hadn't felt safe going back to her apartment, so she'd crashed on a girlfriend's couch and made up an excuse about ducking an old boyfriend. She'd hardly slept at all. And then, in the morning, she'd debated whether to report what had happened. Her editor, Jacques, had finally prevailed on her to call the police, but now she was regretting her decision.

"Did this man want something from you?" the police officer went on. "Did he ask for money? Or do you think he was planning a sexual assault?"

"I think he was just planning to shoot me."

"Did the two of you argue? Was he angry?"

"No, he wasn't angry. He never showed any emotion

at all. This guy was an assassin. He met me in order to kill me. Period. If I hadn't had the Taser, I'd be dead."

"Ah, yes, the Taser," the cop murmured with a reprimand in his voice. "I'm glad you came back to that. Are you aware, Ms. Laurent, that a Taser is a prohibited weapon in Canada? Importing and owning one is a crime. If it's missing as you say, then I suppose I can let it go, but I would strongly advise you not to replace it."

Abbey brushed her mahogany bangs out of her eyes with a swipe of her fingers. "Seriously, you're worried about my Taser? That's what you're taking away from all this? A man tried to kill me. Right here. A *hit man*."

"Well, that's very dramatic, but I'm not sure we can leap to a conclusion like that," he sneered at her. "I understand that journalists like to think they're all characters in a Tarantino film, but if this happened as you say, the most likely explanation is that this man is some kind of stalker."

"Call him whatever you want. The question is, how are you going to find him?"

"As much as we'd like to help, Ms. Laurent, I'm afraid we have very little to go on. Frankly, you're in a better position than we are to identify this man. When you figure out where you crossed paths with him, or if you see him again, then you can let us know."

"Don't you have cameras all over town?" Abbey asked. "I told you what he looked like. I told you when this happened. How hard is it to check the cameras around the bar and try to find him? Maybe he had a car, and you can get a license plate. Maybe he was staying at a local hotel."

The police officer gave her a strangely pained look, as if he wished she would just let it go. "In normal circumstances that might be an option, but I'm afraid there were technology issues in the city last night. Most of our surveillance cameras were offline."

"*Offline*," Abbey said. "Does that happen a lot?"

"No, it's quite rare."

"Starting when? When did the cameras go offline?"

"Sometime before ten o'clock. The issue wasn't resolved until the middle of the night."

"Well, that's pretty damn convenient," Abbey said. "Ten o'clock is the time when *I* was at Château Frontenac. I already told you that. And now there's no way to confirm anything I'm telling you. Look, what happened up there, anyway?"

"There was an incident, but we're not releasing details at this time."

"Why? What's with all the secrets? What are you people covering up? I was supposed to meet someone on the boardwalk who didn't show up, and not long after that, I hear about people getting shot and killed up there. And then somebody pretends to be the person I was supposed to meet and tries to kill *me*? You don't seriously expect me to believe that's a coincidence, do you?"

"If you have questions about the incident at Château Frontenac, or if you feel you should be interviewed, you'll need to contact the public information officer, and she can put you in touch with the appropriate government authorities."

"The appropriate authorities? You mean the Quebec police aren't running the investigation?"

The police officer didn't answer. He simply combed his mustache.

"So what am I supposed to do now?" Abbey went on. "Go home? What if this guy is waiting for me?"

"If you have concerns for your safety, you should certainly call us back," the officer replied with another condescending smile. Then he took a phone from his belt and gave her a look that said he had better things to do. "Otherwise, if you don't have any other information to share, I think we're done here."

Abbey scowled. "Thanks for the help."

"Please remember my warning about the Taser, Ms. Laurent."

"Yeah. Sure."

Abbey stalked away in disgust. When she glanced over her shoulder, she saw the policeman watching her, making sure she was actually leaving. His phone was poised in his hand. She kept walking, her shoes crunching on the gravel path. She passed the park's welcome center, then turned the corner past a stone wall near the outer gate.

When she knew he couldn't see her anymore, she crept back to the corner to listen.

Almost immediately, she heard the policeman on the phone, but it took her a moment to realize it was him, because his voice and tone had changed completely. He didn't sound like a bored, stuffy street cop anymore, handling a citizen's complaint with polite disbelief. He spoke like someone in authority who was used to giving orders. In fact, he didn't sound like a cop at all now.

He sounded like a spy.

The appropriate government authorities.

"I just completed my interview with the Laurent woman," she heard the man say, switching easily to up-scale urban French as he talked. "Oh, yes, they were targeting her, no doubt about that. She described the man who tried to kill her. Stocky, forties, blond hair, gold-rimmed glasses. No, that's right, it's definitely not Cain. Tell the Americans. This was their operation and their mess, let them worry about it."

Abbey didn't wait to hear more. She spun off the wall and ran for the gate, to make sure the man didn't realize she'd been eavesdropping on his call. He'd said the one word that had been in her nightmares for a week.

Cain.

THE area of the boardwalk near the Château Frontenac was still cordoned off with crime scene tape and guarded by police to keep the public away. Abbey tried to stay inconspicuous as she sat on the steps of the statue of Champlain near the entrance to the *funiculaire* that took tourists down the cliff to the lower town. She wore sunglasses to cover her face. She sipped coffee from the Starbucks inside the hotel, and she checked her watch often, as if waiting for someone to join her.

The city police guarding the area were just a diversion. The real investigation was going on beyond the crime scene tape, and the men in charge were definitely not police. They wore suits and had wired headsets connected to radios, and they were all armed. Abbey had been around enough government personnel to know that she was looking at a team of intelligence officers. They were mostly Americans, too. Americans stood out even when they were trying to blend in. In an operation like this, that meant they were probably CIA.

She had no trouble identifying the agent in charge. He barked orders to everyone else. He was a small, hard-looking man, well into his fifties, with a face that didn't look like it knew what a smile was. The sun was out today, but he wore a gray raincoat over his suit and a fedora low on his forehead. He was in pain. That was obvious. He used a cane awkwardly, and she could see his features contort into a grimace whenever he took a step. Abbey took her phone and pretended to be typing a text, while in reality, she zoomed in on the man's face and snapped several pictures.

She had plenty of contacts in the U.S. and Canadian governments. Someone could tell her who he was.

Abbey climbed off the steps and wandered toward the police tape. She took a selfie with the Château Frontenac behind her and then picked the youngest, cutest cop and put on her flirtiest smile. "Wow, what's going on?" she asked him. "I've never seen so many cops around here."

"It's nothing to be concerned about, miss," the officer replied.

"I hope not, but everybody's talking about people getting shot and killed! It's hard to believe. Did you catch the guy who did it?"

"There's no danger to the public."

"Oh, good. That's a relief." Abbey ran her fingers through her loose hair and gave her head a little toss. She knew she was pretty much irresistible when she did that. "How many people were killed?"

"We're not releasing any information. I'd suggest you turn on the evening news, and you'll probably hear all about it."

"Sure, of course. I get that. But is it true they were *shot?*"

"I'm sorry, but we're not—"

"Yeah, yeah, no information, I know. The thing is, I write stories for *The Fort.* The online magazine? Do you read it? You really should. We're always looking for scoops, and I would be a *hero* to my editor if I could bring him something on this. Seriously, a hero. I mean, they must have told you some of the dirt, right? Is there anything you can give me behind the scenes? Totally anonymous. Believe me, you steer me in the right direction, the drinks are on me this weekend."

The young cop looked pained. He glanced both ways to make sure no one else was around. "They haven't told us anything. They're keeping it very quiet."

"Sure, I understand. You're cute, by the way. Maybe we could have that drink anyway. Hey, do you know who's in charge around here? That guy with the limp over there, do you know who he is?"

"Somebody called him Rollins. That's all I know."

"Rollins. He's American, right?"

"They all are."

Abbey leaned close enough that she knew the cop could inhale her perfume. "Did anybody say anything about New York? I heard there might be a connection to that congresswoman getting killed in the park."

"I don't know anything about that."

"What about the name Cain? You hear anyone mention that today?"

The cop looked uncomfortable, as if he'd made a big mistake saying anything at all. "I'm sorry, miss, you better go. If people see us talking, I could get into trouble. We're not supposed to talk to reporters."

"Sure. I get it. Hey, thanks for the help."

Abbey headed away from the boardwalk. Before she'd gone too far into the plaza, she took one last look over her shoulder, and when she did, she froze in place.

The American agent named Rollins was leaning on his cane and staring directly at her.

Like he knew exactly who she was.

SIX

"**W**E have a situation in New York," Miles Priest told Bourne. "We need you to go there immediately. This may be our first opportunity to infiltrate Medusa."

Jason sat at a table in a windowless modular room with Priest and Scott DeRay. The room was a SCIF—a Sensitive Compartmented Information Facility—adjacent to Priest's top-floor office in the West Coast headquarters of Carillon Technology. They could talk freely there without fear of electronic surveillance.

"What's the situation?" Bourne asked.

His friend Scott pushed a folder across the table. "I assume you're familiar with Sofia Ortiz."

"The freshman congresswoman out of New York? Sure. She's made quite a name for herself on social media."

"Yes, she has," Scott went on. "Mostly at our expense. She's been crusading against the data practices at Carillon and other tech companies since she got into office. If she has *her way, the feds will turn Big Tech into nothing more than utilities operating at the whims of Congress."*

"Well, you have what every politician dreams about," Bourne pointed out. "Personal information on nearly every voter."

"Exactly!" Miles Priest snorted. The Carillon CEO got up from his chair and paced between the walls of the SCIF. "This crusade of hers isn't about privacy or consumer protection. It's about power, pure and simple. Believe me, the last people you want anywhere near our data are members of Congress."

Bourne knew that Priest was intimately familiar with the government world. He was a former director of the FBI who'd retired after thirty years inside the Beltway and switched from the public sector to the private sector. He'd taken the reins at Carillon Technology when social media companies were first beginning to flex their muscles. In the fifteen years since then, he'd built Carillon into the backbone of Silicon Valley, providing database infrastructure for nearly all of the social media giants.

Priest himself had become the personification of the money and influence of Big Tech. He was an immediately recognizable figure wherever he went, six foot six, with neatly coiffed gray hair and a long, hangdog face. His tenure at Carillon had also made him a billionaire with homes all over the world, from an estate on his own Caribbean island to a remote castle in the Highlands of Scotland.

"Ortiz has made a lot of noise," Bourne agreed, "but she's still just a freshman. How much influence does she really have?"

"It's not a question of influence," Scott said.

"Oh?"

"Yes, we have reason to believe that Ortiz is working with Medusa. Or Medusa has penetrated her office and is feeding her information. That's why we want you to go to New York. To follow the trail."

"A sitting congresswoman? What makes you think that?"

"Recently, there was a profile of Ortiz in an online magazine called The Fort by a Canadian journalist named Abbey Laurent. Laurent quotes a source inside Ortiz's circle who says that the congresswoman is ready to expose the worst scandal in the history of Big Tech. Ortiz herself wouldn't comment, but now she's scheduled a huge rally in Washington Square Park next week. We think she's planning to expose the data hack."

"She'll use that as the launching pad for legislation against us," Priest interjected. "This will be like the Patriot Act after 9/11. When people find out that the entire tech cabal was victimized—that an encyclopedia of data on nearly every American was stolen—they're going to demand action. It will give Congress the cover they need to put us under their thumb."

"We know Medusa was behind the hack," Scott went on. "We've been able to keep it under wraps for almost a year while we tried to figure out what they were planning to do with the data they stole. But since then, nothing. Silence. As far as we can tell, they haven't tried to use it, haven't tried to sell it. So we still don't know their ultimate plan. But now it appears that Sofia Ortiz is planning to make news of the hack public. This is clearly the first shot in the war."

Priest sat down again and put both of his long arms on the table, with his hands curled into fists. "The leak about the hack didn't come from any of us. If Ortiz knows about it, it's because Medusa gave her the information. They want it out there. Somewhere in Sofia Ortiz's operation is a trail that leads back to them. That's why we need you. That's why we need a spy."

"There are a lot of spies out there," Bourne replied. "Why me?"

"Bringing you in was my idea," Scott explained. "Miles convinced the other CEOs that we needed to hire our own operative to take on Medusa. The feds have had no luck getting inside the organization or learning anything about it. So it's up to us now. We want someone who reports directly to us, with no conflicted loyalties. I said I had the perfect man."

Bourne stared at Scott DeRay with a question. "Do they know about . . . ?"

"Treadstone?" Scott replied. "Yes, they know all about Treadstone."

"Don't look so surprised, Bourne!" Priest interjected with a chuckle. "I was the head of the FBI. You think the CIA can take a piss without me knowing about it? I've been in the loop on Treadstone since their first black ops mission."

"And yes, I told them why you left," Scott went on, with a meaningful glance that Bourne didn't miss. "They know about Nova and what Treadstone did to her. No one blames you for walking away. In fact, as I told Miles, you leaving Treadstone was a gift to us. One of the best intelligence agents in the world was suddenly a man without portfolio. How could we turn that down?"

Jason heard the unspoken message. Scott knew all about the memory loss that had nearly destroyed Jason a few years earlier, but he'd kept the truth about Bourne's amnesia from Miles Priest. Scott was protecting him.

Like Priest, Scott DeRay was former FBI. He'd been on the fast track, buzzed about as a future director and eventual attorney general. But he'd surprised his superiors a few years earlier by quitting the bureau and joining Carillon Technology as their number two executive. Scott was now the protégé and eventual successor to Miles Priest. His FBI colleagues had assumed it was about money, but Bourne knew that Scott's decision wasn't financial. He already came from a billionaire family; he'd gone to exclusive private schools and colleges in Europe. No, Scott had decided in his early thirties that the real future of the world was in technology, not government. So he'd moved on.

They were old friends. Bourne had known Scott throughout his Treadstone days, but their relationship went much further back. They'd spent summers together as teenagers. Scott had showed him pictures from back then, two boys hanging out week after week at the beach, laughing together, arms around each other's shoulders. Bourne remembered none of it. To him, those events may as well have happened to someone else. He had no recollection of his childhood, but he still had Scott in his life as a reminder.

Scott was smooth and handsome. Wavy dark hair. A permanent suntan. He wasn't particularly tall, but he had a politician's charisma. Everyone who met him remembered him. He had limitless energy, fueled by a metabolism that barely needed more than four hours of sleep on any night.

Every day, he'd run in Central Park at five in the morning, pumping through an intense workout. Then, if he wasn't at his Manhattan desk doing venture capital deals for Carillon, he'd be on a plane or helicopter, hopscotching from Washington to Scotland to Nassau to San Francisco with Miles Priest.

His friend was going to rule the world someday. Or maybe he already did.

"What do you say, Bourne?" Priest asked impatiently. "The clock is ticking. We need someone who can find the connection between Sofia Ortiz and Medusa. We need to know what they're planning. Will you help us?"

Jason noticed a little smirk on Scott's face, because his friend knew there was no way he was going to say no. Sometimes Jason thought that Scott knew him better than he knew himself.

"I'm in," Bourne replied.

THAT was two weeks ago.

Now Sofia Ortiz was dead, and Jason was on the run.

He sat in the back seat of an Audi sedan driven south along the Canadian coast by a fat businessman and his twenty-something mistress. Bourne knew where he needed to go. Despite the ambush the previous night, he had to go back to Quebec City. If Medusa had framed him for the murder of Sofia Ortiz, then the only thing he could do was to take the fight to Medusa, and that meant infiltrating their operation. There was one person left who could help him do that.

Abbey Laurent.

She had a source who'd told her about the data hack. She had a source who'd told her about *Cain*. Bourne needed to find out who was passing secrets to her and trace her source back to Medusa.

"Where are we going?" the businessman in the front seat whined, his voice oozing fear. He had sweat glistening on his head, which was mostly bald except for a thin crown of brown hair. "You haven't told us anything!"

"Just keep driving."

"How do we know you won't kill us?"

"You don't," Jason said.

Bourne eased far back into the seat, where his face was partly hidden through the rear window. He watched small towns passing as they headed south, and he eyed the highway ahead for roadblocks and police. They were still more than an hour outside the urban core of Quebec City. His shoulder burned as if a spike had been driven through it, and his head throbbed. He tried to concentrate; he needed a plan. But as he sat in the rear of the Audi, he found himself tormented by flashbacks. His face twitched. In moments of stress, his brain fired a storm of memories at him, one after another. He saw the faces of people from his lost past, people he should have known but who were strangers to him.

And other faces.

People he'd killed.

Jason tried to shut it all out. He had to focus. *Stop it!*

He realized he'd become distracted. When he glanced at the front seat, he saw that the fat businessman's right hand had drifted away from the steering wheel.

"What are you *doing*?" Jason hissed.

He lurched forward, shoving the gun into the man's neck. The man had slipped a cell phone out of his pocket and was trying to dial an emergency number. Jason twisted the man's wrist sharply, forcing him to drop the phone. The car swerved as the man screamed in pain, and a car in the opposite lane blared its horn. Jason grabbed the phone, then put the barrel of the gun against the head of the blond in the passenger seat.

"Give me your phone, too. Any more tricks like that, and I'll shoot you both."

The young woman, unlike her companion, remained cool and calm. She took out a phone from her tight jeans and handed it to Bourne. He shoved both phones in his pocket, then collapsed backward against the seat. The woman turned around to stare at him. She looked him up and down, more curious than afraid.

"You're bleeding," she said.

The businessman, whose thick fingers were clenched around the wheel again, shot her an angry look. "Don't talk to him! Are you crazy?"

"Shut up, Wallace," the girl snapped. Then she said to Bourne: "You should have somebody look at that. I can help you if you want."

"Are you a nurse?"

"Close. My dad's a vet."

Bourne laughed. "That's what you call close?"

"I've helped him in surgery since I was twelve. If I can deal with an angry Siamese, I think I can deal with you."

"Why would you want to help me?" Jason asked.

She shrugged. "Hopefully, you're less likely to kill me that way."

Bourne studied the girl's face. She couldn't be more than twenty-two or twenty-three. Her blond hair was long and straight, and she wore a scoop T-shirt that emphasized her skinny neck and bony shoulders. Her face was pimpled. She had sleepy brown eyes, but she had a street-smart look that told him she already knew a lot about men.

"What's your name?" he asked.

"Amie."

"And who's Wallace here?"

"My boss," she said. She added with a smirk, "Among other things."

"Amie, stop talking to him!" the man behind the wheel demanded again. "He's a psychopath!"

"You're being boring, Wallace," the young woman replied with a lazy glance. She nodded her head toward the car window as she continued the conversation with Bourne. "We're in Montmagny. There's a pharmacy a few blocks away from here. I can get the things to fix you up."

"Are you saying I should let you go inside by yourself?" Bourne asked.

"Well, you could, but I'll be honest. If you do that, I won't come back."

"That *is* honest. Except if I come inside with you,

then I have to worry about Wallace driving off and calling the police."

She smirked again. "You don't need to worry about him. Wallace will be a good boy."

"Because he wants to keep you alive?"

"Oh, no, he'd run out on me in a heartbeat to save his own neck. But you have his phone, and he likes to take pictures of me while I'm sucking his dick. I imagine his wife would find those pretty interesting."

Wallace swore at her over and over in a loud voice.

Bourne smiled. "Have you ever done stitches?"

"Lots of times."

He nodded. "Okay. Wallace, pull into the pharmacy lot when you see it. Don't even think about trying to flag down a cop."

"Wallace, give the man your wallet, too," Amie added.

"What the hell for?" the businessman bellowed.

"That's our deal, baby. You always pay."

They reached the parking lot of the pharmacy, where the signs were in French. Bourne directed the businessman to park near the door so that he could watch the car through the windows. It was early evening, and the store was crowded when they went inside, but the number of people helped him keep a low profile. No one gave them a second glance. He took Amie by the hand in a tight grip, and she played her part, leaning her head against his shoulder as if they were lovers. He noticed an ATM near the wall and remembered he was low on cash.

"Do you know his bank code?" Bourne asked her.

"Sure."

"Take out five hundred dollars."

Amie shrugged. "Make it a thousand. He can afford it."

"You're something else," Jason told her.

He avoided the bank camera as the girl made the transaction. When she handed him the cash, he gave two hundred dollars back to her. She smiled and stuffed the wad of bills in her pocket.

"So what's the deal with you two?" Jason asked her. "You can do a lot better than him."

"I know, but I have champagne tastes. Wallace helps with that. What about you? You want to tell me who you are and what you're running from?"

"It's better that you not know," Jason replied.

"Yeah, I figured."

They didn't take long to buy the supplies they needed. When they were back in the Audi, Bourne directed Wallace to the highway, and they headed west out of town. Not long after, the houses thinned, and they found themselves in a densely wooded area. When they reached a cross street that led deeper into the forest, he directed the businessman to turn away from the coastal road. They drove for several miles, until they were on a deserted stretch hugged by trees on both sides. Wallace parked the sedan on the shoulder, and Bourne could feel the man's panic rise.

"Let me take a look at your shoulder," Amie said.

She got out of the passenger seat, came around to the rear of the car, and straddled Bourne's lap in the back seat. She undid the buttons of his shirt and pushed it off his shoulder, where the bullet wound was bleeding. Using the gauze and antiseptic from the pharmacy, she cleaned the wound, removed the torn stitches, then dipped a needle in rubbing alcohol and poured some over the bullet hole, making him wince with pain. She set about closing him up again, and he was impressed. Her stitches were neater and tighter than the doctor had given him the previous night.

"You're good at that," he said.

"I know." She winked at him.

Then she was done, and it was time to go. She got out of the car, and Bourne pointed the gun at Wallace's head in the front seat. "Get out. Leave the keys."

"Jesus, you're going to shoot me! Shit! Shit!"

"I'm not going to shoot you, but I'm taking your car. You can walk back to town and report it missing. By then, I won't need it. And remember, I still have your phone. Be nice to Amie, or I start texting your wife."

"Shit!" Wallace said again, backing up toward the trees and yanking the belt of his pants over his stomach. Tears rolled down his round face.

Bourne climbed out of the rear seat. He opened the driver's door and gestured at the young blonde. "You don't need him. If you want to come with me, I can drop you anywhere you want."

"Nah. If I don't stay with him, he'll probably get eaten by a bear."

"Well, thanks for your help," Jason told her.

Amie patted the bulge in her front pocket, where she had the cash from the ATM. "Thank *you*."

Bourne got behind the wheel, then rolled down the

window. "Why were you so sure I wouldn't kill you, Amie?"

The girl shrugged. "Dad treats lots of cats."

"Cats?" he said. "So what?"

"Sometimes you look in a cat's eyes and know you better not turn your back on them. But with some cats, you realize that no matter how much they growl and hiss at you, that's not who they really are. I decided you weren't a mean cat."

SEVEN

BOURNE left the Audi in an empty parking lot behind the Musée Nationale des Beaux-Arts in Quebec City. He was confident the car wouldn't be found for a day or more, but he had no intention of going back to it. When the time came, he'd find another way out of town. He left behind all of the phones, too, including his own. He'd used it to call Miles Priest and Scott DeRay, and that meant it could be tracked to him as soon as he powered it on. He'd find a new burner phone along the way.

It was nearly eight o'clock at night. He hiked in the darkness through the old growth trees and shallow hills of the battlefield park known as the Plains of Abraham on his way into the heart of the city. When he reached the downtown streets, the first thing he did was find a cheap hostel near Rue Dauphine, mostly populated by students. He paid cash for a tiny room with not much more than a bed and a shared bathroom down the hall.

As he headed outside, he passed a young couple coming in who smelled of Turkish coffee and marijuana. He told them his phone had died and asked if they'd mind running a quick Google search for him. Ninety seconds and ten dollars later, he had the local address for the online magazine called *The Fort*.

Editor and publisher, Jacques Varille.

Senior writer, Abbey Laurent.

The magazine office was only a few blocks away, in a gray stone building across from Esplanade Park. The cobblestoned Rue d'Auteuil was deserted, but Jason avoided the street and approached the building via the park, where the trees hid him. He watched the neighborhood, alert for signs of a trap. The windows of the building were all dark, including the top-floor offices where *The Fort* was housed. The cross streets looked empty, but Jason let the time tick by before he moved. Patience was how he stayed alive. When he was certain that no one was keeping the building under surveillance, he darted across the intersection.

There were windows in the middle of the twin entry doors. Using the butt of his pistol, he broke the glass, reached around the jagged shards, and let himself inside the building. With his gun in his hand, he took the staircase to the top floor, where he found another door labeled with a sign for *The Fort*. The interior door yielded with a single kick of his boot.

He had a mini penlight in his pocket that cast a weak beam, and he aimed it at the floor, making sure the light didn't pass close to the windows. The magazine office was small, just a single room with half a dozen desks, a supply closet, a mini kitchen, and a laser printer. Cheap tourist posters of Canadian landscapes adorned the walls. The room smelled of pizza, thanks to a delivery box squeezed into one of the wastebaskets. Bourne went from desk to desk, looking for the one that belonged to Abbey Laurent. He found it at the back, and he knew it because of the photographs she kept. He recognized the attractive woman with mahogany-colored hair. The woman he'd saved from a killer in New York. The woman he'd seen through the lenses of his binoculars in the rain at Dufferin Terrace.

The woman who'd led him into an ambush.

Did she know what was going to happen? Was *she* part of Medusa? Or was she another one of their innocent pawns?

He picked up another of the framed photographs on her desk, which showed Abbey standing next to a tall, lean man in a gray suit, obviously a few years older than she was. The man had one arm around her waist in a possessive grip, and he carried a leather briefcase in his other hand. He wore a lanyard around his neck that identified him as part of a United Nations conference. Bourne recognized the background of the photo as inside Grand Central Station. On the photograph itself, someone had written a caption in neat penmanship: *Abbey et Michel, New York*. It was dated the previous year.

Jason had a hard time imagining these two in a relationship. The man in the photograph had the cautious, humorless smile of a diplomat. By contrast, Abbey stared at the camera with the grin of someone who rode life like a roller coaster with her arms in the air. She wore a little black dress with a plunging neckline and flouncy lace sleeves that said, *Look at me*. Even though the two women didn't resemble each other at all, there was something in Abbey's attitude and eyes that reminded him of Nova.

Bourne examined Abbey's desk, which was messy, with hardly a square inch of open space. She had notepads filled with writing, scribbled out of the lines with arrows and bubbles as she thought of new ideas. The borders of her computer monitor were covered over with yellow sticky notes. It all reflected a quick, chaotic mind.

He opened the top drawer of her desk. Inside, he found a dozen matching Uni-Ball pens, two tins of breath mints, and coupons for just about every fast-food restaurant in the city. There was also a digital voice recorder.

Jason took out the recorder and pressed the button for playback.

The voice on the machine sounded loud in the dark, empty space. He quickly switched it to a whisper and held the device to his ear.

"Congresswoman, some people say that in the age of social media, privacy is an archaic notion. I take it you disagree."

He had never heard Abbey Laurent's voice before, but he was sure it was her. The fast, almost breathless way she had of talking matched her face. She sounded as if her mouth were always trying to catch up with her brain.

Bourne kept listening, and the next voice on the recording was one he recognized from television.

Congresswoman Sofia Ortiz.

Her Hispanic-accented voice was slow and measured, like a politician considering her words.

"Yes, I do disagree. Most strenuously. Is there convenience that comes with living our lives online? Have these apps made our lives better? Absolutely. But the question is, who is really in control of all that information? If we are talking about an individual's personal data, then the individual should own it. Period. And I'm afraid that Big Tech has forgotten that simple lesson. These companies are the latest in a long history of monopolistic industries with too much money, too much power, too much influence, too much potential for abuse. They need to be reined in."

"Speaking of abuse," Abbey went on, *"one of my sources tells me that you believe Big Tech has been covering up some kind of large-scale data hack. A theft that affects practically every online user. What can you tell me about that?"*

"I'm not commenting on that," the congresswoman replied. When she continued, Jason could hear the smile in her voice. *"At least not on the record."*

"And off the record?"

"Off the record, people will be shocked to the core by the volume of data that was stolen."

"Do you know who is behind it?"

"No. How can you investigate the perpetrator of something that Big Tech claims never happened? There are obviously foreign actors who would be likely suspects. Russia. China. Iran."

"What are the risks of this data being in the wrong hands?"

"The risks? Incalculable. Online advertisers already synthesize data in order to influence your buying behavior. Imagine if nearly all of your personal data was available to a rogue actor, someone who wanted to influence you for other reasons. To shape what you think, what you believe, how you act, how you vote. That's the situation we face."

"There's already a new social media software that claims to know what you want to do before you do it," Abbey said. *"Prescix boasts that it can predict your behavior. If you don't know what you want for dinner, the app will tell you. I've used it. It's creepy how accurate it is."*

"Prescix," Congresswoman Ortiz replied thoughtfully. *"Yes, I know the software, but the goal of this technology is not to predict what you do. It's not so benign as they would claim. The goal is to tell you what to do. To manipulate you and make you do whatever they want."*

Jason switched off the recorder.

The interview confirmed what Miles Priest and Scott DeRay had expected, that Abbey had a source who knew about the data hack. The question was *who* and whether that person could help him infiltrate Medusa.

He needed a name.

Bourne dug deeper, sifting through folders and notepads on Abbey's desk. She was prolific and had multiple projects under way, but he didn't find any research notes that were connected to her profile of Sofia Ortiz. There was nothing to tell him who her source might be. If she had other materials about Ortiz and Big Tech, then she hadn't left them in the office. He'd have to find her and talk to her himself.

Jason checked his watch. He'd been inside the offices of *The Fort* for ten minutes, and he couldn't stay much longer. But he wanted to see if he could access Abbey's computer. He found the CPU tower on the floor and switched it on, and the monitor on her desk bloomed to life. The login asked for a password, and he didn't have time to crack it. However, he was intrigued by the wall-paper photograph she'd chosen for her screen.

It showed the hills of Red Rock Canyon outside Las Vegas.

The picture sent a chill up his spine. *Las Vegas.*

Bourne knew it might be a coincidence. Millions of people went to Las Vegas as tourists, and Abbey Laurent going there might not mean anything at all. But this was also the city in which Nova had been murdered.

He logged into the computer as a guest. He couldn't access Abbey's files, but he could load a search engine and search the web. He typed in: *Abbey Laurent Las Vegas.* What came up first in the results took Jason's breath away.

THE MURDERER NEXT DOOR:

Inside the Bland Life of America's Worst Mass Shooter

Abbey had done a profile of *Charles Hackman.*

She'd done a profile of the man who had killed Nova, along with sixty-six other men, women, and children.

Bourne felt his breathing accelerate. Another flashback paralyzed him. In his head, he heard the bullets, the screams; he saw the panic as people ran. But they had nowhere to go. They were easy targets for a man in a hotel window.

And he saw Nova, dead in the middle of the chaos, her body being carried away by a man he knew.

A Treadstone agent.

Jason didn't have time to read further. He glanced at the monitor on the desk in front of him and saw a web camera clipped to the frame. The green light on the webcam glowed. It was active.

Someone was watching him.

He grabbed the camera and yanked it out of the computer port and then kicked the power plug from the wall. He didn't have much time. Seconds. He ran for the office door of *The Fort* and took the stairs to the first floor two at a time. Rather than use the front door again, he followed a dusty corridor to the rear of the building and found another exit that led out to a side street. He cracked the door and looked out. The neighborhood was empty. He ran across the street, where an iron fence built atop a stone wall led into the rear yard of an upscale residential house. He leaped for the fence, propped his foot on one of the crossbars, and threw himself to the other side. Then he flattened himself against the wet green lawn and waited.

He didn't have to wait long.

Headlights shot down Rue d'Auteuil. An SUV stopped outside the building where *The Fort* had its offices, and three men jumped out. They all wore beige raincoats. One man headed for the side street and the exit where Jason had just left, and another charged toward the front door with the broken window.

The third man, who was obviously in charge, hung back. He was tall and sleek, with a neat, polished look that Bourne recognized from long experience. It was the look of a killer. The man wore gold-rimmed glasses that he took off and cleaned as he stood outside the building. Then he examined the area around him with the eyes of a hawk, as if he could sense that Jason was still close by. His eyes were so intense that Jason sunk lower into the grass to make sure he couldn't be seen, even under the shroud of night.

Almost a full minute went by before the man with the gold-rimmed glasses joined his colleagues inside the empty building. The street was deserted again.

Bourne pushed himself off the ground and ran.

EIGHT

ABBEY used a pair of ceramic chopsticks she'd bought in Hong Kong to scoop lo mein noodles out of a white Chinese take-out container. With her other hand, she bit into an egg roll dipped in spicy mustard. Nervously, as she ate, she got out of the wheely chair near her computer and went to the apartment window, which she'd done dozens of times since getting home. The blinds were closed, but she pushed them aside and peered out at the fire escape and the narrow alley called Rue Saint-Flavien. The streetlight showed nothing but a bicycle chained to a drainpipe. She saw no one in the alley, but that didn't make her feel less paranoid.

She paced on the worn carpet of her second-floor studio apartment. The space wasn't large. She had a mattress on the floor where she slept and a tiny bathroom that consisted of a toilet, shower, and sink. Her dinette table doubled as her desk, where she kept her laptop. Her garbage overflowed with fast-food wrappers, because the only kitchen appliance she ever used was the microwave. Her refrigerator was mostly empty, and so were the light blue walls. She traveled more than she was at home, so she didn't have much time to shop or decorate. She never liked to be in one place for very long.

The radio was off, leaving the room quiet. Normally, she played loud jazz, at least until the downstairs neighbors pounded on the ceiling to complain. But tonight she didn't want to drown out any noises. Footsteps in the hallway. Cars in the alley. If the killer in the gold-rimmed glasses came back, she wanted to hear him before he got to her door.

She wished she still had her Taser.

Abbey checked her phone. No messages. No emails. She swore under her breath, because she felt cut off from her sources of information. She'd left four messages for the lawyer in New York who'd fed her the story about the data hack and the suspect in the Ortiz assassination, but he wasn't calling her back. The Quebec police had nothing to say about the shooting at Château Frontenac. Neither did her contacts in the intelligence agencies. No one was talking to her. She didn't have any answers.

She knew who she had to call next, but she didn't want to do it.

His name was Michel Marciano. He'd been her on-again, off-again lover for three years, but over the winter, she'd called it quits with him for good. Michel hadn't been happy about losing her. They'd known each other since college at McGill, where she was a journalism major and he was a law student. They couldn't have been more opposite in nature. He was the buttoned-down bureaucrat with his eyes on government work, and she was the free spirit planning to go around the world chasing stories. She suspected that each of them saw in the other a little bit of what they were missing in life.

They'd dated a few times in college, but it hadn't turned into anything serious. Then they'd reconnected three years ago in Ottawa when she was digging into a bribery scandal on export licenses and he was a mid-level lawyer working in the department of global affairs. Michel hadn't given her any confidential information—he would never do that—but he'd pointed her to people who could help her, and eventually she'd broken the story wide open. Not long after that, she'd invited him to dinner as a way to say thanks, and that night they slept together for the first time.

Within a year, he'd asked her to marry him. She'd been tempted. Michel was kind, smart, and successful, and he bought her nice things, took her to nice places, and always knew what kind of wine to order with dinner. Married life with him would have been stable and pleasant, making stable, pleasant friends and raising stable, pleasant children. She would have had a big house overlooking the Ottawa River with a maid, a swimming pool, and not a take-out container to be found in the kitchen.

Even so, she told him no. That wasn't the life for her. She liked her greasy lo mein and her mattress on the floor. That should have been the end of their relationship, but Michel wasn't the kind of man who gave up easily. He kept pursuing her, and she let herself stay on the hook for two more years. It was convenient to keep him in her life, because she could tell her father that she had a boyfriend, and she could have stable, pleasant sex from time to time. But around Christmastime, she'd decided that the status quo wasn't right for either of them, and she'd finally told Michel that it was over.

She knew what would happen if she called him again. He'd want her back.

But Michel also had contacts throughout the Canadian and American governments, and he could get answers for her. If she waited too long, she knew she would chicken out, so she picked up the phone and dialed. He answered on the first ring, and she could imagine his heart racing as he spotted her name on the caller ID.

"Abbey," he said breathlessly. "It's so lovely to hear from you."

"Hello, Michel."

"Where are you? Are you in Ottawa?"

"No. I'm home in Quebec."

"I've missed you."

She didn't answer right away. His voice sounded the same, that cultured private school accent that always said the right thing as if he were reading it out of a book. She could picture him in her head, his neat black hair in a stiff pompadour, his face handsome and mostly expressionless, his silk tie making a tight knot under his chin.

"I'm—I'm not calling to talk about us, Michel," she murmured.

"Well, can't we do that anyway? I mean it. I've missed you."

"I know. Part of me misses you, too. But we decided—"

"You decided," he interrupted her. "This was you, not me."

"Yes. You're right. It was my call."

"My feelings haven't changed," Michel went on. "If anything, not seeing you for months has made them stronger. I've followed what you've been doing. I read your stories from New York, and I can't tell you how worried I was, thinking of you in the midst of that violence. I was immensely relieved to see that you were safe. I just wish it would make you change your mind about things."

"Michel, please, let's not do this. Not now."

She heard him sigh.

"Fine. All right. What do you want, Abbey?"

"Information."

"About what?"

"Something's going on," she told him. "There was a shooting near Château Frontenac last night. No one in the government will talk about it. The Americans are involved. Have you heard anything?"

Michel was silent for a little while. "No."

"Can you make some inquiries? Can you see what you can find out?"

"I suppose so, yes," he replied with obvious reluctance. "Do you know anything more?"

"It may be related to the assassination in New York."

"Abbey, you're swimming in dangerous waters."

"So what else is new?" she replied. "Can you help me, Michel?"

"I'll make some calls, but the Americans hold everything close to the vest. I don't like the idea of you digging into this story. It's not safe."

"I'm fine," Abbey told him, but she failed to keep the anxiety out of her voice. Michel knew her well enough to know she was hiding something.

"Abbey?" he said. "Are you all right? What's going on?"

"It's nothing."

But he didn't believe her. "If you want my help, be straight with me. Are you in trouble?"

"Actually, a man tried to kill me last night."

"*Kill* you? My God!"

"I got away. I'm fine for now. But the police won't do anything. This is all connected to whatever is going on, and that's why I need answers."

"What you need to do is to *stop* looking into something that could get you killed!" Michel told her sharply.

"I don't walk away from stories. That's not who I am. Besides, it's too late for that."

He sighed again. "All right, let me see what I can find out."

"Thank you, Michel. You'll call me tomorrow?"

"No. I'm taking the first flight to Quebec in the morning. I'll meet you for lunch. We'll talk then."

"You don't have to do that," she said.

"It's not up for discussion. One o'clock at Les Vingt Chats."

She opted not to protest, because she knew he wouldn't change his mind. "All right. I'll see you there."

"Be careful."

Michel hung up the phone. Sitting in silence in her apartment, she felt the weight of his absence. It had felt good to hear his voice, like the comfort of putting on an old, familiar sweater. In truth, she liked the idea of him running to her rescue. She couldn't help but wonder if lunch would lead to dinner, and dinner would lead to her spending the night in his hotel room.

Abbey picked up her carton of lo mein.

Then someone pounded on her apartment door. She dropped the carton on the floor, making a mess of noodles and sauce. A husky voice shouted her name. *"Abbey Laurent! Police!"*

She stifled a scream. When she ran back to the window and looked down at the alley, she saw two police vehicles with flashing lights parked beside her building.

"Ms. Laurent!" the same voice called again impatiently, pounding on her door for a second time.

Abbey checked the peephole. Through the fish-eye lens, she could see three uniformed police officers outside her door, but they weren't alone. A man in a dark raincoat and a fedora stood behind them. She opened the door, and when she did, the police officers separated. The other man came forward, assisted by a cane as he limped to her doorway.

It was the American intelligence officer she'd seen on the boardwalk.

"Ms. Laurent? My name is Nash Rollins. I'm with the American government. I want to talk to you."

Abbey studied the expressionless faces of the police officers who were with him. "If I don't want to talk, will I be arrested?"

"Not at all," Rollins replied. "Actually, I brought the police along to make sure you felt safe. I heard about the attempt on your life, so I wasn't sure you'd open the door to a stranger."

"You're right."

"May I come in?" he asked.

Abbey hesitated, then waved her hand to usher him inside. The man limped into her apartment and shot a glance around the messy, impersonal studio. He didn't look like a man who missed much. She didn't invite him to sit down.

"What do you want?"

"First, would you mind closing the door?"

She eyed the open door and the policemen, and then she shut the door quietly. She also noticed her laptop on the table and went and closed the lid.

Rollins was a compact man, with a tough, weathered body coiled tightly like a rope. His knuckles were white where he gripped the head of his cane, and his torso bent like a question mark. With his other hand, he removed his hat, revealing unruly gray hair. He had bushy pale eyebrows, with blue eyes that squinted as if he were being assaulted by a frigid wind. The skin on his face was etched with tight, narrow wrinkles.

"I'll cut to the chase, Ms. Laurent. I know who you

are and what you do, and I know you were supposed to meet a man on the boardwalk last night. I'd like you to tell me if he's been in touch with you since then."

"If you know what I do, then you know I'm a journalist," Abbey replied. "I'm not in the habit of sharing information with someone from the government. Particularly someone who's not even from *my* government."

"This man is dangerous, Ms. Laurent. You don't know who you're dealing with."

"I don't know who I'm dealing with right now, Mr. Rollins. You say you're with the American government, but you haven't shown me any identification. I assume you're a spook, so what are you? CIA?"

Rollins's hooded eyes assessed her with a grudging respect, but he made no move to produce any identification. He tapped the head of his cane on the floor. "You don't trust me. Fine. You shouldn't trust him, either."

"No?"

"No. Let me ask you a question. Are you under the impression that this man didn't show up for your meeting last night?"

Abbey frowned. "That's right."

"Wrong," Rollins snarled. "He was there. He *killed* four of my agents. He shot me in the leg. He was following *you* when we intercepted him, Ms. Laurent. Do I need to tell you what would have happened if he'd caught up with you? You'd be dead with a bullet in your throat."

The information hit Abbey hard. She paled and sat heavily in one of her chairs. "Is that really true?"

"It is."

"Someone came after me later, but it wasn't him."

"Do you think he operates alone? He doesn't. He's part of a very dangerous network. Until we catch him, you're at serious risk. You may not trust me, but I'm trying to help you, Ms. Laurent. Now, you need to answer my question. Has he been in touch with you since last night?"

She shook her head. "No."

"Well, watch your back. He's heading your way."

Her dark eyes widened. "What?"

"He escaped from us last night and took refuge in a town a couple hours north of here. But we think he's on his way back to the city. He may already be here now. I can think of only one reason why he'd take that kind of risk. He's coming after *you*. My question is, what do you know that makes you a threat to him?"

"I don't know anything."

"I think you're lying to me."

"I really don't care what you think. I don't know anything."

"Why were you meeting with this man? What did he want?"

"I have nothing to say about that."

"I'm trying to protect you, Ms. Laurent."

"No, you're not. You don't care what happens to me. You just want *him*."

Rollins shifted on his feet and grimaced with pain. He reached into the inner pocket of his coat and came out with a small white card, which he handed to her. She read it and saw no name, no identification, no agency, just ten numbers. A phone number.

"If he contacts you, call that number," Rollins told her. "Day or night."

"Why? So you can kill both of us?"

Rollins sighed. "Please don't think you can confront this man alone. He's violent, and he's unstable. I've known him for years. He's damaged in a way you or I can't understand. He's a man with no past."

"What the hell does that mean?"

Rollins ignored her question. He limped to the apartment door and put a hand on the doorknob. Then he turned back. "If you hear from him, call that number, Ms. Laurent."

"Wait!" Abbey said. "Who *is* he? Is he Cain? What's his real name?"

"Names don't matter," Rollins told her. "He goes by a lot of names. Cain is just one of them. The only thing you need to know is that this man is a killer."

JASON stood in the darkness at the far end of Rue Saint-Flavien. He sheltered in the nook of a graffiti-strewn doorway, where he was invisible. Police cars with swirling lights blocked the alley on both sides of the apartment building where Abbey Laurent lived, and he heard the chatter of their radios. There was also a dark sedan parked farther away, its lights off. As Bourne watched, the door to the building opened, and a cluster of police officers walked outside. They were followed by a man that he knew well. A man limping from the injury that Jason had given him the previous night.

Nash Rollins.

Treadstone was still here. Still hunting him.

The police got into their cars, and the cars peeled away in both directions. Bourne sank deeper into the doorway as one of the vehicles spun around the corner directly in front of him. That left Nash Rollins and the sedan. Rollins signaled with his hand, and the sedan's lights turned on, as it roared up to the curb in front of him. The back door opened, and Rollins climbed inside, but as he did, another Treadstone agent got out of the vehicle.

The sedan made a U-turn and sped away, but the remaining agent stayed by the door to Abbey Laurent's building. His hands were in his pockets, where he no doubt had easy access to a weapon. Bourne knew the drill. The agent would be there all night.

Jason pulled up his collar, silently left the doorway, and melted into the darkness. He had a plan.

Tomorrow he'd fight back.

Tomorrow he'd take Abbey Laurent.

NINE

THE next morning, Jason watched the watchers.

He spotted a second Treadstone agent arriving to conduct surveillance on Abbey Laurent, replacing the one who'd spent the night there. Jason knew him from a mission they'd done together in Milan. His name was Farnham, and Jason remembered him as cocky and way too sure of himself. He was in his twenties, with brown hair and a baby face that disguised his ruthlessness. He wore a white mock turtleneck and a gray silk suit, looking like an upscale Canadian businessman. He leaned against a parked car half a block away from Abbey's door and talked on his phone in fluent French, using a loud voice and an easy smile.

Bourne knew the rule. Sometimes the best cover was to hide in plain sight.

At nine o'clock, Abbey Laurent emerged into the alley below her apartment. Jason watched her check both directions with a nervous expression. She studied all of the pedestrians coming and going. An old woman walking her dog. Two teenage boys eating chocolate croissants and carrying red backpacks. A man hosing down the sidewalk. Her gaze passed over Farnham without stopping. She shot a quick look at the cloudless sky and then shrugged her purse strap over her shoulder and walked up the hill. Her red hair and cobalt-blue blouse made her easy to spot.

At the corner, she turned right. As soon as she did, Farnham slipped the phone into his pocket and followed. Two blocks behind him, Bourne followed, too. When he reached the next alley, he could see both of them. Abbey walked without looking back, and Farnham stayed about twenty yards behind her on the opposite sidewalk. Near the next intersection at Côte de la Fabrique, Abbey disappeared into a bakery. She wasn't inside for long. When she came out, she had a takeaway cup of coffee in her hand, and again she glanced up and down the street.

This time, however, she zeroed in on a police officer approaching from the opposite direction. She engaged in a brief conversation with the cop, then walked quickly away. Farnham increased his pace to catch her, but he had only gone a few steps when the police officer confronted him on the sidewalk. The cop demanded to know who Farnham was and why he was following a young woman on the street, and while the American agent made loud protestations, Abbey disappeared from view around the next curve.

Bourne smiled. The woman was smart and resourceful. She'd spotted the tail. By the time Farnham got free of the cop, he had to run to locate her again, but he was too late. Bourne kept Farnham in sight as the Treadstone agent hurried to the next intersection, where several streets came together in a busy jumble of cars and people. There was no sign of Abbey Laurent.

As Jason watched, Farnham pulled out his phone to call in a report. Less than five minutes later, a blue Mercedes whipped along the busy street and stopped beside him, and the agent climbed into the passenger seat. The car sped off. Bourne waited to see what would happen next. As soon as the car disappeared, he spotted Abbey emerging from her hiding place on a grassy slope above the Côte de la Fabrique, where she'd been watching the whole thing.

Definitely smart.

With a toss of her deep red hair, Abbey joined the people on the street. Jason gave her plenty of space, but she walked with more assurance now, as if she were confident that she'd shaken the people pursuing her. Her route took her sharply uphill past the Morrin Centre, and eventually she reached Rue d'Auteuil near Esplanade Park, only a couple of blocks from the offices of *The Fort*. As he had the previous night, Jason stayed in the park, rather than on the street, and he shadowed Abbey until she reached the building where the magazine was housed. She observed the broken window on the front door, and the sight obviously unnerved her. She turned around, suspicious again, and made a careful review of the area, as if she could feel his eyes. Then she went inside.

Bourne waited. There was nothing else to do. Waiting was the real art of surveillance. He bought a newspaper; he bought coffee; he found a bench near the Boer War monument, where the trees sheltered him. The morning was cold but bright, and he wore sunglasses. From where he was, he could see the building doors. Whenever Abbey came outside again, he'd spot her.

Soon he had company on the stakeout. The blue Mercedes returned and pulled into a parking place with a similar vantage on Abbey Laurent's building. Someone had obviously reported to Treadstone that she'd arrived at *The Fort*. Two men got out of the Mercedes. One was Farnham; the other was an agent who Bourne didn't recognize. Farnham took the car keys, and the other agent walked away down the cobblestoned street, leaving Farnham alone to take the first shift. Jason watched the young operative get behind the wheel of the Mercedes. The driver's window was open, and he could see the occasional cloud of cigarette smoke drift into the air.

The morning passed slowly.

A few people came and went from the building, but Abbey stayed inside. Farnham didn't leave the car, and he smoked his way through half a pack of cigarettes as he sat there. Bourne eyed the street for other surveillance, but he didn't see anyone else covering the neighborhood. It seemed to be just the two of them.

Then, around twelve-thirty, a newcomer attracted his attention. A woman panhandler shuffled down the north side of Rue d'Auteuil, cupping her palm at everyone she passed and demanding change. She wore a multicolored skirt that draped to her ankles and a heavy crocheted black sweater that was too long for her arms. Her thick black hair fell to the middle of her back, with half a dozen red plastic butterflies braided into the strands. She wore round yellow glasses that kept slipping down her nose. Her back was hunched. When she got to the corner, she stopped, accosting every pedestrian who passed her and swearing at those who didn't give her money.

"Cochon riche! Est-ce que je suis trop sale pour vous?"

The panhandler noticed Farnham in the Mercedes, and with a snort of derision, she approached the car. Bourne saw her stuff her left hand inside the open window. The encounter didn't last long, no more than a few seconds, and then the woman backed away with another curse and disappeared around the corner onto Rue Saint-Louis.

Maybe it was an innocent exchange. Maybe not.

Had she passed Farnham a message?

Jason didn't have time to think about it, because only a couple of minutes later, Abbey Laurent finally reappeared. She turned right out of the building along Rue Saint-Louis, and her pace was quick, as if she needed to get somewhere. Bourne waited for the Treadstone agent in the Mercedes to take up the chase, but the man made no move to get out of the car.

Why not?

There was no way Farnham could have missed her, and yet he was letting her go. Seconds passed. Then a minute. Then two.

Something was wrong.

Bourne headed toward the Mercedes. Inside the car, Farnham still hadn't moved. Bourne listened for the sound of the man talking on the phone, reporting Abbey's position to another agent, but there was no noise from the interior. Jason came up slowly on the open window. If Farnham saw Bourne, he'd recognize him, but it couldn't be helped. He reached the door of the sedan and shot a quick glance at the Treadstone agent, and then he froze where he was.

Farnham's eyes were closed. He wasn't moving.

Jason leaned inside the car window. He pulled aside the flap of Farnham's suit coat and saw a slit in the man's white shirt directly over his heart and a bloodstain spreading across the fabric.

It was a perfect, precise attack, a single killing thrust with a knife through the ribs and into the heart and lungs.

The panhandler was an assassin.

And now she was after Abbey Laurent.

Bourne spun away from the Mercedes and into Rue Saint-Louis, which was jammed with people taking their lunch breaks. Time had passed since he'd seen Abbey leave. Too much time. He'd let her get too far ahead of him. Looking down the sidewalk, he couldn't pick her out, and he half walked, half ran, shoving his way through the crowd and offering excuses in French.

Where was she?

He hurried under the yellow awnings of the quaint stone buildings. Canadian flags snapped over his head. A backup of cars filled the street. He passed doorway after doorway of gift shops, restaurants, and hotels, the volume of people thickening as he neared the tourist heart of the city. Still he couldn't find Abbey, and by now she could be anywhere. She could already be dying in a doorway on one of the side streets, a knife in her chest.

Ahead of him, the street ended in the shadows of Château Frontenac. The statue of Champlain rose over the plaza.

There!

Just for an instant, he spotted a woman darting between the stopped cars, and he saw a flash of red and blue as she passed out of sight. It was her. Bourne ran again, and two blocks later, the street opened into the wide-open plaza that led to the Dufferin Terrace. The castle-like walls of the hotel loomed over his head. Hundreds of people milled in the square, and Abbey was lost in the crowd.

He didn't like it. Crowds were dangerous. People squeezed together, people shouting and laughing, people bumping into each other. One collision was all the killer needed to plunge in the knife. No one would see a thing.

Bourne pushed people aside, going faster and faster through the plaza. The sun was blinding, and the bodies around him were a blur of motion. Men and women passed back and forth in his line of sight, blocking his view. His senses shot into overdrive, feeding him information faster than his brain could process it. Every time he saw red—a red T-shirt, a red balloon, a red backpack— he froze to see if it was Abbey Laurent. But he couldn't find her. Then his eyes locked onto a familiar flash of color. Not red. This was a quick, swirling rainbow of fabric. The panhandler. He recognized her multicolored skirt, the butterflies in her hair, her black sweater—a sweater in which she had a bloody knife secured in one of the sleeves. The woman wasn't shuffling anymore, and her back was no longer hunched. She moved through the crowd with deadly intent. As Bourne watched, she disappeared through glass doors that led into the funicular connecting the upper and lower towns of Quebec City.

She was following Abbey.

He used a gap in the crowd to bolt for the green-and-white building with the huge sign overhead: *Funiculaire*. When he got there, he wrenched open the glass door and shoved past the people in front of him to get down the stairs. Half a dozen people were already waiting for the next car to take them down the sharp slope to the Basse-Ville. He saw the back of Abbey's head; she was at the front, ready to board as the doors opened. Four people back, eyes focused like a laser on Abbey Laurent, was the panhandler, with her hands invisible inside the long arms of her sweater.

One couple was ahead of Jason in the ticket queue. An American in a Chicago Cubs jacket hunted for coins to pay the fare for him and his wife. Jason saw one of the funicular cars rising into view, approaching the station. He was running out of time. When the doors opened, Abbey and the others would board, and the funicular car would descend the cliffside. By the time it got to the bottom, she would have a knife wound in her heart, and her lungs would be filling with blood.

"*Non, monsieur, sept, sept,*" the ticket clerk told the American. "Seven. It is seven dollars for the two of you."

"Seven dollars? That's outrageous!" The man turned to his wife. "I think we should walk. For seven bucks? Let's take the stairs."

"Oh, for heaven's sake, Chuck, just pay the man, will you? My feet are tired as it is."

Grumbling, the man in the Cubs jacket handed over a twenty-dollar Canadian bill.

While the clerk dug in the drawer for change, the doors of the funicular opened. The people inside disembarked. When the car was empty, Jason saw Abbey Laurent walk through the open doors to the far side and stand in front of the windows. The car was small. People squeezed in behind her. Bourne saw the panhandler nudging toward the front, positioning herself for the kill.

Finally, the couple in front of him finished paying. Jason threw a five-dollar bill down without waiting for change. He headed for the turnstile that led to the funicular, but the American couple blocked his way.

"It's crowded," the man told his wife, pointing at the car. "Look at how many people are on there. Let's just wait for the next one."

"There's plenty of room."

"But if we're not at the front, we can't take pictures."

Bourne veered around them, ignoring the couple's protests. He slammed through the turnstile and threw himself onto the funicular just as the doors closed behind him. No one noticed his arrival. They were all staring at the panorama of the old town spread out below them and the deep blue water of the St. Lawrence River beyond the port. The people stood shoulder to shoulder in the tight warm space, which felt like an oversized phone booth.

He saw Abbey in front of the glass. The panhandler was immediately behind her. The woman's black sleeves covered her hands, except for a glimpse of her fingertips. Jason could see that her fingernails were stained with blood.

The car started down the cliff.

Two hundred feet below them, pedestrians dotted the streets of the old town, and boats traversed the river. The ride wouldn't take long. One minute, no more. Jason knew when the attack would come. At the exact moment when the doors opened at the bottom and the people shoved against each other to get out, there would be one quick thrust of the knife. No one would see it happen. The panhandler would maneuver calmly around her and escape as Abbey stood frozen in place. Abbey wouldn't even know what had happened; she'd take a few steps and feel only the odd, sharp pain in her back and find herself struggling to breathe. By the time she collapsed, by the time she died, the woman who'd killed her would have vanished into the streets of the Basse-Ville.

Jason squeezed to the side of the car. He muscled past a woman and her child, using his shoulder to force them away. The mother shot him an angry look and murmured, "*Très impoli.*" The seconds ticked by as he nudged closer, until his breath was practically on the panhandler's neck. He kept his eyes locked on her left arm, and the panhandler kept her eyes locked on Abbey Laurent directly in front of her.

The roofs of the old town grew closer and larger.

Bourne saw the assassin slowly bring up her arm. Her hand, cloaked by the sleeve of her sweater, was positioned below Abbey's left shoulder blade, where the knife could slide into her back. As soon as the doors slid open, she would thrust forward and bump hard against Abbey with an apology. *"Excusez-moi!"*

The knife would go in and out.

Jason held his breath. The funicular car shuddered as it bumped into place. He timed his strike, and as the doors began to open, he pinched the panhandler's elbow bone hard, driving his fingers deep into her pressure points, freezing all sensation. The panhandler screeched in pain, and Bourne heard a metallic clatter as the knife dropped from her limp hand to the floor of the car. Her neck jerked around, her face screwed up in rage, and then her eyes widened as she saw Bourne not even six inches away.

She *knew* him.

The panhandler's mouth twisted into a snarl. Her body swung all the way around, and her right hand came up with a small pistol. He grabbed her wrist, keeping the gun away, and with the heel of his other hand, he snapped her chin back and drove her head into the steel frame of the funicular car.

Her eyes rolled up. Her body slid to the floor of the car.

He couldn't hide what he'd done. People saw it happen; they saw *him*. Bedlam ensued. Shouts for help rose in the station, and inside and outside the funicular car, two dozen people stampeded for the sunlight of the exit.

He saw Abbey Laurent among the crowd. She'd almost reached the streets of the lower town when she heard the scream and the chaos erupting behind her. She turned in confusion and looked back at the funicular car, taking in the sight of the unconscious woman on the floor and Jason standing over her.

Their eyes met across the station, and he watched her face go pale. Then he could see her lips soundlessly form one word.

Cain.

TEN

CAIN.

Abbey had no doubt that it was him. The assassin. The killer who had sent a bullet into the throat of Congresswoman Sofia Ortiz.

She also had no doubt that he was here to kill *her*.

Abbey ran into the streets of the lower town, where the crowd swallowed her and kept her invisible. Once she was there, she walked quickly, keeping her head down. Her red hair stood out, so when she passed a gift shop that had a table of clearance clothes outside, she grabbed a hooded sweatshirt and quickly pulled it over her head. She yanked up the hood, hiding her hair. She didn't dare look back.

The Basse-Ville was a rabbit's warren of uneven streets tunneling between centuries-old brick buildings. When she reached the first cross street, she turned left and hurried beside shop doorways with her hands shoved in the pouch of the sweatshirt. In the plaza ahead of her, she approached an eighteenth-century stone church known as Notre-Dame-des-Victoires. As she passed the church wall, she crossed the steps and took cover in a pedestrian alleyway. Peering around the corner of the wall, she watched the people in the plaza.

Moments later, she saw him. Cain. He ran into the courtyard, hunting for her. Abbey immediately backed away before he could see her and headed down the alley. At the other end, she turned toward the water. She ran across the green grass outside the Royal Battery, past the park's walls and cannons, and then darted through traffic to the walkway beside the cold ribbon of the St. Lawrence River.

Looking back across the street, she saw no sign that he'd followed her. She stayed next to the water as she walked, with the hood blocking her face if anyone looked her way from the city. The wind was fierce and cold, but she was hot from running. The pier was deserted. In the high season, cruise ships docked here, belching out thousands of tourists into the tiny streets, but April was too early for the big ships to come calling. The glass walkway from the terminal crossed over her head and ended at the water. Across the narrow river channel, she could see the hillside marking the town of Lévis. Out beyond the port, the river split in two around Ile d'Orléans as it snaked toward the Atlantic.

Abbey checked her watch. It was already after one o'clock, which meant she was late. Ahead of her, beyond the terminal building, she saw the riverside restaurant known as Les Vingt Chats. Whenever Michel was in town, they met there. He was waiting for her now, and the thought of seeing him gave her an intense sense of relief.

Her phone buzzed in her pocket. She took it out, expecting a message from Michel, but when she read it, she knew who the message was from.

It was the man in the funicular. The man who'd lured her to the boardwalk the previous night.

It was Cain.

I'm not trying to hurt you. You're in danger.

She trembled as she stared at the screen. She stopped where she was and turned around to study the port. Had he found her? Was he hiding near the terminal?

No. She was all alone on the blustery river walk. And yet she felt watched.

Another text came in.

The woman on the funicular was going to kill you. Tell me where you are.

She didn't believe him. She couldn't let him find her. *You're Cain! You're the killer!*

She powered down her phone rather than let him taunt her with more messages. She was distracted now, focused on getting to the restaurant. The sign for Les Vingt Chats called to her, as it had so many times before. The long row of windows in the dining room overlooked the water, and stairs led from the portside walkway to the lobby. She headed there, but then she heard someone calling to her.

"*Abbey!*"

Startled, she tried to find the source of the voice. Then she heard it again.

"*Ici! C'est moi!*"

Far down the pier, she spotted a man by the water, framed against the sun. It was Michel, waving at her. He felt like a lifeline after two days caught in a nightmare. She ran toward him, but as she got closer, she was disturbed by what she saw. Michel, who was always the perfectly dressed bureaucrat, looked disheveled and unshaved. He wore a dirty raincoat; his tie was loose. The wind had blown his coiffed black hair into messy tufts.

"Michel!" She went to embrace him, but instead, he took her by the shoulders.

"What the hell have you gotten me into?" he demanded.

"What? What are you talking about?"

"They threatened to *fire* me. They threatened to *arrest* me."

"Who?"

"The government. They told me to bring you back to Ottawa with me. You need to answer their questions, Abbey. You need to tell them everything you know."

Abbey pried his hands from her and backed away. "Michel, what have you done?"

"Me? What have *I* done? My career is finished. They'll never trust me again. All because I tried to help you."

"Slow down. Tell me what's going on."

Michel walked to the edge of the concrete pier. Out on the river, dots of sunlight glistened on the whitecaps. He ran his hands through his hair and stared at the sky. She'd never seen him like this. She'd barely seen any emotion from him in all the time they'd spent together, and now he was falling to pieces.

"Jesus," he said. "I can't believe this."

"Michel, talk to me. What happened?"

He turned and looked at her. His eyes were sleepless and bloodshot. "After we talked last night, I went to the office. I was there all night. I dug into our intelligence reports to see what information we'd gathered about the assassination in New York. Then I reached out to a few of my American contacts. That was all. I was still at my desk at four in the morning when the phone rang. It was the minister. The minister *himself.* He told me that three CSIS agents would be in my office in ten minutes, and I was to tell them *everything* about the inquiries I'd been making. And he said the answers would determine whether I'd keep my job or spend the next twenty years in Millhaven."

"Oh, my God! Did you tell them about me?"

"They already knew all about you. The CSIS think you're a threat to national security, Abbey. Why do they think that? What the hell have you been doing?"

"Nothing! This is *insane!* I've been following a story, that's all. I tried to set up a meeting with a source, and then someone tried to kill me. Last night someone broke into *The Fort* and searched my desk. Today I was followed as I came here. I barely got away."

"Who followed you?"

"I think it was the assassin from New York. I think it was Cain."

Michel rubbed his chin, and she could see the strain on his face. "Are you sure?"

"No, I've never met him. I don't know what he looks like. But an American intelligence agent visited my apartment last night with the police. He said that Cain was coming to Quebec City to get *me*."

"You know something. You have something he wants." Michel hesitated. "Or you're involved in something criminal, Abbey. Tell me that's not true."

Anger flashed on her face. "You know me, Michel. I'm a reporter. You actually think I'm a spy?"

"I don't know what to think anymore."

"This is all about Cain. The Americans, the CSIS, they both think I can lead them to Cain. That's why he wants me dead."

Michel took her hands. "Then come back with me to Ottawa, and talk to them."

"So they can put me in Millhaven, too? No, thanks."

"It's not like that. Just answer their questions. Nothing will happen to you. I'll make sure they let me stay with you the whole time. It's safer if you're not in Quebec City, based on what's been happening here. Stay with me. We can be together." He paused and then leaned closer to her. "You know I still love you."

Abbey wanted to believe him. She'd spent three years with Michel and almost married him. And yet if it came down to a choice, she wondered if he would sacrifice her with barely a second thought.

"First, tell me what you found out," Abbey said. "You said you reached out to your contacts. What did you find?"

"I didn't find anything."

"I don't believe that."

"It's true. I hit a brick wall."

"You're lying, Michel," Abbey snapped. "You think I can't read your face? The CSIS didn't show up simply because you were asking questions. You *found* something, and whatever it is scared the hell out of people."

Michel didn't say anything, but she could see him breathing hard. His raw nerves made him twitch.

"It scared the hell out of *you*, too, didn't it?" Abbey went on softly. "You have to tell me the truth. I have to know what I'm up against. What did you find out, Michel? What did the Americans tell you about Cain?"

He bit his lip. "Cain is just the tip of the iceberg."

"Then what else is going on?"

Michel leaned close to her and whispered. "Have you ever heard of an organization called Medusa?"

"No."

"Are you sure? It's never come up from any of your sources?"

"Never," Abbey said. "What's Medusa?"

Michel shook his head. "I don't know many details. One of the Americans I talked to assumed I knew all about it, and that's why he told me what he did. When he realized this was new to me, he panicked and said I had to keep it all quiet. But I didn't. I kept pushing, and that's why the CSIS showed up in my office."

"Michel, *what is Medusa?*"

"Nobody really knows. That's what has everyone scared. Nobody seems to know how big the organization is, or how it's structured, or who runs it. It's not connected to any government, or at least no one seems to think so, but they can't be sure. The only thing anyone seems to know is that it's technology-driven. They aim to control people, influence them, shape how they behave, how they think. They've been fomenting unrest. Protests. Riots. They're like an army that uses technology to recruit its own soldiers."

Abbey put a hand over her mouth. "The data hack," she murmured. "Personal information on tens of millions of people."

"Exactly. The CIA thinks Medusa was behind it."

"But *why?*"

"That's what scares them, Abbey. They don't know."

"So this killer called Cain must be part of Medusa."

"The government thinks so," Michel replied. "Do you see why you have to come with me, Abbey? If this organization thinks you're a threat, you're dead. Let me protect you. Let *us* protect you."

She hesitated. *Do I trust this man?*

But she didn't have a choice.

For two days, the walls had been closing in on her, and now Michel was giving her a way out. She'd called him for help, and he was offering help. She couldn't keep running. Not on her own.

"Okay," she said.

"Really? Thank God!"

"Yes, let's go," she told him. "Let's get the hell out of here."

Michel's face flushed with relief. He took two steps along the pier to embrace her.

Then his neck exploded.

The bullet went straight through him, severing his spinal cord. Blood showered over Abbey as if she'd walked into a fountain. The crack of a gunshot rolled over the wind, but she barely even noticed it. Her mouth froze open in horror and shock. Michel was alive, and then he was dead; it happened in an instant. The light vanished from his eyes. Her lover crumpled sideways, and his body spilled from the pier, making a splash in the river water. He disappeared below the surface. Just like that, he was gone. The only evidence that he'd been there at all was the blood dripping down her face.

The killer with the gold-rimmed glasses walked calmly toward her across the empty pier. His coat flew up behind him in the wind. He had a gun with a suppressor in his right hand, and this time she had no Taser to fight back. She needed to run, but her legs felt rooted to the ground. Her brain whirled, unable to catch up to what was happening. Reality broke into a million pieces.

Run!

But she stood there, paralyzed. Michel was dead.

Soon she would be, too. It was as if she were watching herself from far away, screaming commands that her body ignored.

The man stopped right in front of her. His wispy blond hair blew across his head. His cold blue eyes made her shiver. She expected him to raise the gun, but he didn't. The other night, in the park, he would have put a bullet in her neck and been done, but he wasn't going to make it that easy for her now.

"Ms. Laurent," he said in that same flat, emotionless voice. "I believe you and I have unfinished business."

ELEVEN

JASON stood on the Rue du Sault-au-Matelot under a rough cliff that rose like a craggy face over his head. He had no hope of finding Abbey Laurent in the maze of lower-town streets. He checked his new phone, but she hadn't answered his texts. He didn't blame her for that. She thought he was Cain; she thought he was a murderer. He could picture her face vividly in his mind and remember the look of terror as she saw him in the funicular. He'd seen that look often enough in his life.

He also knew that if he didn't find her, she wouldn't make it out of the Basse-Ville alive. Medusa had already sent one assassin after her, and Bourne doubted that the woman in the funicular was working alone.

Save her! She has information you need!

But in truth, it was more than that. He'd watched her face through the lenses of his binoculars. Then, in the funicular, he'd been inches away from her, able to admire the soft curve of her jaw in profile, the choppy red hair, the way her lips always had the same little smile, as if she were thinking of a private joke. She intrigued him.

Don't think like that! Abbey Laurent is an asset, nothing more. She's the gateway to Medusa. Find her!

Bourne switched off his emotions. He had a problem to solve, and he needed to solve it quickly. He dialed a new number on the phone, and a moment later, a male voice answered, "*The Fort.*"

"Abbey Laurent, please," Jason said, letting his voice flatten into a Brooklyn accent.

"I'm sorry, Abbey's at lunch. Can I take a message?"

"Is this Jacques? Jacques Varille?"

"Yes, it is."

"Jacques, this is Matt Schneider calling. Abs gave me your name and said if I couldn't reach her, I should talk to you."

He heard hesitation in the magazine editor's voice. "How can I help you?"

"Well, see, I'm a freelance photographer based in New York. I met Abs last year when she was hanging out at that UN conference with Michel, and I bumped into her again last week when I was shooting pics at the Ortiz rally. Man, that went sideways, but for a photographer, it was like winning the lottery, you know?"

"I guess so."

"Anyway, we were chatting before the rally, and I mentioned that I was going to be in QC today doing brochure photos for Hilton. We talked about getting together, but it was a pretty casual thing. She wasn't even sure she'd be in town. Except then she called me a few days ago and asked if I'd mind bringing along my pics from the riot and letting her go through them. I guess she's trying to ID somebody for a story. We were supposed to meet for lunch, but I'm here with my laptop, and she's not, and she's not answering her phone. You got any idea where I can find her? The thing is, I have to head to the airport at three, and she sounded like she really wanted to see my pics."

"Are you certain she knew it was today, Matt?" the editor asked. "Because she told me this morning that Michel was coming to town and she was meeting him at one o'clock."

"Well, it wouldn't be the first time I got my signals crossed. I was pretty sure we were clear on the date, though. Of course, if Michel's in town, maybe she just forgot. You know where they were having lunch? I could swing over and say hi to both of them and see if she still wants to breeze through my photo library."

"She didn't say specifically, but they usually meet at Les Vingt Chats. It's a riverside restaurant near the port terminal."

"Twenty cats. Got it. Thanks a lot, Jacques."

Bourne hung up. He checked a map on his phone for the restaurant, which was only a short walk from where he was. He hurried through the newer, more corporate section of town, where the Old World charm evaporated and Quebec looked like any other city. As he neared the river, the wind rose up like a slap and turned the air cold. He used an access road past an old pumping station to approach the restaurant, but he hesitated near the door. If Abbey Laurent wasn't alone, that complicated his mission, and if she saw him coming for her, she'd panic. He didn't want her to run.

Find her! Take her!

Then his plan changed. Everything changed.

A suppressor muffled the sound, but the wind carried the noise of a gunshot to his ears from near the river.

Medusa.

Bourne jumped a fence near the town's massive Old Port building, which took him inside an open-air amphitheater that was used for summer concerts. He skidded down the grass to the sunken staging area and sprinted to the opposite side. There, he took the concrete steps two at a time to the top of the theater, where a knoll with overgrown weeds separated him from the pier walkway. He could see the river and a series of white storage silos rising over the industrial port. In front of him was a long, low building that housed a naval museum, which was closed and empty today.

He heard a muffled scream. Bourne threw himself over the next fence and crouched low in the weeds. Two people approached from the river. One was the killer with the gold-rimmed glasses he'd seen outside the offices of *The Fort* the previous night. The other was Abbey Laurent. She had streaks of blood on her face, and she squirmed violently in the man's grasp. A belt secured her wrists tightly behind her back. The Medusa killer held the woman around her waist, dragging her with him as she struggled. His gun wasn't visible, but Bourne knew he had one jabbed into the woman's side.

Twenty yards away, he saw a blue Renault parked near a row of maple trees outside the naval museum. The killer hustled Abbey toward the car. Bourne readied his gun, but Abbey's body was between him and the killer, and he couldn't fire without hitting her. He crawled through the grass, staying parallel to them, waiting for an opportunity when the Medusa assassin was in his line of sight.

"If you kill me, I can't tell you anything!" Abbey hissed on the walkway as she tried to twist free from her captor.

The assassin laughed at her. "Don't flatter yourself, Ms. Laurent. Anything you know comes from *us*. You have nothing we need. You're simply a loose end."

"Then what are you waiting for?" she snarled.

"*Patience*, please. My orders are to kill you, but how I do so is up to me. Since you're so fond of electric shocks, I thought you might enjoy feeling what it's like when fifty thousand volts fire between your legs. Maybe you'll get a *thrill*."

Abbey inhaled and spat in his face. The killer flinched and yanked his gun arm back to whip the barrel across her skull. As he did, his grip on her loosened. Abbey wrenched away, and in the same instant, Bourne fired. He fired and *missed*. The bullet ripped off part of the man's ear, then shattered a window in the naval museum.

The gunshot froze Abbey where she was, and before

she could run, the killer grabbed her again. He pinned her with his arm around her throat and used her body as a shield as he pointed his weapon into the weeds.

"Come out!" he barked. "Come out now!"

Bourne stood up slowly, his gun aimed across the short space of grass and concrete between them, his finger on the trigger. They confronted each other, neither one with an advantage. Jason inched down the grassy slope until his feet were on the pavement. Not even ten feet separated them.

"*Cain*," the man murmured.

"That's a name from my past," Jason replied.

"I'm told you don't have a past."

The killer's glasses glinted in the sunlight, and his lips curled into a smile. Blood poured from his ear. He crushed his arm around Abbey's neck, and her legs kicked wildly as he lifted her off the ground. With her air cut off, panic filled her eyes.

"Let her go," Bourne said.

"Put down your gun, and I will."

"Give me the girl, and I'll let you leave."

"Then we're at an impasse," the man replied.

Abbey's legs flailed. Her body shunted back and forth, slamming against the killer, but he remained rooted to the ground like the trunk of a tree. He lifted her higher. A purple color flushed her cheeks.

"*Stop!*" Bourne shouted.

"Drop your gun. She goes free."

"If she dies, so do you."

"Well, she *is* going to die," the killer replied.

Jason's eyes met Abbey's. Something changed in her expression. Her mouth opened, as if she were trying to form a word, but she couldn't. Then Bourne understood. Abbey's hands were still tied behind her, but he could see her fingers curled like claws, the nails long and sharp. Her body jerked against the assassin, and this time, she snapped her fingers around the man's testicles and crushed them between her nails.

He howled in agony. As he thrashed to dislodge her, she clung to him without letting go. Still holding Abbey by the neck, the assassin cracked the barrel down against the top of her head. As soon as Jason saw the man's gun shift away, he leaped across the space between them. The assassin tried to bring his gun back around, but Bourne locked his fingers around the man's wrist and piled his weight against him, bringing all of them to the ground.

Unconscious, Abbey spilled to the concrete beside them.

Jason was on top, pinning the killer down. He slammed the man's wrist against the pavement until his hand released the gun. The assassin had his own hand locked around Jason's gun, and their arms seesawed for control. Bourne snapped his forehead against the man's nose, breaking it in a mass of blood, but the killer didn't relent. The Renault was right next to them, and Jason rolled, throwing the man sideways and slamming his head into the steel frame of the sedan.

The blow dizzied the man. His grip on Jason's gun hand loosened. Bourne shoved the barrel into the killer's temple and squeezed the trigger. The shot was like a cannon in his ears. Bone, blood, and brain flew. Deadweight, the assassin collapsed on top of him, and Jason shoved away the body and tried to get air into his chest again.

Then his head turned sideways.

Abbey Laurent had disappeared.

Go after her! You can't let her go!

Bourne staggered to his feet. Just beyond the Renault, Abbey limped away, zigzagging, too dizzy to make a straight path. Her hands were still tied behind her. He marched toward her, and when she looked back, she tried to run. But she couldn't. She swayed and fell, and her eyes leached tears as he loomed over her. She struggled to fight him, but her kicks were weak. Jason picked her up under the shoulders and carried her to the Renault, and then he opened the back door and laid her across the seat.

She stared at him with wide-open brown eyes that struggled to focus.

"Are you going to run?" he asked. "If I were you, I'd try to run."

She didn't answer.

"I'm going to tie your legs, just to be sure," he said. "I'm sorry, but I can't let you go right now. We need to talk, and we can't talk here. I'm going to get us out of town."

He slid off his belt and wrapped it around her ankles. She didn't resist as he tied them together.

"Did he hurt you in any other way?" Jason asked. "Do you need medical help?"

Abbey simply watched him with a blank expression. Her face was oddly calm.

"I'm not going to kill you," he added.

Still she said nothing. Her skin was pale. Her red bangs hung in messy strands across her forehead. Her eyes followed everything he did, as if trying to figure him out.

"I'm going to get the keys," Jason told her, "and then we'll go."

He backed out of the Renault and began to close the car door, but then Abbey spoke to him for the first time.

"Hey."

Jason stared at her, waiting.

"What do you like most about Quebec?" she asked.

He allowed himself a quick laugh.

"Those wonderful little maple candies," Bourne replied.

TWELVE

BOURNE drove for hours until it was dark and the Renault was in the hills north of Montreal. He took a dirt road that ended at the shore of a mountain lake, with dense stands of pines filling the slopes over the water. A small wooden pier jutted into the lake, and stars crowded the night sky. Behind him, tied up in the back seat, Abbey Laurent was silent. She hadn't spoken again during the long trip.

He got out into the cold air and opened the rear door. Starlight shined in Abbey's eyes. She was awake, watching him, waiting to see what he would do. He leaned inside and untied the belt that bound her ankles, and then he gently pulled her up by the shoulders and reached around to release her wrists. Slowly, she stretched her limbs, wincing, and she glanced through the car windows. Her eyes registered the remoteness of where they were.

"This looks like a good place to kill someone," she said.

"I told you. I'm not going to do that."

"No? Isn't that what Cain does? You killed that man by the river. Not that I'm complaining, by the way, since he was going to kill me. You killed four people at the boardwalk, right? *Four*. And then there's Sofia Ortiz. You shot her in the throat. As far as I can tell, killing is what you're good at."

"I didn't shoot Sofia Ortiz," Bourne replied. "As for the others, I killed them because they were trying to kill me."

He watched her try to figure out if he was telling the truth or simply letting her believe what she wanted to hear. Her lips pushed together in a frown. Then she fidgeted on the seat.

"Not that you care or anything, but I need to pee so bad you wouldn't believe," she said.

"Sorry. Of course. Go ahead."

"Aren't you afraid I'll run?"

"There's nowhere to run out here, Abbey."

They both got out of the Renault. Abbey held on to the car to steady herself as the blood returned to her limbs. She walked a little way into the trees, and Jason turned his back to give her privacy. He heard the noise of her zipper and then of her relieving herself in the dirt. He headed to the edge of the lake, and he was surprised when she came up beside him after she was done. He'd assumed that, regardless of what he'd told her, she would try to run and he'd have to chase her down.

Abbey knelt at the shore and washed her hands in the cold water, and then she splashed it over her face and did her best to clean off the dried blood. When she was done, she walked onto a sturdy pier, where she sat down and dangled her feet above the water. He followed and sat down next to her.

"I'm sorry about your friend Michel," he said.

Abbey stared out at the lake. "It's my fault. I got him killed."

"Don't blame yourself for that."

"Why not? I asked him to help me, and now he's dead."

"Were the two of you involved?"

She shrugged. "Yes and no. He was kind of like my safety net."

They sat in silence. He watched her try to quash her fear, as her knee jiggled nervously on the dock.

"Is it really true that you didn't shoot the congresswoman?" she asked him finally.

"Yes, it's true."

"The shot came from your hotel room. That's what my source told me."

"You're right. It did."

"So?"

"I wasn't there when it happened."

"Oh, yeah? Where were you? Taking the Circle Line tour or something?"

"Actually, I was saving your life," Bourne said.

Abbey swiveled to look at him. "What?"

"Someone tried to shoot you as you ran from the scene. I knocked you out of the way."

"That was *you*?"

"Yes."

"Why should I believe that?"

"Because you never shared on your social media accounts that somebody tried to kill you. Did you tell anyone about it?"

Abbey hesitated. "Nobody."

"That's why you should believe me. I was there on the street with you. I wasn't in that hotel room. I didn't shoot Congresswoman Ortiz."

"Am I supposed to think that this was just a big coincidence? You happened to show up and be my hero?"

"No. I was following you."

"Why?" Abbey demanded.

"Because you have information I need."

"I don't know anything."

"Yes, you do. You heard what the man on the pier said. He's part of an organization that's been feeding you stories. They played you, Abbey Laurent. You were their pawn. That's why you got the interview with Sofia Ortiz. That's why you knew about the data hack. That's why they told you about me."

"Medusa," Abbey murmured.

Bourne felt a rush of adrenaline. He grabbed Abbey's wrist and twisted. Too hard. "What do you know about Medusa?"

"You're hurting me," she complained.

"Tell me about *Medusa!*"

"I don't know anything about them! The first time I heard the name was today. Michel said that whatever Medusa is, it has government officials scared to death. And oh, by the way, Mr. Cain, they think *you're* part of it."

Jason let go of her wrist, and she massaged it with her other hand.

"I'm sorry," he said. "Regardless of what Michel told you, I'm not part of Medusa. They set me up. They framed me for the murder in New York and put me in the crosshairs of every intelligence agent on the planet."

"You mean like Nash Rollins?" she asked. "He came to my apartment last night."

"I know."

"He said you were a killer and that I should be afraid of you."

"Well, you should probably believe him."

"He said you were damaged. He called you a man with no past. What does that mean?"

"It's not important," Bourne replied.

"The man on the pier said the same thing. He said you didn't have a past."

"You ask a lot of questions."

"I'm a reporter. Asking questions is what I do. Besides, I'm still not sure you aren't going to kill me, so what difference does it make?"

"The less you know about me, the better."

Abbey opened her mouth to say something more, but she stopped. She brought her knees up on the pier and wrapped her arms around them. "What do you think I know? Why did you want to meet with me in the first place?"

"I want to know who your source is," Jason said. "You

have a source in New York. Someone gave you information about the data hack. I think whoever it is can point the way to Medusa. That's where I need to start. That's my *only* lead right now. I need to leverage your source to get inside the organization."

"In order to do what?" Abbey asked.

"Destroy them. Expose the conspiracy."

She studied his face in the darkness and then shook her head. "I'm sorry, who the hell *are* you? Who do you work for?"

"Right now, nobody. I'm on my own."

"Why do they call you Cain?"

"It's an identity from the past," Bourne said.

"Do you have a real name?"

"I did, but that was a long time ago. I'm not that person anymore. I've had to accept that."

"That doesn't make any sense."

"You're right. It doesn't."

She gave an annoyed little sigh at his unwillingness to talk. Then she said, "Did you really save me in New York?"

"Yes, I did."

"And you saved me again today. I guess I should say thank you."

Bourne shrugged. "I saved you because I needed information. That's all it is."

You're an asset. Nothing more.

"Why didn't you show up on the boardwalk?" Abbey asked.

"Because it was a trap."

"Well, how did you know I wasn't part of Medusa, too? Why were you so sure it wasn't me who set you up?"

He turned and stared at her. "I wasn't sure at all."

"Then what's changed? Why do you trust me now?"

"I don't trust you. I think you're a pawn, not part of Medusa, but that doesn't mean I trust you. Generally speaking, I don't trust anyone."

"I guess we're even. Generally speaking, I don't trust killers."

"Smart choice," Bourne said.

"So what happens now?"

"Now you tell me your source in New York. Who told you about the data hack? Who was feeding you information?"

"Journalists don't reveal their sources," Abbey said.

"Unless a source burns you, which this one did. Do you think the attempt on your life in New York was *random*? It wasn't. It was Medusa. You'd outlived your usefulness to them, and they were using the riot as cover to eliminate you."

He could see in her eyes that she hadn't considered that possibility. "You really think they were targeting me?"

"They still are. The man on the pier proved that."

She chewed on her fingernail. "Jesus."

"Who's your source?" Bourne asked again.

"He couldn't be involved. He's *legit*."

"If he's not involved, then he's a pawn like you. But one way or another, he's a link in the chain that leads to Medusa."

"What will you do if you find him?"

"Get him to tell me what he knows," Bourne said.

"What does that mean? Are you going to torture him? Kill him?"

"It depends. I need him to be scared enough to send an alarm up the chain. He needs to reach out to *his* contact. And then I follow that person. That's how it works."

"You make it sound so normal," Abbey said. "Not like twisted bullshit, which it is."

"It's just my world."

She gripped the end of the pier with both hands. "If I tell you his name, how do I know you won't kill me? We're sitting in the middle of the forest where no one will ever find my body. You said yourself you only saved me because you needed me. What makes you any different from Medusa once I've outlived my usefulness?"

"I can't give you any guarantees, Abbey. You wouldn't believe them anyway."

"So what are you saying? I should trust you? You just said I was smart *not* to trust you."

"That's right."

"You know what, Mr. Mystery Man?" she snapped. "You're scarier than the guy on the pier. I knew what his deal was. I knew what he was going to do to me. You, I have no idea. You've killed *how many people* in the past couple of days, and now you sit there like you're not going to hurt me and like you're some kind of hero."

"I'm definitely not that," Bourne said.

Abbey bit her lip. She didn't trust this man, but she knew he was telling her the truth. She'd been set up.

From the beginning, she'd been played. "Okay. His name is Carson Gattor. He's a lawyer and partner at the firm of Davis, Nelvis and Bear in New York."

"How did you get involved with him as a source?"

"I met him in Las Vegas," Abbey replied.

Bourne closed his eyes. Gunfire exploded in his head again. He saw people running, blood on the ground. Sweat gathered on his neck despite the cold night air, and he felt his hands curling into fists. *Nova!*

"Are you okay?" Abbey asked. "What's wrong?"

"Nothing," Bourne said, trying to steady himself. "Why Las Vegas?"

"His firm represented the casino after the mass shooting there. I was doing a profile on the killer, Charles Hackman, and Carson helped me with background. He called me a couple of weeks after the article came out and told me how much he liked it. He said he had a story I might be interested in. In addition to his legal work, Carson is a big shot in New York political circles. That's when he told me that Sofia Ortiz was planning a big rally to take on the tech companies and expose their cover-up of a huge data hack."

"Did Gattor tell you how he knew about it?" Bourne asked.

"No, but the congresswoman confirmed it off the record when I interviewed her."

"I know she did."

"You know?" Abbey asked. Then her face darkened. "It was you. You broke into the magazine office and searched my desk. You found my voice recorder."

He nodded. "I also found out that Medusa has been watching you. Your webcam was hacked. They've been keeping an eye on you, Abbey. Every keystroke on your computer has probably been monitored. You can also assume that your apartment is bugged."

"This is *crazy*!" she replied.

"I know."

"So what happens now?"

"Now I go after Carson Gattor," Bourne said.

"I mean, you've got what you wanted. Do you kill me?"

Jason slipped a hand inside his pocket. He saw her flinch, expecting a gun. Instead, he pulled out the keys to the Renault and let them dangle from his fingers. "Here. Take the car."

Abbey stared at him. "What?"

"Take the car. Drive back to Quebec City. When you get there, write the story. Everything. Write it all down and publish it. Make sure there isn't any secret left that would give them a reason to come after you. Right now, you're a loose end, but if you go public and put whatever you know online, they might decide you're not worth the trouble to kill. But be prepared. They'll come after you in other ways. They'll discredit you. Smear you. They'll paint you as a conspiracy nut, and they may even plant evidence to convict you of a crime. Watch your back, Abbey."

"You're really letting me go?" she asked.

"I told you I would."

"And what the hell are you going to do if I take the car? Sit here in the woods?"

"Why do you care?"

"Call it morbid curiosity. I'm a reporter, remember?"

"We're only a hundred yards from a parking lot for long-term campers," Jason replied with a tight smile. "I have a friend in Montreal. When I came across the border, I arranged for him to leave a car, ID, and cash from one of my accounts."

"You don't leave much to chance, do you?"

"No."

Always have a backup. Always assume you'll need a way to escape. Treadstone.

"And that's it?" Abbey asked.

"That's it."

"You're not worried that I'll warn Carson Gattor that you're coming after him?"

"You took a risk by giving me the name. I'll take the same risk with you. Now get the hell out of here, Abbey Laurent. The longer you stay with me, the more danger you're in."

Abbey clutched the car keys in her hand. She pushed herself to her feet on the dock and didn't say anything more to him. As she walked away, he didn't look back at her. Sitting by the lake, he heard the car door open and shut, and then he heard the purr of the engine. The headlights came on, throwing his shadow over the water. He heard the crunch of the tires in the dirt as she did a three-point turn and drove toward the highway.

Bourne was alone.

That was how it had to be.

THIRTEEN

NASH Rollins waited in the darkness outside the terminal at the north end of the Quebec City airport. A CSIS agent with a pencil mustache stood beside him and conducted an animated phone conversation in French. Rollins leaned on his cane and perused the night sky for the arrival of the Treadstone helicopter. He was more than ready to get out of Canada.

The CSIS agent, whose name was Fontaine, hung up the phone. "The borders are all on alert for your man. This *Cain*."

Rollins shrugged. "You won't find him."

"Don't be so sure of that. We tracked the stolen Renault and its plates on a street cam. The police are searching for the car."

"He'll switch vehicles soon if he hasn't already. You lost him for good as soon as he was out of Quebec."

"Are you suggesting we don't know how to do our jobs, Mr. Rollins?"

That was, in fact, what Rollins was suggesting, but he didn't bother with actual insults. "I'm suggesting that Cain is a professional who knows how to avoid capture. He knows where to cross the border without being detected."

"And why are you so sure he's on his way out of the country?"

"Because he got the woman. He got what he came for. He's done here."

The CSIS agent had an annoying habit of smoothing his mustache with his finger. "Well, if we do find him before he gets across the border, he's ours first. We believe he murdered a Canadian government official when he kidnapped the reporter. He'll need to answer for that, in addition to his other crimes on Canadian soil."

"What about the body at the naval museum?" Rollins asked. "Did you identify him?"

"Not yet. The man had no wallet. But he matches the description the woman gave us of the person who tried to kill her in Artillery Park. The question is why Cain killed *him*."

"Probably because the man saw his face."

"He's quite a dangerous man, your Cain."

"Yes, he is."

"What do you think he'll do with the woman?"

"He'll kill her, too," Rollins replied.

"*Quel dommage.* She's a pretty thing. Spirited, too. The kind of cat who's likely to leave scratches on your back." The agent smoothed his mustache again and smirked, as if he'd made a very amusing joke.

Rollins made no comment. He saw the lights of the approaching helicopter and heard the staccato throb of its rotors. Black and unmarked, it floated down to the helipad in front of them, and Rollins had to hold his hat down to keep it on his head. As the helicopter touched down, Rollins signaled the pilot with a finger across his throat. The engine quieted, and the rotors began to slow.

The CSIS agent extended a hand. "Good hunting, Mr. Rollins."

"Thank you."

"I'd like to say I'm sorry to see you go, but in all honesty, most of us will be happy to see the backs of you and your men. And Cain, too, of course. We have no interest in being part of the American Wild West."

Rollins snorted. "*Au revoir*, Fontaine."

The agent gave him a pained smile. He combed his mustache one last time and headed back to the terminal building. When he was out of earshot, Rollins took out his phone and dialed Treadstone in New York.

"It's me," he said. "I'm heading home."

"The tone of your voice suggests you failed again."

Rollins fumed silently. "Yes. Bourne made it out of the city. He took the journalist with him, and after that, he disappeared. I assume he'll head back to the U.S."

"What's his next target?"

"Unknown."

"Director Shaw won't be happy. He's getting pressure from Congress. One of their own was murdered, and the assassin is one of *ours*. Cain needs to be eliminated. Soon."

Rollins didn't need headquarters telling him what he already knew.

"Activate all of our assets around the U.S.," he told her, "and tell them to keep a close eye on our safe houses. Cain knows all of them. He could show up anywhere. Issue a kill-on-sight order, and make sure we warn everyone who knows him. Jason Bourne isn't Treadstone anymore. He's Medusa."

BOURNE used a penlight to guide him through the trees. Every few steps, he stopped, listening. He had the Medusa assassin's gun in his hand. Even out here, even at night, there were always threats. He didn't know what Abbey Laurent would do now that she was free. She might go back to Quebec City, as he'd told her to do. Or she might pull off the road at the next town and call the police.

It was also possible that his contact in Montreal had turned against him. He and Nova had relied on the man many times, but payoffs had a way of trumping loyalty. Jason kept off-the-books contacts in most cities, but he was a marked man now, and even the most reliable sources could smell a lucrative payday. He didn't know whether to expect a welcoming party when he went for the car.

He turned off the flashlight as he neared the main highway. At the end of the trail, nearly two dozen cars filled a small parking lot used by backpackers hiking into the mountains. He spotted the truck that had been left for him, a beat-up forest-green Land Rover. Instead of heading for the vehicle, he stayed on the fringe of the trees and circled the parking lot, coming up on the Land Rover from behind. He moved silently, leading with the gun.

No one was here.

They hadn't found him yet.

Jason crossed the pavement to the truck. He checked under the chassis for explosives or tracking devices, but found nothing. Then he located the keys in a metallic case under the front bumper and let himself inside the vehicle. The truck had a stale smell of fake pine from an air freshener dangling under the mirror. He checked under the dashboard and found a thick envelope that contained twenty-five thousand dollars in cash from one of his personal accounts.

Time to go.

He turned the key in the ignition and switched on the headlights. When he did, he grabbed for his gun.

Abbey Laurent stood in front of the car.

Jason threw open the door and leaped out, pointing the gun at her chest. She put up her arms and spread her fingers wide.

"What the hell are you doing here?" he demanded.

When Abbey didn't answer, Bourne walked over to her and pressed the suppressor against her forehead. "I said, what the hell are you doing here?"

"Honestly? I don't know."

"What does that mean? You're working with them, aren't you? You're *one* of them."

Her voice was steady as she replied. "I'm not. I swear I'm not. I'm exactly who you think I am."

"Then why did you come back? I let you go."

"Because I want to go with you," Abbey said.

"What?"

Jason saw a fierce determination in her eyes. "Look, I may not trust you, but I trust everyone else even less. Plus, I'm a writer, and this story isn't over. You said you want to expose the conspiracy? So do I. These people killed Michel, and they tried to kill me. I want to find out the truth about who they are."

"You're *insane.*"

"Maybe I am."

"You'll slow me down. You'll wind up dead."

"I know the risks. That's my choice. If I slow you down, then fine, leave me behind. But you might find you can use me. A man traveling alone attracts a lot more attention than a man and a woman together. I'm your cover."

Jason frowned, but he couldn't argue with her logic.

"See?" Abbey went on. "You know I'm right. Take me to New York with you. That's where Carson Gattor is. You already said he's the first link in the chain that leads to Medusa. You know it's not going to be easy to get to him. He's smart. If he thinks you're coming after him, he's going to be on his guard. He doesn't know you, but he knows *me.* I can help you draw him out, Mr. Cain."

He shook his head in disbelief at this woman's sheer

foolish courage. He hadn't met someone like her in a long time.

Not since Nova.

He lowered his weapon.

"I'm not Cain," he told her. "Not anymore. Cain was a long time ago. My name is Jason Bourne."

PART TWO

FOURTEEN

THE CEOs of thirty-six of the world's most influential technology companies sat around a handmade beechwood conference table imported from a Baltic coastal village in Sweden. Thirty of the participants were men, six were women, and they ranged in age from twenty-nine to seventy-five. Their countries of origin were dominated by the United States, but also included representatives from China, South Korea, Switzerland, Germany, and India. The invitation-only group had no name. Outside of this room, it didn't officially exist. The billionaire members called it simply "the cabal."

Four times a year, they came here to discuss technology strategy, in a villa owned by Miles Priest on a private island a few miles off the coast of Nassau. Warm ocean breezes blew through the open-air space that looked down on the island's sand beach, which was now bone-white in the moonlight. Dozens of red-necked Bahama parrots chattered in the palm trees beyond the balcony. Silver platters of coconut-crusted shrimp, fish stew and johnnycakes, conch salad, and guava duff sat in the middle of the table within easy reach, along with carafes of wine, sparkling water, Yellow Bird, and Goombay Smash. There was, ironically, no technology allowed at these meetings. No phones, no laptops, no devices of any kind. The members of the cabal knew better than anyone that people were always listening.

Miles Priest sat in his usual place at the head of the table, his back to the ocean view. Scott DeRay sat on his right, and Nelly Lessard, who coordinated the cabal's communications and meetings, sat on his left. Most of the others in the group wore comfortable tropical attire—flowered shirts, shorts, sandals—but Priest never wore anything except a business suit at these meetings. He was still a product of the FBI culture in which he'd spent thirty years. Always professional. Always driven by stringent rules and values. Many of the CEOs expected hedonistic pleasures during their stay on the island, and Priest had no trouble indulging their distasteful fetishes, but he refused to allow such weaknesses in his own life.

At most meetings, the executives deferred to him as the leader of the cabal. That was high praise in a group whose other members were equally brilliant, arrogant, and über-rich, but Priest's éminence grise persona and his six-foot-six stature managed to keep them in line. So did the fact that Nelly Lessard kept secret recordings of each member's private peccadilloes. A night at a Macau hotel with two seventeen-year-olds? A taste for trafficked

Egyptian antiquities? Nelly Lessard knew all about them. If anyone stepped seriously out of line, they were quietly reminded that certain recordings could be sent to their boards of directors or even the criminal authorities in their countries.

However, tonight Miles Priest was on the defensive.

"A debacle!" Hon Xiu-Le announced from the far end of the conference table. The small forty-year-old with straw-like black hair was the Shanghai-based leader of China's largest social messaging application, representing nearly a billion users. "A debacle, Mr. Priest, there is no other way to describe it! You told us that your operation in New York would help us gain the upper hand against Medusa. We would finally know what they were planning. Instead you played right into their hands."

Priest's sagging bloodhound face showed no expression. "I don't disagree with you, Hon."

"Congress is screaming!" added Tyler Wall, the youngest member of the cabal and the founder of a medical device company specializing in internal microrobotics for surgical procedures. The irony of his focus on small things was that Wall was built like a carnival strongman, with blond hair down to his waist and a full beard. His odd affectation was that he always wore a flowing white robe and carried a walking stick, like a modern-day Moses. "The legislation from Ortiz should have been dead in the water, but after her murder, the bill is gathering momentum in the House. Rumors are all over D.C. that Big Tech was behind the assassination. You think anyone is going to believe us if we say yes, the

killer *was* our agent, but actually he was a Medusa mole
and we had no idea about that when we hired him? How
stupid does that make us look?"

Wall looked straight at Scott DeRay as he said this.

"You're right, I take full responsibility for the recruitment of Jason Bourne," Scott replied. "Obviously, he was
more susceptible to manipulation by Medusa's psychological methods than I realized. The man is one of my
oldest friends, but I misjudged him."

"A lot of good that does now," Wall went on. "If our
involvement in hiring him comes to light, this is disas-
trous! Catastrophic!"

"It won't come out," Priest interjected sharply.

"That seems optimistic, Mr. Priest," Hon Xiu-Le announced to sympathetic rumblings from the others at
the table. The Chinese entrepreneur adjusted tiny round
glasses on his face and folded his small hands together.
"If this man is captured, it seems inevitable that the investigation will lead back to Mr. DeRay—and from him
to all of us."

"Bourne will never be captured," Scott informed them.

"Unless Medusa *wants* him to be captured," Wall suggested. "Maybe that's the plan. Bring him up to Capitol
Hill in cuffs and leg irons to point the finger at the cabal,
and watch them pass legislation to cripple us by voice
vote!"

Priest waited until the unrest settled and the members
were quiet. "We are dealing with Bourne."

"How?" Wall asked, thumping a meaty fist on the table.

"I reached out to Treadstone," Priest replied with a sideways glance at Scott. "I suggested that we have a shared interest in getting rid of Bourne, particularly given Treadstone's recent resurrection. Bourne is a threat to them as much as to us. Director Shaw is in complete agreement. They were nearly successful in eliminating him in Canada."

Hon Xiu-Le scowled. "Nearly?"

"It appears Bourne escaped the net," Scott announced. "He's gone underground again."

More discontent rippled through the cabal.

"He escaped *for now*," Priest continued, "but there's nowhere he can go where we won't be looking for him. Nelly is coordinating the tech resources among our various members to watch for any footprint he may leave online. He *will* be found. As soon as we locate him, Treadstone will take action to remove him. Now, I share your disappointment with our failure in New York, but I suggest we all return our focus to the more urgent issue. Namely, Medusa. Ever since the data hack, we've been expecting them to move against us in a major way. Any congressional action that arises because of the Ortiz assassination will weaken us, but this is only the first step. We still don't know their endgame. I would suggest that we remain vigilant for unusual activity within our companies. Fluctuations in stock price or unusual buying or selling activity. Key personnel departures. Theft of intellectual property. Until we know what Medusa is planning, we're all at risk."

"Speaking of risk," Wall interrupted again, "what is being done about Prescix? You promised us a deal, Miles."

"We've faced a setback on that front," Priest told them, "but we're not done yet."

He nodded at Nelly Lessard to give her report. Nelly was sixty years old, with neat gray hair and a grandmotherly voice that masked a tough-as-nails personality. She wasn't even five feet tall, and she stood up so that the others at the table could see her. Her bones were thin and birdlike. "We extended an invitation to the founder of Prescix, Gabriel Fox, to join the cabal and meet with us here on the island," she told the group. "He declined. In fact, he declined by hiring a blimp to fly over the Carillon headquarters flashing the word *No*. Along with a curse directed at Miles. As we all know, Gabriel is a genius but with the erratic personality quirks that geniuses sometimes have."

"Gabriel is *nuts!*" Wall said flatly. "But who cares? Prescix software is more powerful than anything we've seen in social media in more than a decade. It's been *quadrupling* its user base worldwide every month for the past year. We can't have that much influence out there unchecked and uncoordinated. Prescix needs to be in this room."

"Agreed," Priest replied crisply. "As Nelly says, we'd hoped to recruit Gabriel directly, but he refused. In my mind, that's an unacceptable response. In the absence of Gabriel's cooperation, we've been working to give the company alternative leadership."

Hon Xiu-Le leaned forward, his eyes suspicious. "How do you plan to do that?"

Scott stood up. Like Priest, he always wore a suit to

these meetings. "I've been working with the legal team at Carillon to acquire Prescix. We've been quietly accumulating a large holding of stock under multiple surrogates. And we've made an outreach to the company's COO, Kevin Drake, to support our bid and get a majority of the board to back the takeover. If that goes forward in the next day or so as we expect, then Gabriel will be out, and as the next CEO, Kevin has promised his enthusiasm for joining our group. Prescix will shortly be one of us, ladies and gentlemen. I guarantee it."

Scott's announcement won smiles from the others at the table. In the wake of that news, Priest stood up next to his protégé. "This seems like a good time to break for the evening. We'll reconvene at breakfast. I'm sure you can all find productive ways to spend your night on the island."

As the CEOs began to disperse throughout the estate grounds, Priest leaned closer to Scott. "Have you confirmed with Kevin Drake that everything is on track?"

Scott nodded. "Kevin's in Las Vegas. He'll be breaking the news to Gabriel tomorrow. We'll shortly have majority support on the Prescix board. It's a done deal. Gabriel's gone."

"Excellent," Priest replied. "Nelly, have you arranged some company for Kevin while he's in Sin City? I understand he's rather particular."

Nelly had the smile of a woman who knew men. "Oh, yes. I reached out to a very reliable agency. Kevin should be very pleased."

"Well done." Priest's deeply lined face flushed with

relief. "I don't need to remind the two of you of the stakes here. Prescix isn't simply another social media site. It's the most sophisticated tool for behavior modification that I've ever seen. If Medusa gets their hands on that code, there's no limit to what they can do."

THE nighttime fountains of the Bellagio casino danced to the music of Frank Sinatra doing things his way. Kevin Drake, COO of the Prescix Corporation, got up from the desk where he was working on his MacBook and stood at the floor-to-ceiling windows in his penthouse suite. Thirty stories below him, hundreds of tourists crowded the sidewalk on the Las Vegas Strip to watch the water show. From up here, he also had a panoramic view of the rainbow lights of Paris, Aria, and the Cosmopolitan.

Kevin sipped a shot of Clase Azul Ultra tequila, each little taste just enough to wet his lips. His doughy body was wrapped up in a Versace silk robe that felt as smooth as butter on his skin. Everything else that he needed for the evening had been left for him on the marble bar in a gold-leaf box. Cologne. Body oil. Cocaine. Cialis. He hadn't always been a fan of Miles Priest and Carillon Technology, but he couldn't deny that they had impeccable taste in perks, and perks were what made the world go around. Once you had a few hundred million dollars in the bank, life was no longer about money but about finding the best experiences that money could buy.

The chime sounded on the suite door. Hearing the

bell shot a twinge of excitement through Kevin's body. This was another perk. The best kind.

He padded across the plush carpet in his bare feet and opened the door. There she was. He'd expected gorgeous, but the woman in front of him was a vision. Jet-black hair tumbled to her shoulders and made a few wispy bangs across her forehead. She had blue eyes that looked unusually pale against her ebony hair. Her narrow face curved to a sharp V at her chin, and one little freckle on her jaw gave her the smallest imperfection that made everything else even more perfect. She was much taller than he was and even taller in gold stilettos that matched the shimmering gold of her skintight spaghetti strap dress. A black leather purse dangled from her shoulder.

The raven-haired woman grabbed the thousand-dollar shot of tequila from his hand and downed it in a single swallow. Her lips curled into a smile, showing snow-white teeth.

"Are you Kevin?"

"Yes."

"I'm not an ordinary companion, Kevin. Was that made clear?"

"It was. I—I asked for someone like you."

"I have rules for my appointments. Are you a man who follows the rules?"

"Definitely."

"Then let's be clear on what I require. You will address me at all times as Miss Shirley. Any deviation will result in punishment. Is that understood?"

Kevin blinked. "Yes."

The woman's hand flew like a streak of lightning across his face, and her sharp nails drew blood. "*Is that understood?*"

He staggered back. "Yes . . . Miss Shirley."

She grabbed his head tightly between her two hands and used her tongue to lick the blood off his cheek. "Better."

Miss Shirley sauntered past him into the suite as if she owned it. Kevin followed, unable to rip his eyes away from her long legs. Her gold dress barely covered her ass. She put down her purse, went to the tall windows, and admired the stunning view, with one knee bent and her hands on her hips. Then she spun around, used two fingers to peel away the straps on her shoulders, and let the dress fall into a gold swirl at her ankles. Other than her heels, she was naked. Her rose-tipped breasts swelled like pyramids on her torso, and her build was thin.

Kevin reached for the tie on his robe so he could undress himself, but she held up a hand, stopping him.

"Leave your robe on. I'm the prize in this room. Focus on me."

"I understand . . . Miss Shirley."

"Impress me, Kevin," she directed him.

He stared at her, puzzled, trying to understand what she wanted. In the process, he forgot the rules. "I'm sorry?"

"I want to be impressed. Any man I'm with must impress me."

"What do you want . . . Miss Shirley?"

"Offer me something worthy of me," she snapped.

"I have champagne. Would you like some champagne . . . Miss Shirley?"

"Champagne is a given. It's barely even a start, but open it anyway."

He stumbled to the wet bar and removed a bottle of Krug from the refrigerator. He struggled to peel away the foil with trembling fingers and undo the cage at the top of the bottle. He'd barely touched the cork when it shot out of the bottle and hit the ceiling, and foam bubbled over his hands.

"I trust that's not the kind of performance I can expect from you later," Miss Shirley sneered.

Kevin poured two glasses until they were nearly spilling over the crystal rims and brought one over to her. She was inches away, a naked goddess, and he had to adjust his robe to hide the effect she was having on him. She drank the champagne as she had the tequila, with one swallow, and held out the empty glass, which he scurried to refill.

Her gaze traveled around the dimly lit room. To the laptop. To the dining room and chandelier. To the neon of Las Vegas Boulevard.

"*Impress* me," she said again. "Aren't you an important man, Kevin? They told me you're an important man. Prove it."

"I'm worth nearly half a billion dollars . . . Miss Shirley."

She shrugged. "That sum is below average by my standards. Which is also what I see under your robe. If that's all you can offer me, we can proceed with the thirty seconds it will take me to finish you off, and I'll be on my way."

"Wait!" he begged her, his mind working furiously. No other woman had ever aroused him like this one. He couldn't let her leave. "Wait, I can show you something amazing. This will impress you. See all those tourists down on the street?"

"Yes."

"I can make them take off their clothes and jump in the fountain."

Her head cocked with curiosity, and her fingertips played idly across one of her erect nipples. "Are you serious?"

"I swear! I can do it . . . Miss Shirley."

Kevin grabbed his laptop and a pair of mini binoculars from his briefcase and brought them over to the tall windows. He handed the binoculars to Miss Shirley, who aimed them at the crowd. His hunger for this woman was literally making his mouth water, and he had to clench the laptop hard to stop himself from reaching out to caress her bare skin.

"How does this work?" she asked him.

"I run a company called Prescix," Kevin explained. "It's the hottest social media site out there. . . . You must have heard of it. We tell people that the software knows what you want to do before you know it yourself. The algorithm uses thousands of personal factors—where you are, who you're with, your medical history, your social history, your likes and dislikes—and it calculates what you will want to do next. People call it spooky because it's so accurate, but they don't know the half of what it can do. It can also influence behavior, which is what advertisers love. Watch! I highlight the geographic area right here, and then I submit a prompt in the executive-level code: 'Take off your clothes and jump in the fountain.' I'll also define a few characteristics for the command based on the personality traits and resistance levels needed to carry it out."

With one hand, he tapped on the keys. On the laptop screen, a series of red X's began populating the mapped area on Las Vegas Boulevard. In a few seconds, more than a hundred users had been identified, and their photos and profiles appeared in a separate column on the right side of the screen.

"See, the X's mark the Prescix users within the target area," Kevin explained. "Now, based on the command I selected, the software will use its AI algorithm to assess the likeliest users to respond to that suggestion. It will look at everything, their photo stream, their alcohol purchases, keywords in their posts, arrest records, attitudes toward authority, whatever we know about them. Then it will highlight the users with the greatest probability of success and deliver the prompt to their devices, as well as photos and posts designed to encourage the behavior."

Blue circles appeared around two dozen red X's.

"Watch this . . . Miss Shirley."

There was a long, pregnant pause as she focused on the crowd below. Kevin couldn't see the people clearly from the top-floor suite, but a few seconds later, he could just make out a body in the glow of the Las Vegas lights, jumping over the stone railing and splashing into the fountains.

Then another person did the same thing.

And another. And another.

He could see Miss Shirley's eyes glittering. Her smile showed perfect teeth.

"It becomes a self-fulfilling command, too," Kevin went on. "When one person does it, the resistance level diminishes in the group, and others join in."

By now, he could see almost thirty people wading in the Bellagio fountains and security running to deal with them.

Miss Shirley put down the binoculars. "Kevin, you succeeded. I am impressed."

"Thank you . . . Miss Shirley."

"And you run this company?"

"I'm the number two executive, but the founder is crazy, out of control. I'm in town to squeeze him out. Another company is paying me a fortune to take over the entire operation. As of tomorrow, Prescix will be mine . . . Miss Shirley."

"Well, you're a busy man, so let's not waste time," she told him, loosening the knot on his robe and pushing it off his shoulders. Kevin stood naked in the middle of the floor, and her fingernails began to scrape across his body. He groaned.

"Go to the bedroom right now," she directed him.

"Yes . . . Miss Shirley."

"Do you want to touch me?"

"More than anything . . . Miss Shirley."

"Do you want me on top of you? Do you want to be inside me?"

"I do, I do . . . Miss Shirley."

"Then go. Wait for me."

Kevin practically ran for the bedroom. Miss Shirley followed at a languid pace. He bolted through the doorway and threw himself onto the king-size bed and lay on his back. He squirmed with anticipation. Moments later, Miss Shirley appeared before him, a silhouette in the doorway. Neon from the tall windows blinked on her nude body. She brushed aside her dark hair. Her pale eyes glistened.

"Are you ready for me?"

He spread his arms to beckon her to him. "I can't wait."

She took a step into the room. She had her purse over her shoulder again, and her right hand was buried inside the zippered pouch. She posed for him like a model, her mouth smiling wickedly.

"What did you say?"

"I said, I can't *wait*."

"That's too bad, Kevin."

"What? Why?"

"You forgot the rules," she reminded him. "Forgetting the rules means punishment."

"I'm sorry! I'm sorry . . . Miss Shirley!"

"It's too late for that," she said. "In any case, this punishment doesn't come from me. It comes from Medusa."

"What?"

Miss Shirley's hand emerged from her purse with a gun. She fired a bullet into Kevin's throat.

FIFTEEN

"TELL me about Medusa," Abbey said to Jason.

Her voice came out of the darkness. They sat in the Land Rover, hidden in a dense stand of trees in the Green Mountains. The windows were open despite the cold; if anyone came close, he'd hear them. They'd crossed the border on a smugglers trail in northern Vermont without being noticed, but he was certain that alerts had been posted for him throughout the northern states. He needed to be careful.

In the daylight, they'd head into New York City and prepare their campaign of psychological warfare against Carson Gattor. Panic him. Scare him. Force him to make contact with his superiors.

But for now, they needed rest. They'd been on the road for hours. *Sleep is a weapon. It's as powerful as a gun.*

Treadstone.

"Don't talk," Jason said. "Close your eyes. You'll need to be sharp tomorrow."

"What about you?"

"I want to make sure no one followed us from the border. Sometimes the feds will leave an illegal crossing unmonitored but track it electronically. If we're not alone, we'll know soon enough. Once I'm sure we're safe, then I'll sleep."

"It's too cold to sleep," Abbey complained. "I'm a fricking freezer pop."

He smiled. "Let me check the back. Maybe there's a blanket you can use."

Jason got out of the truck and paused to listen to the woods around them. Then he walked to the rear and opened the tailgate. He found a greasy wool blanket stuffed in a box of oil and tools, and he took the blanket back to the front seat. Abbey said nothing as he draped the blanket over her legs and tucked it in around her shoulders.

"Better?" he asked.

"Thank you."

"Sorry about the cold, but I need to hear what's happening outside."

"I'm okay. You want to share?"

"No, I'm fine," Jason said.

"Right. Tough guy. I forgot."

He smiled again. "Get some sleep."

"First tell me about Medusa. I want to know what we're going after."

"We don't know very much about them," Jason replied. "That's part of the problem."

"Michel said that the intelligence agencies aren't even sure who started it."

"That's true. We've never been able to get close to their leadership structure. They're well funded, which suggests that a foreign government could be involved. But if it's Russia or China, is it their own operation or just a partnership of convenience for both sides? Nobody knows."

"What do they want?" Abbey asked.

"So far, the only common denominator is chaos. Anarchy. For several years, Medusa has been trying to stoke social divisions in North America and Europe, and they've been very successful. They don't lean left or right. They fire up people on both sides, no matter what the issue is. Election fraud. Abortion. Climate change. Racism. Immigration. Their whole point is to create an atmosphere of instability and unrest, which can lead to violence. You saw that in New York, but it's been happening for a while, and it's getting worse. The riots and protests you see on the news aren't just organic. They're not accidents. Medusa is pulling the strings. Most of the time, the people involved don't even realize they're being manipulated."

"But *why*?"

"That's hard to say. They haven't tipped their hand. Maybe anarchy is the end in itself, or maybe they're trying to undermine the Western democracies in order to pave the way for some kind of takeover. It's not clear what that would look like, but the point is, we can't trust anybody in authority. Medusa almost certainly has spies within the U.S. government. That's why we weren't sure about Congresswoman Ortiz. We thought she could be part of Medusa."

"You thought I was part of it, too," Abbey said softly. "Didn't you?"

"Yes, that seemed like a possibility."

"Jason, how did *you* get involved? Where do you come from?"

Bourne sat in silence as he wondered what to say. He closed his eyes, because darkness had always been his friend. Darkness protected him. He hated questions about his life, because none of those questions had simple answers. Once upon a time, long ago, he'd been a man named David Webb, but that man didn't exist anymore. David Webb was dead. Forgotten. Now there was only Jason Bourne. And Cain.

"I used to work for a government agency," he told Abbey. "You wouldn't know its name, and it's better you not know it at all. Just knowing the name can put a target on your back. They're the ones who recruited me, trained me, made me who I am. The man you met, Nash Rollins, he's part of it."

"Your own agency is trying to *kill* you?"

"They think I'm a traitor. They think after I quit them, I joined Medusa."

"Why did you quit?"

"It doesn't matter."

"Based on the look on your face, it looks like it matters a lot. What happened?"

He shrugged. "I lost someone."

"Someone special?"

Jason wanted to stay silent. All he could feel was the pain. *Nova*.

"I worked with one of the agency's operatives in the UK," he told her, unable to stop himself. "My code name on missions was Cain. Hers was Nova. We did a lot of operations together. Europe. Asia. In Canada, too. She was the best agent I'd ever met. But we made a mistake."

"You fell in love," Abbey murmured. "Didn't you? I can tell."

He turned his head and saw that she was staring into his eyes. "Yes. That's not smart in my business. Personal feelings interfere with the job, so you suppress them. Nova and I found we couldn't do that. We kept our affair secret, but we were in love. I've only been in love one other time like that in my life. And both times, the woman died."

"I'm sorry. What happened?"

"Nova was part of an operation in London that went bad. Innocent people were killed. She wasn't to blame, but it was an embarrassment for the agency, and they forced her out. She became a pariah in the intelligence community. Nobody would hire her. She hated it, but on some level, it was also a new beginning for us. With her out, we didn't have to keep our relationship hidden anymore. We arranged to meet in Las Vegas to spend time together. I got there on November 3, 2018."

"November 3." The date took a moment to register with her. "Oh, my God. The Lucky Nickel shooting. Was she there? Did Charles Hackman kill her?"

"The *agency* killed her," Bourne said flatly. "I don't know how it was done, but she was the sixty-seventh victim. Invisible. Unacknowledged. A man from my own agency carried away her body. I *saw* him. I *knew* him. I ran to the casino to see if I could get to the shooter, because I knew they'd cover up what really happened. But I was too late. The area was already locked down, and Nash Rollins was *there*. He had Nova killed."

"But why?"

"They couldn't let Nova stay on the outside. They couldn't run the risk that some other rogue government would take her on."

"So after Las Vegas, you quit?"

Bourne nodded. "I walked away from my past. It wasn't the first time I'd had to do that."

Her face screwed up in confusion. "What does that mean?"

"Nothing. Forget it."

She frowned at his lack of an answer. "What about Medusa? How did you wind up chasing them?"

"An old friend approached me recently. He's part of a group of powerful technology companies that Medusa is targeting. Stealing their data. Looking to gain control of their operations and their software. They decided the government was too impotent or too compromised to stop Medusa, so they hired me. The operation in New York—Sofia Ortiz—that was supposed to be my way in. Instead, Medusa set me up. It was perfect. A damaged rogue agent, upset over the murder of his lover, taking revenge on the government. A killer. *Cain.* Now everyone is gunning for me, and they won't stop until I'm dead."

Abbey didn't look at him, but her hand snaked out from under the blanket and took hold of his hand. Her skin was warm and soft. It felt odd to enjoy a human touch again. To be close to a woman.

"Thank you for telling me all of this," she said.

"Don't thank me for anything. Staying with me is likely to get you killed. You should get as far away from me as you can. It's not too late, but once you call Carson Gattor tomorrow, there's no going back."

"I know." She paused and then went on. "I'm sorry about Nova."

"Well, I'm sorry about Michel. We've both lost people."

"At least you were in love. I've never been in love. Michel and I, I don't know what that was, but it wasn't love. He loved me, but I didn't want to let him get that close. I'm not sure I could ever let down my guard long enough to let anyone in."

"I would have said the same thing about myself," Jason replied, "but I was wrong."

"Why won't you tell me who you really are? About your past. Is the Bourne identity some kind of secret?"

"I can't tell you what I don't remember," Jason said.

"I don't understand that."

Bourne didn't answer her. There were places he didn't go. There were places he *couldn't* go. Instead, he said, "I've been doing all the talking. Tell me about you."

He heard a slight coolness take over her voice. "Isn't that a little disingenuous?"

"What do you mean?"

"Well, are you saying that you don't already know everything about me? That you don't have a file on me? Because I find that hard to believe. You're a spy. You would have researched my whole life before you got in touch with me."

He thought to himself again that Abbey was smart. Formidable.

"That's true," he admitted. "I know a lot of facts about you. But facts are bloodless things. Human beings are more than facts."

"What do you know about me?"

"I know you were born in New York. French-Canadian father, American mother. After your mother died, you and your father moved to Ottawa. You went to McGill for journalism school, and then you settled in Quebec City to take a job with a start-up online magazine called *The Fort*."

Abbey shrugged. "See? You know everything there is."

"Actually, I don't know much at all," Jason replied. "I don't know why you seem to be largely estranged from your father. I don't know why you're still working at a small operation like *The Fort* when you've had offers from *The Atlantic* and *Vanity Fair*. I also don't know why a smart, funny, very attractive thirty-two-year-old woman hates the idea of a serious relationship."

"Did you think that last one would soften me up for the others?"

"No."

"So what are you saying? I'm pretty but I'm screwed up?"

"I just want to know who you really are."

"I'm a writer going after a story," Abbey said. "That's all. That's my life."

"I'm not sure that explains why you're helping me."

She shrugged. "Maybe I can't really explain it to myself. Did you think about that? Maybe sometimes I leap at things and can't explain why I do it."

He smiled at her. "Now that I can believe."

"I'll get you to Carson Gattor. Beyond that, nothing else matters, does it?"

"You're right. Nothing else matters."

"Okay, then. I'm going to sleep. You said I need to sleep."

She closed her eyes and turned her head away from him. She looked tense and restless now, and he could hear her breathing harshly. Her body had grown warm under the blanket, and she kicked it off. Jason stayed awake, waiting until her breathing slowed, going in and out as she slept, but it took a long time.

Then he closed his eyes, too. He noticed that she hadn't let go of his hand.

SIXTEEN

ABBEY tried to calm her nerves as she sat on a stone bench in Washington Square Park the next day. The fountain reflected the park's giant arch in the water like a blurry photograph. Hundreds of people came and went around her, and to her eyes, everyone looked like a threat. High-rises loomed over the trees, making her think of sniper rifles aimed from the windows. Being in the park again, where she'd witnessed an assassination, where she'd nearly been killed herself, made her want to get up and run away. She had to grab hold of the bench to stay where she was.

More than a week later, she could still see the after-effects of the riot. Scorched ground from the fires. Protest signs stacked next to the overflowing garbage cans. Boarded-up windows in the buildings surrounding the park. The echoes of violence brought it all back for her. She flinched, remembering the shot that had killed Sofia

Ortiz, seeing the blood spray. She heard screams again and the noise of panic around her.

"*You look nervous,*" a voice said in the receiver hidden in her ear. Jason. She could see him in the trees on the other side of the fountain. He wore a baseball cap, and his eyes were hidden by sunglasses.

"I am," she murmured, barely moving her lips.

"*You'll do fine. Your call to Gattor was perfect. He'll be here.*"

Abbey checked her watch and saw that it was nearly three o'clock in the afternoon. Carson Gattor was due for their meeting.

If he was planning to show up at all.

If he hadn't simply called Medusa to target her while she was waiting in the park.

"I'm too exposed. What if they try to kill me?"

"*I'm watching the area, Abbey. Right now, there are no threats. If I see anything, I'll move in immediately. Remember, the only thing Gattor knows is that you need to see him. Even if he called Medusa, they'd tell him to take the meeting and find out why you're here and what you want. You're safe.*"

"I'm not sure. There's a man near the hot dog cart. See him? With the T-shirt and the goatee? He's watching me."

"*I see him. He's not Medusa.*"

"How do you know?"

"*Because I know how operatives behave. I already ruled him out. He's watching you because you're attractive, Abbey. That's all. His eyes follow every pretty girl who shows up in the park.*"

She shook her head. "I don't know if I can do this. I said I could, but now I don't know."

"You can. Just stay focused on the strategy. This is Phase One. We need to throw Gattor off balance. We need to get him so panicked that he goes running to his contact at Medusa. Remember, this is a man who's almost certainly in it for the money, not ideology. He wants to keep his hands clean. If he thinks he's going to be exposed, if he thinks his comfortable life is at risk, he'll crack."

"Will he believe me?" Abbey asked. "Will he buy the story we made up?"

"That's up to you. You need to sell it."

"What if he knows I'm working with you?"

"Unlikely. There's no way he's high up enough for that kind of information."

She glanced through the crowds in the park and recognized Carson Gattor heading toward her. "I see him. He's coming."

"You'll be fine. Just do it like we practiced. I'll be watching and listening the whole time. If anything goes sideways, I'll be there in seconds."

Abbey stood up from the bench and gave the lawyer a little wave. Carson nodded from near the fountain as he spotted her. He affected a calm, rich, self-confident walk, as if the world couldn't touch him, and she wondered if she'd really be able to shake him with her lies. She felt nervous again about what she was doing. Then she reminded herself that this man had used her. He'd set her up to do Medusa's dirty work and put her in a position to be killed. She wanted to make him shiver with fear all the way down to his Ferragamo shoes.

"Hello, Carson."

"Abbey," he said, giving her a quick, awkward embrace. He'd never done that before. It made her think that, underneath his cool exterior, he was nervous, too, wondering why she'd called him and what she wanted.

They both sat down. Carson draped an arm around the back of the bench and crossed his legs and smoothed the cuff of his pants. He was medium height and skinny enough that his clothes looked loose. He had a long, narrow head, which looked even longer because his black hair was greased straight back, leaving him with a high forehead. His five o'clock shadow was dark and pronounced. He was forty years old, which was a tough age for a New York lawyer. He hadn't made enough money to retire, but to keep up with colleagues and friends, he had to spend his cash as if it were never going to run out.

"*He's already spooked,*" Bourne said in her ear. "*That's good.*"

Abbey suppressed a smile, because she'd been thinking the same thing.

"I appreciate your meeting me on short notice," she told Carson.

"Of course. You made it sound important."

"It is. I need your help."

"What's going on?"

"Well, first of all, I want to thank you for all of the information you've given me," Abbey told him. "It's been dead-on. You can't believe the attention I've gotten for my recent articles. I'm grateful. It's been a career maker."

"Good for you, Abbey, but all I did was point the way. You did the rest."

"A lot of doors are open to me now. A lot of people are coming out of the shadows with story ideas."

"I'm pleased to hear it. If I can be useful, you know I will be. Is that what you need? More information?"

"No, that's not it. I don't need your help on a story." She lowered her voice and took Carson by the wrist. "Actually, I need your help as a lawyer."

"Are you in trouble?"

"It's not for me. It's for someone else." She pretended to study the people in the park, and she let anxiety creep onto her face. "Did you tell anyone you were meeting me? Do people know where you are?"

"No. No one. Abbey, you can always count on my discretion."

"Okay. Here's the thing. I assume you have contacts inside the Justice Department, right? And the FBI?"

"Some, yes. What is this about?"

She bit her lip, as if struggling to get the words out. "Have you ever heard of an organization called *Medusa*?"

Carson was good, but not good enough. The muscles in his face made the smallest twitch, and then he recovered. His pale lips squeezed into a frown. "No, I don't think so. What is it?"

"Apparently, it's some kind of anarchist group trying to stir up violence and social unrest. Like the riot here after the assassination. I'm told they were involved in that. We're not talking about a handful of nutjobs passing around manifestos from their parents' basement. This is a well-funded, well-organized extremist faction with deep technology resources and tentacles throughout the government."

Carson made a show of skepticism. "It's hard to believe an organization like that could operate in secret. Wouldn't everyone know about them?"

"A lot of people in government do know, but they're not saying anything. I know what you're thinking, but this isn't just a wild conspiracy. Medusa is real. I can *prove* it."

His eyebrows flicked with curiosity. "You can prove it? How?"

"I have a mole."

This time she scored a direct hit. He couldn't keep the surprise off his face. "A mole? You mean—"

"I have a source *inside* Medusa," Abbey told him.

"Who?"

"I can't say. Not yet."

Carson backtracked. "Oh, of course. Obviously."

"But my source is high up in the organization. He says he was a true believer, but the violence has gone too far for him. He thought New York—the assassination, the riot—was a mistake. He saw my articles and reached out to me, because he wants the story to come out. The thing is, this guy knows *everything*. He knows details of their operations and how their technology works. Plus, he's got a list of contacts in the government and private sector who have been compromised by Medusa."

"Impressive," Carson replied evenly, but she could imagine the ocean wave of terror rolling through his mind. "Did he give you any names on this list?"

"Not yet."

"Well, how exactly can I help?" Carson asked.

"My source is going to need a lawyer. Someone who can guide him through the system. You know this story is going to lead to hearings, criminal investigations, prosecutions. He'll need immunity in order to talk. Plus witness protection."

"Yes, definitely," Carson replied. Then he added with studied casualness, "Did you already give him my name? Did you tell him you were going to talk to me?"

"No, I just said I knew a lawyer who could help. I wanted to reach out to you first. I'd like to get the two of you together. Would you be willing to meet with him?"

"Of course, but I need more details before I do that."

"*No more details,*" Jason said in her ear. "*He's hooked. He's scared. Let him twist.*"

Abbey bolted to her feet from the bench. "I'll get back in touch and tell you everything soon. I just needed to know you were in, Carson. Thank you."

"Abbey, wait, if I'm going to research the legal issues, I need to know more of what we're facing. What is this person's role inside the organization? What crimes has he been involved with? That will affect any immunity discussions with the feds."

"Let me talk to him first," Abbey replied. "He's cautious, because his life is in danger as soon as he goes public. I'll share everything you told me, and I'll make sure he knows he can trust you."

"Abbey, you have to be careful what you say to him. There could be legal conflicts with me or my firm that need to be cleared before we can move forward. I'm worried about my name getting out before I know who I'm dealing with."

"Don't worry, Carson," she said. "I'll be careful. We'll work it all out. I'm sorry, I have to go. I'll call you, and we'll meet soon."

"When? Where?"

Abbey didn't answer him. She put her head down and disappeared into the crowd.

PHASE One was done. Now it was time for Phase Two.

Once a target is off balance, keep him that way. Don't let him recover.

Treadstone.

Bourne fell in behind Carson Gattor as the lawyer headed under the arch out of Washington Square Park. The man walked as if in a daze up Fifth Avenue, not looking behind him. Abbey had done well. Gattor was scared. His pace was quick; he needed to get back to the safety of his office; he needed to make a phone call to Medusa.

Now it was time to ramp up the fear.

At the stoplight, Bourne came up immediately behind the lawyer. He whispered in his ear. "You handled that well, Mr. Gattor."

The man began to spin around in shock, but Bourne hissed, "*Don't look back*. The feds could be watching. Take out your phone and pretend you're making a call."

Gattor did as instructed, but Bourne could see sweat on the back of the man's neck. "Who *are* you? What's going on?"

"We've been watching Abbey Laurent. We were wondering who she would meet with."

"*Why?*"

"You heard her. This is a *mole hunt*, Mr. Gattor. We've known for some time that we had a leak. Operations have been compromised. Agents have been killed. Whoever it is has been very careful, but now he's shown himself. When Ms. Laurent calls you again, we need you to set up a meeting. We'll have someone standing by to eliminate both of them."

"My God! You're *Medusa*. . . . You mean, this is *real*? There's a mole?"

"There is. Be glad Ms. Laurent reached out to you, Mr. Gattor. It puts you in the clear. Some of us were convinced that *you* were the mole."

"Me? Never! I would never!"

"We'll be in touch again before the meeting. Take precautions until then, and assume you're under surveillance."

"Wait! You can't leave it like that. I have questions."

"We can't talk here. The light is green. Walk. Don't look at me. When you get to the Church of the Ascension on the next block, go into the courtyard and around to the far corner of the building. I'll be there."

Bourne pushed past Gattor and continued northward until he reached the Episcopal church, where he let himself inside the gate and took cover behind the trees. He didn't have to wait long. The rapid tap of Gattor's leather shoes announced his arrival, and as the man came around the building, Bourne grabbed him and shoved him against the brick wall.

Gattor's eyes widened with recognition. "Oh my God, it's you! You're *Cain!*"

"Of course I am. I told you, you did well, Mr. Gattor. You've played your part perfectly up until now. Don't blow it."

"My part? What are you saying? You're supposed to be *dead!*"

"Yes, that's what we wanted everyone to think. The setup worked just as we hoped, thanks in large part to you, Mr. Gattor. The information you gave Abbey Laurent worked exactly as intended. Medusa is grateful. But now we have a problem."

"I don't understand. Why are you here? There's never supposed to be direct contact! I'm a resource, nothing more. She swore to me I was safe!"

She.

Gattor's contact at Medusa was a woman.

"Your previous terms of engagement no longer apply," Bourne informed him. "The mole changes everything. You're on a list, Mr. Gattor. You're *blown.*"

"My God, what do I do?"

"I told you, as soon as the journalist calls you again, set up a meeting. We'll take care of the rest."

"But what if she gives him my name? What if he knows me? You just said I'm blown."

"If she gives him your name, it won't be the mole at that meeting. It'll be the FBI. You'll be under arrest. And don't get any ideas about cutting a deal with them, Mr. Gattor. We can get to you anywhere."

"This is *madness!*"

Bourne slid out the gun he'd taken from the Canadian policeman. Gattor squirmed, seeing the weapon, and Bourne held him in place against the wall. He pressed the butt of the gun, which was empty now, into the lawyer's hand. "Look, there's a slim chance you may need to take care of this situation on your own."

"*What?*"

"The mole is part of Medusa. That means he'll be cautious. If he suspects a trap, he may contact you outside the scheduled time and place, when we don't have a wet team ready to go. In that case, we'll need you to eliminate him yourself. The woman, too, if she's with him."

"Eliminate them? You want me to *kill* them? That was never part of the deal! I don't even know how to fire a gun!"

"If he thinks he's dealing only with you, he's less likely to expect an ambush. That's your advantage. As for the gun, it's easy. Point and shoot. Be careful, the trigger is sensitive, so don't put your finger on it until you're ready to fire. A forehead shot is best, so you'll need to be close. Anywhere else, and he'll take time to bleed out, so he may have an opportunity to grab his own weapon and kill you."

"Jesus!"

"Good luck, Mr. Gattor," Bourne told him. "We'll be watching."

Jason left the lawyer a quivering mess inside the shelter of the trees. He melted back onto the New York streets. As he walked downtown, he slipped his phone into his hand and sent a text to Abbey.

Phase Two complete. It's a go.

Carson Gattor was in full panic mode. The lawyer would be screaming into his phone soon and demanding a meeting, but not with Abbey Laurent.

The only thing he could do now was reach out to Medusa.

SEVENTEEN

IT was *Cain!*" Carson Gattor screamed into his phone after he closed and locked the door of his twentieth-floor office near Union Square. "He's in New York. He confronted me on the street. He said he was *part* of Medusa. He said you're looking for a mole inside the organization who knows about *me*. My God, is that true?"

The sultry voice of his contact showed no emotion. She never did. "Are you certain it was him, Carson?"

"Of course I'm sure! You're the one who gave me the information about him. I thought he was going to kill me!"

She didn't answer right away. Her silence told him that calculations were going through her mind. "But in fact, he didn't kill you. How interesting."

"*Interesting?* That's all you have to say? This isn't how it's supposed to work! This isn't our deal! I was just supposed to be a go-between. I wasn't supposed to deal with people like Cain."

"Calm down, Carson. If Cain wanted you dead, you'd already have a bullet in your throat."

"I won't calm down. Was he telling the truth? Is there a mole inside Medusa who can expose me?"

"No, he was simply trying to rattle you, and obviously he succeeded."

"But *why*?"

"That I'm not sure about. It's a curious puzzle."

Carson shook his head. "You need to help me. Mole or not, I'm at risk. You need to get me out!"

"*Quiet!*" the woman insisted, in a voice that didn't allow for any protest. He knew better than to open his mouth again when she used that tone. In person, it was a tone that brought swift punishment.

Carson waited through an interminable length of silence. He heard nothing on the phone but the smooth, measured sound of her breathing, which he knew well. That sound always aroused him. Her breath was like that when she straddled him, her eyes closed, when she teased him with her interminably slow movements up and down, postponing the aching moment of relief.

They'd met exactly six times. Every meeting was memorable. Every one ended the same way, with depraved, glorious sex in a hotel room and information passed to him on a thumb drive for distribution to a contact in the media or government. Money always showed up in his bank account a few days later, although in truth, he would have paid *her* for the experience. She was that good.

The very first time had been in Las Vegas. He'd been

in town for a meeting with one of his clients, and a taxi had taken him to an upscale casino outside the city. He'd played the blackjack tables and lost big. He'd never had such a losing streak in his life, but he found that he couldn't stop, not even when the rational part of his brain told him to walk away. The deeper he dug the hole, the more he believed that his luck had to turn, and when it did, everything would go his way. But his luck never changed. He played and lost throughout the night, raising the stakes higher and higher with each hand, until he was down by more than one hundred and fifty thousand dollars. He didn't have that kind of money.

That was when he met her.

She showed up at his side, incredibly tall, sleek and gorgeous, with black hair and pale eyes that sent a surge of blood between his legs. She wore a barely-there thigh-high black dress that clung to her bony curves, and when she bent over, he could see everything.

"You seem to have a problem, Mr. Gattor."

How did she know his name?

Carson hadn't put it together at the time. He was in too much of a fog. It was only later that he realized that he'd been set up, that he'd been *chosen* and steered to the casino and manipulated and cheated out of his money. No, all he knew at that moment was that he was turned on by this woman and facing a debt he couldn't pay.

"I have a solution. I have a way for you to satisfy your debt in full and make a great deal more money beyond that."

"What do I have to do?" he asked, although it didn't

matter. Whatever it was, he was going to do it. He couldn't say no to her.

"We'll talk about details soon. For now, I only have one demand."

"What is it?"

"You must remember at all times when we are together to call me Miss Shirley."

Then she'd taken him up to a penthouse suite in the hotel that overlooked the mountains and introduced him to a night of pain and pleasure unlike anything he'd ever experienced. In the morning, she'd given him a first-class airline ticket and told him to strike up a conversation with the man in the seat next to him.

That was all. Build a relationship.

That was his first mission for Medusa.

"You did the right thing by calling me, Carson," Miss Shirley told him when the waiting on the phone had gone on for more than a minute. "Your assessment of the situation is correct. We need to extract you."

"You'll pull me out?"

"Yes. Obviously, your work for us has become known, and that means you're at risk. You can't stay in New York."

"Where will I go?"

"Initially, you'll join me in Las Vegas. I'll send the jet for you tonight. Someone will debrief you about your interaction with Cain and Ms. Laurent. And then we'll find you a new location and identity. You'll start over, Carson. Do you like Asia? Perhaps we can send you to Bangkok. I suspect you'd find diversions to entertain you there. Of course, our relationship will need to end. We won't talk again."

"I—I don't know—" He found himself horrified at the idea of never spending another night with her.

"The alternative is another meeting with Cain," Miss Shirley replied. "Is that what you want?"

"*No!*"

"Fine. Do exactly as I say. There's a wine bar in Greenwich Village called Villiers. Be there tonight at ten o'clock. In the meantime, I'll make plans for your departure, and I'll text you further instructions when you're in place. Walk, don't take a cab. We need to make sure you're not being followed."

"Are you sure it's safe?"

"Relax, Carson. Haven't I always taken care of you?"

"What if he contacts me again?" Carson asked. "What if he simply shows up somewhere? What do I do?"

He heard the smile in her voice. "You said Cain gave you a gun. Use it."

MISS Shirley hung up the phone.

She lay naked on a chaise lounge in a white-walled estate in the Las Vegas hills. The ninety-degree sun beat down on her bronzed body. She climbed off the chaise lounge and walked in her sandals to the diving board of the Roman-inspired pool, which was surrounded by stone urns, erotic fountains, and statues of goddesses. She kicked off her shoes, mounted the board, and made a clean dive, her lean body slicing into the turquoise water. Like the Olympic swimmer she was, she swam forty laps freestyle and used the ladder to climb out of the pool again, not winded at all.

Water dripped from her breasts and wet hair. She dried herself with a towel, retrieved her sandals, and returned to the chaise at an unhurried pace.

She picked up the phone and dialed a number.

"Restak," a voice answered.

"It's me."

"What can I do for you . . . Miss Shirley?"

"I'm coming to New York," she replied. "Cain is there. We need an incident arranged for tonight."

EIGHTEEN

"**HERE** he is," Bourne told Abbey, stealing a glance through binoculars at the Broadway entrance of the high-rise off Union Square.

A cold rain fell in the New York night. Carson Gattor wore a beige trench coat and opened an umbrella over his head. He joined the crowd of pedestrians and turned left across from the park, heading west past a row of retail shops. He walked quickly and nervously, looking back over his shoulder every few steps.

Jason didn't move.

"Shouldn't we follow him?" Abbey asked.

"We will. First I want to see who else is following him."

Bourne waited patiently, assessing the others in the crowd near Gattor. When he was satisfied, he took Abbey's arm, and the two of them hurried along Fourteenth Street without crossing the street, keeping an eye on the lawyer across the late-evening traffic. They'd done a rough color job to change Abbey's hair from red to black, and she wore a dark hoodie pulled up to hide her face. Jason wore a wool cap pulled low on his forehead and an Islanders jersey. Despite checking his surroundings repeatedly, Gattor never looked in their direction. He wasn't skilled at identifying surveillance.

They stayed behind him for two long blocks until he got to Sixth Avenue, where he turned left toward the heart of Greenwich Village. Rain spat through the streetlights, and the passing cars threw spray over the curbs. The short southbound blocks passed quickly, and the farther Gattor went, the more careless he got about looking back. It was easy to keep him in sight. When he reached the clock tower of the Jefferson Market Library, he turned onto Tenth Street and continued through the leafy streets of the Village. The pedestrians thinned, and Jason allowed the gap between them to increase. Gattor walked several more blocks past parked cars that were squeezed together on the street and trash bags piled on the curb. On the other side of Seventh Avenue, they watched him disappear into a small wine bar with tall windows facing the sidewalk.

Jason and Abbey sat down next to each other under the awning of a shipping store across the street, where they had a vantage on the bar. The place was packed. As the door opened and closed, they could hear piano music. Jason put an arm around Abbey's shoulders and nudged her head against him, so they looked like lovers taking a respite from the rain. From where they were, they could see the One World Trade Center tower jutting into the sky.

"Do you think he's meeting someone?" Abbey said under her breath.

"It looks that way."

"Medusa?"

"Most likely."

She saw the concern on Jason's face. "You don't look pleased. Isn't this what you wanted?"

"He's alone," Jason said. "Nobody followed him. Just us. He isn't being watched. I don't understand that. If he's meeting anyone from Medusa, they'd make sure the area's secure."

"Do you think it's a trap? For us?"

"If they wanted us, this place would already be surrounded. It's not."

"What do you want to do?" Abbey asked.

Jason shot his gaze across the narrow street toward the wine bar and its flashing neon sign with the name *Villiers*. The lights were bright inside, and a crowd of twenty- and thirty-somethings made the place standing room only. Several high cocktail tables dotted the floor and a railing circled the perimeter for people who were standing up. He could see Carson Gattor near the rear wall, his coat over his sleeve. The lawyer had a glass of white wine in his hand, and he closed his eyes as he drank. He looked relaxed now. Relieved.

But he was still alone. No one had approached him. The size of the crowd squeezed into the small bar made it impossible to tell whether Gattor was being watched.

"Take a walk outside the place," Jason told Abbey. "Both directions. Don't stop or look through the windows, but have your phone out and do a continuous burst of photographs of the interior. I'd like to see who's in there with him."

"You think someone from Medusa is already there?"

"I don't know, but Gattor's not here for the chardonnay. Do you feel comfortable doing this?"

"Sure."

Abbey got to her feet and dodged a couple of cars as she ran to the opposite corner of Tenth near the wine bar. She wandered past the blue-painted walls of Villiers and pretended to be having a conversation on her phone as she fired off multiple photographs of the people inside. Then she acted as if she'd gotten lost and retraced her steps, repeating the process from the other direction. Bourne smiled. She had good tradecraft.

She rejoined Jason and huddled close to him again. Rain dripped from the awning.

"Carson is at the back. He's not talking to anybody, and I didn't notice anyone paying attention to him."

"Do you know if he lives near here?"

"No. Other direction. He told me he has a place in Chelsea."

"I don't like this," Jason said.

They waited as time ticked by, first half an hour, then an hour. Nothing changed inside the wine bar. Periodically, Jason kept an eye on Gattor, and he noticed that the man's relaxed demeanor evaporated as the evening wore on. The lawyer grew anxious, checking his watch and his phone. He was being stood up, and that obviously unnerved him. When the clock passed eleven, Gattor made a call to someone but obviously got no answer.

Still, he made no effort to leave.

"Jason!" Abbey whispered urgently. "Across the street. Under the scaffolding."

Bourne shifted his gaze that way. Two men had arrived on the corner, with eyes glued to their phone screens. Both were young, probably not even twenty-five, dressed completely in black. One was tall and skinny, with messy brown hair streaked with neon green. His companion was a squat Asian with a chin beard and dark buzz cut.

When Jason looked the other way up Seventh Avenue, he saw a third man, also in black, his head shaved bald and his neck covered in tattoos.

Then, only seconds later, an Uber car pulled up to the curb on the far side of the street, and two muscular young women emerged from the back seat. Also in black. One slipped a Guy Fawkes mask over her face, but her friend spoke to her sharply, and she removed it and secured it in the pocket of her black jacket.

The five of them stood in the rain up and down the street, not communicating directly with each other but obviously together.

"What's going on?" Abbey asked. "Are they looking for us?"

"I don't think so, but something's going down."

Bourne leaned back and checked inside Villiers with his binoculars. Gattor had his phone in his hand now. He tapped out a text. The lawyer waited, and a few seconds later, his face broke into a smile of relief. He took his trench coat and slipped his arms into the sleeves. He shook out his umbrella on the floor.

"Gattor's getting ready to go," Jason said. "He got a text with new instructions. I want you out of here, Abbey. Right now, before Gattor leaves."

"What? Why?"

"Things are about to get violent. I don't want you in the middle of it. I want you safe."

"These kids? They're *Medusa*?"

Bourne shook his head. "No, they look like street thugs, but them showing up now isn't a coincidence."

"I'd rather stay with you," Abbey said.

"That's not an option. Listen to me. There's an apartment complex near Gramercy Park that Nova and I used once. We can stay there tonight. A block away, you'll find a twenty-four-hour bistro on Park and Twentieth. Take a cab there, and wait for me."

"What are you going to do?"

"Get some answers for us. Now go. Please."

Abbey hesitated, obviously reluctant to leave, but then she got to her feet and walked with her head down, back along Tenth the way they'd come. He kept an eye on her until he saw her flag down a cab and head safely away. Then he returned his attention to Villiers, where he saw Carson Gattor walk out of the wine bar into the rain. Jason slumped against the shop wall. Through slitted eyes, he watched what was happening at the intersection. Gattor crossed the street, his umbrella up, heading down

Seventh. The lawyer paid no attention to Jason, who was sprawled on the sidewalk like one of the city's homeless. As Gattor passed him, Jason saw the two men at the corner checking their phones and signaling to the others.

Gattor was definitely the one they wanted.

All five of them followed. The three men on the west side of Seventh stayed half a block behind the lawyer, while the two women kept pace on the east side of the street. Jason sprang to his feet and fell in a few steps behind them. Halfway down the block, Gattor veered to the other side of Seventh, and the three men did the same. The lawyer never looked back, not seeing the five thugs in his wake. In a gap between the traffic, Gattor hurried past the Stonewall monument and disappeared down the steps into the Christopher Street subway station.

As soon as the lawyer was out of sight, the five young people who were following him donned black bandanas and masks. Two produced knives from their pockets; two had chains; one had a length of lead pipe. They ran for the subway. Jason held back until the five of them had reached the steps, then ran to catch up. Rainwater poured down the stairs into the station, and a dank smell billowed from the underground. As he entered the station, Jason could see Gattor heading through the turnstile toward the northbound tracks. Four of the five masked attackers took off in the same direction, but the fifth was slow. Jason slid out his gun and came up behind him and cracked the barrel sharply over the thug's skull. The bald man with the neck tattoos crumpled to the ground, and

Jason pocketed his gun again and jumped the turnstile to follow the others.

He approached the bottom of the steps cautiously. Ahead of him, on the northbound platform, Carson Gattor checked the station clocks as he waited for the number 1 train. The tiled walkway was brightly lit, but the tracks between the platforms were dark, divided by rows of green steel I-beams. Jason saw four black-clad aggressors converging on Gattor. The lawyer was preoccupied and didn't even notice them until they were practically in his face. Then, when he spotted the bandanas and masks, his expression twisted with confusion and fear, and he backed away down the platform. But there was nowhere for him to go.

"Look what we have here!" the Asian man shouted from behind his mask. "A piece-of-shit white nationalist who thinks he can hide behind his nice suit. Hey, Nazi, you want us to show you what we do to fascist pigs?"

Gattor's eyes widened. He looked over his shoulder at the tracks, but there was no train coming to give him an escape. "What are you talking about? You're wrong! *Jesus*, you're wrong!"

"You think you get a free pass because you're a lawyer? You defend fascists. You defend Nazis. That makes you one of them."

"I don't! I'm not!"

But the Asian thug's arm shot out, whipping a two-foot length of chain through the air. Gattor didn't have time to duck. The chain hit him across the side of the head, opening up a huge cut that sprayed blood onto the platform floor. The second of the four thugs moved in immediately, punching the lawyer in the mouth with a fist hardened by a ring of brass knuckles. Gattor screamed, coughing out blood and teeth.

Bourne leaped for the nearest of the four assailants. It was one of the two heavy-set women, and he threw her head against a steel I-beam, where she groaned and collapsed, unconscious. The attackers spotted the new threat behind them, and two of them shifted their focus from Gattor to Bourne. One was the other woman; the other was the man with green streaks like lightning bolts through his messy hair. With a knife outstretched, the skinny man jabbed at Jason, who dodged the assault and used the heel of his fist to rap the man's head sideways. Dizzied, the man stumbled, and Jason lashed out with his boot to kick the man off the platform onto the train tracks.

With Jason's back turned, the woman with the Guy Fawkes mask unleashed a rebel scream and leaped at him with a lead pipe held high over her head. Jason twisted as she swung it down, but the blow landed hard on his shoulder, freezing it and shocking his brain with pain. The woman aimed for his head, but he grabbed her and wrestled her to the ground. He slammed her head against the platform floor, but she shook off the impact and fought back with insane passion, using her fingernails like blades on his back. Her head rose off the ground, and he had to rear back as she chomped her teeth and tried to bite his face. He drove his knee into her stomach, making her gasp, and then he punched her head down again, once, twice, three times. Finally, her eyes rolled back, and she lost consciousness.

Jason shoved himself off the woman and stood up, trying to keep his balance. He shook life back into his left arm. Twenty feet away, the Asian man stood over Gattor, who lay motionless on the ground. With the chain in his hand, the assailant lashed the lawyer repeatedly around the head, and there was so much blood now that Gattor's face was unrecognizable.

"*Stop!*" Bourne shouted.

The Asian man saw Jason coming toward him. His eyes gleamed with something like amusement. Above his chin beard, his mouth broke into a coffee-brown grin. The chain dropped from his fingers and rattled to the platform floor. In one swift motion, the man dug a pistol out of a holster at his back and pointed the gun at Carson Gattor. His finger jerked, and a bullet burned into the lawyer's throat.

Medusa!

Bourne already had his own gun back in his hand, and as the Asian swung the pistol around, Jason squatted and squeezed off a single shot that caught the Asian man between the eyes. The man's body dropped on top of the dead lawyer.

Behind him, Jason heard running footsteps. He turned and saw the thug with the green-streaked hair climbing out of the well of the train tracks and staggering in a zigzag fashion for the platform stairs. Bourne charged after him. Just as the man got to the steps, Jason took him down hard against the concrete. Ignoring the pain in his own shoulder, he grabbed the man and wrenched him onto his back and shoved the barrel of his gun into the man's forehead.

"*Who sent you?*"

The man spoke between bloody lips. "Nobody sent me."

"You're lying. You're *Medusa*."

"What the hell's that? I don't know what you're talking about!"

"The Asian. The one with the gun. Who was he? What was his name?"

"His profile said his name was Cho. I never met him before!"

"Profile? What profile?"

"His Prescix profile. We got the alert that some white-power lawyer was in the neighborhood and a few of us got together to rough him up. There weren't supposed to be guns. We weren't going to kill him, just beat the shit out of him!"

Jason heard police sirens getting closer outside the station. He didn't have much time. He dug in the man's pocket until he found his phone. "*Show me.*"

The man tapped on the phone with one finger to unlock it, and he selected an app that opened with a black screen and a close-up photograph of a human eye. Inside the iris, a single gold word appeared letter by letter.

PRESCIX

When the intro screen dissolved, Jason saw a local map and a list of users scrolling down the right side of the phone. In the news timeline was a photograph of Carson Gattor, with a flashing message in red below the picture.

Action Alert! Fascist Lawyer in the Village!

"You attacked a stranger because an *app* told you to?"

"Hey, you bring that white-power shit around here, you pay the price," the man said.

"Did you know any of the others who were with you?" Jason asked.

"Nah. Just their profiles."

Bourne shook his head. He still had nothing.

He heard screaming behind him as a train unloaded at the station and the arriving passengers spotted the bodies on the platform. It was time to go. With a quick snap of his gun, he knocked out the man on the steps, and then he climbed over him and took the stairs back to the station, which was a frenzy of panic. He calmly pulled his Islanders jersey over his head and stuffed it into a trash can.

Then he left the station into the rain just as he saw the first of the police cars arriving.

NINETEEN

JASON slid into a seat across from Abbey at the all-night bistro near Gramercy Park. She had a plate of eggs in front of her, but she'd left it untouched. Her face bloomed with relief when she saw him.

"Oh, my God! I was so worried!" She looked around the mostly empty restaurant and lowered her voice. "I heard people talking about a shooting at the subway in the Village. Was that you?"

"Let's not talk about it here."

He twisted his head to check the street, and a shiver of pain shot up his neck. Abbey noticed the grimace on his face.

"Are you okay? Are you hurt?"

"I'm fine, but we need to get out of sight. There's a safe house a block away we can use. It's run by the British. Nova knew about it."

"Okay."

"Put your hoodie up when we go. I don't want your face on any street cameras."

She nodded quietly. Before pulling up the hood, she combed her fingers through her hair in a gesture that was unconsciously sensual. The look she achieved was messy and perfect. Her black bangs dipped over her forehead, and he could see hints of red among the black. Her mouth was serious now, just her lips pressed softly together. Her wide dark eyes stared across the table at him, and he found it hard to look away from her face.

Then she brought the hood gently over her head. "That okay?"

"Yes. Fine."

The two of them left the restaurant and walked down Twentieth Street in the rain. Neither one of them said a word, but he could feel something strange happening between them. The narrow street was dark, but lights glowed in the apartments overhead. A car passed, kicking up spray without slowing down. When they reached the park, he steered her next to the wrought-iron fence. Trees covered them and held back some of the downpour. Parked cars filled every spot, and he watched for any sign that someone was watching the area. He didn't think that anyone at Treadstone knew about this safe house, but he couldn't be sure.

The twenty-story building was at the end of the block.

"Keep your head down when we go inside," Bourne told her. "Don't look at the man at the desk."

He buzzed for entry. When the guard came on the intercom to query him, he used a name that was supposed to give him access to the building, any day, any time. After a tense moment of waiting, the door opened. Jason slipped inside, keeping Abbey behind him, and went over to the man at the desk. He repeated the name and laid out three thousand dollars in cash, which he hoped would buy them anonymity.

"No records," Jason told him. "We're not here. Okay?"

The man said nothing, but he took the money and handed over a key. Jason pocketed it and guided Abbey to the elevator. No one else was in the lobby. When the elevator doors opened, he went first, conscious of the camera looking down at them. He kept his head down and turned around, only to see Abbey raising her hands toward her hoodie to slip it down. Immediately, he moved toward her and took hold of both of her hands to stop her. He meant nothing personal by touching her. This was about keeping them safe, nothing else.

But that was a lie.

He bent down close to her. She tilted her chin, meeting his eyes. The message passing between them was unmistakable. Her lips moved and parted, inviting him, and he put his mouth on hers. The kiss started soft and slow, then grew intense. Their fingers were still laced together, and she pressed forward with her body against his. As she did, the hoodie slipped down, but he didn't notice. They stayed that way, their lips exploring each other, until the elevator doors opened on the fourteenth floor.

He let go of her hands. Abbey backed up, embarrassed, a flush on her face. They got out of the elevator and walked silently to the end of the hall, where the room was. He undid the lock and murmured, "Stay here while I make sure it's clear."

Her eyes stared at the floor. "Okay."

Jason went into the one-bedroom apartment. Nothing had changed, not the paint, the furniture, the curtains. It was the same as it had been when he was here with Nova. He went back to the door and held it open so that Abbey could come inside. He closed the door behind her and did the dead bolt.

"Are we safe here?" she asked softly.

"I think so."

"Good."

"Do you want anything? They usually keep the fridge stocked."

"No, thanks."

"I'll sleep on the couch. You can have the bed."

"Okay."

"Abbey, listen, I'm sorry."

She shoved her hands in her pockets. "Don't be. You got the signal right."

"It's better if nothing happens between us."

"Definitely," she replied. "Definitely better. Sure."

"I kill people," Jason said. "Don't forget that."

"I haven't forgotten." She went to the window and looked out at the lights of the city. "Did you kill Carson?"

"It wasn't me. But he's dead."

"Medusa?"

Jason nodded. "One of them was definitely Medusa.

His job was to make sure Gattor died. The rest, I don't think so."

"Then who were they? Why were they after him?"

He sat down at the apartment's dinette table and pulled out the phone he'd taken from the last of the assailants. Abbey sat down next to him, and she pulled her chair close enough that their legs brushed together. He unlocked the phone using the code he'd seen the man enter, and he opened the app for the Prescix software.

As he scrolled through the man's news feed, Abbey whistled, seeing the photos and articles about Carson Gattor. "He was a lawyer for white power groups? I never would have guessed that."

"That's the thing, I don't think he was," Bourne replied. "These articles are all deepfakes. So are the photos. This incident was manipulated. Someone knew where Carson was going, and they put him in the crosshairs for a bunch of anti-fascist thugs who love to go around beating up Nazis. Look at these posts. The software targeted these people, fed them sophisticated misinformation, and sent them after Gattor. And then Medusa included one of their own just to make sure they got the result they wanted. Gattor dead."

"Software can do all that?" Abbey asked.

"Apparently so. With the right code and the right people pulling the strings."

"Prescix," she murmured. "Congresswoman Ortiz talked about Prescix. Are they part of Medusa?"

"I don't know. Medusa obviously has people who can hack parts of the Prescix system."

"There was a news station on TV in the cab. A top exec at Prescix was found murdered in Las Vegas today."

"Whatever Medusa is planning, they're moving forward," he said.

"But what do we do now? Carson was our only link to Medusa, and now he's dead."

Bourne frowned. "I know. Medusa outplayed us."

Abbey looked deep in thought, and he found himself unsettled by how attractive she was. Then she took the assailant's phone out of his hands and reopened the Prescix software. "Hang on a minute, Jason. Don't be so sure."

"What do you mean?"

She scrolled to the very end of the thread and then turned the phone around for Jason to see. "Look at this last photo of Carson. The one they posted to make sure the thugs could find him. It was taken *at* Villiers. Medusa was there."

He studied the phone and saw that she was right. The photograph showed Carson Gattor in the wine bar, his coat over his arm, his wineglass in his hand. The lawyer looked down at the hidden camera without realizing it was there.

"Let's go through the photos you took outside the bar," Jason said. "Maybe we can figure out who was watching Gattor."

Again they leaned next to each other, both of them conscious of their closeness. Abbey took her phone from her pocket and scrolled slowly through the dozens of photographs she'd taken in a burst as she walked past the wine bar. The first time through they found nothing, but then Bourne reexamined the angle of the photo in the Prescix post. He opened up Abbey's pictures again.

"The man at that table with his laptop open. See how Carson is looking down? The person who took it was seated. It's him. He used the laptop to grab the photo and post it to Prescix."

Abbey enlarged the photograph of the man in the wine bar, who didn't look older than thirty. It was impossible to tell how tall he was, and the picture she'd taken was in profile, but they could see a long, slim nose, the untrimmed line of his beard creeping down his neck, and his sandy-blond hair pulled into a short ponytail on top of his head. He wore a rust-colored sweater with a collar and zipper.

"He's Medusa?" Abbey asked.

"I think so."

"So how do we figure out who he is?"

Bourne stared at the man in the photograph. There was only one way to find him. "I have to talk to an old friend," Jason said.

BEFORE sunrise, Jason sat behind the Hans Christian Andersen statue near the boat pond in Central Park. The rain had stopped overnight, but the ground was still wet. The luxury apartments of Fifth Avenue loomed above the trees. He'd arrived early, but he didn't have to wait long before he recognized the jogger approaching on the concrete trail. The man wasn't tall, but he ran with a fast, confident athleticism. He was dressed down, so no one would recognize that he was one of the most powerful men in the country. The man stopped at the Conservatory Water, ran his hands through his wavy dark hair, and rested for a minute with his hands on his knees.

"It's good that you're a creature of habit," Jason called.

Scott DeRay spun around. "Jesus Christ."

"Sorry to ambush you, Scott, but we need to talk."

"Of course, yes. Definitely."

Scott took a plastic bottle from his belt and drank a squirt of Gatorade. He checked to confirm that the two of them were alone and then headed to the bench where Jason was sitting. He sat down next to his childhood friend.

"I didn't shoot Sofia Ortiz," Jason said.

Scott hesitated. "If you say so, I believe you."

"But?"

"But I'm sorry, Jason. No one else will believe it. There's too much evidence. The FBI has video of you in the hotel, fingerprints in the room and on the gun. And as for your background—well, we both know you fit the profile."

"Medusa framed me. They set me up."

Scott waited to answer. He drank another shot of Gatorade, and his face glowed with sweat. "It's my fault. I shouldn't have gotten you into this. But my hands are tied. Right now, it doesn't matter to the cabal whether Medusa framed you or recruited you. The effect is the same. They want nothing to do with you. A member of Congress was *assassinated*. I'm heading to Washington this morning to reassure a bunch of furious politicians that Big Tech had nothing to do with it. If any actual evidence comes out that you were working for us, it will be devastating."

"I get that," Jason replied. "I'm an outcast. Me being dead would be better for everyone. Treadstone is trying to kill me, did you know that? Nash Rollins is hunting me. Is that Miles Priest's handiwork?"

Scott frowned. "Yes. Miles talked to the director, and Shaw sent Nash after you. He knows the two of you have history."

"Well, can you call off the dogs? Give me some breathing room?"

His friend stood up from the bench. Dawn lightened the sky, creating reflections on the boat pond. "Do you remember all the times we came here as kids? Sorry, what am I saying, of course you don't remember. But we did. It seems like a long time ago."

"For me, it was a different lifetime."

"I know. The point is, you were my best friend, Jason."

"Is that your way of softening the blow that you can't help me?"

Scott looked down at him. "I wish I could. I wish I could set you up with a new identity somewhere, but I can't. What's going on is bigger than both of us. If any of this is traced back to me, I'm finished. I'm afraid you're on your own."

"I don't want to escape," Jason replied. "I'm not running."

His friend's face showed surprise. "Then why are you here?"

"I'm still chasing Medusa."

"Alone? That's crazy."

"Well, everyone thinks I *am* crazy, don't they? Psychologically damaged. A prime candidate for terrorist recruitment."

"Look—Jason—"

"Medusa is on the move, Scott. Ortiz was step one. *I* was step one. But whatever's coming next is much bigger."

"Do you know what it is?"

"No, but I suspect the Prescix software is involved. Someone at Medusa manipulated the Prescix software last night to arrange the death of Abbey Laurent's source. They knew I was coming after him. Oh, and I heard about the murder of the Prescix executive, too. You and Miles better be careful."

"We are." Scott glanced at the boat pond and saw other early-morning runners heading in their direction. "I need to go. We can't be seen together. What do you want, Jason? You obviously want something if you took the risk of coming here."

"I need to identify someone. I think he's Medusa. I have a photograph but nothing else. I was hoping someone at Carillon could access the facial recognition systems across the cabal and get me a name and background."

"And if you find him, what will you do?"

"Follow him up the chain. See where it leads me."

Jason could see his friend weighing the pros and cons. Everything had a cost and benefit in Scott's world.

"There's a coffee shop across from the Carillon lobby," Scott said finally. "Be there in three hours. One of my techs will find you."

"What's his name?"

"No names. I'm not putting my people at risk. You meet this man, and he'll get you the information you need."

"Will the FBI be meeting me, too, Scott?"

"Don't worry, you're safe. I won't turn you in, for the simple reason that nobody wants you in custody."

"Just dead," Jason said.

Scott shook out his legs, getting ready to start running again. "I trust your skills, so I'm sure you'll monitor the area before you move in."

"I appreciate the help."

"This is a one-time offer," Scott replied. "For old times, Jason. After that, we're done. But be forewarned. Once this query launches, you'll be leaving footprints online. Nothing is private anymore. Whatever or whoever you're searching for, Medusa will find out about it. Quickly."

TWENTY

THE new Carillon Technology building rose twelve hundred feet in the air over midtown, its sharp silver angles making it look as if it had been carved out of quartz. The company had teased half the cities in the country with the prospect of landing its second headquarters, but ultimately, they'd followed the money to Manhattan. Now the company's twin towers in California and New York stood like ultramodern palaces on either coast, with Miles Priest presiding over one and Scott DeRay ruling the other.

Jason watched the mass of pedestrians on Forty-Second Street. He was alert for the possibility of a trap. The location made him nervous, because the easiest kill of all was an innocent collision at a crowded intersection. Gun. Knife. Poison. No one saw a thing, and the ensuing panic covered the assassin's escape.

Crowds favor the hunter. You're never safe in a crowd.

Treadstone.

"Do you see any threats?" Abbey asked.

"Not right now."

"Do you trust Scott?"

"I don't trust anyone," Bourne replied.

The light changed. They crossed the street to the sprawling coffee shop on the opposite corner from the Carillon tower. Jason surveyed the tables through the glass windows before he took Abbey by the elbow and led her inside. They waited to purchase drinks and then found an empty table where he could watch the entrance. Abbey drank her latte, but he didn't touch his own drink. He could tell that she'd picked up on his anxiety, because she didn't speak to him or interrupt his concentration.

Twenty minutes later, Jason spotted a man entering the shop with an open laptop in his hands. He wore a lime-green dress shirt buttoned to the neck and black jeans. His glasses matched his shirt, and they kept sliding down his long nose. He was short and skinny and had a mop of curly brown hair. He typed one-handed as he waited in line.

"That's him," Jason said softly.

"How do you know?"

"I saw him at a meeting with Scott once. He's a tech savant. Be nice to him. If you tailgate him on the freeway, he can slice your credit rating in half before you get to the next exit."

"I'm not sure you can cut a negative number in half," Abbey commented with a smirk.

The young man from Carillon spent a ridiculous amount of time at the counter specifying how the barista should prepare his drink, eliciting eye rolls from the people in line behind him. When he finally got his soy mocha, he went straight to Jason's table without looking at anyone else in the shop. He'd obviously been prepped for the man he was supposed to meet.

"Scott sent me," he said as he sat down. He checked out Abbey from behind his green glasses. "Who's the girl? Scott didn't say there would be anybody else."

"She's with me," Jason replied.

"We're inseparable," Abbey added, smiling.

The tech studied both of them with condescending eyes. His lone typing hand made a frenzied attack on the keyboard, and he was quiet for almost a minute. Then he sat back in the chair. "Abbey Laurent. Canadian journalist for *The Fort*. Birthday, October 2. Studio apartment in Quebec City, behind on last month's rent, credit card debt exceeding eight thousand dollars. Savings account balance one thousand two hundred and forty-two dollars, checking account balance eighty-nine dollars. Most common online password is ImAbs1002. Had an unusual result on her Pap smear three years ago, but further testing showed no issues. On the pill. Three full-frontal nude photos sent to a college boyfriend twelve years ago. Very nice."

The smile disappeared from Abbey's face. "You piece of shit."

Jason put a hand on her arm and murmured, "Easy."

"You both need to understand that I'm not to be messed with," the young tech snapped. "Got it? As far as your lives go, I am God."

"We just want to identify someone," Jason said, "and we can pay for the privilege."

"Carillon pays me four hundred and fifty thousand dollars a year, plus options. Keep your money, Mr. Bourne. Yes, I know who you are. I'm here to do a favor for Scott, and that's all. Now show me the man you want to hack."

Her face dark with anger, Abbey took out her phone and scrolled to the picture of the Medusa operative in the coffee shop. "This is him. I can text you the picture."

The tech shook his head. "I already have it. I transferred everything from your phone while I was waiting in line."

"You little—" Abbey began, then stopped without saying anything more and clamped her lips together.

"Don't worry, we needed to dump the phone anyway," Jason said. "We'll get new burners this afternoon."

The tech ignored their conversation. "Did Scott explain the timeline? If anyone is monitoring this person's online records, they'll know you've located him. You won't have much time to get to him before his identity is erased and rewritten. I'm masking our geographic signature here, but it will also take them about ninety seconds to override that and figure out where you are."

"Then we better move fast," Jason said.

The tech used his index finger to push his green glasses up his nose. He typed one-handed again, still drinking his latte and only occasionally looking at the screen. He said nothing as he worked. Almost five minutes passed, which was longer than Jason expected, and he saw a small crinkle of surprise on the tech's face. Obviously, Medusa kept their records more secure than the Canadian health service did.

Meanwhile, Jason kept an eye on Forty-Second Street through the coffee shop windows. He knew they didn't have much time before someone crashed the party.

"Interesting," the tech said finally.

"Did you find him?" Jason asked.

"Yes, but I had to break into archives to recover his deleted records. He went to a lot of trouble to remove himself from the grid."

"Who is he?"

"His name is Peter Restak. That's an alias. Fingerprints don't match anyone else on file, so his previous identity is unknown."

Like me, Bourne thought.

"Restak is a hacker," the tech went on. "And an impressive one, I have to say. He didn't leave many breadcrumbs behind. He's used multiple online personas on different social media platforms, but he rarely uses any of them more than once. He's a chameleon online, sometimes young, sometimes old, man, woman, trans, whatever. Once he's inside a fake persona, he establishes relationships with similarly situated real people. He feeds them posts that reinforce their biases, and he recruits them for extremist activities. He was heavily involved in the Ortiz riot. The people he's interacted with now have multiple arrest records. A couple of them have been killed. It's like group behavioral modification. Very cool stuff."

"Does that include the murder of a lawyer in the Village last night?" Jason asked.

"Carson Gattor. Yes, Restak orchestrated that."

"Did he use Prescix to do that?" Abbey asked.

"He did, but that's only one of his tools. You have a Prescix account, too, I see. Nine months ago, you bought a very expensive bottle of French perfume, which you couldn't afford. You probably don't even know why you bought it. In fact, you were part of a paid Prescix sponsorship that inserted that particular French perfume into your life at multiple touchpoints. It took twenty-three touchpoints and four days before you purchased the bottle. Don't worry, most of the other buyers cracked more quickly than you did. The company sold seventeen thousand units that week, which is nine times their typical average U.S. weekly sales."

Abbey stared at him, and her face flushed deep red.

"Let's get back to the reason we're here," Jason interrupted. "Restak. What else did you find about him?"

"I told you, very little. Even where he leaves footprints, the identity leads to a dead end. Last night he was an anarchist sympathizer with the handle KillAllNazis. That profile is now inactive. I'm sure he won't go back to it."

"We need to locate him," Jason said.

"That won't be easy. As far as the world is concerned, Peter Restak has no real life. No credit cards, no bank records, no permanent address, not even a past address.

He knows how hackers like me identify people, because he's exactly *like* me. I doubt he stays in any one place for a long period of time."

"There must be something," Abbey interjected. "What about friends? Or a girlfriend? You people can't spend every night playing Call of Duty and searching for mommy videos on Pornhub."

The tech's fish eyes drilled into her again. "Do you really want to antagonize me, Abbey Laurent? Does that seem like a good idea?"

"I want you to stop showing off and tell us what you found. Because we all know you found something. There's no way you're going to sit here and tell us that this Restak is a smarter hacker than you. You've got too much ego for that. So how do we find him?"

The tech's nostrils flared with annoyance. "I don't like her, Bourne."

"That's too bad, because I'm liking her more and more," Jason replied. "Now answer her question. How do we find Restak?"

The young man sighed. "You won't find him directly, like I told you. But he did make a mistake. It *was* a girl-friend. I found a few matching photos of him with a woman named Holly d'Angelo. He scrubbed their relationship online, so there's nothing on social media, but he must have forgotten to check photo processing services. They showed up together in the background of several photos taken by other people that were uploaded to a photo-printing database for a national drugstore. I got them with facial recognition."

Abbey shook her head. "Unbelievable."

"Where do we find Holly d'Angelo?" Jason asked.

"She has a one-bedroom apartment in Flatbush, and she works at a medical clinic in the city. After her job most days, she works out at a women-only fitness studio on Twenty-Third. Then she takes the train home."

"You have her picture?" Abbey asked.

The tech nodded. "I already sent it to your phone. I sent you the photos of Restak, too. Are we done?"

"We're done," Jason replied. "Thanks for the help."

"Thank Scott, not me." He slapped his laptop shut and gave Abbey another disgruntled stare from his cold eyes as he stood up. Abbey stuck out her tongue at him, which triggered an angry hiss from the tech.

As the man turned away, Jason grabbed his wrist in an iron grip.

"By the way," Bourne said, "*your* name is Aaron Haberman. You have a condo on Thirty-Third Street in Kips Bay, and you have a cabin in the Finger Lakes that you like to visit on weekends. See, I make it a point of knowing about the people in Scott's circle, Aaron. So if you have any ideas about messing with Abbey's online life, then be aware that I will insert myself into your *real* life. And believe me when I tell you that is something you do *not* want."

NASH Rollins stood on the Battery Park walkway and watched boats navigate the wavy waters of the Hudson River. It was a cool, breezy afternoon, with clouds moving fast overhead. On the far side of the channel, the Statue of Liberty lifted her torch like a salute. Rollins leaned on his cane, as stiff and unmoving as a statue himself.

A man came up next to him at the railing. He was wiry and medium height, with choppy black hair, a prominent nose, and thick dark eyebrows. His skin was the color of olive oil. He wore black corduroys, a black T-shirt, and a loose-fitting untucked checked shirt with the cuffs rolled back. The shirt, Rollins knew, made it impossible to see that the man had a holster and weapon in the small of his back. He also had two knives, one in his pocket, one at his ankle. He had a holster on his other ankle for a smaller backup pistol.

Standard equipment for Treadstone.

"Benoit," Rollins murmured, staring at the New York view and not at the man next to him.

"Boss."

The two of them had worked together for more than a decade. Rollins had recruited him from the French intelligence service at the suggestion of Cain. Whatever else was true of Cain, the man knew how to assess the value of people. Even inside Treadstone, Rollins had to be careful about the agents he trusted, and Benoit was one of the few whose reliability was beyond question.

In the old days, Rollins had trusted Cain, too.

"What's going on?" Benoit asked. "I had to break off an assignment in New Orleans to get back here. I don't recall your ever sending the jet for me before."

Rollins squinted into the sunlight. "I texted you a photograph."

Casually, Benoit removed his phone from his pocket and checked it as he pretended to take a picture of Lady Liberty. The picture that Rollins had sent was taken from a camera feed in an elevator. The man in the picture had his back to the camera, but the woman was clearly visible, a hoodie slipping down to reveal her face.

"That was captured on an internet-enabled video feed overnight," Rollins murmured. "The computers flagged it for manual review, which we did this morning. The woman is Abbey Laurent. The man with her is Bourne."

"Okay."

"The video came from a UK safe house near Gramercy Park. You need to be ready if they go back there."

"What are my orders?"

"Termination."

"Just Cain or the girl, too?"

Rollins had learned long ago to shove his conscience down into a place where it didn't gnaw at his soul. "Take them both. We can't afford loose ends. Shaw thinks there's too much risk of this getting out and destroying Treadstone. We've only recently gone back in business, and there are a lot of people in Washington who wish we'd been shut down altogether."

"Understood."

But Benoit didn't move from where he was. He stayed on the walkway with his hands clenched around the railing, and he watched the harbor as the wind mussed his dark hair.

"Is there something else?" Rollins asked.

"I've never questioned an order from you, Nash."

"Then don't start now."

Benoit turned and violated protocol by staring directly into Rollins's eyes. If there were cameras, it would be clear that the two of them were together. And Rollins knew that there were always cameras.

"I know Jason Bourne," Benoit said. "I've worked with him many times. He's the best. Even after what happened to him, he never lost a step in the field. What I'm saying is, are you absolutely certain he's turned? Because that doesn't sound like the man I know. Even when I was watching him in Las Vegas, I didn't see any evidence of it. Yes, I know, he's good, and he knows how to keep cover. But the alternate explanation is that he was innocent then and still is."

"Do you think I *like* this?" Rollins snarled. "I know Bourne, too. I've known him for years. But he has *changed*, Benoit. Medusa recruited him, or manipulated him, or whatever it is they do. Regardless, he's not on our side anymore. I saw the FBI report on Congresswoman Ortiz. It was *Cain*. His room, his fingerprints, his gun. There is zero room for doubt."

Benoit casually trimmed a jagged edge on one of his nails. "Does Bourne know the truth about Las Vegas? And about Nova?"

"No."

"Maybe you should have told him what was really going on."

"That wasn't an option. Given his behavior since then, I'm not questioning my decision. For all we know, he was *already* Medusa when he was in Las Vegas. Did you think about that? It's very possible that Cain is the one who ordered the hit on Nova."

Benoit shrugged. "You make strategy based on data, Nash. You believe what the computers tell you. I act based on people. I'm not saying you're wrong. I'm just saying you're not describing the person I know."

"Do you have a problem with this assignment? Do I need to get someone else?"

The Treadstone agent shook his head. "No. Don't worry about me. I'm quite clear on the assignment. Bourne and the girl are dead."

TWENTY-ONE

MILES Priest and Nelly Lessard sat on the outdoor terrace of Gabriel Fox's fifteen-million-dollar estate high in the desert hills of Henderson, Nevada. The founder of Prescix had designed the home himself. It was bone-white, boxy and geometric, with a sweeping view across the Las Vegas valley. From where they were, they could see the lineup of casinos on the Strip, from Mandalay Bay in the south to the Stratosphere in the north. All of the glass towers glinted in the sunshine. On the other side of the valley, barren hills rose over the city, and snow capped the peak of Mount Charleston.

The décor of the estate reflected Gabriel's quirky personality, in addition to his money. Half a dozen bighorn sheep wandered in the private acreage of the mountain above them, and the animals had free run of the house. The multilevel swimming pool featured fountains and a wave machine so Gabriel could surf at will. There was a black-light bowling alley. One room had been finished to look like a Polynesian coastline, including genuine statues imported from Easter Island and walls that were actually 4K screens live-streaming footage from the Pacific. Another room re-created a 1950s Hollywood party, featuring wax figures of actors like Marilyn Monroe, Cary Grant, Katharine Hepburn, Kirk Douglas, and others, built for Gabriel by Madame Tussauds.

On the table in front of Miles and Nelly, an air-conditioned conveyor belt brought a steady stream of cocktails and eclectic appetizers from Gabriel's four-star kitchen. Morimoto sushi. Hong Kong dim sum. Texas brisket. Minnesota lutefisk. Rum shots, craft beer, and glasses of five-hundred-dollar wines.

Priest hated the over-the-top ego on display. To him, it was a monument to excess. He tugged at the collar of his dress shirt as the ninety-degree heat beat down on them. He hated heat, too. He preferred the cold days and nights of his castle in Scotland. Nelly, on the other hand, thrived on it. She'd grown up in Phoenix, and she took in the view without even breaking into a sweat. She also seemed to have no problem with the lavish surroundings. Priest ate and drank nothing, but Nelly calmly sampled the drinks and hors d'oeuvres passing on the belt in front of them.

"Do you want me to do the talking, Miles?" Nelly asked, noting the discomfort on his face. "You don't do too well around Gabriel. He pushes your buttons."

"The man is insane," Priest replied.

"Maybe so, but he's also a genius, and he has what we want. Namely, Prescix. So you have to indulge him."

"Yes, because he has so little indulgence in his life," Priest replied sourly.

"You know what I mean."

The two of them looked up as Gabriel Fox made his entrance onto the terrace. He was dressed in the uniform of a World War I infantryman, including a helmet on his head and a rifle and bayonet in his arms. The brown fabric of the uniform was torn and soiled with mud and bloodstains.

He sat down across from them and smiled pleasantly, with no indication that his attire was unusual. "Miles, Nelly, always a treat to see you."

"Hello, Gabriel," Priest replied. "Are you doing some kind of reenactment?"

Gabriel's face creased with genuine puzzlement. "Reenactment? Reenactment of what?"

"It's nothing," Nelly interjected, shooting a glance at Priest. "We were very sorry to hear about Kevin Drake."

The CEO of Prescix shrugged. He flipped open one of the compartments on the conveyor belt and removed a plate stacked with crispy-fried black bites. It took Priest a moment to realize that the food on the plate was actually a mound of crickets. He had to look away and cover his mouth as Gabriel popped two between his teeth and ate them with a loud crunch.

"Oh, that. Well, we all have to go sometime."

Gabriel took off his helmet and rubbed some of the

sweat on his bald head. He was only in his mid-thirties, but stocky, with a round, sunburned face and a bushy brown mustache. Five years earlier, he'd literally been living on the Las Vegas streets and writing his software in the public library, and now he was a billionaire eating bugs in a Big Tech version of Wonderland. Priest shook his head.

"You don't sound very upset about his murder, Gabriel. Kevin was your partner. He took Prescix public. He made all this possible."

Gabriel flicked his hands as if he were typing on a keyboard. "These are what made Prescix possible. These fingers. Kevin was an accountant. A number cruncher. The only thing he knew about software was what I taught him. And he was trying to steal the company away from me and hand it over to you, Miles. Do you think I don't know that?"

"It's business," Priest replied.

"*My* business."

"So did you have him killed?" Priest asked.

The Prescix founder stamped the barrel of his rifle on the ground with a loud crack. "*I'm* not the one who goes around shooting members of Congress, Miles."

Priest opened his mouth to fire back, then scowled and didn't answer.

"We're getting off track here," Nelly interjected. "As Miles says, this is about business, Gabriel. It's true that Carillon has wanted to acquire Prescix for some time, and you're right that Kevin was sympathetic to our interests."

"He was sympathetic because you bought him off."

"Regardless of his motives, you can't deny there's synergy between our companies. Prescix has amazing potential, and with Carillon behind it, the reach of your software would be almost limitless. We want you on board. We want to finalize a contract, and you would find the terms extremely favorable. This doesn't have to be a hostile takeover. It can be a deal built around our mutual goals. The fact is, you're already part of Big Tech, whether you like it or not. If Congress starts regulating us, they're not going to leave you out of the mix. We all need to speak with one voice."

"I speak with my own voice," Gabriel snapped. "I designed and built Prescix. I run Prescix. Your little *cabal* is not going to get your hands on it."

"We're happy to negotiate an independent management agreement as part of the acquisition," Nelly said. "You'd still be calling the shots."

"Pass," Gabriel replied, popping more crickets into his mouth.

"Would you rather see the company in Medusa's hands?" Priest asked. "Because that's the alternative. They're already infiltrating and using your code. They're manipulating your vision, Gabriel. Is that what you want? Imagine what they can do if they're able to take over the company itself."

Gabriel chuckled. "Medusa, Medusa, Medusa. It's an obsession with you, Miles. Are you sure it's not just a myth?"

"Tell that to Congresswoman Ortiz," Priest replied. "Medusa ordered her assassination, not us."

"That's not what I'm hearing from Washington."

"Don't believe them. Medusa is inside the Beltway *and* the intelligence agencies. Their power is growing."

"Or maybe you just need a bogeyman, Miles," Gabriel retorted. "Give the people some new threat to be afraid of, so they don't notice that the real threat is you."

"Do you think Kevin's murder was just coincidental timing?" Priest replied. "He was killed by Medusa to stop our takeover so they can move on the company themselves. Right now, they need you, but once they're successful in acquiring Prescix, you'll be gone so they can put their own man at the top. And by *gone* I mean they'll find you at the bottom of your wave pool."

Gabriel shrugged. "Prescix has always been independent, and that's the way it's going to stay. I've already taken steps to assure that."

"What does that mean?"

"I'm in final negotiations with an equity group to take us private again. No more hostile takeover attempts, Miles. Prescix will be its own master."

"What private fund has that kind of leverage?"

"They're quiet, but their resources are vast. Face it, Miles, you're too late. You've been outbid and outmaneuvered."

"You're making a mistake, Gabriel," Nelly told him gently.

"She's right," Priest added. "Whatever group you're talking about, Medusa must be somewhere in the background. You're giving them exactly what they want."

"What I want is to keep my company and my software

away from *you*," Gabriel replied with a smile. He placed his World War I helmet back on his bald head, and he stood up with his rifle across his chest. "Now, don't worry, Miles. This isn't personal. As Nelly says, this is just business. The two of you can feel free to stay here as long as you want. Enjoy the amenities of the estate. Me, I have to get back to planning a party."

"A party?" Nelly asked.

"Yes indeed. I'm getting married in a couple of days. Stick around for the celebration, if you'd like."

"*Married?*" Priest grunted. "You?"

"That's right. My fiancée works for the equity group that is partnering with me to take Prescix private. She leads their security services. We met shortly after I started negotiations with the group a few months ago."

"Who is she?" Nelly asked.

Gabriel threw another cricket in the air and caught it in his mouth. "Her background is rather mysterious, but that simply adds to her charm. She's Czech. What is it about Czech women that they all screw like porn stars? Not to be crude, but she's the most voracious sexual partner I've ever experienced, and that's saying a lot."

"What's her name?" Priest asked him.

"Oh, her last name is unpronounceable," Gabriel told them. "So I just call her Miss Shirley."

YOU'RE certain about the location?" Miss Shirley asked, perching on a twelve-inch ledge atop a Gramercy Park apartment building, nineteen stories above the street.

Her gaze focused on the tower of the safe house rising over the trees on the other side of the park.

"It's the fourteenth floor," Peter Restak replied, his voice cracking with a nervous flutter as he watched her on the narrow strip of concrete. "Southeast corner. We confirmed it with our sources in the UK . . . Miss Shirley."

"Excellent."

The gales through the New York canyons swirled unpredictably, but Miss Shirley remained in perfect balance on the ledge. She bent one knee and pointed her other leg, then spread her arms flat as she knelt into a Warrior II yoga pose on the rooftop. She held that pose for nearly a minute. When she was done, she stood up straight and extended her arms over her head with her palms flat together.

"I sent you the video we hacked from the safe house feed," Restak added. "Just so you know, we believe Treadstone has it as well . . . Miss Shirley."

"If we had faith in Treadstone taking action, then I wouldn't be here," she replied.

Miss Shirley brought her arms down in front of her breasts and then slowly lifted her left foot and braced it against the inside of her right thigh. She stood one-legged in the Tree Pose, her tall, lean swimmer's frame swaying gently like a gyroscope. On the surface of the roof below her, she heard a gasp of discomfort from Peter Restak.

"Does this bother you?" she asked.

"It doesn't look very safe . . . Miss Shirley."

"There's no such thing as safe or unsafe. There's only

experienced and inexperienced, ability and inability. Come up here. Join me."

"I'd rather not . . . Miss Shirley."

Her dark eyebrows slanted at a fierce downward angle, and her blue eyes zeroed in on him like a predator. "Did that sound like a request, Restak?"

"No . . . Miss Shirley."

She saw the hacker wiping sweat from his hands. Almost hyperventilating with fear, Restak put both hands on the ledge and pulled himself up, his entirely body trembling. He squatted on the edge of the roof, shivering in the fierce wind. By instinct, he kept looking down. The wind made the entire building seem to move back and forth around them.

"Stand up."

"I don't think I can . . . Miss Shirley."

"Stand up. I won't let you fall, Restak."

She watched him unbend his knees, which were tense and locked. His fingers turned white as they pressed against the ledge. She could smell his fear, sense his mind spinning. He rose only a few inches before he screamed and pitched forward, but Miss Shirley locked a hand around his forearm and held him in place. He dangled, half on the roof, half off, moaning. Slowly, she dragged him onto the ledge and lifted him until he was vertical, standing beside her on wobbling knees. Tears of terror streamed down his face. His eyes were closed.

"Well done, Restak," she told him. "Now open your eyes."

"I can't . . . Miss Shirley."

"Open your eyes!"

Restak's eyes shot open, staring straight ahead.

"Good. You may get down now."

She held his wrist and guided him off the ledge. When he got back to the roof, he collapsed and threw up. Miss Shirley did a final pirouette and then gracefully jumped down. She put the toe of her shoe on his forehead as Restak lay on the ground.

"We must have absolute trust in one another."

"Yes . . . Miss Shirley."

"You did excellent work in eliminating Gattor. The Prescix incident worked precisely as I wished."

"Thank you . . . Miss Shirley."

"But your work in New York is over. Cain is aware of your identity. You need to return to headquarters to be reassigned."

Restak wiped his mouth and looked up at her with another wave of fear. Miss Shirley gave him a smile of reassurance.

"If your usefulness to me was at an end, you'd be on the street right now, Restak. Consider this a promotion. Now let's go back inside, shall we?"

She held the man up, because he wasn't able to walk, and they crossed the rooftop patio to the door that led into the building's penthouse suite. They took glass stairs down one level to the apartment's lavish living area overlooking the park. The sixty-two-year-old apartment owner lay where she'd fallen on the carpet, her throat cut. Miss Shirley knelt and recovered the knife from beside the body, then wiped it on the woman's blouse and secured it in her pocket again. She took the elongated case for her sniper's rifle from the floor and put it on top of the walnut dining room table. Unlocking the lid, she opened it and caressed the full length of the slim, hard barrel with her fingertips.

Her head turned, gazing through the apartment windows at the tower beyond the park. She calculated the location of the corner room on the fourteenth floor, which was in clear sight. In the background, hundreds of high-rises dotted the skyline.

"I love New York," she said.

Restak said nothing. A foul odor emanated from his clothes.

"Go take a shower and clean yourself up, Restak. Then we'll have sex, and you can take care of your apartment."

"All right . . . Miss Shirley."

"Sex is what you want, isn't it?"

"Yes . . . Miss Shirley."

"Take a pill from my purse. I suspect you'll need it."

Restak slunk away from her. She watched him dig inside her purse and swallow one of the tablets from an unlabeled plastic bottle, and then he shrugged off his soiled clothes and disappeared into the apartment's palatial bathroom, with its walk-in shower and marble bench. She heard the noise of the water, and she felt a tingling anticipation of all the things that lay ahead. The vigorous sex. The gun, long and sleek in her hands. The shooting and the eruption of blood.

It had been that way with Sofia Ortiz, too.

She took her phone from her pocket and played the video that Restak had sent her. She saw the two people in the elevator inside the UK safe house. They kissed, slowly and then quite passionately, like two people who were very attracted to each other. She found it surprising for a man like Cain to be entranced by someone whose beauty was so ordinary.

At the end of the video, the woman backed away, the hood slipping down. Her cheeks were flushed with excitement, her eyes wide with desire. Miss Shirley froze the playback of the video and studied the woman's face.

"Abbey Laurent," she snarled. "Well, well, aren't you the little slut."

TWENTY-TWO

ABBEY recognized Holly d'Angelo from the photo that the Carillon tech had loaded on her phone. Peter Restak's girlfriend looked like an Italian firecracker, tiny and explosive. Her feet pounded on the gym treadmill as if she were running a hundred-yard dash, small legs pumping, sweat glowing on her face and dripping from her hooked nose. Her eyebrows were thick and black, and her long dark hair bounced in a ponytail behind her. She wore a red tank top and formfitting shorts.

The room was loud with the metal clang of exercise equipment, but Holly seemed too deep in concentration to notice anything outside her workout. When Abbey mounted the treadmill next to her, the other woman didn't turn her head. Abbey switched on the machine and ran beside her at a much more relaxed pace. Every couple of minutes, she glanced over with a smile, but Holly paid no attention.

Half an hour later, Holly still showed no signs of slowing her relentless run. Abbey dialed down the speed on her own machine to a walk, and after another ten minutes, she noticed Holly finally doing the same thing. Abbey climbed off the treadmill and did a series of stretching exercises as she waited for the other woman to finish. When Holly turned off the machine, her entire outfit was soaking wet, and her face was beet red. She did cooldown exercises of her own, and when she was in the midst of pelvic squats with her hands on her hips, Abbey decided to make her move.

"Excuse me."

Holly looked up at Abbey. When she spoke, her voice had a nasal Jersey accent. "What do you want?"

"I apologize for bothering you, but you look so familiar. I knew it as soon as I saw you on the treadmill. I'm sure we've met somewhere."

"We haven't met," Holly replied. "And if this is a pickup line, it needs work."

Abbey laughed. "No, no, seriously, I know you. It's Holly, isn't it?"

The woman's face showed surprise. "That's right. Who are you?"

"Britney Jenks," Abbey lied.

"I don't remember you," Holly said.

"Oh, I don't suppose you would. It was at some party last year. Tribeca, maybe. All those lofts look alike. I remember you were there, because you were with your boyfriend, and I knew him from one of my social groups on Prescix. Pete Restak."

"You have an account on Prescix?"

"Doesn't everybody?" Abbey said.

"And you remember Peter?"

"Sure. Tech guy, really smart, one of those hacker wizards, right? Dirty-blond hair, man bun."

"That's him," Holly replied.

"Are you two still seeing each other?"

"Why do you want to know? Do you want to ask him out?"

"Me? Oh, no, I've got a boyfriend. I just noticed that Pete had dropped out of my Prescix feed. He was always good about helping me when I had computer questions. I'm pretty hopeless about that stuff. I was actually thinking about reconnecting with him, but I realized I had no way to get in touch."

Holly took a long time to reply. She wrapped a towel around the back of her neck and held on to the ends with her hands. "Well, Peter and I broke up months ago. I dumped his ass."

"I'm sorry. That's too bad. This is probably a little awkward, but you wouldn't still have contact info for him, would you? My laptop seems to have bad juju right now, and I don't have a few hundred bucks to replace it. I thought maybe Pete could perform an exorcism or something."

Abbey smiled. Holly didn't. Her flushed face never moved. "Yeah, I probably have his number. My phone's in my locker. Come on back, and I'll get it for you."

"Thanks, that's great. I appreciate it."

Holly led the way. The woman walked quickly, the

same way she ran on the treadmill, and Abbey hurried to keep up with her. They pushed through doors on the other side of the studio into the changing room, where stainless steel lockers gleamed on the nearest wall. Two or three other women were inside. Abbey followed Holly along a row of wooden benches to the far end, where Holly opened the combination lock on one of the lockers. Her street clothes were inside, along with a gym bag and purse.

"My phone's in here," Holly said.

She dug in her purse, but then with the speed of a cobra, she twisted around and grabbed Abbey by the shoulders and threw her against the lockers. Abbey's head banged against the steel. Holly pressed her forearm hard into Abbey's throat, and with her other hand, she brought the tip of a miniature Swiss Army knife up to within an inch of Abbey's eye. Holly's face contorted with anger, and her breath was warm and sour.

"Okay, who the hell are you?"

Abbey choked as she tried to get out the words. "I already told you."

"What you told me was a *lie*. Anybody who knows Peter Restak knows he doesn't go by Pete. He's never Pete. And Peter never had a Prescix account under his own name. No way. He told me if I wanted to stay safe, I should keep my life offline, the way he did. He said Prescix messes with your head."

"I—I must have made a mistake."

"A mistake? I don't think so. Who are you, and what do you want? And how the hell did you get my name?"

"I told you . . . a party."

Holly shook her head. "Me and Peter? A loft party? We'd never be caught dead in that scene."

One of the other women in the locker room shouted from the showers. "Hey, Holl, you okay? You want me to call 911?"

Holly pushed even harder with her forearm against Abbey's throat. The blade of the tiny knife loomed huge in front of Abbey's pupil. "What do you think? Should I have her call 911? Because I'm pretty sure you wouldn't be very happy explaining yourself to the cops. You've got five seconds to decide. Start talking, or we get the NYPD over here and you can talk to them."

Abbey tried to nod. "Okay. Okay. I'll tell you the truth."

Holly glanced over her shoulder and called to the other woman. "It's all right, Steph. I've got it under control."

She let Abbey go, then took her by the wrist and shoved her down roughly on the bench. Abbey rubbed her throat and inhaled loudly. Holly folded up the knife and stuffed it back in her purse, and then she sat down next to her. The dank smell of her sweat was in Abbey's nose.

"You're one of *them*, aren't you?" Holly asked.

"Who?"

"Peter's group. The ones he wouldn't talk about."

"You mean *Medusa*?"

"Is that what they're called? Peter never gave me a name. He never told me anything. But whoever they are, they're into some serious shit."

"I'm not part of them," Abbey told her. "I swear."

"Then who are you?"

Abbey sighed. Jason made covers and disguises look so easy, but it was different when you were face-to-face with a stranger. "My name's Abbey Laurent. I'm a reporter. The fact is, I'm trying to *expose* that group. Right now, Peter Restak is the only contact I have that I know is Medusa. I need to find him."

"Peter won't tell you anything. He's a true believer."

"Do you know anything about what he's doing?"

Holly shrugged. "You said it yourself. Peter's a hacker. Sometimes he'd be up half the night on his computer, and it always seemed like something bad would go down the next day. He'd have the news on, watching some protest turn violent, and it was like he *knew* what was going to happen. I'd ask him about it, and he'd just say that the system was rotten and the only way to cleanse it was to get rid of the dead flesh. Pretty creepy stuff."

"Is that why you broke up with him?"

"That, and he was cheating on me with some bitch from the group."

"Do you know who she was? Did you get a name? Or did you see them together?"

"No, I only know that she was a serious whack job. He had bite marks and bruises all over his body after she screwed him. He tried to give me some lame-ass excuse to cover for it like I was an idiot. I told him if that was what he wanted in bed, he wasn't going to get it from me. So I kicked him to the curb."

"When did you last see him?" Abbey asked.

"Six months ago. We broke up, but that wasn't the end of it. About a week later, I got the crazy feeling that I was being followed. I was pretty sure somebody had been inside my apartment, too. Honestly, if you put me in a chair and made me swear, I think they still have cameras in my place. Sometimes I just get this weird feeling that I'm being watched. So when you showed up and started asking about Peter, I freaked."

"I understand."

"If you're trying to expose this group, you better be careful."

"Yeah. Believe me, I know, but I really do need to find him. Do you have any idea where he's living?"

"He moves around a lot," Holly told her. "He never leaves forwarding addresses. That should have been a red flag, right? After I dumped him, he moved a couple of weeks later, like he didn't want me to be able to find him. But I didn't like the idea of not knowing where he was. Somehow I always figured a day like this might come, when somebody would be looking to track him down. So I hung out in a park where I knew he liked to do his coding, and I spotted him. I followed him when he left. He was in a new place, an apartment on Tenth in Alphabet City. I don't know whether he's still there, though."

"Thank you, Holly."

"I have to shower and catch my train. I'll get you the address."

Holly scrolled through a few screens on her phone to find the exact address for Peter Restak's apartment. As Abbey keyed the address into her own phone, Holly kicked off her sneakers, then peeled the damp red tank top off her torso and rolled off her shorts and underwear. Abbey's eyes flicked casually across the woman's naked body, and she couldn't help but stop and stare when she spotted a tight round scar in the fleshy part of Holly's shoulder above her left breast.

"I'm sorry," Abbey said. "I don't mean to pry, but is that a *bullet* wound?"

Holly looked down at her chest. "Oh, yeah. I got shot. Let me tell you, when boys compare their scars at the bar, I always win. They hate that."

"How did it happen?"

"I was in the wrong place at the really, really wrong time. Peter's a car buff, and he wanted to go to this antique car show. It was in a big empty lot across from the Lucky Nickel hotel in Las Vegas. November 3, 2018. That ring any bells?"

Abbey felt a wave of nausea and had to sit down on the bench. "You were there when Charles Hackman killed all those people."

Holly rubbed the scar like it was some kind of charm. "Yeah. I was there. Believe me, I try to forget, but it's tattooed on my brain. If that bullet had gone in another three inches lower, Hackman would have killed me, too."

TWENTY-THREE

*H*ACKMAN?" Bourne asked Abbey when they met up at an outdoor table across from the Flatiron Building. "Holly d'Angelo was one of the people who got shot by Charles Hackman in Las Vegas?"

"Yes. And here's the thing. Peter Restak was in the crowd, too. Holly said it was his idea to go to the car show."

Jason closed his eyes. He was back there again, lost in the chaos, hearing the cracks of the rifle and seeing people fall. "Restak knew the shooting was about to go down. All this time, I've thought Nova was killed by *my* agency, but maybe I was wrong. Maybe *Medusa* killed Nova. But *why?* And damn it, I saw one of my own people carrying away her body!"

"Jason, I know you said it wasn't safe to tell me the name of your agency, but I want to know anyway. Please."

Bourne stared at the young woman in front of him. A

woman he liked. A woman he was attracted to. He thought about the women he'd loved in his past lives. Marie. Nova. They'd died because of him. It was an inevitable cycle, repeated over and over. He got close to a woman, he pulled her into his world, and she paid the price. They were the sacrifices for his sins. He didn't want that fate for Abbey Laurent.

"It's my choice, Jason," she went on, as if she could feel his reluctance. "I know the risks."

He felt as if he were signing her death warrant by saying the word. "Treadstone."

"You worked for them?"

"They trained me. They made me who I am. They made all of us that way, custom-designed to be killers. For a long time, I believed in them, even when everyone in Washington was trying to shut them down. I believed in what I was doing. And then they murdered Nova. Or at least, that's what I thought happened. Now I'm not sure. I need to get to Peter Restak and find out what he knows. If he was in Las Vegas during the shooting, he has the answers."

"I'm coming with you," Abbey said.

"That's not a good idea. I should go alone."

"Jason, I told you, I'm *in*."

He wanted to argue with her. He wanted to tell her that it wasn't safe. He also knew that if he found Restak, he would have to break the man to get him to talk. Torture worked faster on some people than others, but with a Medusa operative, Bourne was certain he'd have to inflict excruciating pain before the man cracked.

He didn't want Abbey to see that. He didn't want her to see that he was capable of those things, but she already knew who he was.

"Okay," he said. "Let's go find him."

They crossed the sidewalk park to Fifth Avenue and hailed a cab, and Abbey gave the driver the address in Alphabet City for Peter Restak. The early evening traffic crawled as they headed east across town. Horns blared around them as backed-up vehicles stalled at the lights, and pedestrians streamed around the cars across the intersections. When they reached Second Avenue, they made faster progress until they got to the East Village. There, only a few blocks from Restak's apartment, traffic ground to a standstill. The taxi driver threw up his arms in disgust.

Not far away, Jason heard sirens, and he made a snap decision.

"We're getting out here," he told the driver suddenly, pushing cash through the slot. He took Abbey's arm and dragged her onto the sidewalk. They were near the playgrounds and basketball courts of Tompkins Square Park.

"What's going on?" Abbey asked. "Why get out here?"

"Don't you smell it?"

Abbey turned her face up, inhaling the air. Her mouth bent into a frown. "Smoke."

"There's a fire close by," he said.

"That could be a coincidence."

Bourne shook his head. "It's not."

He took Abbey's hand as they hurried down the next

long block, past a lineup of cars and frustrated drivers. A few winter trees on the sidewalks interrupted the concrete. As they got closer to the address where Restak lived, the smell of smoke intensified, and they could see a crowd of gawkers gathered at the intersection. Three fire trucks blocked the traffic, and torrents of water streamed from fire hoses. Over the heads of the people on the street, Jason could see black smoke billowing from a top-floor window in a redbrick building on the corner.

He checked the street number on the nearest doorway. "The fire is in Restak's building. I'm willing to bet it's his apartment. They're erasing the evidence."

"With him in it?" Abbey asked.

"Good question."

They pushed through the crowd. When they got to the front, they could see that the firefighters hadn't been able to get the blaze under control. Flames shot through a broken window on the other wall of the building. Anything that Peter Restak had left behind was already incinerated.

Medusa was still one step ahead of them.

Abbey shook her head in frustration. "Are we done? Do we leave?"

"Not yet." Jason's stare went from face to face, studying the people watching the fire on the three corners surrounding the building. "Sometimes an arsonist likes to stay behind to make sure everything goes as planned."

He saw no one suspicious in the crowd. Even so, his senses told him to linger.

Always trust what your instincts tell you. Your brain sees clues that you don't.

Treadstone.

He led Abbey across the street behind the fire trucks. They could feel the heat of the fire blowing on their skin. More sirens whined in the distance, and overlapping emergency radios squawked around them. Police officers kept the crowd squeezed behind a makeshift barrier. Jason's eyes tried to penetrate the sea of people, all of them moving, talking, blocking each other, making it nearly impossible to spot one single individual among all the others.

He saw *something*. But what?

There!

Halfway down the block, a cloud of vapor puffed from the recessed frame of a garage entrance, indicating that someone was hiding there, observing the fire. As Jason watched, the man stepped out far enough to offer a fleeting glimpse of his profile.

A long nose. A blond beard spreading over his neck and cheek like a weed.

"*Restak*," Jason said. Then, as he observed the doorway, the Medusa operative stepped out of the recess, and Jason could see his head swinging their way. "Turn around," he hissed to Abbey. "*Fast!*"

The two of them spun, letting the rubberneckers in the crowd fill in around them. If Restak looked, all he would see were their backs among dozens of other people on the sidewalk. Jason counted slowly in his head, giving the man time to assess his surroundings and make sure he was safe. *One, two, three . . .*

When Jason got to twenty, he twisted around and glanced down the street. Restak was walking east on Tenth, heading toward the river. He wore baggy black jeans and a blue-striped Baja poncho with the hood pulled up. Another vapor cloud trailed behind him.

"Wait here," Jason told Abbey.

He took off after Restak. When he was past the fire, he crossed to the opposite side to make his pursuit less noticeable. Restak walked casually, seemingly unconcerned that he was being followed. The man reached Avenue D, where he was stopped by a red light. A group of kids played basketball in a fenced court near the corner, their voices loud. Bourne stopped, too, feeling exposed on a stretch of naked wall that offered no hiding place. Restak didn't look back. He had his vape pen in his hand and looked pleased with himself.

The fire had done its work. He was free.

Then one of the kids on the court missed the basketball as it was passed to him, and the ball slammed into the fence with a loud clang. Startled, Restak dropped his vape pen on the sidewalk. He bent down to retrieve it, and as he picked it up, his gaze swept across the street and settled on Bourne.

Restak's eyes widened in shock. Instantly, the Medusa hacker shot across Avenue D just as the light changed. Bourne took off, too, but he lost time dodging three cars that bolted through the red light. When he finally made it across the street, Restak already had a head start. The man raced east on Tenth past a series of drab brown apartment towers.

Jason ran, too. Restak looked back, spotting him, his eyes wild with fear. They ran in tandem for one more block, and Jason slowly closed the gap. Restak was about thirty feet away when the street dead-ended at the FDR, but the man didn't even break stride as he leaped over the concrete barrier into the middle of the parkway. Horns wailed, and brakes squealed. Restak rolled over the hood of one car, and an SUV in the next lane swerved to avoid him, crashing at high speed into a truck in the left lane. The accident triggered a chain reaction as vehicles banged into each other with screeches of metal, and one car flew onto its side as the driver overcorrected.

Bourne stopped short at the parkway, unable to cross. The lanes in front of him were littered with crashes. Ahead of him, Restak jumped the barrier into the northbound lanes and then did a running leap to a wrought-iron fence and threw his body into the East River Park. Not slowing down, he took off toward the water.

Jason ran up a ramp to the pedestrian overpass. When he made it to the park, he didn't see Restak. He cursed and took off toward the river, but he made it all the way to the wide jogging path by the water and didn't see the Medusa operative anywhere. He stopped to catch his breath and slapped the railing over the East River in frustration.

Runners came and went in both directions in the waning light of dusk. Not far away, the Williamsburg Bridge arched across the water. He walked another hundred yards north, looking for someone hiding in the trees, but the Medusa operative had vanished.

Peter Restak was gone.

IT was dark by the time Jason and Abbey made it back to the safe house. They stopped at a diner for dinner, but neither one of them said anything to the other. They rode the elevator in silence, too. It was only when they got to the apartment door that Abbey said what was on both of their minds.

"What now? What do we do?"

Jason shrugged. "I'm not sure. I don't have a plan yet."

"Can you talk to your friend Scott again?"

"No, he made it clear that his help was a one-time thing. I'm on my own."

"You mean *we*."

"No. I don't. You need to go back to Canada. I have no more leads, and the only thing you're going to do by staying with me is put yourself at greater risk. You helped me, Abbey. You helped me a lot. But there's nothing more for you to do now."

She brushed her bangs from her eyes. "Is that what you really want? For me to go?"

He said the one thing he shouldn't say. The one thing that made no sense. "It's not what I want. No. But it's the way it has to be."

Abbey shook her head. "I don't care. I'm staying."

Jason used the key to open the apartment door. He

left the lights off. The curtains at the window looking out over Gramercy Park were open, letting in the glow of the city. He realized he was tired. Bone-tired. Days of pain had caught up to him. His body was a mess of bruises. He could feel a throbbing where he'd been shot, and his headache was back. His shoulder felt numb where the woman in the Guy Fawkes mask had struck him with the lead pipe. He wanted to sleep for days, but he knew he couldn't.

In another hour, they'd leave the city. They'd drive all night.

To go where? He didn't know.

"I'm going to take a shower," Jason said, hearing the weariness in his own voice. "Keep the lights off. We need to go soon."

He went to the bedroom and pushed the door partly closed and stripped off his clothes. In the shower, he scraped off the dirt and then stood under the rainfall showerhead with his eyes closed. The hot water revived him, and some of his muscles relaxed. He felt better when he returned to the bedroom and dressed in fresh clothes. Through the crack of the door, he saw only darkness in the other room.

"You can shower, too, if you want," Jason called to Abbey.

She didn't answer.

"Abbey?"

He still heard only silence from the living room.

Jason went to the bed and took his gun in his hand. He pointed it straight ahead as he crept to the door. He listened carefully and heard a low disturbance on the other side. Someone crying softly. Breath coming in ragged bursts.

"Abbey?" he called one more time. "I'm coming out."

Bourne slowly opened the door into the semidarkness of the living room, leading with the gun.

"*Jason!*" Abbey said, her voice choked with tears.

He could see her near the front door, bathed in the bright city glow through the window. Her eyes pleaded with him. She was on her knees, her hands laced together on top of her black hair.

A Treadstone agent stood behind her.

He held two guns, both with suppressors. One was aimed across the apartment at Bourne. The other was jammed into the back of Abbey's head.

TWENTY-FOUR

"**B**ENOIT,**"** Jason said. "It's been a long time."

"Hello, Bourne."

"The woman's not part of this. It's me you want. Let her walk away, and as soon as she's free, I'll lower my weapon. You can take me out. Quick. Clean. I'm a man of my word, you know that."

"Jason, *no!*" Abbey shouted from the floor.

Benoit's arms were rock-solid. No flutter or hesitation. His dark eyes were unblinking. "Unfortunately, my orders are for both of you."

"So lie to Nash. Tell him Abbey wasn't here."

"I wish that was possible, but I'm a man of my word, too."

Bourne nodded. "That's true."

Jason knew this man well. They'd been in the field together many times. They'd saved each other's lives more than once. He'd met Benoit when the man was still a French agent, and the two of them had gathered intelligence on a terror cell from a stone farmhouse in the rural countryside outside Lyon. The stakeout had been blown by the barking of a stray dog, and Bourne had found himself in the midst of a midnight firefight while Benoit was half a mile away conducting night-vision surveillance. Rushing back in the middle of the assault, Benoit could have chosen to stay out of it, rather than intervene to rescue an operative from a different country. Instead, Benoit saved Bourne and took gunshots in the arm, hip, and leg that nearly killed him.

That was the first time they'd been together.

The last time he'd seen Benoit was under very different circumstances.

Benoit was the agent who'd carried away the body of Nova from the killing ground in Las Vegas. The sixty-seventh victim, never acknowledged.

Shoot him!

A lust for revenge screamed in Bourne's head. All he could see was Nova draped over Benoit's shoulder, her eyes closed, blood on her face, her long hair swinging as this man took her away. Ever since that moment, he'd wanted the opportunity to come face-to-face with Benoit again, and now here he was.

If Bourne pulled the trigger, all three of them would die in an eruption of gunfire. Jason wouldn't miss; neither would Benoit. But Bourne knew that he and Abbey were going to die anyway.

Another woman in his life had been sentenced to death.

"Kill me if you want," Benoit said, reading the look on Jason's face. "That won't change anything."

"I should kill you. You deserve to die."

"We're all going to hell for the lives we've led, Bourne."

"Maybe so, but not Nova. She was *out*. She wasn't a threat to anyone. But Nash and the director couldn't let her go. So you murdered her."

"I didn't shoot Nova. Charles Hackman did that."

"Does it matter? Hackman was Treadstone, wasn't he? Isn't that why the word came down to whitewash his past? You couldn't let the public find out that the worst mass shooter in history was actually one of our own intelligence assets."

"Hackman was never Treadstone," Benoit snapped. "He was *Medusa*. Like you, *Cain!* All those people died because *you* put your lover in the firing line. Nash thinks you ordered the hit yourself. Is that true? Did you want her dead? Were you afraid she suspected who you really were?"

"You're a *liar!* What's going on, Benoit? Are you taping this? Does Director Shaw want a recording he can play to the congressional oversight committee? You were *there*. You were in Las Vegas. Am I supposed to believe that's a coincidence? You just happened to be in the crowd when Nova was shot? Nash just happened to be waiting outside the hotel where the shooter was holed up?"

Benoit shook his head. "I admire the act, but you're smarter than that, Bourne. You know exactly why Nash and I were in Las Vegas."

"Really? Tell me."

"We were watching *you*."

Bourne felt the words like a blow to his chest. "*What?*"

"That's right. Look, we all knew Treadstone was dying. The director was tucked away in some basement office, and our budgets were bleeding away. That meant we had a lot of agents out there who were prime targets for recruitment by Medusa. We didn't know who to trust and who was a traitor. We still don't. But let's just say your *psychological* history made Nash doubt you. I didn't want to believe it, and neither did Nova. But Nash didn't think we could take any chances. That's why I was there, to watch you, to observe you, to follow you, to see if you'd been turned."

Jason's mind spun as he tried to process the revelations. He heard the words, but he couldn't understand them. Benoit was an experienced agent. He was playing with his head, using lies to throw him off balance. If Jason lost his concentration for even a moment, he and Abbey would both be dead.

Shoot him!

"I'm not Medusa," Bourne said. "I never was."

"You shot Congresswoman Ortiz."

"They framed me."

"Nash says the evidence points to you."

"I'm sure it does," Jason agreed. "That's what Medusa wanted. Go ahead, Benoit. Kill me. Do their bidding. But let Abbey go."

"I can't do that."

But still Benoit didn't pull the trigger. He didn't fire. The standoff continued, guns pointed at each other, death inevitable. There was no way out for any of them. This would end only one way, with three bodies on the floor.

Benoit is *Treadstone!*

Nova is dead because of *him! Shoot him!*

But Jason didn't pull the trigger, either. He aimed down the barrel at Benoit's dark face, a face he'd known for years, and he couldn't do it.

"Jason."

Abbey called softly to him. He couldn't look at her, couldn't take his eyes away from Benoit, but he heard her voice, which was measured and unemotional. He no longer heard panic or tears. She was on her knees, about to die, but she didn't sound afraid.

"Jason, this man doesn't want to kill us."

Bourne barely shook his head to tell her she was wrong. He stared at Benoit, and Benoit stared back. Their whole history flashed through his mind. "You don't know him, Abbey. He's Treadstone. He's a killer. He does what he's told. Just like me."

"He *wants* to believe you," she insisted.

"No, he wants me to put the gun down. That's all. Then he'll kill us both, and he gets out of here alive."

"Jason, if that was his plan, *I'd already be dead*. He could have killed me the instant I answered the door, but he didn't. He could have shot me and gone to the shower and shot you. That's what a cold-blooded assassin would have done. He should have been in and out of this room in thirty seconds. Instead, he *waited*. He made me go on my knees, and he waited for you to come out here. He knew you'd have a gun. He knew he was giving you the chance to kill him, too. He wants the truth."

Bourne faltered. He looked for confirmation in Benoit's face, but the man gave nothing away. "You're wrong."

"No, I'm not. Jason, if this was your assignment, if you were here to kill the two of us, what would *you* have done?"

He hesitated, because it was true. Benoit's actions made no sense. They were the opposite of everything Treadstone had trained them to do. *Delay is your enemy. Delay means failure.* Abbey should have been dead on the floor five seconds after Benoit entered the apartment, and Jason should have been dead another ten seconds after that. By now, Benoit should be back on the New York streets, his job done.

Instead, he was still here, with Jason aiming a gun at him. Benoit knew that waiting was the equivalent of signing his own death warrant, but he'd done it anyway.

Why?

"Jason, you're *not* the man he thinks you are," Abbey said. "Prove it to him."

"How?"

"Put down your gun," she said.

"That's insane."

"It's not. You have to take a leap of faith. He already took his, Jason. Don't you see? We're still alive because he let us live. You have to trust him, too."

Jason studied the man. "Is that true, Benoit?"

The Treadstone agent didn't say a word. He was a

poker player, not showing his hand, because he couldn't. That was part of the test.

Slowly, reluctantly, Jason lowered his arm. He knelt, putting his pistol on the floor, and with one tap of his boot, he kicked it away across the carpet. Then he put both of his hands in the air, surrendering. He waited through the next tense, excruciating moment, unsure if the bullets would follow. First Abbey, then him. If this had all been a game, then Benoit would want him to see Abbey die first.

Instead, Benoit removed the gun from Abbey's head and holstered it under his shoulder. He holstered the other gun, too, behind his back. Abbey sprang off her knees and ran across the room and threw her arms around Bourne.

"Oh, my God!" she murmured. "Oh, Jason."

He held on to her tightly, enjoying her warmth. She kissed his cheek and then kissed his lips. On the opposite side of the room, a grin creased Benoit's face.

"Jesus Christ, Bourne, I really thought you were going to make me kill you."

"I'm damn glad you didn't, but what are you going to tell Nash?"

Benoit shrugged. "I'll tell him he's a stubborn ass, and he nearly lost one of his best agents. Two, actually, since I didn't figure I'd get out of here alive. We can talk to him together if you're willing. I can set up a meeting. But it has to be off the grid. I wasn't lying. Nash literally doesn't know who to trust, even inside Treadstone."

"There's something I need to know first," Bourne said.

The other agent frowned. "Nova?"

"Yes. You said you didn't want to believe I'd turned, and *neither did Nova*. What the hell does that mean? Nova was already out of Treadstone. She was forced out after the operation in London went bad. Why would she still have been in touch with anyone inside the agency?"

Benoit hesitated. "This should come from Nash, not me."

"I need to know the truth, old friend."

Benoit ran his hands through his choppy black hair. "All right. You're right, you do deserve to know the truth. I told Nash that. The fact is, Medusa has been running rings around all of the intelligence agencies. We haven't been able to get close to them. So Nash decided to run a sting. Off the books, unauthorized. *Nova* was the sting."

Bourne shook his head. "I don't understand."

"Nash didn't trust many people, but he trusted Nova. And me. For what it's worth, we both said he should bring you in, too, but he was concerned about the damage from your memory loss. He thought it made you vulnerable. So he kept you out of the loop. The operation involved the three of us, that's all. Nova, Nash, me. Nash didn't even tell Director Shaw about it. There was no assignment in London that went bad. That was a ruse. We piggybacked on top of an industrial accident and put out the word in the intelligence community that it was a big Treadstone failure. We put the blame squarely on Nova.

Not long after that, we pushed her out in a very public way. We wanted everyone to know she was damaged goods. Untouchable."

"For God's sake, *why*?" Bourne asked.

"Because we needed to give her a convincing cover story. We wanted to put an enormously talented agent on the street, bitter and unemployable. Don't you see? The whole idea was to get *Medusa* to reach out to her. To recruit her. We'd finally have one of our own people inside their network. That was how Nash planned to destroy them."

Jason shook his head in disbelief.

Suddenly, he had no idea whether anything Nova had told him was true. She'd lied. She'd concealed her real mission. She'd left him in the dark.

She'd told him she was in love with him.

Was that a lie, too?

"Did Medusa take the bait?" he asked.

"They did. That's why Nova was in Las Vegas. That's where they brought her for recruitment. She bought a house near the airport to run the operation undercover, and she thought she was in. She thought they *trusted* her. But then something changed. She began to get nervous; she began to worry that her cover was blown. That somehow they'd figured out she was a mole. We didn't know how it happened, or who could have exposed her, but Nash thought you were the prime suspect. You and Nova were involved. Who knew what information you'd been able to glean about the operation without her knowing it? So I was in town to check you out. For what it's worth, Nova never wavered. She never had any doubts about you. She was afraid that *you* were the one who was in danger."

"Instead, Charles Hackman got to her first," Jason said.

"Yes. I'm sorry. Nova told Nash that she'd heard some big operation was planned. She heard a reference to the Lucky Nickel. That's why he was in town. To prevent whatever was going to happen. But we were all too late."

Bourne said nothing more. Abbey put her warm hands on his face. "Jason? Are you okay?"

"The last eighteen months have been a lie," he said, trying to process the deception, as well as his own mistakes. "Nothing I believed was true. I blamed Treadstone for killing Nova. I was chasing the wrong enemy."

"That's not true," she reminded him. "You've been after Medusa all along. So was Nova. And now you know where to go to get them."

"Las Vegas," Jason said.

"We should get out of here," Benoit interjected. "If we know about this place, it's likely that Medusa does, too. I'd rather not stay here any longer than we need to."

"Agreed."

Jason crossed the room to retrieve his gun. Benoit headed for the apartment door from the opposite direction. In a wild accident of timing, they both passed across the line of sight of the window at the exact same moment.

The glass shattered.

The nighttime air roared in, along with a cloud of razor-sharp fragments.

The sniper's bullet meant for Bourne went into the base of Benoit's skull, which exploded with blood. As Jason threw himself down and Abbey screamed, Benoit collapsed. He was dead before his body hit the floor.

TWENTY-FIVE

THE head of Medusa pulled his black roller bag into the men's room on Concourse C at Dulles International Airport. He was alone inside. Near the entrance, tape had been strung to close off the restroom, and a man in a dark suit with an earpiece watched to make sure no one entered behind him.

This was Washington, D.C. No one questioned things like that.

He stood in front of the urinal with his hands on his hips, and as he did, his phone rang in his pocket. He knew who was calling; very few people had this number. He tapped the earbud in his left ear to take the call.

"Yes?"

"I'm afraid it's bad news."

"That's not the report I expect to get from you, Shirl."

He was the only man on the planet who called her anything but Miss Shirley without fear of punishment.

"Yes, sir. I apologize."

"Why did you fail?"

"Treadstone interfered. One of their agents was in the room to confront Bourne. I hoped he would do the work for us and kill them both, but he didn't. Instead, he crossed my line of fire as I took the shot on Bourne, and I hit him. There was no chance for a follow-up shot. I'm afraid Bourne and the woman are both gone. They're on the run."

"That's extremely unfortunate."

"Yes, sir. We'll be looking for tech signatures to see where they go next. However, I don't believe they have any information that would threaten us."

"This is Bourne. Don't be so sure."

"Yes, sir. I've made certain that the evidence in the shooting points to him. Treadstone will still believe he's working for us."

"Anything else, Shirl?"

"I've pulled Peter Restak out of New York, per your request."

He could hear in her voice that there was more to the story. "But?"

"Well, it was a close call. Restak torched his apartment, so there was no evidence left behind, but Bourne was there and nearly captured him. Fortunately, Restak was able to get away. He's safely on the way to Las Vegas now."

"Maybe I was wrong," the head of Medusa mused. "Maybe I should have had you eliminate Restak, rather than evacuate him."

"His skills are valuable in our operations," Miss Shirley reminded him. "Once we have complete access to the Prescix code, I expect Restak to lead our team in correlating it with the data from the hack. We need him."

"That being the case, the risk of his capture was unacceptable. You didn't move fast enough, Shirl."

"No, sir."

"Is this going to be a habit with you?"

"No, sir. I kept Restak in town to help me set up the shoot. That was a mistake. I should have sent him away immediately."

"Don't be coy with me. You kept him in town to have sex with him. Correct?"

Miss Shirley hesitated on the phone. "Yes, sir."

"I indulge your appetites, Shirl, but if this is going to interfere with your work, then we have a problem."

"It won't be a problem."

"Are you sure? Are you letting Bourne go free because you want to keep him for yourself? Is that why you missed?"

"No, sir. That had nothing to do with it. Although I confess I wouldn't mind getting rid of that little bitch he's running with."

The head of Medusa shook his head. "Stay *focused*, Shirl. We're at a critical juncture, the culmination of years of planning. Prescix is nearly ours. That means we're ready to take the next step against the tech cabal. You need to lead the operation. That's our priority."

"Yes, sir."

"Don't disappoint me again."

"No, sir."

He ended the call.

When he glanced to his right, he saw that another man had taken up a position at the urinal next to him, as planned. The man was in his sixties, tall and morbidly obese, with a crown of white hair, a large bulbous nose, and several chins. He wore a brown suit that hung loosely on him despite his size. When he spoke, his accented voice sounded like he had a mouthful of oatmeal.

"Miss Shirley?" the man asked.

"Yes."

The man guffawed. "What an interesting woman! I don't mind telling you, I'd love to see what that one is like in bed."

"She'd kill you, Fyodor."

"Ah, but what a way to go. Besides, I have more stamina than you think."

"I'm sure you do."

Fyodor shook his hips and unleashed a stream of urine that roared like Niagara Falls. Russian men were oddly proud of their ability to piss. Fyodor Mikhailov was the number two man in the Russian embassy, and as such, he had the diplomatic clearance to travel all over the world. However, his real role was as the head of Russian interference operations mounted against the United States and Europe.

He was also a disgusting human being, crude and cruel, and the head of Medusa detested him. But for now, Fyodor and the Russians were a means to an end.

"So what is the update, my friend?" Fyodor asked.

"Are we finally going to see a return on our sizable investment in your operations?"

"Everything is proceeding according to schedule. Prescix will be ours very soon. The government is doing their part, too. The proposed regulatory framework laid out in the Ortiz legislation plays right into our hands."

"And the tech cabal?"

"We expect to move on them in days. At that point, we'll have everything we want. Psycho-profiling, manufactured news, deepfake videos, online bots customized to an individual's background. Hackman showed us the extent of what was possible. Soon we'll be able to manipulate and radicalize people en masse. Social debates. Legislation. Elections. Violence."

Fyodor finished his work at the urinal and zipped himself up. "They'll be so busy hating each other they won't even notice as we begin reclaiming our lost territories."

"Exactly."

"Chaos is only the beginning, my friend. It's not enough to wound the beast. That can make him more dangerous when he recovers. No, we must split him apart, tear him down, and then start rebuilding from the ashes. Civil war. Never forget our goal, my friend. All this violence must lead to civil war. That's the whole point of the conspiracy."

"We're well on our way."

A broad grin broke across Fyodor's face. "You do good work. I knew it as soon as we met all those years ago. I will share my positive report in Moscow."

"Thank you, Fyodor. I'm honored."

I can't wait to let Miss Shirley kill you, you old fool, the head of Medusa thought. *The only thing that will rise from the ashes is a new world led by us. No countries. No governments. Just technology. The future is not Russia, Fyodor. The future is Medusa.*

The two men turned around and went to the row of sinks. Fyodor stood in amusement as the head of Medusa carefully used soap and water on his hands. After he was done, the Russian casually stuck out his own unwashed hand to be shaken. It was a reminder of who was still the boss.

"What about Jason Bourne?" Fyodor asked as they shook hands. "I understand you've failed to remove him despite several attempts. Is that a concern?"

"Don't worry about Bourne," the head of Medusa replied. "It's just a matter of time before we take him down. He's not a threat to our plans."

PART THREE

TWENTY-SIX

AFTER driving straight through out of New York for twenty-four hours, Jason and Abbey finally took a break at a motel off I-20 near Amarillo, Texas. They'd stopped only for gas and to visit a safe-deposit box at a bank in D.C., where Jason retrieved cash, a driver's license and passport under a different name, and another gun. By midnight, they were still twelve hours from Las Vegas, and they needed sleep.

He got them a room with two beds, close enough to the stairs that he could hear anyone coming their way. He left the window open, letting in warm, sticky air and the buzz of mosquitoes. Neither of them bothered to undress. They simply stretched out on top of the blankets and tried to clear their minds. But an hour later, in the deep darkness, Jason was still awake, and he could tell from the sound of Abbey's breathing in the other bed that she was awake, too.

They'd said little on the road. After Benoit's death, Abbey had stared at the blood and brains on the apartment floor with a kind of numb shock, but after he dragged her away, she'd insisted on staying with him as the hunt for Medusa led to Nevada. For an entire day since then, they'd traded off driving, but they hadn't really talked, even though there were definitely things to talk about.

They both felt something happening between them.

They were both pretending it wasn't real.

"I know you're questioning everything you knew about Nova," Abbey murmured in the darkness, just loud enough for him to hear.

He didn't answer, and she waited a long time before saying anything more.

"What Benoit told you doesn't change anything, does it? She still loved you. You loved her."

"I did love her," Jason replied finally. "I suppose on some level, I still do. Beyond that, I'm not sure what's true anymore. Nova was a good operative. She was more than capable of fooling me into thinking her feelings were real. Even if she did love me on some level, she didn't trust me. As Benoit said, Treadstone thought I'd turned."

"He also said Nova didn't believe that."

"Maybe, but if she was sure I wasn't part of Medusa, she would have told me what she was doing. I could have helped her. I could have watched her back. Instead, she walked into a trap, and there was nothing I could do to protect her."

"It sounds like she was protecting *you*," Abbey said.

"No, she was keeping secrets from me."

He listened to her breathing. Abbey was invisible just a few feet away.

"Jason, what happened to your memory?" she went on carefully, as if tiptoeing into a minefield. "You talk about having no past. You say you don't remember who you are. What does that mean?"

He tried to decide what to say to her. He'd known that she would go back to the subject of his past sooner or later. She was a reporter; she asked questions for a living. She needed to know the truth about the people she was with, in order to profile them and study them, like insects in an experiment. Or maybe it was something else. Maybe not every human motive hid something dark.

He wanted to tell her the truth. He hadn't felt that desire with anyone in a long time.

"I was shot in the head during a mission," he explained. "The injury caused amnesia. I lost everything. I had no identity, no way to explain who I was, the skills I had."

"Did your memory come back?" she asked.

"Only bits and pieces of it. Disconnected images. Eventually, I found out who I was, and people told me the details of my past, but that's not the same as remembering it. I know about my past the way you know about reading something in a history book. You can memorize the facts. You can look at the pictures. But it may as well have happened to someone else. The man in those photos is a stranger. I spent a long time trying to force myself to remember, but it doesn't work that way. And what's the point? The person I was no longer exists. I'm Jason Bourne. I'm the man that Treadstone created. That's who I am. That other identity, the one I started my life with, isn't real to me anymore."

Abbey was silent.

He heard the rustle of blankets on the other bed. The floor in the old motel creaked as she stood up, but she was as dark as a ghost. Telltale sounds gave her away. The noise of clothes being removed, the rattle of a zipper. The springs of the bed he was in squealed as she joined him there. She molded herself against him, and by instinct, he put his arm around her. Her face was on his shoulder, her breath on his neck. He moved his hand down her body and felt nothing but bare skin. She was naked.

"You also said you don't really know who *I* am," Abbey whispered.

"Yes, I did."

"Was that true, or was that a lie? Because I know you're like Nova. You're more than capable of fooling me into thinking that your feelings are real."

"It's true," Jason told her. "I want to know who you are."

Abbey took a slow, deep breath.

"Well. Let's see. You said I seem to be estranged from my father. You're right. I love him, but I don't respect him. I don't even particularly like him. Before my mother got sick, he was cheating on her. She knew about it. I know that him betraying her didn't give her cancer, but on some level, I can't help but think it took the fight out of her. He was supposed to be the love of her life, and his love turned out to be hollow. I can't forgive him for that."

"What about Michel?" Jason asked. "Why did it not work out with him? Did he remind you of your father too much?"

She gave a quiet laugh. "You're good. Yes, that was probably part of it. Life with Michel looked an awful lot like the life my parents had, and look how that turned out. That's probably unfair, but it's how I felt. Besides, I wanted something else out of life."

"What?"

"If I figure it out, I'll let you know," Abbey replied.

"You obviously don't care about getting a big job," Jason went on. "You had a shot at top magazines, and you turned them down. And yet you don't strike me as someone who's afraid of risks."

"I'm not."

"You won't quit your job, but you hate standing still. You stay in Quebec, but you don't do anything at home except sleep."

"Maybe I like being an enigma."

"Or maybe you're like a skydiver," Jason said.

"How so?"

"You love the idea of jumping. You can't wait to feel that freedom as you fall. You're excited by the thrill of cheating death. You can't believe there's anything more boring than a life spent on the ground, and you're sure that once you take that first step, it's going to be the most incredible experience ever."

"But?" she asked.

"But that first step is scary."

Abbey turned his head toward her and found his mouth in the darkness. As they kissed, her hands worked on his clothes, undressing him quickly and urgently. He helped her, shrugging off his shirt, kicking off his pants. She found the skin of his chest, and her fingertips traced over old wounds and scars like an explorer. Her lips were on his face, his shoulders, his neck. When he was naked, like her, she took his hand and pulled him on top of her, and her body rose up to meet him and guide him inside her.

"First steps are always scary," she whispered.

NASH Rollins pulled open the rear door of the stretch limousine parked in front of the New York apartment building where they'd found Benoit's body. He looked both ways up and down the street, then climbed into the back and shut the door behind him. He shifted painfully in the seat and folded up his walking cane. Through the smoked windows, he saw the flashing lights of a dozen police cars.

"Good evening, Nash," Miles Priest said.

"Hello, Miles."

The CEO's hangdog face looked longer and sadder than usual. "You have my sympathy about Benoit. He was a good man."

"Yes, he was."

"Do you know what happened?"

"Bourne shot him. I should have seen it coming. He knew we'd see the video feed from the safe house, knew we'd send someone after him. He staked out an apartment across the street and waited for Benoit. He took him out through the window. This is war. Bourne's declared war against us. Which means Medusa has, too."

Rollins heard himself spitting out the words. He'd actually questioned his judgment about Bourne's innocence, but Cain had now erased those doubts for good. Rollins's anger was like a fire, but he had to purge his emotions. He wanted nothing in his brain now but cold calculations.

"Just to be clear, are we quite sure it was Bourne?" Priest asked.

"He left a fingerprint on the sniper rifle."

"That seems rather careless of him."

"It wasn't careless," Rollins snapped. "It was deliberate. He was sending me and Shaw a message. He wants us to know that he was the one who killed Benoit. Just like he did with Congresswoman Ortiz."

"He fooled all of us, Nash. Scott convinced me that Bourne was the right man for the job. We made a mistake."

Rollins shook his head. "The director and I both warned Scott to find someone else. I told him that Bourne wasn't the same man anymore. But he let his history with him get in the way of his judgment."

"Do you have any idea where Bourne is headed next?" Priest asked.

"No. We're tapped into police databases, but he knows we'll be looking for him. That's why I called you, Miles. I'd like your people looking, too. Put some of those damn computers and databases to work to help me."

"I imagine Bourne is too smart to be found that way," Priest replied.

"Maybe so, but he's not alone. We think he's still with the Canadian woman. Abbey Laurent."

Priest's brow furrowed. "That's interesting. Is she a hostage?"

"It doesn't look that way. She appears to be with him voluntarily. She's the softer target, so if we find her, we find him."

"I'll do what I can to help," Priest replied.

"Good. If you locate them, call me. We'll take care of the rest."

Priest fixed the knot in his tie and folded his arms across his chest. "You haven't been too successful with that up until now, Nash."

"What are you saying?"

"I'm simply reminding you that your earlier attempts have failed. You have to ask yourself why. We're both thinking the same thing—that Medusa has a spy inside Treadstone."

"Or you do, Miles."

"Meaning what?"

"Meaning no one inside Treadstone knew about the Nova operation in Las Vegas other than me and Benoit. But *you* knew, Miles. I told you about my plan when I asked for technology help on the surveillance. Someone betrayed her, and it wasn't me."

Priest frowned, as if this were a possibility he hadn't considered. "Regardless, it doesn't change where we are now. Cain has to be removed. So make sure your team is reliable."

"I will. Hell, I'll kill him myself if I have to."

"You? You're an old man, Nash. And I say that as an even older man myself. The last time you went up against Cain, he took pity on you. He shot you, but he left you alive. I doubt he'll be so charitable next time."

Rollins felt his anger surging again, but only because Miles was right. "Trust me, I'll take down Medusa. And Bourne, too."

"I hope that's true."

"If you find anything about where they are, let me know."

"I will."

Rollins reached for the door handle of the limousine, but then he turned back. "A word of warning, Miles."

"About what?"

"I read about the Carillon deal with Prescix collapsing. I heard about Kevin Drake's murder. Medusa is on the move. You better be ready for them to come after you. You're used to being the king, but your Scottish ancestors could teach you a lesson."

A little smile played across Priest's face. "What would that be?"

"Kings have a way of getting their heads chopped off."

TWENTY-SEVEN

A SCORCHING November sun beat down on Las Vegas, as if summer had never left. Jason walked hand in hand with Nova through the thousands of people crowded around the Phaetons, Bel Airs, Hornets, and Thunderbolts at the antique car show. What was normally a vacant lot steps away from the I-515 was a boisterous festival that day. The air was sweet with the smell of cotton candy. Twangy country music played from the stage, and the partiers drank yard-long margaritas. Nova wore a red bikini top and black short shorts, exposing most of her deep brown skin and taut physique. Her lush black hair hung loose around her shoulders, and she hid her dark eyes behind oversized sunglasses. She walked in high heels, but he was still a foot taller than she was. Her mouth broke into a big smile as she watched children running around them.

"I think I want kids," she said.

Jason was surprised. She'd never expressed an interest in

children before, but Nova was a woman of many dimen-
sions. A ruthless killer, a voracious lover, but also a woman
who could cry at a Schumann concerto and play chess with
old men in the park. One of the things he loved about her
was that she was impossible to predict.

"Someday," she added, reading the look on his face. "Not
today, Jason."

"That's a relief," he said, grinning.

"I'm serious, though. Think about it."

"I will."

She dragged him toward a gleaming 1931 Cadillac
roadster and posed for a picture beside the car's owner. Her
body was voluptuous, attracting stares from the men nearby.
The sixty-something car owner in a plaid cap let his hand
wander while Jason took the picture, and Nova just laughed.
She looked happy. No worries, no fears. Jason felt happy, too,
but happiness also dulled his reactions. Happiness meant
letting his guard down. That was how he made mistakes.

As he took Nova's picture in front of the Cadillac, every-
thing changed, and he missed it entirely. He didn't even
notice what had happened until he looked at the photograph
later that night. One instant, she was smiling at him. The
next instant, as he snapped the photo, her smile had van-
ished. She was staring at something over his shoulder, her
lips in a frown. Her whole body was tense.

By the time he put away his phone, she'd pasted a smile
back on her face.

"Those margaritas look amazing," Nova said, which
was unusual, because she rarely drank. "Would you be a
love and get me one?"

"Come with me."

"Oh, you know I can't wait in lines. I get impatient and say nasty things about people. Make it a tall one, and float some Patrón on top."

"Okay."

As he turned away, Nova grabbed his wrist and pulled him back. Her arms snaked around his waist. Her skin glowed from the heat. "I love you, Jason Bourne," she whispered.

Those were the last words he heard her say.

He threaded his way to the tent on the far side of the festival where they sold margaritas frozen and on the rocks. Most of the people in line were loud and not on their first drink. When he looked back over the crowd, he couldn't see Nova near the Cadillac anymore. She'd disappeared, lost among thousands of others.

He should have been worried, but he wasn't. He was happy.

The band onstage played a cover of a Brad Paisley song. A skinny twenty-something black man in a cowboy hat talked with a wizened old man in overalls about his 1950 Studebaker Land Cruiser. Three kids no more than ten dodged the people in line as they squealed and played tag. Two teenage girls danced to the music. He smelled smoke; someone was sneaking a cigarette. Across the street, sunlight glimmered on the windows in the tower of the Lucky Nickel hotel.

Bourne heard the first shot as soon as it happened. Nobody else did.

The report of the rifle wasn't even as loud as a firecracker, easy to miss, but he knew what it was. His head snapped around as he tried to pinpoint the source of the gunfire. The echoes played with the sound, as if it were coming from everywhere. Definitely a long gun. Definitely high up.

It had to be the hotel. He surveyed the windows, looking for the weapon.

A few seconds later, the shooter fired again.

The black man in the cowboy hat collapsed. It happened too fast for anyone to realize he'd been shot in the head. He simply fell where he stood, his hat covering his face. Another muffled pop rolled over the festival, barely loud enough to hear.

"Gun!" Bourne shouted. "Shooter! Take cover!"

Hesitation gripped the people around him. Not fear, just a frozen moment of uncertainty. No one understood what was happening; no one believed it was real. Then a woman grabbed her chest, and when everyone saw the spray of blood, the screaming began. Parents grabbed children. People ran, and shoved, and fell, trampled in a stampede. The fence around the lot penned them in, and there was nowhere to hide. More bullets rained down, faster now, one after another, randomly spraying the crowd, cutting down human beings like paper targets in an arcade. Metal pinged as rounds thudded into Fords and LaSalles.

Bourne had only one thought.

Nova.

He raced through a scene of wild panic. Bullets missed him by inches, and more bodies fell. He searched the faces, trying to find her. Look for the calm one; she wouldn't run.

She'd be helping others, dragging children behind cars, ripping off shirts to tend to the wounded.

Where was she?

Already, sirens wailed on the streets as police scrambled for the scene. Only a couple of minutes had passed since the carnage began, but every few seconds brought more death, more blood. He stopped and stared at the Lucky Nickel tower. He could see where the shooter was now, could see the reflection near the top floor and the fire of the barrel. He waved his arms, trying to draw the attention of whoever was behind the riflescope. Shoot at me, take me, leave the others.

Leave Nova.

But the gunfire went elsewhere. He shouted Nova's name, barely audible above the tumult of voices. He found the Cadillac roadster where she'd been standing minutes earlier, but she was gone. Dozens of people lay flat on the hot pavement behind the car, covering their heads, covering their children, hiding from the assault.

The car owner in the plaid cap lay beside his prize car. He was dead, a bullet in his throat.

"Nova!" Jason screamed, turning in every direction.

Then, with the crowd parting like a curtain, he saw her. His world turned black. Someone carried her, her body slung over a man's shoulder, her hair swishing back and forth as he took her away. He could only see half her face, but what he saw was streaked in blood. Her lifeless arms hung down. Her sunglasses had fallen off; her eyes were closed.

Jason choked out her name again. "Nova!"

The man carrying her turned around. Their eyes met. Jason's grief erupted into fury, and his heartbeat took off like a rocket. He knew that man. He knew that face; he'd spent days, weeks with him around the world. An agent like him. A killer.

Benoit.

Treadstone was here.

Treadstone was taking away the woman he loved. She was dead, and they were stealing her body. More than that, he knew—he knew beyond any doubt in his mind—that the agency had killed her.

They'd done this. Whoever was in the sniper's lair was Treadstone.

Bourne took off after Benoit, but two other men collided with him. They all fell to the ground, crushed as people stampeded over them to escape. His head struck the concrete hard. His teeth clamped shut. He fought his way back to his feet, but by the time he did, Benoit was gone. Nova was gone.

He headed for the street. A car would be there, ready to whisk the body from the scene. He ran, shoving his way through the crowd, pushing toward the fence bordering the lot. At the open gates, he saw people flooding out of the festival grounds, escaping in every direction. But he saw a car, too, emerging from the underground parking lot of the Lucky Nickel.

There was Benoit. And Nova.

The rear door of the sedan flew open. Benoit shoved the lifeless body inside and followed. Jason ran along the fence, trying to keep the car in sight as it inched through a stream of people escaping from the festival. It couldn't go fast; it couldn't go far. He made it to the gate, where he wasn't even fifty yards away. He closed on the car, shouting Nova's name, but then a gap opened up in the crowd, and the sedan accelerated. Bourne thrust out a hand for the door, but the car shot forward, disappearing toward the freeway. All he could do was stand there and watch his life taken away from him.

Bourne stared up at the Lucky Nickel. The shooting was over. A man with a rifle was dead on the floor. The broken hotel window was quiet. He knew the cover-up would happen next. The evidence would be erased. He needed to get inside, needed to see the man who had done this.

Would he recognize him?

Would he know the assassin?

Jason ran for the Lucky Nickel. He jumped the closest fence and dashed across railroad tracks toward the rear of the hotel. Police cars already had the building sealed, the front and back blocked off by dozens of emergency vehicles. There was nowhere to go. He could see frightened guests huddled in the parking lot; he could see people flooding from the hotel doors. His eyes went from face to face, watching them, memorizing them.

An instinct. A reflex.

Then he saw a man he knew. A window in a sedan in the hotel parking lot went down, and Bourne saw who was behind the wheel. Nash Rollins.

Treadstone.

Nash saw him, too. The man's face was hard, devoid of any emotion as he looked back at Bourne.

Then the window shut, and the car sped away.

———

JASON stood in the vacant lot with Abbey. They were the only ones here. The scene of the massacre had been their first stop as they drove into the city. It was a shrine now, where strangers stopped and left flowers. From where they were, he could see the fifteenth-floor suite in the Lucky Nickel where Charles Hackman had built his sniper's lair. Memories of that day jolted through him like bolts of lightning. He could still close his eyes and see every face. The living and the dead.

Abbey followed the path of his eyes. "Sixty-six people. It's unimaginable."

Jason shook his head. "Sixty-seven. They never counted Nova. She was never on the lists of the dead."

"Do you believe Benoit?" she asked. "Do you think Nova was working undercover to infiltrate Medusa?"

"I do."

"Is that why she was killed?"

Bourne nodded. "It has to be. She got inside the organization, but somehow they figured out she was a spy. So they executed her. Now we just have to hope she left some clues behind. Something to point us in the right direction."

"Wouldn't Treadstone already have searched her place?" Abbey asked.

"I'm sure they did."

"So what do you hope to find?"

"Something they missed," Jason replied. He turned away from the Lucky Nickel and stared south, toward the

Stratosphere and the gleaming hotels of the Strip. "We're closer to the heart of the conspiracy than we've ever been before. Medusa is here in Las Vegas. We need to find them."

TWENTY-EIGHT

THEY located Nova's house on a dusty open lot south of the McCarran airport. It was a stucco rambler with a red clay roof. Some of the other nearby tracts had been snapped up and converted into luxury estates, but this house dated to the old days in Las Vegas. The windows had been boarded up and painted with *No Trespassing* signs. Garbage filled the yard, which was nothing but a square patch of flat, rocky dirt with a scattering of mesquite bushes and drooping palm trees. A mesh fence surrounded the entire lot.

Jason drove two blocks past the house and parked the Land Rover where it wouldn't be seen, and then they walked back along the deserted street. He checked the area for surveillance and didn't see any, but he also spotted tire tracks in the dirt. They weren't the first to investigate here.

"You think this was where Nova was based?" Abbey asked.

Bourne pushed aside a section of the fence so they could squeeze inside. "Benoit said she bought a place near the airport. This house was purchased four months before Nova was killed, and the property tax records show the owner as Felicity Brand. That's an alias she used on one of the missions we did together."

"But you didn't know about the house?"

He shook his head. "No."

Jason led them to the front door, which hung ajar on one of its hinges. A lizard ran across his dirty boot. The air inside was hot and stale, and the boarded-over windows left the interior dark. The furniture had all been removed, either taken by Treadstone or hauled away by thieves. Nothing was left to remind him of Nova. What was still here—some old blankets, a shopping cart, empty food bags—had obviously been left by squatters looking for a place to spend the night.

He turned on a flashlight, which caused another scattering of lizards. A few wasps clung to the bare walls. He did an up-and-down survey of the hardwood floor with his light. Many of the beams had splintered in the heat.

"What are you looking for?" Abbey asked.

"Hiding places."

Jason paced slowly, tapping floor panels with his boot, looking for the hollow reverberation of a storage area. He found nothing. When he was done in the living room, he repeated the process in the dining room and then in each of the house's bedrooms. In the kitchen, he pushed aside the abandoned refrigerator, disturbing a scorpion. He checked the toilet tanks in the bathrooms and found only dank brown water. There were no secret areas.

And yet he knew Nova. She would have kept a place to hide the information she was gathering.

"Let's check the garage," he said.

They took a narrow hallway to the musty single-stall garage. Wooden shelves had been assembled on one wall, but they'd collapsed, spilling a few paint cans. When he turned his flashlight to the floor, he saw interlocking rigid tiles, an unusual upgrade in what was otherwise a downscale house. A dusting of plaster had gathered on the tiles. He saw overlapping footprints.

Jason got on his hands and knees and began pushing the tiles with his fingers. Abbey saw what he was doing and got on the floor next to him and did the same thing. Together, they checked every tile. When they reached the center of the garage, where a vehicle would normally be parked, Abbey murmured, "Jason, look at this."

He shined the flashlight where she was pointing and saw that two tiles were loose, as if they'd been removed and replaced many times. He handed the flashlight to Abbey and then pried back the tiles, revealing the concrete floor underneath. The light showed a square metal panel that had been installed in the concrete, along with hinges on one side and a circular ring on the other that could be used to lift the panel from the floor.

Abbey kept the light aimed at the floor as he squeezed his finger into the ring and pulled back the metal cover.

As he did, Abbey said, "That's strange."

"What?"

"A red light just went on down there." An instant later, she continued: "Jason, that's a *camera!*"

Jason dropped the metal cover. He got to his feet and pulled Abbey with him. "We need to get out of here. They're coming."

He avoided the front door and instead led Abbey out the back. The two of them hurried across the rocky yard, which was littered with burnt wooden posts, old tools, dried palm fronds, and one rusted hubcap. When they reached the fence at the back of the lot, he separated the mesh and pushed Abbey through ahead of him. There was a low stone wall marking the neighboring property, and he helped Abbey over the top and then climbed after her. On the other side, they waited.

"Who's coming?" she whispered.

"Either Treadstone or Medusa. That was a motion-sensitive camera. Somebody just got an alert that there was movement in the house."

"So they know we're in Las Vegas?" Abbey asked.

"Hopefully the flashlight beam blocked our faces."

Not far away, they heard the rumble of a car moving fast. Whoever was watching the house had wasted no time. Bourne peered over the edge of the stone wall and saw a brown SUV screech to a stop on the empty street a hundred yards away. Two men got out, one tall, one short, both dressed in the yellow reflective uniforms of utility workers. A ruse. He was sure they were both armed. The men squeezed through the fence and tramped across the yard, where the structure of the house hid them.

"Treadstone?" Abbey murmured.

Jason shook his head. "No. These guys are hired muscle, not pros. That probably means Medusa. If we were still inside, we'd either be dead, or they'd be taking us out to be tortured and questioned in the desert. And then killed."

He waited. A few minutes later, both men returned outside. They toured the perimeter of the house, and Jason ducked below the wall as the two men hiked to the rear of the yard, not more than ten feet away. He heard them near the fence, and the one man talked on the phone in an irritated voice.

"Nah, nobody's in the house. They split. I'm telling you, we were here in like ninety seconds. If they spotted the camera, they booked it out of here. We can hang around if you want, but they ain't coming back."

There was a long stretch of silence, and then Jason heard: "All right, I'll send someone to watch the house overnight. If they show up again, we'll get them."

Bourne heard the crunch of footsteps as the two men headed back to the SUV. He checked over the top of the wall and saw the truck driving away. He waited another ten minutes to make sure the men weren't planning to return, and then he took Abbey's hand and led them back over the wall and out of hiding.

"So Medusa cleaned out the house and set a trap," Abbey said.

Jason nodded, but he didn't say anything. He stared at the debris littering the backyard.

"What now?" she went on. "Even if Nova left something, Medusa already found it."

He still didn't answer.

"Jason?"

He walked to the mesh fence and pushed inside the yard again. Abbey followed him. He made his way to the old hubcap that was pressed into the dusty soil like a sundial. The monsoons and blistering summer sun had chewed away at the metal and left it brittle and rusted, but he could still make out the bow-tie Chevrolet logo.

"What is it?" Abbey asked.

"That's a Nova hubcap," Jason said.

"Do you think that's a coincidence?"

"No, I don't."

He looked around the yard and saw a hand trowel. He didn't think it had been left there by accident. He grabbed the trowel and dug it into the earth to pry away the hubcap, and then he stabbed at the rocky soil with the pointed edge of the spade. He didn't have to go far. An inch down, the trowel scratched against something hard, and when he cleared more dirt, he saw the molded shell of a fireproof box with a combination lock. Digging his fingers down into the earth on both sides, he worked the box out of the ground.

"I'll be damned," Abbey said.

"Come on, let's get back to the car. I don't want us staying in the open."

Jason carried the safe under his arm, and they returned to the street. He kept an eye on the intersections to make sure that no one had been sent to watch the house. They walked two blocks back to the car, and he turned on the engine and opened the windows. It would have been safer to go elsewhere, but he didn't want to wait to see what was inside the box.

"Do you know the combination?" Abbey asked.

"I hope it's something she'd expect me to know. If she really trusted me." He keyed in several different combinations, and on the fourth try, he heard the lock unlatch.

"Your birthday?" Abbey said with a smile.

"She knows that wouldn't mean anything to me. She used the date we met. In reverse order, just to be difficult."

He put both hands on the lid of the security box.

"It wouldn't be booby-trapped, would it?" Abbey asked. He could tell that she was only half joking.

"If it is, we'll never know."

"Optimist," she said.

He opened the safe. Seeing the meager contents, he was disappointed. He wasn't sure what he expected, but he was hoping that something inside would remind him of Nova. She could have left behind hidden fragments of who she was. Passports. Driver's licenses. Anything to let him see her again. But there was nothing like that. In fact, there was no useful material inside for an intelligence agent at all, no identifications, no cash, no gun. The only thing in the box was a thick manila folder.

"I don't get it," he said.

"What?"

"I was expecting a getaway box. You keep things in it you'd need if you have to run."

"Do you have something like that?" Abbey asked.

"Ten of them," Bourne said. "They're in different cities, different countries. You never know when you'll need them. But this is something else."

"What's in the folder?"

He removed the folder from the box and opened it so they could both study the contents. The first thing he saw was a surveillance photo of a man getting into a beat-up Cutlass. He didn't recognize the location, but it was in the desert, somewhere remote, with craggy hills in the background. The man himself was tall and slightly stooped, in his fifties, with an unruly mop of gray hair. He wore loose jeans and a shirt and string tie.

"That's *Charles Hackman*," Abbey said.

Jason dug further into the folder. Everything he found was related to Hackman. Phone records, credit card statements, printouts from his social media pages. Nova had compiled a complete dossier on the Lucky Nickel shooter.

"This makes no sense," Abbey said. "Are you sure it was Nova who left this? Could it have been someone else?"

He shook his head. "This is her work."

"But she died in the shooting," Abbey pointed out. "How could she have gathered information about Hackman? Until November 3, he was a complete nobody. He came out of nowhere and didn't leave any clues behind."

Jason pointed at the computer date on the bottom of the printouts. *October 28.*

"Nova was doing research on Hackman *before* the massacre," Bourne said. "Somehow, she already knew who this guy was before anyone else did. She knew he was being groomed for something."

TWENTY-NINE

ABBEY knocked on the door of Sylvia Hackman's apartment in the seamy heart of North Las Vegas. There were bars on her windows, and the neighborhood around her was ground zero for gang activity in the valley. This wasn't a place anyone chose to live unless they couldn't afford to live anywhere else. When Abbey had first met Charles Hackman's wife, the woman had owned an upscale house in Summerlin, but money had obviously grown tight after her husband became a notorious killer.

The woman answered the door from behind a chain. Her eyes were suspicious. "What do you want?"

"Mrs. Hackman, my name is Abbey Laurent. I visited you once before when I was working on an article last year."

"I remember. I told you back then that I don't talk to reporters."

"Yes, I understand that, but I have some new information to share with you. Maybe if we put our heads together, we can get some answers."

"I don't care about answers," Sylvia snapped.

"Don't you want to know what really happened to your husband?"

"I already know. I was married to a monster. He killed all those people. He ruined my life. End of story."

Sylvia began to close the door.

"I can pay," Abbey went on quickly. "Five hundred dollars. Just to talk. It looks to me like you could use the money."

The woman hesitated. "Off the record? You leave me out of it?"

"Sure."

"Let me see the cash."

Abbey dug in her pocket for a wad of folded bills and pushed it through the crack in the door. Sylvia Hackman took it, undid the chain, and opened the door. "I'll give you fifteen minutes."

The woman led Abbey into the small apartment, which was neat as a pin but sparsely furnished. The television was on, and she switched it off using a remote. She took a seat on a worn sofa near the barred windows, next to a fat orange cat that was sound asleep. Abbey pulled a wooden chair from the kitchenette and sat near her. She glanced around the apartment and saw nothing personal here. No family photographs. Nothing from the woman's past.

Sylvia was tall and slim. She had short gray hair and

wore glasses, and her makeup and nails were carefully done, even though she didn't look as if she went out much. Her orange blouse and beige pants were old but clean and wrinkle-free. Abbey got the impression that Sylvia was a woman clinging to the tiniest bits of who she'd once been.

"I'm sure the last eighteen months have been very difficult," Abbey said.

Sylvia frowned and stroked the cat's fur. "You have no idea. I was fired from my job. I had to sell my house. It was partly for the money, but also because people kept breaking the windows and painting obscenities on the garage. My neighbors didn't want me around anymore. My children haven't spoken to me in a year."

"I'm sorry."

"No one can seem to believe that I didn't have the faintest idea what Charles was planning. I'm as disgusted and horrified as anyone. Everyone tells me, 'You must have known! You must be guilty, too!' Well, I didn't know. I didn't have a clue. Whatever broke inside his head, it came out of nowhere. I'll tell you what I told the FBI, Ms. Laurent. I wish I could help you, but I can't. I have no idea why Charles did what he did. If the government couldn't figure it out, I really don't see how you think *you* can."

Abbey looked around the apartment and wondered if it was bugged. By Treadstone. By Medusa. By the FBI. "I think the government knows more about your husband's motive than they're saying," she told Sylvia.

"Are you one of those conspiracy nuts?" the woman asked. "Because if that's all this is, you can leave now."

"No, there's more. I know that an intelligence agent

was investigating your husband *before* he killed all those people."

Sylvia stared at her. "That's impossible. You're mistaken."

"I saw the information this agent gathered. She was looking into his whole life. The material was dated several days before the massacre."

"Charles didn't have so much as a parking ticket before the shooting. How could anyone have known what he was planning?"

"That's what I'm trying to find out," Abbey said.

"Who was this agent? Who did she work for?"

"I can't say. But I do have some questions for you. I think you can help me."

Sylvia looked shaken. "Yes, all right. I still can't believe this is true. If someone in the government knew about Charles, why didn't they stop him? Why didn't they *do* something?"

"I'm not sure if she knew what he was going to do. She simply knew he was involved in something."

Sylvia shook her head. "What can I tell you? What information do you want?"

"Did Charles ever mention an organization called Medusa?" Abbey asked.

"No."

"The name never came up? You never saw it in any papers he had?"

"No, I've never heard of it before. What is Medusa?"

"I think they may have been involved in recruiting or manipulating your husband to do what he did."

"Recruiting him how?"

"It may have started online. That seems to be their specialty. Are you familiar with a social media software called Prescix?"

A shadow crossed Sylvia's face, and her lips tightened with disgust. "Oh, yes."

"Do you know if Charles used it?"

"All the time. He signed up almost as soon as it came out. He thought it was a joke, this idea that software could predict what you were going to do next. But he couldn't believe how accurate it was. Charles was an actuary, so he was impressed at the statistical modeling that was built into the code. He said it was like Prescix knew him better than he knew himself. What started out as a hobby became kind of an obsession for him. At first, I thought it was just a professional thing, trying to reverse engineer how they did it. But it became personal, too. He used Prescix all the time. He'd spend hours going through the feed, seeing what others were saying, going into chat rooms. I told all this to the FBI, you know. I told him this was where Charles's problems started."

"What do you mean?" Abbey asked.

"He became a different person because of Prescix. He was addicted to the software and obsessed with trying to understand its algorithms. He started pulling away from me. His entire world went online. But I never thought he was at risk for anything like what he did. I still can't imagine *why* he killed those people."

"Did you know he'd purchased guns? That he was training with rifles at gun ranges?"

"I had no idea."

"The FBI said he wasn't particularly religious and didn't seem to have any strong political beliefs."

Sylvia nodded. "Yes. Charles didn't care about those things. He was a scientist."

"Were there any groups of people he didn't like? Or that he spoke out against?"

"No, nothing like that," she said. "Actually, he was frustrated by the divide in the country. He used to say that the left and the right were so far apart that maybe it would be better if we all just divorced before we wound up in another civil war."

Abbey took her phone out of her pocket and found a photo that Jason had texted to her. It was a picture of Nova. There was something about the woman's fiery, confident face that made her a little jealous. She realized that she felt that way whenever Jason talked about her. She could see the emotion in his face when he did, and most of the time Jason seemed disconnected from any emotions at all.

She showed the picture to Sylvia Hackman. "Do you ever remember seeing your husband with this woman? Or do you remember seeing her anywhere else?"

Sylvia studied the photograph. "I don't think so. She has a distinctive face. I think I'd remember."

"What about this man?" Abbey asked, pulling up a picture of Peter Restak.

"No."

Abbey sat back in the chair and frowned. She knew more about Charles Hackman than she ever had before, even when she was researching him for *The Fort*, but she still felt as if she knew nothing at all. Somehow Medusa had recruited him out of millions of other prospects because of his psychological profile. What had Hackman said to his wife? *Prescix knew him better than he knew himself.* Somehow, thanks to Prescix, Medusa had found him and brainwashed him. Radicalized him. Set him up in a hotel with a rifle.

That wasn't just a software operation. It was more complicated than that. It may have begun online, but there had to have been a direct contact somewhere, too.

"Did you ever see your husband's Prescix account?" Abbey asked.

"He wouldn't let me see it. Typically, he and I used the same password on all of our online accounts, but he used a different one for Prescix. I tried to log in, which was how I found out he'd changed it. I asked him why, and he got upset. He said he deserved privacy and that I shouldn't be checking up on him. I figured he must be having an affair with someone he'd met out there. But I never saw his account in order to know who it was. And of course, he deleted the account before the shooting. Or somebody deleted it."

"Somebody?" Abbey asked. "What do you mean?"

"Oh, it was all very strange. The FBI asked if I was sure about Charles using the Prescix software, because they hadn't been able to locate his account. They couldn't even find archives of it anywhere. It's like it never existed. I swore to them I wasn't wrong. Charles used Prescix every day. If they couldn't find the account, then somebody removed it. For all I know, it was the company itself. I'm sure they were worried about all the lawsuits if it came out that Charles was influenced by things he did online."

Abbey shook her head. The social media trail had been wiped out of existence. *Leave no clues.* Even so, someone must have reached out to Hackman in real life. They had to have spent hours together, and that was harder to conceal. There had to be evidence. Witnesses. A location where they met.

"Was Charles away from home a lot during those last few months?" Abbey asked.

Sylvia nodded. "Yes, he'd be gone for long stretches of time. Often overnight."

"Did you ask him where he went?"

"He said it was client work."

"Did you look at his credit card statements?"

"I did, but wherever he went, he must have paid cash. There was nothing out there. I looked, Ms. Laurent. So did the FBI."

"I understand, but the thing is, I'm convinced your husband didn't do this alone. I think he had help. I need to know *who* helped him and *where* they met. Because this organization called Medusa is not done. The massacre wasn't an isolated event. Whatever they do next is likely to be even worse."

"I wish I could help you," Sylvia replied. "But Charles took his secrets to his grave."

"Did you ever follow him?" Abbey asked.

"What?"

"You said he'd be gone for long stretches of times. You were concerned. You thought he was cheating on you. Did you ever follow him to see where he went?"

Sylvia looked away, as if she were embarrassed. "Once."

"Did you tell the FBI?"

"No, because it turned out to be nothing. Charles told me he had to visit a client, and he said it was a long drive, so he was going to stay overnight rather than make the round trip. I thought maybe he was meeting a woman. So yes, after he left, I followed him. As it happens, that was one time he wasn't lying to me. He really did go to a client's location. I felt stupid about it, so I went back home and never followed him again."

"Where did he go?" Abbey asked. "Who was the client?"

"A casino in Mesquite called the Three Mountains. They were a new client, but they were generating a lot of business for him. He had to go out there almost every week."

Abbey frowned. "Charles was an actuary, right?"

"Yes, he did complex statistical modeling. Anticipating risk. He was a brilliant man. He had an incredible mind for math."

"Had he worked for casinos before?"

"In Las Vegas? Of course. They're obsessed with balancing risk and reward."

"You said the Three Mountains casino was a new client. A lucrative one. Do you know how they picked Charles to work for them?"

Sylvia shrugged. "It was a referral. That was how he got most of his business."

"Who referred him?"

"He'd built a relationship with a New York lawyer who had connections at a number of the casinos in town," Sylvia replied. "They'd known each other for several months. Charles got bumped up to first class on a flight to LaGuardia, and this man sat in the seat next to him. It was totally coincidental, but sometimes that's how the best connections happen."

Abbey didn't think the meeting on the plane was a coincidence. Not where Medusa was concerned.

"What was the lawyer's name?" she asked.

Sylvia hesitated as she tried to place it in her memory. "It was an odd name," she said finally. "Gattor, I think. Yes, that was it. Carson Gattor."

THIRTY

JASON stood atop the hills directly across from the Three Mountains casino in the small desert town of Mesquite. He focused his binoculars on the neon-lit back door, watching elegantly dressed players come and go. It was nearly midnight, but that hadn't slowed the arrival of high rollers. He saw limousines from Las Vegas bringing Arab and Chinese customers, each of them greeted by stunning escorts, sometimes male, sometimes female. The casino knew the sexual preferences of its best clients. An occasional private jet roared overhead, landing at the small Mesquite airport to ferry what the gaming industry called whales. They were the ones who didn't blink at playing blackjack at ten thousand dollars a hand.

A posse of guards in suits, obviously armed, roamed the porte cochere to keep out ordinary players. Anyone who tried to go inside at the rear door was politely redirected to an entrance on the other side of the building, where they could find penny slots and keno. There were two hotel towers rising above the casino, a taller one for the average tourist and a smaller venue that couldn't be booked by outsiders. There was nothing about it online.

"This definitely isn't a sawdust joint," Abbey commented, borrowing the binoculars. "Most of these people must be putting seven figures in play. How can a hole-in-the-wall casino in Mesquite handle that kind of action?"

"Deep pockets," Bourne replied. "Medusa."

"You think this is their headquarters?"

"Probably not, but it's part of their operation. They went to a lot of trouble to get Charles Hackman here, so I'm guessing this is where he was recruited. Look at the people going in the door. I'm sure they're hand-selected. Everyone brings something different. Political influence. Corporate power. Technical expertise. Military background. Wealthy connections. Bring them in, ply them with drinks, drugs, women, money. That's how you create leverage. Medusa is expanding its reach all over the world. It starts behind those doors."

"So what are you going to do?" Abbey asked.

"Go inside," Bourne replied.

Abbey turned and stared at him in the darkness. "Are you crazy, Jason? They'll recognize you as soon as you set foot inside the casino."

"I hope so. That's my plan. I need to go in there as Cain."

"But *why?*"

"Medusa put out the word that I'm the one who murdered Congresswoman Ortiz. I'm counting on the people in there knowing that. It should be enough for them to roll out the welcome mat."

"But that was a *lie*," Abbey protested. "You were set up. They framed you."

"Yes, but very few people inside Medusa are likely to know that. I'm betting there can't be more than a few top people inside the organization who realize that Cain *wasn't* actually a Medusa killer. As far as everyone else is concerned, I'm one of them."

"What if those top people are inside the casino?" Abbey asked him. "The ones who set you up?"

"I know it's a risk, but I'd only expect mid-level operatives at a place like this. This is still a Nevada casino, which means they have to worry about regulators dropping in unannounced. You don't put your top people in offices where the Gaming Commission might come calling."

"And what do you hope to accomplish by going inside?"

"We need information. A name. Or some hint about what they're planning next. The clock is ticking, Abbey. I don't know how much time we have. That casino is a Medusa hub. If Cain shows up looking for connections, they'll point me up the chain."

"Or they'll kill you," Abbey told him. She added quietly, "Do you have a death wish, Jason? Is that what this is about?"

He didn't answer her. He wasn't sure if he had an answer.

"I'll leave my phone with you," he said. "I don't want any devices inside. If I *don't* come back, talk to Nash Rollins. Use that number he gave you. Tell him what we found."

Jason left before Abbey could protest further. He headed down the hillside toward the casino, his shoes kicking up dust as he walked. He chose not to go straight in through the private door, where the high rollers were. He hadn't admitted it to Abbey, but he wasn't at all sure whether his cover as Cain would keep him alive. If he gave them his name outside, he'd be in the middle of a dozen armed security guards who could take him down in seconds if the word came back that Cain was to be killed.

No, he needed to get inside another way.

He crossed the parking lot toward the other casino, where the ordinary gamblers played. There would be cameras everywhere, but he wore sunglasses and a baseball cap, which he hoped would buy him time before he was recognized. As he neared the doors, he spotted a rowdy group of young men, and he veered across the lot to intercept them. One of them wore an Imagine Dragons T-shirt, and Jason offered up his hand for a fist bump.

"Dragons rule!" Jason shouted, taking on a slightly

slurred, drunken tone in his voice. "Hey, you go to their last concert at the MGM?"

"Are you serious?" the man shouted back, as if they were long-lost friends. "Hell, yes!"

"Dan Reynolds is the *man!*"

"He is, brother!"

Jason kept up the banter as they passed through the doors into the crowded heart of the casino floor. He shoved his hat down, and the eyes of the security guards passed across the whole group with no interest.

To avoid detection, blend in with others. A man who isn't alone attracts less attention.

Treadstone.

Bourne split off from the Imagine Dragons fans when the men gathered around the roulette wheel. He did a casual circuit of the downscale casino, sizing up the locations of the guards, doors, and cameras. Every now and then, he stopped and played ten dollars at one of the slots. To anyone watching, he looked like a gambler hunting for a loose machine. It didn't take him long to spot two double doors with smoked glass at the end of a short hallway, which was guarded by a heavyset security guard who looked more trained and serious than the others around him. On the other side of those doors was the private casino.

The Medusa casino.

Still wearing his hat and sunglasses, Bourne approached the guard, noting the bulge in the coat of his uniform and the radio wire in his ear. The guard sized him up; he knew a threat when he saw it. The man's body tensed. His fingers flexed, ready to dive for his gun.

"Can I help you, sir?" the guard asked warily.

"Looks like a private party through there," Jason replied.

"Invitation only, sir. Sorry."

Jason removed his baseball cap and sunglasses. "Actually, I think I have an invitation."

"I'm afraid you don't," the guard told him. "I know every face who belongs in there. Yours isn't one of them. Now please step back, sir, or I'll have you escorted from the building."

"You're right, I'm not on your list," Bourne acknowledged. "I didn't know I'd be here tonight. Mine's more of a standing invitation. Why don't you check with your boss and see what he says?"

The guard hesitated, his eyes narrowing. He didn't want to make the mistake of offending a whale, even one who showed up without an appointment.

"What's your name, sir?"

"Cain."

"That's it?"

"That's it. Call it in, buddy. I'm getting impatient. Trust me when I say you don't want that."

The guard stepped back into the dark recess of the hallway that led to the other casino. His voice was a murmur, and Jason couldn't hear what he was saying. When the guard returned, his entire demeanor had changed. He was submissive now. "I'm very sorry for the delay, sir. You're welcome to go on through."

"Thank you."

Jason tipped the man a hundred dollars. He headed

down the hallway to the glass door, unable to see through to the other side. When he pushed it open, he found himself in a completely different world. The drab décor of the rest of the building disappeared, and he found himself in a glittering venue, populated by people who were rich and beautiful. The atrium ceiling soared two stories over his head. The artwork on the walls, and the sculptures set among tranquil fountains, had to be valued in the millions. The gaming tables were leather-bound and hand-carved. Waitresses in cocktail dresses, all of them attractive enough to be L.A. actresses, passed silver trays of appetizers and champagne.

As he had in the other room, Bourne quickly assessed the casino security, looking for the armed guards and exits. If he needed to leave quickly, he wanted to know where to go, but his options were limited. Medusa left nothing to chance. He also noted the extensive lineup of cameras and knew that he was already being scrutinized by people in the private hotel tower over his head.

He wasn't alone for long.

A slim Asian woman in a low-cut burgundy dress zeroed in on him from across the casino floor. She had flowing raven hair and diamonds dripping from her earlobes. She walked on sky-high red heels, and her dark eyes gave him a direct, knowing stare. Her smile was equal parts friendly and suspicious.

"Welcome," she said. "My name is Nomi. It's our pleasure to serve you, Mr. . . . Cain."

"Thank you."

"Please forgive our man outside. You took him by surprise. A man of your stature typically doesn't arrive here without advance warning. I hope you weren't offended."

"Not at all," Bourne replied. "I should have called, but I had an unexpected opening in my calendar."

"How lucky for us. Would you like to play some blackjack? I have a table waiting for you."

"I confess I came woefully unprepared with cash," Bourne said.

"No matter. I'm sure credit can be extended."

She put an arm through his elbow and guided him across the casino to a luxury chair at an empty blackjack table. The dealer was another Asian woman, this one with long chestnut hair and a body that spilled out of a formfitting pink dress. She wore an emerald bracelet and a matching necklace on a gold chain.

"This is Shay," Nomi told him. "She'll take good care of you. Would one hundred thousand dollars suffice to start?"

"Fine."

Shay pushed a stack of chips across the table. She hadn't spoken yet, but she had smart eyes.

"Would you like me to bring you a drink?" Nomi asked.

"No, thank you."

"Well, then I'll leave you in Shay's good hands."

The dealer nodded at the hostess as she left, and Shay welcomed Bourne with a smile as she stared down at the table. Their eyes didn't meet. "We have a little tradition here, sir. The first bet is on the house. Shall I play five thousand dollars for you?"

"Go ahead," Jason told her.

She withdrew a single chip from her tray and put it on the lush felt in front of him. From the shoe, she dealt Bourne a ten, then drew a three for herself on the up card. Bourne took another card, which was a king, and he stood. Three cards later, the dealer busted. Shay smiled as she paid him his winnings, but she still never looked at him.

"I trust your luck will continue in the same vein," she said.

"I hope so, too," Jason replied.

"Fortune favors the risk-taker."

"Sometimes."

"Shall we play?"

"Let's."

Bourne found himself playing five thousand dollars a hand, and his luck did continue. Within a few minutes, he was thirty thousand dollars ahead. As they played, he tried to read the dealer's face, and he could see that Shay knew exactly who he was. He'd been put at this table, with this dealer, for a reason.

"People seem surprised to see me here," he said finally. "Why would that be, Shay?"

She dealt him another winning hand. "I couldn't say, sir."

"Something tells me you could say."

She manipulated the cards and chips and showed

nothing on her pretty face. "Perhaps because some of us wondered if you were still alive. It isn't often we're visited by a ghost, Jason Bourne."

"I'm very much alive," he told her.

"We're all pleased to know that. Your work in New York was . . . impressive."

"Thank you."

"However, it isn't a wise thing to show up here where you could be seen. Some of our players have government connections. It's possible someone might know who you are."

"Your security seems up to the task," Bourne said.

"Even so."

The two of them went silent. Bourne began a losing streak across several hands. He dropped nearly back to even before pulling ahead again.

"You must have a reason for coming here," Shay said. "Would you like to tell me what it is?"

"Maybe I'm just looking for a good time."

"In which case, you're very welcome. Stay. Gamble. Drink. If you want companionship, you have many options."

"Including you?" Bourne asked.

This time, Shay's eyes grazed across his. "If you wish."

"Actually, I'm here for another reason. I have urgent information to pass along to Medusa. It can't wait."

Shay's hand froze over the cards. "Some words are not to be spoken here."

"I understand, but I told you. This is urgent."

"If you have information, it should be passed on to your contact. There is protocol. Why come here to deliver your message?"

"Maybe my Prescix account told me I was going to pay you a visit."

Shay's lips turned downward. "You're not funny, Mr. Bourne. Again, I would encourage you to bring your concerns to your contact."

Bourne remembered Carson Gattor talking about his Medusa contact. A woman. "What I have to say is above her pay grade."

He saw surprise on Shay's face. And a little suspicion. "Very little is above *her* pay grade. Certainly no one at the Three Mountains."

"Who's in charge here?" Bourne asked.

"That would be Mr. Yee. He is upstairs."

"I'd like to see him."

Shay hesitated. He watched her face and realized she wore a small earpiece, in which she was obviously receiving instructions. "If you wish to speak to Mr. Yee, he would be honored to make your acquaintance."

"Thank you."

Shay looked over his shoulder and sent a message with a single blink. Like phantoms, two security guards in suits arrived, one on either side of Bourne. "These men will take you to him," she said. "Shall I cash out your winnings? It's fifteen thousand dollars."

"Keep it for yourself, Shay."

"That's very generous of you." She scooped up the chips and gestured to the two guards, who waited with stoic faces as Bourne got out of the chair. "One word of warning, Jason Bourne."

"What's that?"

"You're very good at what you do, but so are these men. Please don't give them a reason to kill you."

THIRTY-ONE

AS soon as the guards led Bourne off the casino floor, they searched him and took his gun. Holding his arms tightly on both sides, they guided him to a key-card elevator and stayed with him on the ride to the top of the tower. The elevator opened onto a lushly decorated hallway that ended at double doors covered with red silk, on which had been painted an elaborate Chinese landscape. Bourne suspected that behind the expensive cloth, the doors were made of bulletproof steel.

He noticed a camera observing their arrival. He also assumed he was being scanned for electronic listening devices and other weapons and his identity confirmed through facial recognition. A few seconds later, a click sounded, and the doors both swung inward automatically. The guards let go of his elbows, and Bourne walked alone into a large office that hummed with white noise.

Behind him, the doors swung shut and the locks clicked back into place.

High-definition video screens took up one wall of the office, and he could see views of the high-roller casino alternating every few seconds among the screens. The rest of the office was decorated with gold leaf and jade. Behind the cherrywood desk, floor-to-ceiling windows overlooked the Mesquite Mountains.

A short, thin Asian man got up from behind the desk and approached him. "Cain," the man said. "Or do you prefer I use the name Jason Bourne? Regardless, you honor us with your presence."

"My apologies for arriving unannounced. It couldn't be helped."

"So I'm led to understand. Well, you are always welcome. I am Andrew Yee. I run the casino here."

Among other things, Jason thought.

Yee didn't look more than thirty years old. He wore a royal-blue suit with a narrow striped tie, and his leather shoes were polished to a bright shine. His black hair was shaved very short on the sides and left long on top, with a gold earring in one ear. He had thick, angled eyebrows above round spectacles, a long face, and a dimpled chin. His expression was respectful but nervous. Yee wasn't accustomed to freelance killers showing up in his office.

"May I offer you something?" Yee asked. "Spirits? Food?"

"No."

Yee waved at the leather chair in front of his desk. "Please, sit."

Jason did, and Yee returned to the other side of the desk and sat down, too. His desk had little on it except a phone and a twenty-seven-inch iMac Pro. He was a neat, organized man. Yee sat straight up in his chair and adjusted his tiny glasses uncomfortably as he studied Bourne.

"Friends like you are always welcome, but it *is* a surprise to see you here. I do have some concerns."

"Such as?"

"Well, to be candid with you, Cain is a wanted man. If your presence here were to become known to the authorities, it might provoke scrutiny we would rather avoid. As I'm sure you're aware, we are . . . fanatical . . . about protecting the privacy of everyone associated with this operation. It would have been better had you called first, and we could have arranged a discreet entrance."

"In this case, it couldn't be helped," Jason replied.

"Yes, I heard what you told Shay. You say you have urgent information, and I'm anxious to explore this with you. However, you also said a very strange thing."

"Oh?"

"You said your information was above *her* pay grade. If that's true, it's certainly above mine, too."

Bourne smiled. "Obviously, that was a test. I wasn't sure who I was dealing with."

"I understand. But then why not reach out to Miss Shirley directly? She does not appreciate interference in her affairs by those of us who are not in the inner circle."

Miss Shirley.

A name. A contact. Someone in the upper echelon of Medusa.

"It may be time to bring you into that circle, Mr. Yee," Jason said.

"You flatter me, but I don't have the skills that she does. Or you, for that matter. Cain is a legend. I'm no more than a casino executive. A businessman. My role is limited, and I have never complained about that."

"Regardless, we have a problem, and I need your help," Bourne told him, inventing a new story on the fly. "I'd rather not involve Miss Shirley unless we can't resolve it here."

Yee frowned. "What is it?"

"I was nearly killed in New York. My security has been compromised."

"That's very distressing to hear."

"Someone talked. A Treadstone agent knew how to find me." Bourne gave the man a cold stare. "The leak came from here at the casino."

Yee leaned forward in his chair. "*Impossible!*"

"It's true. I've gone off the grid in response to the threat. No electronic contact whatsoever. I can't afford to put Miss Shirley at risk. It's one thing for me to be in danger, but obviously, we can't take a chance on exposing her. That's why I had to approach you directly. I don't suspect *you*, Mr. Yee. Your loyalty is beyond question. But others can be influenced all too easily. A dealer, a waitress, a guard hears a conversation and passes it along."

The casino manager shook his head fiercely. "That cannot happen. I make every hire personally. They are all monitored. All under constant surveillance. Personal behavior, finances, family. I know every aspect of their lives."

"Regardless, you missed something. I interrogated the Treadstone agent before I executed him. He knew about the Three Mountains. The feds are watching this place, Mr. Yee. They must have someone on the inside."

"No! I refuse to believe that. No one gets into the private casino who hasn't been vetted. They would never breathe a word."

"It may not necessarily be one of your people. It could be an outsider, deliberately trying to get inside the organization. The way *Nova* did. You remember what a catastrophe that was."

"I had nothing to do with that!" Yee protested. "You know my role! Medusa identifies the recruits. *Prescix* identifies them. I'm given names and background and told how to proceed. The strategy comes from above. We follow Miss Shirley's instructions to the letter."

"Even so, a mistake was made," Bourne said. He let violence creep into his voice. "You understand the consequences of that, don't you?"

Yee's eyes widened with fear. "Is that why you're here? To kill me?"

"I don't want to, but I need to know how much of our strategy may have been exposed."

"We can't expose what we don't know," Yee replied.

"No one in this building is privy to Medusa's operations. Not even me. The leak had to come from elsewhere."

"Are you telling me the suites in the tower aren't bugged?"

"Well, of course they are, but the recordings go directly to *her*. No one else."

"You've never listened? A little insurance policy, maybe?"

"Never!"

Bourne debated how far to push the man. "I'd hoped to avoid taking this step, but Miss Shirley needs to be in the loop. You and I need to talk to her."

Yee picked up the phone. "Of course. I'll call her now. You'll see, wherever the mistake was made, it wasn't at the casino."

Bourne grabbed the phone out of Yee's hand and put it back in the cradle. "Not by phone. In person. We need to visit her together."

"In person? That violates every protocol. She'll kill both of us. Even you, Mr. Bourne."

"I told you, we need to stay off the grid. Treadstone is monitoring everything. So is the tech cabal. Did you think they wouldn't fight back? You need to take me to her, and I'll deal with the repercussions."

Yee shook his head. "What you're asking is out of the question."

Bourne came around the desk and towered over the casino manager. "I killed a United States congresswoman, Mr. Yee. Do you think I'd hesitate even for a moment about killing you? My life, your life, is inconsequential. What matters is *Medusa*."

Yee's head bobbed with fear. "Yes. Yes, of course."

"We need to go. Now."

"All right, whatever you want. We can take my limo to Las Vegas."

Yee pushed a button under his desk and the double doors to the hallway opened inward. The two guards who had brought Jason to the top floor were still there, their faces like stone. Bourne stayed close to Yee as they returned to the plush corridor, but he was concerned that the man's nervous demeanor might attract attention. If that happened, if anyone grew worried, calls would be made. The truth about Bourne would be exposed. He'd be dead before they got out the casino doors.

When they reached the elevator, Jason held out his hand to the guard who'd taken his gun. The man eyed the casino boss, and Yee nodded with an uncomfortable frown. The guard hesitated, obviously concerned by the change in Yee's behavior, but he reached inside his coat anyway and returned Bourne's pistol.

They waited for the elevator.

It finally came, and when the doors slid open, the elevator car wasn't empty.

Peter Restak was inside. The New York hacker with the scraggly beard and man bun had a phone in his hand and his attention was glued to the screen, but when he looked up, his eyes widened with recognition.

"Bourne!"

Then he shouted to the guards: "Kill him, you fools!"

Next to Jason, Yee's mouth dropped open in disbelief. Bourne grabbed the casino manager by the shoulder and launched him off his feet toward the guards. One dodged away, but Yee landed hard against the other. The first guard reached under his coat for a gun, and as the pistol came free from its holster, Bourne lashed out with his foot, driving his heel hard into the man's groin and eliciting a howl of agony. He grabbed the man's gun hand and slammed it against the wall until the pistol fell to the carpet. With his right fist, he delivered an uppercut to the man's jaw, groaning as bone landed hard against bone.

Behind him, the elevator doors began to close.

If they closed, he was trapped.

Bourne leaped through the narrow space, and the doors reversed their track. The second guard, who had freed himself from Yee, aimed into the elevator and fired multiple rounds. The mirrored wall at the back of the elevator shattered. Restak threw himself sideways, but not before one of the bullets burrowed into his shoulder. Bourne heard the thunder of footsteps as the heavy guard ran for the elevator and leaped inside. There were three of them now as the elevator headed down.

The guard bounced off the elevator wall with surprising speed, kicking the gun from Jason's hand before he could fire. Jason took hold of the man's wrist, clamped his teeth over the guard's hand and bit down hard. The man's fingers unlocked. The gun fell, but with his other fist, the guard landed a blow to Jason's chin that knocked him into the wall. Dizzied, Jason spotted Restak huddled in the corner of the elevator. The hacker scooped up Jason's gun and jerked the trigger, unleashing a wild shot that missed Bourne entirely but shattered the guard's elbow. As the guard writhed, Jason jabbed a fist into the man's throat and then brought the man's head down sharply against his knee. The guard collapsed, his body landing heavily on top of Restak.

Before the hacker could wriggle free and fire again, Bourne wrenched the gun out of the man's hand and dragged Restak to his feet.

The elevator kept going down.

Jason eyed the overhead camera and knew what was waiting for him on the first floor. He stabbed the button for the floor above the hotel atrium and shoved the barrel of the gun into the underside of the hacker's chin.

"Who's Miss Shirley?"

"Fuck off," the man gasped.

"Where do I find her?"

"She'll find you, Bourne."

The elevator opened on the third floor. Jason had no time to ask more questions. He cracked the steel barrel into Restak's forehead and let the man sink to the floor. He exited the elevator into a quiet hotel corridor. Already he could hear voices and the pounding of footsteps in the stairwell.

They were coming for him.

He ran to the first hotel room door in the corridor, pushed his gun against the lock, and squeezed the trigger. Wood and dust exploded, and he shoved through the door with his shoulder. He found himself in a lavish suite that looked like something out of a European palace.

"*What the hell?*" bellowed a voice from the bedroom.

An eighty-something man with a thick head of snow-white hair appeared in the bedroom doorway. He was stark naked, but he had a revolver in his hand, and Bourne quickly lifted his own gun and aimed at the man's chest.

"Drop it now. Do it, or die."

The old man knew when he was outgunned. He put the gun down and raised his hands over his head. "Son of a bitch, you're Jason Bourne."

Jason took another look at the man. He recognized the barrel-chested octogenarian who'd spent years in the Defense Department. Retired air force general Philip Kahnke. Medusa had its fingers in high places.

"Better get some clothes on, General. Half a dozen men will be coming through that door in about ten seconds."

Not breaking stride, Bourne marched for the floor-to-ceiling windows on the far wall and shot a bullet through the glass, turning it into popcorn and letting warm, dry air whistle through the cool room.

He took one glance at the ground two floors below him and jumped.

THIRTY-TWO

MILES Priest stared out the window of his cliffside castle in the far western Highlands of Scotland. From here, he could see craggy hills, some still topped with snow, and the jagged seacoast that threw wild surf against the spit of land below the castle ramparts. On the green grounds of the estate, he could see the cemetery surrounding the ruins of a sixteenth-century stone chapel.

The window was open. He liked the cold air. Nelly Lessard, who didn't, sat in a musty armchair by the vast old library fireplace. She warmed her hands in front of the flames and tugged on the sleeves of her rust-colored sweater. Scott DeRay sat on the other side of the huge room, underneath an Elizabethan oil painting of a boy in a red velvet robe. On either side of him, bookshelves with leather-bound volumes climbed to the chambered wooden ceiling.

"I don't think you have a choice about this, Miles," Scott told him, flipping the pages in a vintage edition of Fielding's *Tom Jones*. "We need to have an emergency meeting of the cabal to discuss strategy."

Nelly adjusted a heavy, scratchy blanket over her lap. "I agree with Scott. It's imperative that we find a way to block the Prescix takeover."

Priest didn't take his gaze away from the Scottish coast. "What do we know about this private equity group that Gabriel talked about?"

"They're hiding behind a fog of confidentiality," Nelly replied, "but that's not surprising, given the sums involved. Their management team appears to be all experienced players, but they're hiding some very questionable investors. I think we have to conclude that Medusa is behind the takeover."

"Which means if the deal closes, Prescix is in their hands," Scott added. "Combine that with the data hack, and I don't see how we stop them. The cabal needs a plan, either to make a competing bid and hope Gabriel is willing to consider it, or to have a strategy for what action we can take if the deal goes through. As much as we hate it, maybe we should get behind the regulatory moves in Congress."

Priest came away from the window and poured himself a glass of twenty-eight-year-old Laphroaig whisky. "No, the whole point of the legislation is to tie our hands and hobble us from fighting back. That's why Medusa had Bourne kill Ortiz, to move the new regulatory framework forward. Meanwhile, they play their little games behind the scenes. If we support it, we play right into their hands."

"Then what do you suggest, Miles?" Nelly asked.

Priest frowned, because he had no solutions. He'd spent his career finding solutions, first in law enforcement, then in technology. In his mind, there was no such thing as an insoluble problem. It only took creativity, courage, and resourcefulness to find an answer. But it seemed as if Medusa had found a way to outmaneuver him at every turn, as if the group could get inside his head and know what he was thinking.

"What about this Miss Shirley?" he asked. "What do we know about her?"

Nelly offered a cynical chuckle. "Well, much of her background is a mystery, but what we do know makes her out to be quite the dangerous adversary. As Gabriel told us, she's Czech. Mid-thirties, we think. She was a swimmer in the Summer Olympics when she was nineteen and likely would have medaled, but she was disqualified for stabbing an opponent's coach."

"*Stabbing*?" Priest asked.

"Oh, yes. The coach nearly died. After that, Miss Shirley spent a few years doing Czech porn, dominatrix hardcore, not the kind of thing you want to watch on an empty stomach. Then she vanished. She's essentially been a ghost since then. We got a few hits on facial recognition from social media sites across Europe. She mostly appears to hang out with extremely rich men who like to be treated roughly."

"Well, that sounds like Gabriel."

"There's also an interesting coincidence with regard to some of the locations where we've identified her. I'd have to say she's a wet agent. She's been in several cities at the same time as a couple dozen high-profile assassinations."

Priest shook his head. "Definitely Medusa."

"It seems that way."

The CEO of Carillon gave a long sigh. "All right, I agree with you. We need to get the cabal together. Let's make it in two days. Nelly, go to the island and get everything ready. Issue the invitations, and don't accept any whining about the short timeline. Scott and I will take the helicopter from Nassau once we're ready to get underway."

Nelly got to her feet and shivered a little as she stepped out of the warming circle of the fire. "I'll head out immediately. I know you love it here, Miles, but the Caribbean sounds quite a bit better than this drafty old castle."

Priest smiled at her. "I'm a drafty old castle myself."

"We both are."

Nelly left the room, and Priest was alone with Scott. "Do we know anything more about Bourne?" he asked quietly, sipping his whisky.

"No. We're not sure where he and the Canadian woman went after New York."

"You haven't talked to him?"

Scott gave him a quizzical look. "Of course not."

Priest took his glass of Laphroaig across the room, and he opened up his phone to show Scott a photograph.

It was a picture taken in New York's Central Park, showing Scott and Jason Bourne together near the boat pond.

"Anything you want to tell me?" Priest asked.

Scott didn't apologize. "He's my oldest friend, Miles. He came to me for help."

"He's also a liability to the whole tech cabal. What did he want?"

"Access to facial recognition databases. He wanted to identify someone. I put him in touch with one of our people at Carillon. It was a one-time offer of assistance. For what it's worth, by the way, Jason says he didn't murder Ortiz. He claims he's still chasing Medusa."

"He's manipulating you, Scott. He did it when you hired him, and he's still doing it now. And candidly, even if it *were* true, we're way beyond guilt or innocence now. If Bourne is found alive, it blows back on us, which we can't afford in the current circumstances. I think you know that."

"I told him the same thing."

"I'm glad we're on the same page," Priest replied. "Bourne is a distraction we don't need. The sooner he's out of the way, the better. The bigger issue is that we only have two days until the cabal meets on the island. We need a strategy to keep Gabriel Fox from giving up Prescix to Medusa."

"Actually, I've been thinking about that, Miles. I have an idea."

"What is it?"

"I think we should invite Gabriel to join us on the island," Scott said. "Let him meet with the cabal face-to-face. Perhaps as a group, we can finally persuade him that he's better off with us, not against us."

Miles sipped his whisky as he reflected on this idea. "Interesting plan. And what if he still says no?"

Scott shrugged. "Then we have no choice. We kill him."

THIRTY-THREE

JASON winced as Abbey wrapped an elastic bandage around his ankle, which he'd twisted in his jump from the hotel window. When she was done, he got to his feet, limping through the brush. They were back in the red hills, looking down from the heights of the mesa at the Three Mountains casino. The Land Rover was parked on an unpaved trail behind them. They were invisible in the darkness.

He focused the binoculars on the private casino and saw what he expected to see. Panic. Guards roamed the parking lot, shining lights into cars. High rollers were being escorted out the door and whisked away. He wondered what excuse they were using to hide what had really happened. Gas leak. Bomb threat. Computer failure. Even so, someone must have heard the gunshots in the tower; rumors had to be flying.

General Kahnke, whose hotel suite Bourne had crashed,

left almost immediately, his face hidden by sunglasses and a hoodie. The general climbed into the back seat of a town car, accompanied by a redheaded mistress who'd probably been with him in the bedroom. Jason didn't think the general was likely to survive the night. In the morning, he'd be found dead in a respectable Strip hotel. Heart attack probably. The general had seen too much.

He'd seen Bourne.

"You're waiting for something to happen," Abbey murmured as he continued the surveillance. "What?"

"This was an assault on one of the Medusa nerve centers. They're going to have to assess the damage up close."

"Meaning?"

"They'll send someone."

Another hour passed as he surveilled the property. It was the middle of the night. Finally, Jason spotted headlights approaching, and he knew this wasn't one of the limos that had been coming and going since he escaped. When he focused on the vehicle through his binoculars, he saw a black SUV with smoked windows, and he recognized the profile of a Volvo XC90. He suspected it was the heavy, armored version, nearly ten thousand pounds in weight, built to withstand bullets and explosives.

Medusa had arrived.

"Now it gets interesting," Bourne said.

The SUV pulled to a stop outside the casino doors like an ominous black spider. To Jason's surprise, no one got out, and the engine didn't shut down. Instead, two people emerged from inside the casino and headed toward the vehicle. The first was Peter Restak, the color drained from his face, his wounded shoulder bandaged and in a sling. The second was Andrew Yee, still in his royal-blue suit, his expression fearful. As Bourne watched, the rear door of the SUV swung open. The two men got inside, and the Volvo pulled away. The entire process took less than thirty seconds.

"Come on," Jason said, pushing himself to his feet. He stumbled on his bad ankle, and Abbey held him up.

"Where are we going?" she asked.

"The question is, where are *they* going? You'll need to drive this time. Keep the lights off for now."

He tossed her the keys, and Abbey got behind the wheel of the Land Rover. She drove down the dusty road, the truck bouncing on barren terrain. The land sloped sharply through scattered cacti and mesquite, and she squinted to avoid driving them off a cliff's edge. When they reached the flatland, they were nowhere near the gate they'd used originally, and the paved road was on the other side of an aluminum fence.

"Drive over it," Jason told her.

Abbey gave him one sideways look of concern, then gunned the engine. The Land Rover jolted over the uneven ground with a burst of acceleration, took down the fence as it plowed forward, and dragged it behind them before finally breaking free. They were on a divided road not far from the casino entrance road, which was hidden behind the mesa. There was no other traffic.

"Pull onto the median and wait. Keep the lights off."

Abbey followed his instructions. Not long after,

Bourne saw the armored SUV pass through the stoplight ahead of them, leaving the casino and heading west.

"Give them plenty of space, but you can use your headlights now."

She switched on her lights and bumped off the median onto the road. At the stoplight, she turned right, and Jason could see the taillights of the SUV half a mile away, bending around a curve past housing developments that butted up to the hills. Abbey stayed behind the truck for another mile, and there were still only the two vehicles on the road. He knew that made their pursuit obvious.

"The driver will be a pro," Jason said. "Odds are, he's already spotted you back here. He knows you picked them up right outside the casino, and that's going to raise a red flag."

"Does he suspect we're following them?"

"He will if we stay on the same course much longer. We're far enough away that he can't see what we're driving, and that's a plus. But in another minute or so, he'll start slowing down to draw you closer so he can ID the vehicle."

"And then what?"

"Then he'll see if we stay behind him. If we do, either he'll ambush us himself, or he'll call ahead and have someone waiting to take us down in the desert."

"So what do we do?"

"Hang on." Bourne took out his phone and began checking maps of the area.

"Jason, he's *slowing*. Should I slow down, too?"

"No. Then he'll know it's a tail." He glanced up and spotted the SUV a couple of hundred yards ahead of them, and the gap between the two vehicles was closing fast. "There's a cross street ahead. Start signaling right, and then you can slow down."

Abbey used her turn signal and tapped the brakes.

"Turn here," Jason told her.

She swung into the turn lane and turned right. Ahead of them, the taillights of the Volvo got smaller as the SUV accelerated again.

"Now what?"

"There's a sharp left ahead. Take it, and keep driving as fast as you can."

Abbey accelerated, and the Land Rover fishtailed as she turned the wheel hard at the next left. She followed the road through an empty shopping complex. As they approached another intersection at high speed, Jason told her, "Go right and then take your next left and turn off your lights again as you do."

She followed his instructions, and a few seconds later, she braked to a stop at a major intersection.

"Go across the street, and make an immediate U. Then put your lights back on and turn right. If he sees you behind him at all, it should look like you're coming from a completely different direction."

"You think he turned, too?" Abbey asked, eyeing the lonely road as she crossed the intersection in the darkness.

"I think he's heading for the freeway."

Soon Abbey was back on the road with her lights on.

Jason used the binoculars to identify the taillights of the Volvo, which was now almost a mile ahead of them. As he expected, the SUV made a right turn to merge onto I-15, heading west through the mountains toward Las Vegas. Abbey accelerated to narrow the gap. Even in the middle of the night, there were other cars on the freeway, giving them cover. The developed land ended quickly, and they found themselves in the middle of rocky desert, pitch-black except for the lights of the vehicles around them.

"We'll be out here for a while," Jason said.

And they were. They passed a couple of other small towns on their route, but the towns came and went quickly and left them back in the dark hills. The driver of the SUV gave no indication that he was aware that he was being followed; he kept the vehicle at a constant speed through the empty land. More than an hour went by before they saw the sky brightening as they neared the fiery glow of the Las Vegas valley.

"You'll need to get closer," he told Abbey. "It will be easy to lose them in traffic as we hit the city."

She gradually pulled within a few car lengths of the SUV, but she kept at least two other vehicles between them. Jason smiled; she had the raw instincts of a spy. He kept a close eye on the Volvo, wondering if it would exit the freeway soon, but the SUV stayed on I-15 past Nellis Air Force Base and the northern suburbs, continuing into the heart of Las Vegas. They passed the towers of the Strip hotels from north to south, and finally he saw the SUV take the sweeping exit that led them onto the eastbound section of I-215. They were heading to the city of Henderson.

The Volvo left the freeway in the Green Valley area, in a densely commercial section of town. Jason and Abbey kept it in sight through a series of stoplights, but then the SUV turned toward the MacDonald hills, climbing sharply into an area of million-dollar estates carved out of the mountains on terraced stretches of land. He could see the lights of the properties above them, widely spread across vast lots.

"Guard gate," Abbey said, slowing the Land Rover.

Two blocks ahead of them, Jason saw the SUV pull to a stop at a gated access to an exclusive neighborhood called Sensara, monitored by guards who looked like ex-military. That was as far as they could follow. They watched the gates swing wide to allow the SUV to climb higher into the hills, and then the gates closed again, cutting them off. Jason motioned Abbey to turn the Land Rover around and head back down the hill, and once they were out of sight of the gates, they pulled to the curb on the steep access road. She turned off the engine.

"Medusa's up there?" she asked.

He nodded. "Either that, or someone high up in the organization lives there."

"But we don't know where if we can't follow them."

"We'll research the area tomorrow and see what we can find out."

"What do we do now?" Abbey asked. "Do we leave?"

"No, we wait, just in case the Volvo comes back. Why don't you try to sleep, and I'll keep an eye on the road."

"Why don't *you* sleep? Looks like you could use it."

Jason smiled. "Yeah. Okay."

She was right. He was exhausted. He reclined the seat in the Land Rover and closed his eyes. Over the years, he'd mastered the art of sleeping in almost any condition, and he was out in seconds. He dreamed the way he always did, in photographs, the same way he remembered his life. Images passed through his head, of Nova, of Benoit, of Scott, of people from the past who he had known at some point and long since forgotten. He dreamed of Abbey, too, her deep red hair, her eyes wide as she stared at him, her face so close to his that he could see every lovely imperfection.

He started awake.

"Jason," Abbey said. Her hand was on his shoulder. "The Volvo just passed us."

He shook away his dreams and noticed the clock. Not even an hour had passed. They were still more than an hour from dawn.

"Did they see you?"

"I don't think so. I ducked down when I saw headlights. Do you think they're heading back to Mesquite?"

"Go after them, and we'll see. If that's where they head, we'll let them go. We don't need to go all the way back there."

But when they caught up with the Volvo, the vehicle headed in a different direction into the hills that led toward Lake Mead and the Hoover Dam. Traffic was light on this stretch of two-lane road, and without Jason telling her what to do, Abbey held back, keeping distance between the two cars. Rocky hills loomed like silhouettes in the darkness on both sides. Jason kept an eye on the SUV's taillights ahead of them, but then the lights abruptly disappeared. He saw no evidence of where the armored vehicle had turned.

Abbey saw it, too. "Where did they go?"

"I'm not sure."

"Do I keep going?"

"Yes, keep the same pace."

She drove for another mile, but the SUV had vanished from the road. Somehow they'd passed it. Jason told Abbey to pull to the dusty shoulder, and he got out of the Land Rover and studied the land behind them. On the slope of one of the dark hills, he spotted the pinpoint glow of a flashlight moving up and down. Not long after, headlights bloomed to life, and he saw the Volvo inching back down a steep slope toward the road. When it got to the highway, it turned toward Las Vegas.

Jason got back in the Land Rover. "Turn around, go slowly."

Abbey retraced their route for almost half a mile, and then Bourne said, "Stop."

The two of them got out of the vehicle. Jason spotted a rough track up the hillside that the SUV had followed. He began to climb, and Abbey climbed with him. The night was warm and silent except for their footsteps. He swung his flashlight back and forth across the desert land, seeing nothing but the scrub brush. Then, almost a hundred yards from the road, a reflection glinted back at him when he shined his light behind the rocks.

Jason hiked off the trail. He didn't have to go far. The reflection came from a pair of glasses on a man's face.

"Oh, shit," Abbey said when she saw the body in the beam of his flashlight.

The manager of the Three Mountains casino, Andrew Yee, lay in the desert, his body stripped naked. He'd been shot in the throat.

THIRTY-FOUR

WHAT did you say you do, Mr. Briggs?" the Henderson realtor asked Jason the following morning.

Bourne whipped off his sunglasses and gave her a grin. He dropped a little Texas twang into his voice. "Construction engineering, darling. Mostly in Dubai and Qatar. They love their big glass buildings over there."

The Indian realtor, whose name was Iniya, smiled back with extremely white teeth. She was well into her forties but wealthy enough to look thirty. She had shoulder-length jet-black hair, overly red lips set against honey-colored skin, and smoldering green eyes. She wore a formfitting emerald designer dress, probably imported from Milan, and her breasts had been surgically enhanced to the size of small watermelons.

"And this would be . . . *Mrs.* Briggs?" Iniya asked, nodding at Abbey with pointed curiosity.

Abbey's expression was severe. She had her hair tied

tightly behind her head, and she wore an expensive two-piece navy suit they'd purchased in the Green Valley shops an hour earlier. "I'm Mr. Briggs's attorney."

"Oh, I see. Yes, of course."

"Abigail here is a Harvard Law grad," Jason went on. "I can't say as I'm much of a fan of Hahvud types generally, but this gal is as smart as they come. My deal in Doha last fall? She out-negotiated some construction law hotshots from London twice her age on the procurement contracts and cut my sub costs by a third. The fact that she's also mighty pretty to look at is just a bonus."

"And you're interested in building a house in the Sensara neighborhood?" Iniya asked.

"I am. Looks like my kind of homes up there. I like to have elbow room."

"I understand, and you obviously have good taste, Mr. Briggs."

"Charlie. Call me Charlie, Iniya. If we're working together, we should be on a first-name basis."

The realtor touched Jason's shoulder with her long fingernails. "Okay. Charlie. Now, I do need to mention that the Sensara neighborhood is the most exclusive community in the Las Vegas valley. Privacy and security are both at a premium. You can expect to spend a minimum of seven to ten million dollars on a property there, and some of the homes have cost much more. Upwards of twenty million or even higher. Is that a price range with which you're comfortable?"

Jason nodded toward Abbey. "Am I comfortable with that, Abigail?"

"It's fine."

"Abigail says it's fine," Jason told the realtor. "I leave the dollars and cents to her."

"There's also a background check before a prospective buyer can move forward. A rather extensive one."

"Good to know. Every club has its membership rules, right? But of course, I have nothing to hide."

"I'm sure," Iniya said.

"How about we go take a look-see at the home sites? I assume the powers that be wouldn't object to that?"

"Of course, that's fine. You'll need to leave your IDs at the guard gate. And I assume you're not armed? Guests can't bring weapons into Sensara."

Jason smiled. "You're talking to a man from Texas, darling. We're always armed. But I left my guns at the hotel suite. Figured they might make my future neighbors nervous."

"Then let's go."

The three of them used Iniya's red Mercedes sedan to drive into the upper reaches of the Henderson hills, where the Volvo had gone the previous night. At the guard gate, Bourne supplied a driver's license for himself and a passport for Abbey, and he hoped that her name didn't trigger any red flags on a watch list. The guards took a close look at their faces but didn't otherwise react. When they'd passed inspection, Iniya drove them through the gates, and they found themselves in a world of custom multimillion-dollar homes set amid the rocky peaks. Many of the homes were finished; others were in the process of being built.

"There are still a number of homesites left throughout the hills," Iniya told them. "Most feature unobstructed views of the Strip."

"I can see that," Jason said.

"Did you choose the Las Vegas area for a particular reason?" she asked.

"Oh, I like it hot. Usually, I'm in Dallas or the Middle East. I'm a bit of a gambling man, so I like having a place to stay that I can call my own when I come to town."

"Naturally."

"Mind if we stop for a minute and let me stretch my legs, Iniya? I like to have boots on the ground when I judge a place."

"Yes, of course, Charlie."

The realtor parked the red Mercedes on one of the streets that curved around the hillside terraces. Bourne and Abbey both got out, and Jason put his hands on his hips and sighed loudly, as if admiring the views. He strolled up the street and surveyed each of the estates looming above him, one by one. They were all lavish, multistory mansions clinging to the sides of the mountain. Any of them could have been home to Medusa. Or perhaps all of them were. Then he spotted one particular estate higher than the others, with a commanding location above the valley and all of the wealthy neighbors situated below him. It was much larger than the rest, built in modules of rich stone and marble, with a series of flat roofs. On one of the roofs, he could see a helicopter, so the owner didn't have to deal with the Las Vegas traffic. From where he was, he could also see a lineup of catering trucks parked on the road that led to the estate.

"Looks like somebody's having a party tonight," Jason said.

Iniya followed his gaze. "Oh, yes. A wedding reception actually."

"Who's getting married?"

The realtor hesitated. "I'm afraid I can't give out any names, Charlie. As I mentioned, privacy is paramount here. Should you choose to build, of course, you'll find the residents here very welcoming."

"Sure, sure." Jason continued to study the house at the top of the mountain. "Definitely the primo spot up there."

"Yes, it was the first house built in the community."

"Are those bighorn sheep I see? Wandering on the grounds?"

Iniya flushed with embarrassment. "Yes, the owner created something of a preserve for the animals."

"Guess we all have our quirks," Jason said.

Abbey arrived at Jason's side, and she leaned close enough to whisper in his ear. "Check out the *eye*."

Bourne took another look at the sprawling estate above them, and he saw it now. An elaborate series of fountains sprayed like geysers from one of the swimming pools, and the water in the centermost fountain formed a kind of screen on which was projected a huge, ultra-high-definition video image of a single human eye. As he watched, the eye actually winked at him.

He'd seen that eye before, on the phone he'd taken

from the thug in the New York subway. It showed up on the welcome screen for the Prescix software.

Jason and Abbey exchanged a glance. Then he smiled at the realtor.

"So this reception tonight," he said. "Are you going, Iniya?"

"I am, actually. My husband and I are both going. I've been the principal sales agent on the entire project, so I know everyone here. A limo will be picking us up and whisking us to the party. It's all very lovely. You'll discover that people in Sensara know how to do things right."

"Must be a hot ticket."

"Oh, it is. Several hundred people, I believe. Guests are flying in from all over the world."

"Wish I could go and meet some of my future neighbors," Bourne said. "Any chance you could snag an invite for me and Abigail?"

"Truly, I wish I could, Mr. Briggs, but it's simply not possible."

"I understand completely," Jason replied. "No worries at all. I'm sure you and your husband will have a nice time. Where did you say you two live again?"

GABRIEL Fox," Jason announced as he checked the fit of the black tuxedo jacket in the mirror. "The founder, designer, and principal shareholder of Prescix. He's the one who lives in the castle on the hill in Sensara. I found a reference to his house in a tech magazine."

Abbey replied from behind the curtain in the private dressing room. They were in an upscale boutique in the Forum Shops at Caesars. "It fits, doesn't it? Medusa uses Prescix, so it makes sense that the founder would also be involved with Medusa. Maybe that was the whole point of building the software."

"Maybe."

"You don't think so?"

"I think if Medusa already owned Prescix, the tech cabal would know about it. Prescix is part of Medusa's plan, but they don't have what they want yet."

"Then why did the SUV pick up the casino manager and take him to Gabriel Fox's estate to be murdered?"

Bourne frowned. "I don't know. Hopefully, we'll find out at the party tonight."

"Assuming they let us in," she said.

"Don't worry about that."

"I'm coming out," Abbey called from the dressing room. "Are you ready to be dazzled?"

Jason smiled. "Ready."

He waited as Abbey pulled back the curtain and emerged wearing a purple cocktail dress with flowers and swirls beaded over the fabric. The fringed hem fell only to the middle of her thighs and showed off her legs, and the deep V revealed the swell of her breasts. She did a little spin in her matching high heels, making the fringe fly, and then she smirked and balanced one hand on her hip.

"Well?"

"Wow," Jason said.

"Does that mean you approve?"

"It means I'm concerned no one will be able to take their eyes off you. You may look too beautiful."

"Thank you, sir," Abbey said as she came and stood next to him in front of the mirror. "You know this thing costs like six months of my rent."

"You're worth it. We need to look the part."

"I need to get my hair done, too. Men can get away with the scruffy look, but not women."

"Our next stop is the salon," Jason said. "We'll have them package up the clothes and be on our way."

"Are you going to tell me how you plan to get us into that party?" Abbey asked.

"You probably don't want to know."

"Tell me anyway. I mean, we don't have an invitation."

"But Iniya does."

Abbey looked confused as she thought about what he meant. Then she inhaled with a sharp gasp as she understood. "Jesus. You're not going to kill her, are you, Jason?"

"No."

"It's one thing to kill people from Medusa. They're trying to kill *us*. But this woman isn't Medusa."

"You're right. At least I don't think she is. My plan isn't to kill her, Abbey. If I had to do something like that, I'd go there alone. Not with you."

Abbey was quiet for a while. "Because sometimes you *do* have to do things like that. Right?"

"Sometimes."

"You kill innocent people."

"I'm not going to lie to you, Abbey."

"Would you have killed me if I got in your way?"

Jason said nothing.

She stared into the mirror and admired how she looked in the dress, but the sparkle had gone out of her eyes. "I don't know how you can live in your world. I really don't."

"There are days when I don't know either," he said.

She didn't look at him as she walked back behind the curtain. "Well, I signed on for this. I came with you."

He heard her changing, and he switched out of the tux into his other clothes as she did. A few minutes later, she came out from the dressing room, and she was Abbey Laurent again, not a fashion model. The cocktail dress hung on a hanger, and she gave it to him to pay for without a word. Her face was unhappy. He'd seen that face on women in the past. Women who'd discovered the man he really was.

"Are you okay?" he asked.

"Fine."

"I can do this myself. You don't have to go."

"No. It's a party. You're less obvious if you're not alone, right? Isn't that what it says in your *Life According to Treadstone* book?"

"Yes."

"So let's go."

Abbey headed for the display area of the store. He knew, right then, at that moment, that she hated him. He was bothered enough by her reaction that he forgot about the camera he'd spotted in the ceiling of the boutique. He didn't remind her to keep her head down and her face out of sight.

NASH Rollins didn't see a caller ID when his cell phone rang. Normally, the Treadstone phones could unmask the number of anyone who was calling, but not this time. He took the call and barked, "Who is this?"

"Hello, Nash," Miles Priest said in his gravelly voice.

"Ah. Miles. Of course. Do you have information for me?"

"I do. You wanted us to focus on the woman. That was a good call. She's in Las Vegas. We caught her on facial recognition in the Forum Shops."

"Are she and Bourne still together?"

"So it appears."

"Do you know what they're doing there?" Nash asked.

"No."

"Las Vegas," he said. "I'm not surprised that Cain would go back there, since we think it's a Medusa stronghold. All right, I'll take care of it."

"See that you do," Miles replied.

The phone went silent as Miles hung up. Nash immediately dialed another number. "Get the jet ready," he told the woman who answered. "Tell the director I have to go to Nevada tonight."

THIRTY-FIVE

'M sorry about this," Jason told Iniya as he secured the realtor and her husband to the headboard of their bed. He made sure the duct tape was secure, and he checked the gags on their mouths. "It should only be a few hours. When I'm done, I'll call the police and let them know you're here. They'll release you."

The Indian woman's green eyes were wild with fear.

"Your husband will be fine," Jason added. "He should wake up in a few minutes."

The realtor's husband had fought back despite a gun aimed at his chest, and Bourne had been forced to incapacitate him with a blow to the head that left the man bloody. He was still unconscious on the bed next to his wife.

"I'm sorry," Jason said again.

He went back downstairs, where Abbey waited for him, looking perfect in her purple cocktail dress. She held the hand-lettered invitations to the Gabriel Fox party in her hand. Their keys to the Prescix kingdom, which Iniya had given them at gunpoint. When Abbey looked at him now, there was something different in her eyes, as if she needed distance from Jason to keep herself safe. She came up to him with a serious expression and said, "There's blood on your face."

Abbey wet her finger and wiped it off.

"The limo's outside," she told him.

"We should go."

They didn't talk as the car drove them to Sensara. A long line of cars waited at the guard gate, stretching for almost a quarter mile. This time, the guards simply confirmed that the occupants of the vehicles had their invitations and waved them into the neighborhood. There were no searches, no metal detectors. That was what he'd expected, so he'd taken the risk of keeping his gun in the holster on his back, rather than leaving it behind. The limo dropped Jason and Abbey at the gates outside Gabriel Fox's giant property, where servers welcomed them with champagne. Abbey held Jason's hand as they wandered onto the estate grounds past an elaborate cactus garden. Her grip was limp.

Dozens of people in upscale finery surrounded them as they neared the house. The lights were low, creating romantic shadows. Night had fallen, and a vast map of lights came on throughout the Las Vegas valley far below them. The air had turned cooler, and a stiff breeze swirled across the mountaintop. When they got to the estate, they found their way to one of the balconies behind the swimming pools, and Jason did a survey of the guests around them. He saw faces he knew from the business world, from government, from the media, and a few celebrities, too. Some of them might have recognized Bourne if they'd looked closely, but the dim light provided cover, and when anyone looked at the two of them, they saw Abbey, not him. She was a beautiful vision in her dress, and she knew how to play the part.

Even so, he hated the coolness he felt from her. That told him something that he didn't want to face. His feelings for her were real.

"It looks like our hosts have arrived," Abbey murmured.

Jason followed her gaze.

Gabriel Fox and his bride joined the party in spectacular fashion. A gleaming cylindrical steel tower rose slowly from the middle of the swimming pool fountains, rotating slowly as it ascended, until it stopped high above the crowd of guests, thirty feet in the air. White spotlights shined on two people standing on the small platform at the top, behind a gold railing.

One was Gabriel Fox. The squat, pudgy CEO of Prescix wore a black-and-white leopard print tuxedo with black silk lapels, with a matching leopard print pillbox hat on top of his head. Fox carried a flaming metal torch that looked as if it had come from the Olympics, and he raised it high as the tower slowly made another circle over the crowd. The heat of the fire made his round face glow. He grinned below his thick brown mustache.

Bourne was more focused on the woman with him. His bride.

She was incredibly tall and sleek, so thin as to look gaunt. Her coal-black hair was pulled behind her and tied in a tight knot, and a diamond tiara sat on her head like a crown. She wore a jeweled see-through lace top that left her torso essentially nude, and below, she wore a leopard print miniskirt that matched Gabriel's tuxedo. Her smile showed only pale peach lips, and her icy blue eyes missed nothing. She didn't move or wave or acknowledge any of the people below her.

"I think that's the scariest bitch I've ever seen," Abbey said.

Jason couldn't take his eyes off the woman. Abbey glanced his way and saw his fixation.

"Are you okay?" she asked.

"I know her."

"What?"

"I know her," he repeated.

The woman with Gabriel Fox was unforgettable, and he'd seen her before. Just once. She'd been there on one of the worst days of his life. When he ran for the Lucky Nickel hotel after the shooting, he'd found the parking lot crowded with people screaming as they bolted from the exits. It was chaos; the people were in panic. But not all of them. There had been one woman who walked calmly away, utterly unfazed by the violence around her. One woman, tall, cold, confident. Their eyes had met for a brief moment. She'd seen *him* and given him the strangest smile, both erotic and chilling. He'd wondered who she was, but a moment later, he'd spotted Nash Rollins, and the thin, blue-eyed Amazon had disappeared from his mind.

Until now.

Bourne knew. Seeing her here, he knew the truth.

"She killed Nova," he said.

He didn't have time to say anything more or to answer the questions on Abbey's face, because at that moment, Gabriel Fox spoke into a microphone that broadcast his voice around the estate. "Ladies and gentlemen, thank you for joining me here today. The party will last all night, and I want you to enjoy all the amenities of my home. What I have is yours. If you're wondering what to do next, well, just check your Prescix account for advice. Because Prescix will know before you do."

A wave of nervous laughter rippled through the crowd.

"Before we kick off the celebration, let me introduce you to the woman who is now my partner in sex, love, and life . . . especially sex. Trust me when I tell you that you don't want to call her by any other name than this . . . the incredible *Miss Shirley*."

The woman next to Gabriel on the tower held up her hand to wave like a queen, still with the same frozen smile. She might as well have been a statue, perfectly carved. Simultaneously, fireworks shot from the roof of the estate, making multicolored flowers in the night sky and causing rippling waves of thunder under their feet. Around them, the entire crowd burst into applause.

"Miss Shirley," Abbey murmured, eyeing the woman on the platform. "Holy shit. That's her. She's Medusa."

"I'm betting she runs the whole Las Vegas operation," Bourne said.

"You can't let her see you," Abbey told him. "She'll know who you are. We'll never get out of here alive."

"I know."

"What did you mean when you said she killed Nova?"

"She was at the Lucky Nickel. I *saw* her. I don't know if Hackman pulled the trigger or if she did, but she was there."

"Do you think Gabriel knows who she is? *What* she is?"

"We need to find out."

Jason watched the elevated platform slowly descend to the level of the fountains. When it did, stepping-stones emerged out of the water that allowed Gabriel Fox to lead Miss Shirley back to the patio. He saw them mingling with the guests one by one, but he noticed that Miss Shirley never looked at the person she was talking to. Instead, like a predatory reptile, her eyes moved constantly, as if looking for prey. He took Abbey's hand and backed away into the shadows, where they couldn't be seen.

"I have to get Gabriel alone," he said.

"How do you plan to do that?"

Bourne studied the sprawling grounds of the estate. There seemed to be people everywhere, wandering in the darkness. He saw lights in every room, and all the walls were made of glass, allowing others to look inside. Then he glanced at the multilevel roof, which was unlit. No one was up there, not even security.

"Find one of the servers," Jason told Abbey. "Tell them to deliver a message to Gabriel Fox. For him only, no one else. Say that Miles Priest has an urgent private message for him, and he sent someone who's waiting on the roof."

"Do you think he'll come?"

"If he's *not* Medusa, he'll come. If he is, well, he'll tell Miss Shirley, and she'll send others."

Abbey's lips pushed into a thin line. "Okay."

"Can you do this?"

"Of course."

"After you've delivered the message, wait for me near the gates. There's a cactus garden down there that we passed as we were coming in. Stay out of sight. I'll be there as soon as I can. We may need to leave quickly."

He expected her to argue as she had in the past. He half wanted her to say that she wouldn't let him go alone, that she wanted to be with him. But she didn't. Not this time. Instead, she brushed back her hair and told him in a calm voice, "Don't get yourself killed, Jason."

Abbey disappeared into the crowd. He waited until she was gone, and then he made his way to the nearest glass doors leading into the estate itself. He passed through bizarrely decorated open spaces as he hunted for stairs that led to the next level. On the second floor, he did the same. And then again. When he got to the top floor, he found exterior stairs that took him to the roof.

From up here, he had an unobstructed view of the

people, the grounds, the Sensara neighborhood, and the rest of Las Vegas. Near the estate wall and the outer gates, where limousines continued to deliver more guests, he could make out the silhouettes of towering saguaros, chollas, and prickly pears in the cactus garden. Pinpoint snow-white lights shimmered in the breeze. He couldn't see if Abbey had made it there yet. He wondered for a moment if she would leave without him and he would never see her again. Maybe that would be better for both of them.

Jason checked his watch and waited.

Half an hour passed, and he was still alone. He found himself pacing, letting the mountain breeze wash across his face. When an hour had passed, he began to think that Gabriel Fox had chosen to ignore his message.

Then he heard footsteps approaching on the roof stairs. He reached for the holster in the small of his back, but he heard only one set of footsteps, rather than the boots of Medusa's army. A few seconds later, the CEO of Prescix joined him. Gabriel took off his pillbox hat and draped his leopard print tuxedo coat over his arm. He approached warily, but he also had a curious expression.

"Jason Bourne. I don't recall seeing your name on the invitation list. Then again, what's a wedding without a party crasher?"

"You don't sound surprised to see me."

"I'm not. Remember, my business is tech. Do you think anything happens on my estate that isn't observed and recorded? I knew you were here from the second you stepped foot out of that limousine."

"And yet you let me in," Bourne said. "You could have had security turn me away."

Gabriel assessed Bourne like an exhibit of bones in a museum. "Frankly, I was curious about why you're here. Are you going to kill me? Is that the plan?"

"No."

"Well, good," the man replied with a chuckle. "I don't mind missing the party, but I'd sure hate to miss the wedding night."

Bourne frowned. The easy confidence in Gabriel's attitude bothered him. The CEO knew Jason was at the party, and yet he'd come to the roof alone to confront an assassin, seemingly without concern or fear. Something was wrong.

"Anyway, you dragged me up here," Gabriel went on in the same casual drawl. He twirled his pillbox hat in his fingers. "I assume Miles Priest didn't really send you. So what do you want?"

"I came to warn you."

"About what?"

"Your wife," Jason said.

Gabriel's mouth broke into a wide smile. "Ah, you know Miss Shirley, do you? People who meet her rarely forget the experience."

"I know she's Medusa."

The tech billionaire wandered toward the edge of the roof and stared down at the party. "You and Miles. All these fairy tales about Medusa. We've become a society addicted to conspiracy theories."

"Medusa is real, and your new wife is in the middle of

it. If she married you, it's because you've got something they want, and we both know what that is. Prescix."

Gabriel shook his head impatiently. He spoke without turning around. "I'm surprised at you, Bourne. Do you really think I would get involved with a woman—even a woman as *talented* as Miss Shirley—without knowing everything about her? Believe me, I know exactly who she is and what she's done."

"Do you know she's a killer?"

Gabriel chuckled as he walked back to Bourne. "And a very good one, too."

"You don't care?"

"Care? It was one of the things I found most attractive about her. Did it never occur to any of you that a killer is what *I* need? You and Miles seem to think that Miss Shirley is using me, that Medusa is using me. I'm one of the most successful entrepreneurs in the world, Bourne. I know what I'm doing. The fact is, I'm using *them*."

"To accomplish what?"

"To take over the tech cabal, of course. To turn the game around. Tomorrow, Miss Shirley and I will head to Nassau, where Miles and his friends will try to persuade me to join forces with them. I intend to do just that. Say what you want about Miles, but strategically, he's always right. The tech companies need to stand as one. But when all is said and done, I plan to be the person in charge, not him. Prescix will call the shots and start acquiring the other companies. And once that's done, Miss Shirley and I will launch the next part of our plan."

"Namely?"

"We'll take over Medusa, too. Me and her together."

Bourne could see the depth of the man's ego. He wasn't just a rich, harmless eccentric. He was brilliant but also a megalomaniac. Everything that Prescix could do, all the damage it could cause, had been in this man's head all along. He'd intended from the beginning to write software that would let him control people.

But that was the kind of power that others wanted, too. Once Pandora's box was open, it couldn't be closed.

"You're making a mistake, Gabriel."

"Am I?"

"Medusa is stronger than you are. Right now, they're giving you what you want. They're letting you think you're in control. But once they have what they need, you're expendable."

"Actually, you're the one who's expendable, *Cain*. You're a chess piece who's stayed on the board much longer than necessary. Pawns don't win the game. They get sacrificed. Which is what happens next."

"Or I could kill *you* right now," Jason said, reaching behind his back for his pistol.

Gabriel shrugged and began to place the pillbox hat back on his head. "You do what you have to do, Bourne."

Jason stared at the CEO in confusion. And then he realized. The hat was a signal. Gabriel hadn't shown any concern about meeting him, because all along, he'd had Bourne in the gunsights of another assassin. *When I put the hat back on, take him out.* Jason lunged forward just as the bullet from a rifle hidden in the hills cracked past the back of his head, missing him by a millimeter. He launched himself into Gabriel, knowing the tangle of bodies bought him a couple of seconds to grab his own pistol. Then, as he broke free and charged for the roof stairs, he laid down a continuous rain of fire toward the assassin's lair in the dark hills. Shot after shot went wild, but the cover was enough. He threw himself down the steps just as a cloud of stucco blew off the wall where the shooter barely missed him again.

He thundered level by level through the estate, pushing through the crowd of panicked guests on his way to the garden. He only had seconds to get there.

If they knew Bourne was here, then they knew Abbey was here, too.

ABBEY felt a little bit of a chill. High up on the mountain, the air was cooler than on the valley floor. She followed a figure eight sidewalk through the cacti sprouting from the rocks, retracing her footsteps the way she'd been doing for more than an hour. One part of her mind told her to leave right now. To go through the gate and go home to Canada. To forget about Jason Bourne and whether he lived or died.

But another part of her mind made her stay. That was the part that realized she was falling in love with him.

Fool!

She told herself that, but it didn't matter. She felt something for Jason, and she couldn't turn it off or walk away. It didn't matter who he was or what he'd done.

When she heard footsteps approaching on the garden path, her heart sped up with relief, and the only thing she wanted to do was run to him. She'd been terrified that he wasn't coming back. That she'd lost him forever.

But when she turned around, it wasn't Jason standing there.

It was Miss Shirley.

"Abbey Laurent," the woman said from behind her arctic blue eyes. "What a treat. I've been wanting to meet you for a while now."

Instinctively, Abbey took a step backward. Miss Shirley kept coming closer atop her high heels. The woman had a hand hidden behind her back. Her white dress glowed under the garden lights, but her face was in shadow.

"You did such a good job for us, Abbey," Miss Shirley went on, taunting her. "The articles you wrote. About Hackman, about Ortiz. What a good little stooge for Medusa you were. I chose you myself, you know. I told Carson to find you. I told him what to say. You did everything we hoped for, except for one little thing. You forgot the fact that you were supposed to *die* a while ago. We tried in New York. We tried in Quebec. And yet here you are. I'm really rather upset that you're still alive."

"Go to hell, you crazy bitch."

"Oh, Abbey. So foolish. So brave. I wouldn't have thought it. Is that Jason's influence? You've spent a lot of time with him lately. I really have to know, are you sleeping with him? Did he fall for that girl-next-door look of yours? Did you seduce a cold-blooded assassin?"

"You don't know who he really is."

"Oh, I know exactly who he is. You're the naive one."

"Go to hell," she said again.

Miss Shirley smiled with just her lips. Her hand emerged from behind her back, with a knife clutched in her fingers. The knife had a two-foot blade that was curved like a crescent moon. "You're very attractive, Abbey. If we had more time, I'd show you what a real woman is like in bed. All it would take is one night, and trust me, you'd never want to be with a man again. Even Bourne."

"Robots don't turn me on," Abbey snapped.

"You'd be surprised."

"Are you jealous? Is that it? You want Jason for yourself, and you know you'll never have him?"

"There are very few things I want that I can't have," Miss Shirley replied. "Right now, I want *you*. Bleeding. Begging me for mercy."

Abbey spun away to run, but when she did, she found herself trapped by a huge security guard in a black suit who gathered her up in his arms. She hadn't even heard him sneak up behind her. He turned her around so that she had no choice but to face Miss Shirley. Abbey squirmed furiously but couldn't get away. Miss Shirley came up directly in front of her. Her breath was on Abbey's face, and she was close enough to scrape the point of the knife gently over the skin of her shoulder, leaving a red trail.

"Such a lovely dress," she said. "Did Jason buy it for you?"

She flicked the knife and cut away one of the straps,

making the dress slide down Abbey's chest, exposing one of her breasts.

"Beautiful. Pert and perfect."

"Stop playing games," Abbey said. "If you're going to kill me, kill me."

"Oh, let's not get ahead of ourselves. I could just slice open your throat, of course, and you'd be gone in a couple of minutes, but where's the fun in that? I told you, I want to hear you beg. Now, where should I make the first cut? Your fingers? Your delicate little ears? I could take each of your breasts first, how about that? This is a very, very sharp blade. Two little swishes, and they'd be gone. Imagine how terrible it would be for Jason to find you that way. Seeing that naked body he enjoyed desecrated in so many ways."

Abbey spit in her face, and Miss Shirley simply wiped it away and laughed. She cocked the knife, and Abbey squeezed her eyes shut, anticipating the agony.

Then a voice hissed from the darkness. "*Get away from her right now.*"

Bourne emerged from the tall cacti. His gun was inches from the back of Miss Shirley's head. Abbey couldn't help herself. Tears of relief streamed down her cheeks.

"Ah, Jason, I was wondering if you'd be able to join us," Miss Shirley said. "The hero returns in the nick of time. I'd hoped that our shooter would take care of you once and for all, but apparently not. What a shame. Abbey and I were just getting to know each other."

"Drop the knife."

"Of course. If that's what you want."

Miss Shirley opened her fingers, and the knife clattered to the paver stones at her feet. Jason pressed the barrel hard into her neck. "Tell your man to let her go."

"It's all right, Terence," Miss Shirley instructed the guard in the black suit.

The guard removed his arms from around Abbey, and she stumbled across the trail to Jason, her heels tripping on the stones.

"Stay behind me," he told her. "We're heading for the gate."

"You'll never get there," Miss Shirley told them. "At least ten more guards are on their way. You're trapped."

"If I don't make it, neither do you," Bourne replied.

"I'll tell you what, Jason. Let's do a deal. Leave me the girl to play with, and you can go."

Abbey had to swallow down an urge to tell Jason simply to pull the trigger, so they could watch this woman die. She sensed from the tautness of his muscles that Jason was struggling with the same desire. As Abbey held on to his belt, Jason wrapped an arm tightly around Miss Shirley's throat and dragged the woman backward, using her body as a shield. He pointed the gun into her temple as more guards closed in on them from three sides. Abbey acted as his eyes, pulling him backward step by step until they reached the wrought-iron gates of the estate.

There were other guests there, staring wide-eyed at what was happening.

"Open the door on the nearest car, Abbey," Jason instructed her. "Get inside and make sure the driver's ready to go. Tell him I'll shoot him if he hesitates for even a second."

She was sure that Bourne would do just that.

Abbey opened the first limo door and scrambled inside, and she left the door open. Jason dragged Miss Shirley all the way up to the car.

"I should kill you right now," he said.

"You could, but then my men will fire. Everybody loses."

"Jason, let's go," Abbey shouted. "*Hurry.*"

She watched him put one hand on Miss Shirley's back. He shoved hard, pushing her toward the Medusa men. In the same instant, Jason threw himself inside the limo and covered her as he dragged the door shut behind him. The guns were already firing. Bullets shattered the glass all around them and hammered the steel on the doors, and the limo sped away.

THIRTY-SIX

"THEY'RE calling it a failed assassination attempt," Abbey said, scrolling through the news feed on her phone. "'The man believed to be responsible for the shooting of Congresswoman Sofia Ortiz was thwarted by armed security last night in the attempted murder of Gabriel Fox, CEO of Prescix Corporation.'"

"Who do they think I'm working for?" Bourne asked.

"The feds blame 'rogue elements inside Big Tech.'"

Jason shook his head. "Medusa is using this to advance their plan. Do they mention you?"

"I'm an anonymous kidnap victim you used in making your escape," Abbey replied. "I'm not identified by name."

"They're sending you a message by keeping you out of it. You're safe now, but next time, they'll claim you're part of the conspiracy. That's the choice you have to make."

Abbey said nothing. He knew she was wrestling with what to do.

The sky had begun to lighten over the hills with the pink glow of dawn. They sat in the Land Rover in a Henderson parking lot, where they had a vantage on the access road leading in and out of the Sensara community. For hours, a steady stream of vehicles had come and gone. Limousines. Police. FBI. There was no sign yet of Gabriel Fox, but sooner or later, Bourne knew that the man would emerge from seclusion. Along with Miss Shirley.

"Thank you, by the way," Abbey said.

"For what?"

"You saved my life again. It's becoming a habit with you."

"I'm the one who nearly got you killed," Jason said.

"Yes, but I didn't want you to think I don't care. If you hadn't been there, I'd be dead now. That woman—Miss Shirley—do you really think she would have done the things she said? I mean, not just kill me, but . . ."

"Yes, I do. She's a sadist and a psychopath."

"My God. Who are these people? What's their plan?"

"I don't know yet, but I'm hoping Gabriel Fox and Miss Shirley will lead us to the answers."

"Us," Abbey murmured.

He heard the change in her voice, and he turned and stared at her. "I mean *me*. This is my fight, not yours."

She took a long time to say anything more. "I know I insisted on being part of this, Jason, but now I—I think I need to go."

"Of course you do. I *want* you to go. I want you to be safe."

"It's not for the reason you think," Abbey went on. "I'm scared, but I'm not running away. I realized something last night. I'm putting you in danger by being here. I think you know I feel something for you. It's not just attraction, not just sexual. I'm drawn to you, and whatever the feeling is, it's strong. I tried to push it away. I tried to be cold, because some of the things you have to do—they horrify me. But I can't pretend. And the thing is, I think you feel something for me, too."

There was nothing Jason could say to that.

"I know you can't admit it," Abbey went on when she saw that he wouldn't answer her. "That's okay. But I also know that if I'm in danger, that's going to change what you do. Just like it did last night. You're going to put me first, and the result of that is you're more likely to get killed. I can't live with that. I don't want you sacrificing yourself for me."

Jason knew she was right. That was lesson number one they'd drilled into his head.

Emotion is your enemy. Emotion kills. You have to switch off that part of yourself.

Treadstone.

The next part of the journey belonged to him alone. He'd already decided that. He would have left Abbey behind in the night if he had to, to make sure she didn't put herself in any more jeopardy. That was how it had to be.

"There they are," Abbey said, pointing across the street. "They're on the move."

Bourne lifted his binoculars. He saw the vehicle they'd followed two nights ago, the armored Volvo SUV, emerging from the winding road that led to Sensara. He couldn't see through the smoked windows to identify who was inside. This time, there was more than one vehicle leaving the estate. Two other identical SUVs followed the first, like a convoy.

"Let's see where they go," he said.

He pulled into traffic two blocks behind them. As early as it was, there were enough cars on the roads to keep the Land Rover anonymous. The three matching Volvos all followed the same route westward across the city. None of the vehicles had any identifying markings, and the windows were all black. The convoy made slow progress through the city traffic, but when they reached the flat, empty desert land in the far south of the valley, they accelerated. It was easy to keep the three vehicles in sight, and Bourne stayed half a mile back, watching them turn toward Henderson's executive airport.

Before the convoy reached the airport itself, the first of the vehicles turned into the driveway of a large, windowless warehouse. Jason pulled the Land Rover to the curb and watched them. The three SUVs all parked outside a loading dock halfway down the length of the building, and the passengers got out.

He could see them now through his binoculars. Gabriel Fox was there, accompanied by Miss Shirley. The others were security, including faces he recognized from the previous evening. These weren't ordinary guards;

they were clearly trained black-ops men. He counted nine of them.

Medusa.

Miss Shirley walked up to the loading dock and unlocked the door with a key. Two of the guards rolled up the white metal door on its rails, and two others opened up the rear panels of the three Volvos. Then Miss Shirley and Gabriel led them all inside, while one of the guards stayed outside as a sentry.

"Can you see inside the warehouse?" Abbey asked.

"No."

A few minutes later, the guards emerged, pushing hand trucks loaded with wooden crates. One by one, they stored the crates inside the SUVs, and by the time they were done, they'd squeezed two dozen crates into the rear of the Volvos. At that point, they closed the loading dock door, and Miss Shirley relocked it. The vehicles headed back out to the road, and Bourne followed.

"I saw labels stamped on the crates," Abbey said. "What did they say?"

"They were brand names for French vineyards. Champagne."

"Another party?"

"Maybe."

This time, the convoy headed for the airport. Jason stayed behind them until they drove to the fenced area leading to the taxiways, and then he pulled into the airport parking lot and used the binoculars again. The gate slid back, giving the SUVs access, and the Volvos drove in tandem toward a Gulfstream jet parked inside the airport fence. There, Gabriel Fox and Miss Shirley met two uniformed pilots, and the four of them got on board the jet.

Meanwhile, the guards in the SUVs loaded the crates of wine into the baggage compartment of the plane. When they were done, they climbed the steps into the passenger area. The door closed behind them.

Not long after, the jet taxied to the runaway and roared into the sky over the Las Vegas mountains.

"You want me to sweet-talk one of the ground crew and see if they know the flight plan?" Abbey asked.

Jason shook his head. "Gabriel told me that he and Miss Shirley were heading to a meeting of the tech cabal in Nassau. Scott told me they meet on some private island down there."

"You're going to go there, too, aren't you?" Abbey asked.

"Yes." Then he added, "Just me."

Abbey bit her lip, but she didn't protest.

"I'll charter a jet and go after them," Jason said, "but there's something I need to check out first."

Bourne took the Land Rover out of the airport. He retraced the route that the Volvos had taken to the unmarked warehouse a mile away. The parking lot was deserted. He found the loading dock where the convoy had brought out their cargo, and he stopped the Land Rover just outside the door.

He and Abbey both got out. Jason retrieved a crowbar from the back of the truck, and then he went to the loading dock door and used two metal pins from inside his wallet to manipulate the tumblers on the lock. It took him a couple of minutes, and when the lock clicked open, he bent down and threw the door up on its metal rails.

They cautiously entered the dark storage area, which was almost completely filled with wooden crates that matched what had been loaded on the jet. They were all labeled with the names of French wineries. Jason glanced toward the ceiling and saw a series of red lights go on as their motion activated the security cameras. "We don't have much time before we get a lot of company in here," he said.

"What are you looking for?" Abbey asked.

Bourne didn't answer. He went to the nearest crate, which had an ink stamp on the outside for Sarcennes Blanc de Blancs champagne. He wedged the forked blade of the crowbar into the top seam of the crate and pushed hard to loosen the nails on the upper panel. Then he pushed the crate open and shined his flashlight inside.

There was no champagne in the crate.

Instead, he saw military rifles nestled in dense foam, plus magazines and boxes of ammunition.

"Shit," Abbey murmured. She stepped back and assessed the quantity of crates stacked against the wall. "Medusa has enough firepower here to start a war."

"I think that's the plan," Bourne said.

THIRTY-SEVEN

THE jet that would ferry Bourne out of Las Vegas was almost ready to go.

He'd called in a favor from a CEO whose son had been kidnapped in Guatemala a few years earlier and then rescued in a Treadstone mission that Jason had led. The man was happy to arrange a private flight from McCarran to Nassau, no questions asked.

"Take the Land Rover," he told Abbey. "I put twenty thousand dollars in cash in your bag. Drive home. Go back to Quebec City and *The Fort*. Forget about Medusa, and forget about me."

"That's not going to happen," Abbey replied. "You need to call me when this is done."

"If we stay in touch, you're at risk. If anyone thinks they can get to me through you, they'll come after you."

"I don't care. You need to let me know you're safe."

He nodded. "I will if I can."

"*Call* me. Because if you don't, I'm going to assume you're dead."

"I'll call you."

Abbey shook her head in frustration. "I suppose there's no point in telling you to walk away from this. You don't owe anything to the people who hired you. They betrayed you; they tried to have you killed. Let someone else go after Medusa. Not you."

"I'm not doing this for the tech cabal. It's not about them. If I don't stop Medusa, I'll spend the rest of my life running. Always looking over my shoulder. And after what we've found here, this is personal to me, too."

"Because of Nova," Abbey concluded.

"Yes. Medusa killed her. *Miss Shirley* killed her. I can't let that stand."

Abbey came up to him in the McCarran parking lot. He was aware of how achingly pretty she was. Her big eyes were wide and serious. Her bangs hung in messy spikes across her eyes. Having her close to him reminded him of how it felt to have her body in his arms. "You do have a choice, you know. Nova wouldn't want you to die for her. If she really loved you, she'd want you to be free. You have money. Contacts. Skills. Even if you're on the run, you could disappear. I'm sure you know how to do that. Put an end to this, live on a beach somewhere. Anywhere in the world."

"Abbey—"

Before he could say anything more, she put her hands

on his face and whispered to him. "If you asked me, I'd go with you. You get that, right? I'd leave everything behind."

"That's why I can't ask." Jason glanced at the corporate jet, which was in a remote corner of the airport grounds. The pilot flashed him a thumbs-up. "I have to go."

"If that's what you need to do, then go."

Abbey kissed him. He could feel the passion as she held him and the longing as her mouth moved against his. It was a kiss that said she wanted him to stay, a kiss that almost changed his mind. When they broke apart, she took a last long look at him, and then she turned and walked away without another word. She didn't look back. He watched her until she got to the Land Rover, and when she peeled away from the parking lot with the tires screeching, he watched the vehicle until it was lost in the Las Vegas traffic.

"Goodbye, Abbey Laurent," Jason said.

Bourne picked up his duffel bag and slung it over his shoulder. He put on sunglasses and marched through the airport gate onto the tarmac. The jet was waiting for him.

It was time to fight.

ABBEY filled up the Land Rover at a gas station off Paradise Road before heading to the freeway. Her mind was full of Jason, and she was equal parts angry and lonely. She didn't really think about what she was doing. She took cash from her wallet and went inside to prepay, then waited impatiently as the pump dribbled gas into the tank. As it did, she wandered into the middle of the parking lot and watched as a 737 glided over her head to land on the runway at McCarran. She could have waited to see Jason's jet leave, but she didn't want to see the plane that was taking him away from her.

When the tank was full, Abbey went to collect her change and then walked back to the Land Rover. She didn't give a thought to the gas station security cameras, which had a clear view of her face and of the license plate on the SUV.

Traffic crawled on Tropicana heading west to the I-15. Hot air blew through her open window. Eventually, she reached the freeway and headed north past the Strip hotels, reversing the route that she and Jason had taken two nights ago from Mesquite. Road construction slowed her down, and she found a radio station playing fast songs to distract her.

As she passed each exit, another traffic camera registered her vehicle.

The freeway took her out of the valley into the desert hills, where she put the Land Rover on cruise control. Driving back to the cold of Canada would take her several days, but she was in no hurry. She'd continue on I-15 into Utah, head across the mountains toward Denver, and then traverse the flat midwestern lands through Lincoln, Des Moines, and into Chicago. She'd cross the border in Michigan north of Detroit and be back home for the final leg through Ontario into Quebec.

She didn't pay much attention to her surroundings as

she drove. Her mind was elsewhere. Then, half an hour outside Las Vegas, she noticed a black helicopter hovering above the scrubland near the freeway. It was surprisingly low to the ground, with no markings to identify it. After she passed it, she kept an eye on the machine in her mirror, until it disappeared from view as she crested a shallow hill. There was nothing else around her in this section of the road. Utility poles dotted the plains, and rust-colored stone mountains bordered the highway on both sides. She was miles from the nearest town.

Not long after, she noticed something odd. Traffic had completely disappeared from the southbound lanes of the freeway. There wasn't another vehicle to be seen anywhere. When she looked in her mirror, she realized the same was true in her own lane. All the trucks and cars that had been playing tag with her since she left the valley had vanished. She was literally alone in the desert.

Abbey tapped the brakes, feeling a strange sense of foreboding. As she slowed down, a deafening roar erupted outside the Land Rover, so loud and sudden that she screamed. The black helicopter reappeared and shot over the SUV, barely twenty feet above her roof, creating a downdraft that forced her to cling hard to the wheel to avoid driving off the highway. Ahead of her, two SUVs sped toward her, going the wrong way in the northbound lanes, blocking her passage. She slowed as the SUVs wheeled to a stop, angled across both lanes of the freeway directly ahead of her.

When she glanced in her mirror, she saw two more

SUVs approaching from behind and blocking the road from the other direction.

All Abbey could do was stop.

Men with assault rifles poured from the four vehicles, and she screamed again. They were dressed in helmets and paramilitary gear, and they had their guns pointed directly at her. Spreading out, and keeping a safe distance, they surrounded the Land Rover. Meanwhile, the unmarked helicopter drifted to the ground barely fifty yards away, kicking up a fierce cloud of dust in the dry land just beyond the freeway guardrail. The engine cut off, and the whirling rotors slowed.

A voice on loudspeaker boomed from the helicopter.

"Abbey Laurent! Open the door, and keep both hands visible as you exit the vehicle!"

Terrified, Abbey undid her safety belt, pushed open the driver's door of the Land Rover, and stretched out her arms into the warm air as she got out of the SUV. She kept her arms up, her fingers spread wide, as she inched away from the truck.

"Get on your knees! Hands on top of your head!"

Abbey sank to the ground on the hot blacktop and laced her fingers together on her head. "I don't have any weapons!" she shouted. "I'm alone, and I'm unarmed! He's not with me!"

The men approached her slowly, squeezing the circle tighter. Half of them closed on the Land Rover, checking the undercarriage and then pointing their guns in the windows. The other men came close enough to Abbey to brush the barrels of their rifles against her body. One, a large Hispanic man with charcoal smeared under his eyes, shouldered his weapon, then shoved her facedown onto the highway lane. He gave her an invasive pat-down while she lay on her stomach, and then he flipped her over and repeated the process on her front, digging his fingers into her breasts and between her legs.

"Having fun?" Abbey hissed.

The man said nothing.

"I told you, I'm unarmed," she went on. "I know you're looking for him. He's not here."

She lay on her back, her skin burning where her flesh touched the hot pavement. As she watched, the men searched the Land Rover, and when they'd cleared it, one of them relayed a message to the helicopter. A voice responded on radio, but Abbey couldn't make out the words. A moment later, the Hispanic man yanked her off the ground and secured her wrists behind her in cuffs.

"Go," he ordered, pushing her forward with a hard shove. Abbey stumbled, then righted herself and walked across the freeway lanes, with the rifles of the guards following her. They led her to the steel railing, and she climbed awkwardly over it, accompanied by half a dozen men. Footing was treacherous on the rocky ground, and when she slowed, she felt the jab of a gun in the small of her back.

They pushed her toward the helicopter.

As she got closer, the passenger door of the machine opened, and a man got out into the desert.

It was Nash Rollins.

The Treadstone agent leaned on his cane and clutched a fedora in his other hand. His eyes were hidden behind sunglasses. She'd first met him in Quebec City only a few days ago, but somehow he looked older now. The men with guns pushed Abbey forward until she was standing in front of Rollins, and then he dismissed them with a flick of his fingers. The military men retreated, and the two of them were alone by the helicopter.

"Ms. Laurent," Rollins said. "I'm pleased to see you again. Let's make this quick. Where is Jason Bourne?"

THIRTY-EIGHT

BOURNE walked along one of the dozen crowded piers that stretched into the heart of Nassau Harbor. Hundreds of boats bobbed in the pale green water, ranging from beat-up fishing charters to sleek two-hundred-foot yachts. Two soaring highway bridges arched over the inlet's narrow channel, and the pink towers of the Atlantis resort loomed over the white-sand beach of Paradise Island. From where he was, he could see several cruise ship behemoths docked at Prince George Wharf.

The warm late-afternoon sun beat down on his face. He wore a dirty green tank top and loose-fitting cargo shorts, along with a fraying baseball cap, sneakers, and no socks. He hadn't shaved. He'd swapped his leather duffel for an old canvas bag with a shoulder strap. With that look, he blended in as just another Nassau beach bum, one of those urban escapees who'd traded in the nine-to-five world for a downscale island life.

Halfway down the pier, he found what he was looking for, a thirty-foot catamaran with smoked black windows on its bridge and the name *Irish Whiskey* painted along its gleaming-white hull. The owner kept it in pristine shape. The flat boat deck was empty, but someone had been stretched out in the sun recently, leaving behind a half-full pink drink in a hurricane glass and a rippled Tom Clancy paperback that had obviously spent time in the water.

Bourne stepped from the pier onto the boat, feeling it rock under his feet. He didn't announce himself, because if he was in the right place, the owner already knew he was here. He'd talked to half a dozen locals as he tracked down the man on the catamaran, and he was sure that the man's spies had warned him that a stranger was coming his way.

Except Bourne wasn't a stranger.

He dropped his bag on the deck and made his way to the glass door leading to the boat's interior. He opened it, stepped inside, and immediately felt the barrel of a gun pushed against the back of his head.

"Cain," the boat's owner said cheerfully.

"Hello, Teeling."

"I'd say you were getting sloppy, because you made it so easy for me to spot you. But you're never sloppy, are you? That means you wanted me to know you were coming. Presumably, that means you want me to think you're not a threat."

"You're right. I just want to talk. I'm not a threat."

"Well, that's where you're wrong, because the Jason Bourne I know is always a threat."

"My gun's in my bag outside," Bourne told him. "Otherwise, I'm unarmed."

"How'd you find me?"

"You're not as anonymous as you think you are, Teeling. Director Shaw made sure we kept an eye on you after you left. I heard you hopscotched around South America for a couple of years, then landed here. Retirement suits you."

The man grunted. "Seriously? And all this time, I figured if Treadstone ever found me, they'd kill me. Or if they didn't, then the commies would."

Teeling pulled the gun from Bourne's head and gestured toward a white leather sofa that stretched below the boat's slanted windows. The floors and cabinets in the interior were all varnished oak. Bourne sat down, and Teeling went over to the boat's mirrored wet bar and grabbed a bottle of his namesake whiskey. He held up a glass. "You want a shot?"

"No, thanks."

The agent poured one for himself, then sat down at a safe distance. He was well into his seventies, but Bourne wasn't about to underestimate the threat posed by any Treadstone man, and Teeling had been one of the best. They'd only overlapped by a year before Teeling left the agency, but the stories of the man's operations in Russia in the post-Gorbachev era were legendary.

Teeling was around five feet ten, and he'd maintained

a strong build. He wore no shirt, exposing a deep tan interrupted by multiple scars. His turquoise swimsuit came down to his bony knees. He had long gray hair that hung to his shoulders, but his bushy mustache and eyebrows were still mostly black. He had a wrinkled face, with dark eyes that were sharp and bright. He kept his gun loosely in his fingers, pointed at the floor.

"You're a hot commodity these days, Cain," Teeling told him.

"Oh?"

"Yeah, I've been reading about you in the news."

"Don't believe everything you read. I didn't shoot the congresswoman."

"Well, I assumed the stories were bullshit, but I was wondering what was up. The fact that you're here makes me think you'd rather I didn't pick up the phone and call any of our old colleagues."

"You're right."

"Okay. So what do you want from me? No offense, Bourne, but I'm out, and I like being out. I've got money in the bank, a few good spots on the water for yellowtail and snapper, and a couple of local girls who think gray hair is sexy. I'd rather not mess any of that up."

The man made it sound as if he'd left the intelligence world completely behind, but Bourne doubted that was true. Out was never really out at Treadstone. You could leave the life, but it never left you. If only for his personal protection, Teeling was bound to keep a close eye on who was coming and going in Nassau. Bourne was counting on that.

"A private jet probably arrived at Pindling this morning from Nevada," he said. "The jet's owner is Gabriel Fox, CEO of the Prescix Corporation. Did you happen to hear anything about that?"

Teeling grinned. "Any chance Mr. Fox was accompanied by a woman who looks like a major-league ballbuster?"

"A very good chance."

"Well, in fact, word of such an arrival did cross my phone."

"Where did they go?" Bourne asked.

"They headed for the billionaires' marina on the south side of the island. Just them, nine serious dudes, and some crates of thousand-dollar champagne."

"It's not bubbly inside those crates. It's guns."

Teeling shrugged. "Well, this is the Caribbean, Bourne. The curtains don't usually match the carpet."

"Are they still in the marina?"

"No, they boarded one of the mega-yachts moored over there and headed out about two hours ago."

"Going where?"

"That I don't know. There's a lot of water around here and a whole lot of private islands where boats can dock without people keeping an eye on you. You could charter a plane and hope you get lucky, but you don't have much daylight left. So unless you've got a satellite to do a fly-over, you're not going to find them."

"I don't think they're on their own," Bourne said. "They're going to a meeting with other leaders in the tech world. So I suspect there have been other departures from the same marina in the last day or so. Helicopters, too. That sound familiar?"

"It does. Happens a few times a year, actually. This one seems off schedule, though."

"Do you know where they go?"

"You must think my curiosity is endless, Bourne," Teeling said. "Why would I care where a bunch of CEOs go to have deviant sex and plot world takeovers?"

"In other words, you do know."

Teeling got up and poured himself another shot of whiskey. "They pay a lot to shut up the servants and the girls, but rumors go around anyway. It's a beautiful little rock between here and Freeport. I tried to track the ownership, but it's buried under a dozen or so shell companies."

"I think the island is owned by Miles Priest."

Teeling whistled. "Ah, Miles. I should have guessed. He keeps his fingers in every pie, doesn't he? We clashed several times when he was running the FBI."

"Have you ever been out to the island?"

"I sailed close enough to get them nervous once. They've got a pier for the yachts and a helipad, too. There's a big estate up on the hill, but it's mostly hidden in the trees, so you can't catch more than a glimpse from the water. I was close enough to attract some armed security to the beach. Miles values his privacy."

"I need to get out there," Bourne said.

"In other words, you want me to take you?" Teeling asked.

"That's right."

"You got cash? I don't do things like this for old times' sake."

"I've got cash."

Teeling rubbed his chin as he sipped his whiskey. "I assume you don't intend to sail right up to the marina and say hello."

"No."

"Well, I can take you around the other side of the island. There's nothing but rocks back there, but I can only get so close."

"That's okay."

"Odds are, security will see you coming."

"I'll take that chance," Bourne said.

"What exactly do you think is going on out there?" Teeling asked.

Bourne debated how much to say. "Is an organization called Medusa on your radar?"

"I've heard the name, but not much more than that."

"From Treadstone?"

"Actually, no," Teeling told him. "An old Russian comrade retired down here like me. Very much on the QT. We get drunk on Baikal vodka every now and then. He let the name slip last year like it was a hush-hush operation out of Moscow. Made it sound like it was the next stage after their election interference. But even scarier."

"The Russians and Medusa? That's interesting. Did you tell anyone?"

Teeling shrugged. "Why would I? I'm out of the game. What do you think Medusa is planning on the island?"

"I think they're going to open those crates of champagne," Bourne said.

"A party, huh?"

"Sort of."

Teeling's mustache wrinkled. He capped the bottle of whiskey and grabbed a white captain's hat from behind the bar. He shoved it low on his forehead over his long gray hair. The patch on the front of the hat read: *Cut Bait*.

"Guess we better haul ass and get you out there," Teeling said.

BY the time Bourne saw the lush green island rising out of the water ahead of them, it was nearly sunset. The small piece of rock was shaped like a question mark, surrounded by miles of empty ocean. Through the binoculars, he saw a strip of white sand and dense foliage covering the shallow hillside. The roof and upper floor of a large estate barely cleared the tree line. A sleek yacht was docked at the pier that stretched from the beach into the deeper water.

Bourne handed the binoculars to Teeling. "Is that the boat?"

"That's the one. Looks like they've unloaded some of those crates you were talking about. I don't think we want to stay out here in plain sight for very long."

"All right, let's head around to the far side. Move in as close as you can, but don't draw attention to yourself."

"Not my first rodeo, Bourne," Teeling replied with a

wink as he revved the boat's engine. The wind made his long gray hair fly. "Seems like you're going up against an army. You want some backup in there?"

"I don't want to mess up your retirement, Teeling."

"Well, I appreciate that, although to be honest, there are days when I do miss the game. Tell you what, I'll find a quiet spot on the horizon to drop a line. You need a round-trip ticket, you let me know, okay?"

"Thanks."

Teeling navigated the catamaran westward until the beach disappeared from view, and then he steered closer, making the small island loom larger in front of them. The water got choppier, and the boat rose and fell like a bucking bronco with the waves. On this side, the island looked like a lonely patch of wilderness looming out of the ocean. Bourne saw trees crowded together and whitecaps breaking on the rocks at the shore. No one was visible.

As the catamaran neared to within a hundred yards of the island, Bourne slipped off the boat into the cool ocean water. He'd changed into a black neoprene wet suit, and he had his gun, knife, and shoes secured inside a waterproof pouch in the zippered jacket. He waited as the boat passed him and veered toward the open sea, and then he swam for the island with measured strokes. The late-evening shadows and cresting waves kept him out of sight. He reached the rocky beach within a few minutes, but he lingered off the coast before emerging from the water, in case a welcoming party was prepared to meet him.

However, the isolated beach seemed quiet. Too quiet.

He was sure that Miles Priest would maintain surveillance on any craft drawing near to the island, particularly if a meeting of the tech cabal was underway. He would have expected the catamaran to draw guards to the beach, even if the craft made no attempt to land. Instead, there was no one. He was alone.

Bourne shouldered his way out of the water. He retrieved his gun from inside the jacket and felt better with it in his hand. He looked up and down the thin, ragged coastline, which ended in a green wall of Caribbean pines, mahogany, and palm trees. Surf slapped on the shore, and a light, humid breeze blew across his wet skin. Birds chattered loudly over his head, as if agitated.

Something felt wrong.

Not far away, he saw a break in the trees that marked a trail leading inland. He spotted a flash of color near the path, and when he looked more closely, he recognized red stripes on the tough rubber frame of a Zodiac that had been dragged from the water and hidden inside the brush. He wasn't the first visitor on the island. Bourne kept low as he jogged for the trees where the boat had been stowed. He thought about disabling it with his knife, but he decided to leave it intact, in case he needed to use the craft for his own escape.

He continued deeper into the trees, but he hadn't gone twenty feet before he spotted a body sprawled across the sandy path.

He stopped, listening for other movement. He spun, slowly, with his gun arm outstretched. When he was convinced he was alone, he approached the body and saw a muscular black man in the beige uniform of a security guard. The man's gun holster was empty, and his throat had been cut in a deep red slash. Bourne checked for a pulse and found none, but the body was still warm. The assault had been recent.

Medusa was already making its way into the heart of the tech cabal.

Still crouched by the body, Bourne looked up sharply as he heard the crack of gunfire from the eastern side of the island.

He got to his feet and ran through the jungle.

THIRTY-NINE

MISS Shirley perched on the white-sand beach with her hands on her hips. Gabriel Fox stood next to her, in a red Chinese silk robe decorated with a fierce dragon. From behind her sunglasses, she watched the posse of the tech cabal arrive to greet them. Five of the group's CEOs piled out of a Jeep, and two others exited a second Jeep, along with two security guards in uniform. Seeing the guards, Miss Shirley casually tapped two fingers on her hip in a wordless signal to the Medusa operatives standing next to the artillery crates stacked on the pier. She saw the leader of the team acknowledge the signal with the barest of nods, and her men began using crowbars to loosen the lids.

She'd long ago memorized the names, biographies, and corporate histories of the CEOs who met on the is- land. Tyler Wall led the group, his hair and beard nearly to his waist. He was dressed as he always was, in a flowing gown with a staff that made him look like Moses returning from the mountain. Hon Xiu-Le, the diminutive social messaging wizard from Shanghai, walked beside him, dressed in black despite the warm day. The two appeared to be the appointed spokespeople for the cabal, with the other five executives hanging back beside the security guards. Four were men; one was a woman. They were all Americans.

Miles Priest wasn't among the welcoming party, which likely meant that the Carillon CEO hadn't yet arrived on the island. That was a setback, but she couldn't let it delay their plans.

"Gabriel!" Tyler Wall announced in a booming voice, striding up to them and extending his hand. "How are you, man? Good to see you. Welcome to the island. You'll love it here. I may not always see eye to eye with Miles about things, but he and Nelly don't skimp when it comes to entertaining."

Gabriel stepped forward to let his fingers get wrapped up in Wall's burly hand. "Tyler, how goes the world of microrobotics? I heard a doctor at Mayo took one of your latest critters on a test-drive through somebody's innards. No more cameras up your ass, just swallow a robot and let it cruise through your colon."

"Good to see you keep up on my work, Gabe," Wall replied.

"Oh, trust me, I keep up on everybody's work."

"Well, that's what partnership is all about, buddy. Hey, have you met Hon Xiu-Le?"

"I haven't, but I'm looking forward to it."

Xiu-Le stepped forward and made a slight bow. Miss Shirley noticed the jaundiced look the Shanghai entrepreneur gave Gabriel's robe, which was tied loosely with a sash over his ample waist and only dropped to his mid-thighs. "Mr. Fox, we are honored by your presence at long last. I hope this is the beginning of a close and trusting relationship among our various companies."

Gabriel winked. "Your messaging data, Hon, and my behavioral algorithms. Now, that's a marriage made in heaven. Oh, and speaking of marriage, I need to introduce you folks to my wife and business partner. Me, I'm just the eye candy around here. She's the one with the brains and the balls. Gents, this is Miss Shirley."

Miss Shirley gave the two CEOs a frigid smile and offered up one hand to be kissed. Their eyes traveled over her body, which was barely contained by a Brazilian bikini tied with the skimpiest of white strings. Wall didn't hide his hunger as he looked at her. Hon Xiu-Le was more discreet, but he made a deep bow, with his face close enough that he could have licked her breasts like an ice cream cone.

"I've heard stories about you, Shirley, but they don't do you justice," Wall told her, shaking his head in awe.

"It's *Miss* Shirley," she instructed him.

"Well, isn't it really *Mrs.* Shirley, now that you two have tied the knot?" the CEO replied with a chuckle.

"No," she said in a tone that brooked no argument.

Wall laughed again, but he looked uncomfortable when he realized that she wasn't joking.

"You're going to want to remember what she says

about that, Tyler," Gabriel warned him. "Miss Shirley is particular about how you address her. That's not a mistake you want to make more than once. When I did it, I felt those nails of hers in places you do not want to feel nails, believe me."

"Okay, that's good to know, *Miss* Shirley," Wall said. "I have to tell you, all of us here are curious about the people you work for. A private equity group with the resources to make a play for Prescix? Impressive. But you know, the members of our little cabal don't lose very graciously. I think we'd all like to find a way to bring Prescix into our fold. Who knows, maybe we can lure you away from your current employers and get you on our side."

"Unlikely."

"Well, wait until you hear our offer before you say that," Wall replied with a wink.

"Where is Nelly Lessard?" Miss Shirley demanded, cutting him off. "Isn't she the one coordinating this meeting? I assumed she would be here in person for our arrival."

Wall gestured into the trees from where the Jeeps had emerged. "Oh, Nelly's up at the estate with the others. She's getting everything set up for us. If you know Nelly, you know every detail has to be perfect."

"And Miles Priest?" Miss Shirley asked.

"Inbound. Weather delayed him and DeRay out of Glasgow, so they didn't get to Pindling until an hour ago. He and Scott should be arriving at the helipad in a few minutes."

"Everyone else is here? All of the other CEOs?"

"Oh, yeah. Nelly wouldn't take no for an answer about attending this meeting. Everyone canceled plans to be here. That's how important this is, Gabriel. We figured we'd have a little cocktail get-together before we get down to business. We have some serious things to discuss, but serious things usually go better when they're washed down with a little coconut rum. Of course, I see that you've brought along some of the best bubbly, too. We'll definitely want to open some of those bottles tonight."

"What about security?" Miss Shirley asked, as if he hadn't said anything at all. "What measures have you taken?"

Wall shrugged. "Don't worry about that, Shirley. The island is secure."

"*Miss* Shirley. How many men, and what weapons do they have?"

Hon Xiu-Le knitted his brow with suspicion and crossed his arms over his skinny chest. "I'm sorry, but why do you wish to know that?"

"I'm responsible for Gabriel's safety," Miss Shirley replied. "If I'm not satisfied with the security arrangements, we're leaving."

She snapped her fingers at the two guards who had accompanied the CEOs in the second Jeep. "*You two.* Over here. Now."

The guards exchanged glances and then approached the group across the sand. The taller one, who had dark close-cropped hair, seemed to think he was James Bond and gave Miss Shirley a condescending look as he sized up her body in the bikini. The shorter one, who was heavyset and Hispanic, was more cautious and had his hand close to the butt of his gun. He was obviously the smarter of the two.

"You need help with something, ma'am?" the Bond look-alike asked.

"The details of your security. Number of men, where are they located, what is their weaponry."

The guard gave her a tight smile. "Sorry, sweetheart. That's confidential. But don't you worry, we've got everything under control."

Tyler Wall interrupted them. "Trust me, Shirley, I've been coming here for years, and there's never been a problem."

"That's two," she said.

"Sorry?"

"You've now called me Shirley two more times following my warning. It's *Miss* Shirley. A third time will result in punishment."

Wall laughed, making his large body shake. "Shit, Gabe, this one's a hell of a spitfire. You're a lucky son of a bitch."

"She's not kidding, Tyler," Gabriel told him cheerily.

Wall's eyes took another slow tour around Miss Shirley's bikini, and then he rubbed his big hand up and down the handle of his walking staff in a deliberately suggestive manner. "Well, I didn't get where I am without taking risks. I think I might actually enjoy a little punishment from someone like you . . . *Shirley*."

Miss Shirley sighed.

She wore a white leather Prada purse over her shoulder, and she dug both hands inside the main pouch. When her hands emerged again, she had a gun in each one. She aimed the first gun at Tyler Wall's throat and fired a single shot that severed his brain stem and spinal cord, dropping him dead to the sand. With the second gun, she delivered a shot to the center of the forehead of the Hispanic guard, and he collapsed with equal speed.

In the same instant, the half-dozen Medusa operatives on the pier bent over the crates at their feet and grabbed automatic rifles, which they began firing toward the five CEOs who were waiting near the first Jeep. The startled executives tried to run toward the jungle, but the hail of bullets cut them down and left their bodies twitching.

The gleaming white sand ran red with blood.

The James Bond look-alike guard finally awoke from his total shock and reached for his Glock, but Miss Shirley placed the barrel of one of her guns between his eyes, and he immediately raised his hands in surrender.

Hon Xiu-Le's face twisted into a mask of terror and disbelief as he stared at the bodies and the blood. Miss Shirley pointed her other gun at his throat and said calmly, "What's my name?"

"Miss Shirley! Miss Shirley!"

"Excellent." She focused on the remaining guard. "Security details please."

The remaining guard couldn't talk fast enough. "They've got cameras on the beach, so they've been watching since you arrived. They know what just happened, and that means they'll be calling in backup. They'll seal everything up and hold you off until the cavalry arrives. You'll never get through the gate."

"Let me worry about that. How many men?"

"Four men doing shifts on the island perimeter, a dozen more men inside the estate with body armor and semi-automatic rifles."

"Wonderful. Thank you for the information."

Miss Shirley squeezed the trigger and shot him in the head.

She gestured toward the men on the pier to join her on the beach and then separately signaled toward the jungle, where three other Medusa operatives emerged from the trees. They had rifles in their hands, and their clothes were already streaked head to toe with blood.

The guards on the island perimeter were no longer a problem.

"Shall we?" Miss Shirley said to Gabriel Fox.

"Absolutely, my love."

The team prepared to move out, and she nudged one of her guns against the neck of the Chinese CEO. "Lead the way to the Jeeps, Mr. Xiu-Le. Medusa would like to meet the rest of the tech cabal."

THE silver Airbus helicopter carrying Miles Priest and Scott DeRay flew low enough to make whirlpools on the ocean water as it howled toward the island. As they got closer in the waning daylight, Priest saw the profile of the yacht docked at the pier, and it annoyed him that

Gabriel had arrived ahead of them. Priest prided himself on his punctuality, with every meeting starting right on time.

"I hope your plan works, Scott," Priest said.

Scott, in the rear seat next to him, looked equally unhappy with their delay. "I'm not sure we have any alternatives."

Priest rubbed the long chin on his drooping face. He knew they were running out of time. "Our lobbyists in Washington tell me that the Senate has the votes to pass the tech reform bill, despite all the calls I've made. The House was a given, but we'd been hoping to stop it in the Senate. We'll all be dogs on congressional leashes if this goes through. Except for Prescix, of course. If Medusa grabs hold of Prescix and takes it private, they'll be able to operate with a fraction of the oversight on the rest of us, and there won't be a damn thing we can do to stop them. Which I'm sure was the plan all along."

"I'm afraid that's not the only bad news," Scott told him. "The feds are taking the war to another front, too."

Priest scowled. "Namely?"

"I just got an email from one of my sources in the AG's office. He says the Justice Department is threatening antitrust action against several of the largest players in the tech cabal. Starting with Carillon."

"Outrageous!"

"It'll be a long battle," Scott said. "This will be a huge legal fight."

Priest shook his head. "That's the whole point. It will be another expensive distraction. We'll be battling the government instead of battling Medusa. The timing is no coincidence. They're trying to bleed us with a thousand cuts."

"Looks that way."

"It isn't about the other companies," Priest added, staring at the water below them. "It isn't even about Carillon. It's me they want. This is a personal vendetta against me. I'm the biggest obstacle to their plans, and they want me gone."

"They know you're the face of Big Tech," Scott replied. "They need to take you down."

"Sir."

The voice of the helicopter pilot crackled over both of their headsets, interrupting them.

"What is it, Tom?" Priest asked impatiently. "Why aren't we heading for the helipad?"

"There's a problem on the island."

"What problem?"

They felt the helicopter slow sharply, and the pilot increased altitude, climbing vertically so that the island pier and beach came into view below them. At first, Priest didn't understand what he was seeing, but as the picture became clear, he sucked in his breath with a distraught hiss. *"Jesus.* Are those bodies?"

"Yes, sir."

"Go lower! Let me see!"

"Negative, sir. We can't take the risk."

Scott found a pair of binoculars in one of the compartments of the helicopter. He used them to peer out the window. "Holy shit. There's blood everywhere,

Miles. I count six of the cabal, and they appear to be dead. That includes Tyler Wall."

"*Medusa!* It's a massacre!"

"If we hadn't been late, we'd be dead, too," Scott murmured.

"Tom, get us out of here!" Priest roared.

"*Yes, sir.*"

Before the helicopter could move, Priest stared down at the appalling carnage on the beach again. He barked into the microphone. "Wait a minute, wait, hold your position. What's that?"

Immediately below the helicopter, Priest saw a man dressed in black break from the cover of the trees. The man ran across the sand toward the nearest body, and then his face tilted skyward to stare at them as they hovered over the island. From their altitude, he was little more than a stick figure on the beach.

"Who is that?" Priest asked.

Scott focused the binoculars again. When he spoke, his voice had a dark cast. "It's Bourne, Miles. It's Jason Bourne."

FORTY

BOURNE expected gunfire from the silver helicopter. Instead, seconds later, he watched it veer away from the island and head back across the ocean.

When it was gone, he kept his gun trained on the yacht, anticipating a new assault. But the boat looked dark and quiet against the huge expanse of water. He made his way through the murder scene on the beach and found no survivors. The bodies of the CEOs lay sprawled near the trees, where they'd been cut down as they tried to run. Shadows lengthened over the corpses like funeral shrouds.

The assassins had already moved inland. He saw tire tracks in the sand, leading to a winding road that headed up the slope of the island. He sprinted in pursuit around a series of tight curves, his arms and legs pumping furiously. Half a mile later, he stopped as he spotted two Jeeps parked at an angle, blocking the road ahead of him.

He waited, observing the scene, then silently moved closer.

Behind the Jeeps, Miles Priest's lavish estate rose above the Caribbean jungle. It was five stories high, painted in sea foam green, with airy balconies on every level to take advantage of the ocean breezes. The estate was surrounded by a high-tech security wall constructed of nine-foot steel pillars built side by side to let the light in but keep intruders out. Cameras topped the spiked pillars at regular intervals, providing a complete surveillance picture inside and out. A high two-paneled gate stretched across the entrance road. Bourne wasn't sure how Medusa planned to invade the estate or how they expected to remain unseen.

He moved off the road into the trees and picked his way toward the gate. When he was close, he focused binoculars on the interior grounds. The entire estate had been possessed by an eerie quiet, as complete as a ghost town. Nothing moved. The walking trails and swimming pools were empty. But as he examined the upper balconies, he saw a red pinpoint light come and go. The guards were armed and waiting, with telescopic sights surveying the area inside the wall.

The tech cabal wouldn't go down without a fight, but they were training their guns on the main gate, and Medusa wasn't there. Miss Shirley and her team had vanished.

Where were they?

Bourne followed the estate wall. He navigated the dense jungle, picking apart the branches. Every few steps, he stopped to listen for the noise of the assassins ahead of him, but he didn't hear a thing. The wall continued without interruption for at least two hundred yards, until he finally reached a corner that marked the edge of the estate grounds. He still saw no way to breach the wall and no sign that Medusa had done so.

Then he realized he had company.

He smelled the man before he saw him or heard him. The breeze across the hilltop brought the musk of body odor. Bourne froze. He sank low to the ground, hidden inside the web of leaves. On his belly, he crept forward an inch at a time, peering upward until he spotted a man in camouflage six feet away, a rifle cradled in his arms. He wasn't an island guard. He was Medusa. The man was muscular and tall and wore a headset connected to a radio unit on his shoulder. With a word or a scream, he could give Bourne away, and anonymity was Bourne's only asset right now.

Bourne silently drew a hunting knife from a scabbard on his calf. He moved another inch. Then another. If the man looked closely into the jungle at his feet, he would see him. Bourne brought one knee up, poised to spring off the ground. He waited until the man's head swiveled, and then he uncoiled his body and struck like a snake. His left hand closed over the guard's microphone as he locked his forearm around the man's throat, and his right hand simultaneously plunged the blade into the side of the man's neck and severed the carotid artery with a quick, backward slice. A fountain of blood sprayed Bourne's face, and the only sound was a grotesque gurgling. He held on tightly as the man twitched as blood poured out, before the body slumped into deadweight and he lowered him to the ground.

He grabbed the headset and radio and took the man's rifle. He made a quick circle with the gun, anticipating an assault from a different direction, but the man had been left behind while the others went forward.

A sentry.

Guarding *what*?

He was in the middle of dense jungle on the wrong side of the estate wall. And yet there was no sign of the other Medusa assassins.

Bourne heard a voice through the headset and recognized the icy woman's voice. Miss Shirley.

"We're in."

They were already inside the estate. *How?* Then the next communication used a word that explained everything.

"Jersey, all clear at the tunnel?"

A tunnel.

Somewhere close by was a tunnel leading under the wall and into the heart of the estate. He realized there had to be a way to get people out without relying on the main gate, but a tunnel leading out could also be used as a way in if someone knew where it was and how to get it open.

Which told him something else.

Medusa had a mole inside the estate.

Bourne heard Miss Shirley's impatient voice through the headset again. *"Jersey? Report!"*

The Medusa leader expected a reply from the dead man at his feet.

"Clear," he told her in a muffled voice.

"Prepare for detonation."

Bourne didn't have time to prepare for anything. Almost immediately, an earthquake rumbled under his feet, nearly throwing him over. The boom of an explosion rippled across the island. Not even five seconds later, a twin explosion from the same direction rocked the island again, near the gates of the estate. A burnt smell filled the air, and black smoke rose above the crowns of the trees.

He knew what it was. The Jeeps.

They'd wired and blown up the Jeeps. It was a diversion. Focus the guards on the gate, and while they steeled themselves for a frontal assault that was never going to come, Miss Shirley had already led her assassins inside the heart of the estate.

The *tunnel!*

He had to find the tunnel.

Bourne surveyed the thick jungle, knowing that he could be practically standing at the tunnel entrance without seeing it. And yet the guard should have been waiting right at the portal. He pawed through the bushes that grew together in a tight net and found nothing. Overhead, the parrots laughed at him. Somewhere beyond the wall, he heard a rattle of gunfire and knew he was running out of time. The firefight inside the estate had already begun.

There!

At his feet, he spotted a concrete bunker, carefully disguised so that it blended into the forest floor. The only reason he spotted it was because the bunker's armored door, secured with an electronic lock, was open.

Medusa definitely had a spy clearing the way for their assault.

Below the open door, a stairwell led ten feet down to a tunnel that headed in the direction of the estate. When he climbed down, he saw lights near the ceiling, but the lights were off. There was no power, not even from a backup generator. He assumed that meant the internal and external surveillance cameras were down, too.

The men defending the estate were blind.

Bourne switched on his flashlight and ran through the tunnel. At the far end, he found another fire door, which led him to a utility room underneath the estate, surrounded by steel machinery. The underground room, like everything else, was unlit. He used his flashlight to find a stairwell, and he took it upstairs and carefully emerged into a shadowy hallway on the ground floor of the estate. The hallway led to a catering kitchen, where he found half a dozen bodies on the floor.

Chefs. Servers. All dead. All shot. Broken glass sprinkled the ceramic tile like popcorn. In the doorway that led out of the kitchen, he found two guards, dead on the floor, their weapons taken.

He heard Miss Shirley's voice in the headset again.

"Philly, New York, Chicago, clear the downstairs, make sure no one comes up behind us. Kill anyone you find. We're heading to the next level."

Bourne exited the kitchen into a huge interior courtyard that was open to the evening air beneath a retractable roof five stories above him. Stone railings on the upper floors of the estate rose over the atrium. The square courtyard space had been set up for a nighttime cocktail party, but it was empty, just palm trees, black-draped tables, and Caribbean sculptures in wild colors. White columns bordered the space, leading to hallways on all sides.

He ventured into the courtyard. Gunfire immediately erupted from his right, chasing him across the pavers. He dived for cover behind a stone urn, and when he stole a look over the rim, he saw one of the estate's security guards firing from behind a column on the east wall. To the guards, Bourne was a threat. He had no way to let them know he was on their side.

Then the guard made the mistake of breaking cover. He crossed from one column to the next, but a gunshot cracked across the courtyard from an entirely new direction, and the guard dropped with a bullet in his head.

Bourne heard a voice, not on his headset, but ten feet away from inside the courtyard. Someone was there, invisible on the other side of the stone urn.

"Jersey? That you? Why'd you leave the tunnel?"

If the Medusa man got any closer, he'd see that Bourne was an outsider, not one of his own. Bourne steadied the rifle in his hands. He expected the man to be wearing body armor, so there was no point in going for anything but a head shot. He whirled to his feet with the rifle balanced against his shoulder and fired. Two shots, one that missed over the man's shoulder, one that landed square in the middle of the assassin's forehead. The man died with a surprised expression on his face.

Bourne grabbed a second rifle from the assassin and slung it around his neck. He ran to the far side of the courtyard and found a hallway built with salmon-colored stone tiles. The pastel yellow wall was interrupted by a series of double doors all made of intricate stained glass. He opened the first door and found a small leather-furnished den that was empty. He continued to the next room and found a patio with an interior swimming pool and a series of floor-to-ceiling windows that led outside to the grounds of the estate. When he listened, he heard a low whimper of scared, labored breathing. He spotted a wet bar near the patio doors and found a young woman in a flowered cocktail dress hiding behind the bar. When she saw him, saw the blood on his face and the rifle in his arms, she began to scream, and he quickly clapped a hand over her mouth to stifle it. He whispered into her ear.

"I'm here to help. Don't be afraid. Stay right here, and you'll be fine."

He peeled away his hand, and she nodded silently at him.

"Where would the execs be?" he asked her. "Where are they hiding?"

She pointed a finger upward. "Top floor."

"Don't move. It'll be over soon."

Bourne got up from the bar. As he did, he spotted two Medusa operatives on the other side of the patio doors, patrolling the estate grounds. The men spotted him, too, and fired, shattering the glass, scoring the room with a rapid, deadly stream of fire. At his feet, the young woman screamed, and Bourne hit the floor and rolled away, drawing the bullets from her. He rolled until he found cover behind one of the wide legs of a cherry-wood pool table, but a hail of bullets ricocheted around him, and he felt a searing pain in his calf. He spun away again, his shoes slipping on the floor, then fired back with one arm, sending bullets wild but driving the men to the ground.

He shot again and hit one of the men, but the other operative unleashed a new battery of fire. Bourne threw himself down and scrambled away, the bullets pinging after him across the floor and getting closer. He stood no chance, until he heard the assassin's rifle jam, and the rain of bullets suddenly stopped. As the man tried to clear his gun, Bourne sat up and calmly took aim. Seeing the threat, the man broke into a run, but Bourne led him with the barrel shot by shot and took him down with a bullet in the neck.

That was four.

By his count, Medusa still had five other men inside the building. Plus Miss Shirley and Gabriel Fox. All of them were heading upstairs to kill the members of the tech cabal hidden on the top floor.

Bourne hurried back to the hallway. When he looked at the pink tile at his feet, he saw drops of deeper red, and he realized he was trailing blood. He'd been shot in the leg. Running made his heart beat faster and made him lose more blood, but he couldn't stop. He half ran, half limped as he hunted for the stairs, passing more bodies as he did. Staff. Guards. Maids. When he found a marble staircase near the house's palatial entrance, he recognized a man dead on the steps, the Indian CEO of an online retail giant who'd been mowed down before he could escape to the upper floors.

He climbed higher. Everyone on the second and third floors was dead, too. There was nothing but silence and blood around him. As he neared the fourth floor, he heard an explosion of gunfire over his head, muffled by the walls of the mansion. He'd caught up to the Medusa team. Bourne followed the sound of the shooting back to the atrium that rose over the interior courtyard. Slipping to his knees, he slithered across the tiled hallway to the stone railing and assessed the action on the far side of the open space. At least three or four estate security guards had barricaded themselves in the opposite corner, and the Medusa team had split in two and was closing on them from both sides. The columns built along the hallways gave them cover. The gunfire in both directions was intense.

He counted four Medusa operatives, two in each hallway. He didn't see Gabriel Fox. He didn't see Miss Shirley.

Bourne felt his head spinning as pain came in waves from his leg. He tried to focus. He jutted the barrel of a rifle through a gap in the stone railing and saw the head of a Medusa assassin appear in the crosshairs of his scope across the atrium. The man in his sights was focused on the guards. He didn't know Bourne was there.

Breathe in.

Slowly breathe out.

Ease back on the trigger.

The man's head exploded.

The new burst of fire should have alerted the others, but they were too caught up in the adrenaline of the fight to realize that the game had changed. Bourne refocused, re-aimed, sighting down the barrel at the next of the Medusa operatives taking cover along the same atrium corridor.

Another shot. Another kill.

But now they'd spotted the new threat.

One of the two remaining Medusa assassins trained fire across the atrium, and the corridor around Bourne exploded with bullets, rock, and tile. He felt a fragment slice across the back of his hand and leave a gash of blood. He rolled away, his world turning upside down, but he had nowhere to go. With his body mostly exposed, he aimed through the stone railing again and fired back. A hail of bullets burned the air. He never should have survived the exchange, but he got lucky. One of his bullets nicked a column, flaking off a jagged arrowhead of stone that ricocheted into the assassin's eye. The man wailed and staggered back, and the estate guards in the far corner immediately shot him down with a deafening burst of fire.

Bourne had to run. He had to get to the stairs and

then to the next floor. That was where Miss Shirley was. He crawled, stumbled, then found his feet and limped to the next corner and into the middle of the hallway.

But the last Medusa assassin was waiting for him.

The man pulled the trigger. Gunfire erupted around him. Bourne waited to die. This was the end.

Then, in the same instant, shot after shot lit up the atrium like fireworks. The tech cabal guards burst from their barricade in the corner, and Bourne saw the Medusa assassin fall, riddled with bullets. The firefight was done. He tried to get up, tried to keep going, tried to run, but as he pushed himself to his feet, his legs buckled under him.

His head hit the hard floor.

Everything went black.

ONE floor up, Miss Shirley spat out a single curse. "*Fuck!*" She ripped the headset from her head, threw it to the floor, and kicked it away. She felt an urge to pull the trigger on her rifle, just to shoot up the walls in fury, but she held her fire. At that moment, eight expert assassins should have been converging from the lower floors for their final assault on the tech cabal. They should have been about to embark on a last orgy of killing, a frenzy she would feel like electricity between her legs.

Instead, the three of them were alone. Miss Shirley, one last Medusa agent, code-named Dallas, and the utterly worthless Gabriel Fox.

Fox stared at her, his face suddenly filled with fear. "What the hell's going on?"

"They're off the air," she said. "All of them. Jersey, Philly, Chicago, New York, Memphis, the whole fucking lot of them, they're all gone. Nobody's coming to re-group with us. There's no backup. It's just us."

"What are you saying?"

"I'm saying they're *dead*. This is a catastrophe. A disaster."

She stared down the open-air hallway on the estate's top floor. At the far end was a locked door, and on the other side, she knew, was the entire tech cabal. These were the people she'd come here to kill, and she'd failed.

The head of Medusa, the man who'd been her lover for almost twenty years, would never forgive her.

"We need to go," she concluded.

"Are you out of your mind?" Gabriel demanded. "What about our plan? What about you and me taking over the cabal?"

"Oh, Gabriel, shut your lunatic mouth for once in your life. Don't you get it? We need to get to one of the helicopters and get the hell off this island. If we don't, we'll be dead, too. We've lost."

Gabriel shook his head, his face screwed up with rage. "You underestimated them!"

Miss Shirley signaled Dallas to lead the way toward the stairs. She grabbed Gabriel's arm and dragged him with her. "I underestimated nothing. We knew exactly what we were walking into. Don't you get it? This isn't the tech cabal, you fucking fool. They're not the ones who did this."

Gabriel tried to keep up with her, but he stumbled over his own feet. "Then who did?"

Miss Shirley didn't answer, but she knew exactly who'd destroyed her plan. She could picture the man's face in her head, expressionless, infuriating. He was the man she was going to kill slowly, taking him apart limb by limb.

"Bourne."

FORTY-ONE

THE barrels of half a dozen rifles surrounded Bourne. He regained consciousness in an open-air terrace that looked out across the darkness of the island. The only light around him came from a dozen flickering candles, which cast strange, giant shadows. The dark crowns of jungle trees waved on the other side of the railings. A warm breeze blew across his bare skin; he wore only shorts. When he went to get up, he discovered that his wrists and ankles were tightly bound to a wrought-iron chaise where his body had been carried. He stared into the dirty, bloody faces of the estate security guards who'd survived the Medusa assault. They kept their guns focused on him. Meanwhile, an attractive doctor tended to his wounds. She'd already removed the bullet from his leg and bandaged the other gashes on his body.

When the doctor was done, two of the guards moved aside, and Nelly Lessard approached him, her face pale and tired. He'd met her during his meetings with Scott and Miles. Another guard brought her a chair, and she sat down next to Bourne with her short, birdlike legs squeezed together. She wore an elegant dark suit that was torn in several places, and her coiffed gray hair was in disarray. Nonetheless, she projected an aura of calm authority as she waved a hand at the security team.

"I appreciate the abundance of caution, gentlemen, but I think we can dispense with the guns. Also, please untie Mr. Bourne's hands and legs."

The guards freed Bourne, and he sat up slowly, fighting off another wave of dizziness and nausea. The doctor had anesthetized his wounds, but the pain wouldn't stay away for long. He studied his surroundings and noticed the glint of broken glass on the terrace floor and furniture tipped over. He spotted three of the tech cabal's CEOs hovering in the background, pacing near the top-floor railings with a kind of shell shock.

"Medusa?" he asked, hearing the ragged sound of his own voice.

"Gone," Nelly told him. "Gabriel Fox and that awful woman hijacked one of the helicopters. They kidnapped the pilot and escaped."

"How many dead?"

"Sadly, we're still counting. The carnage is appalling. Fortunately, the majority of us—not just the tech cabal but most of the estate staff—were able to take refuge on the top floor when the assault began. Medusa never got to us, but that's only because you wiped most of them out. Had you not arrived when you did, I have no doubt that we'd all be dead right now. We're enormously grateful."

Bourne said nothing.

Nelly looked as if she were trying to make sense of the man in front of her and all she could find were contradictions. "Obviously, I was wrong about you, Jason. We all were. We were convinced that Medusa had exploited your psychological damage and turned you against us."

"It was a setup," Bourne replied. "A very good one."

"Yes, so it seems. We should have been helping you, and instead—"

"Instead, you were trying to kill me," he replied.

"I'm afraid so. I won't apologize, because we both know that's how the game is played. We make choices based on the information we have. I doubt you would have expected us to act any differently."

"You're right."

"Nonetheless, I'm curious, Jason, why you went to so much trouble to save us."

He shrugged. "It wasn't selfless on my part, if that's what you're thinking. I don't care what happens to you. The only way out for me is to expose the conspiracy. Until then, I'm a wanted man. I'd rather not live the rest of my life on the run."

A smile played around the edges of Nelly's lips, as if she didn't believe him. "Well, whatever your motives, I'm glad you were here."

"Are the police on their way?" Bourne asked.

"Oh, yes. Bahamian police and navy. FBI. CIA. We'll be inundated soon enough. I waited as long as I could, but there's no way we could keep an incident like this under wraps. It's going to be worldwide news."

He nodded. "I can't stay here. I need to go."

"Yes, I assumed that was the case. I wish I could help you, but the authorities won't take my word for your innocence. If the U.S. government finds you, you'll be arrested, and after that, I suspect you'll simply disappear. Anyway, I've arranged for fresh clothes and any supplies you may need. Do you want a transport back to Nassau or Freeport? I can get you shuttled there discreetly and put on a private plane wherever you need to go."

Bourne shook his head. "A friend of mine is waiting for me on a boat offshore. At least, I hope he still is. If you have a sat phone, I'll call him."

"Are you sure? The least we can do is arrange your getaway."

"No offense, Nelly, but I don't trust anyone in the tech cabal."

"I suppose we deserve that," she said.

"It's not just because you've been trying to kill me. You're compromised. You have a spy."

Nelly looked around to make sure they were out of earshot. "What do you mean?"

"Medusa has someone inside the cabal."

"Are you sure?"

"There's no other explanation. The assault team knew too much. They knew where the tunnel was and how to get through. They knew the power specs for the island. They were familiar with your defenses and the layout of the estate. Someone on the inside had to give them that kind of information. It could have been someone on the security team, but it could have been one of your CEOs, too."

"I can't believe that's possible," Nelly said. "I know these people backward and forward."

"Like you knew me?" Bourne asked.

She frowned. "That's a fair point."

"All I'm saying is, you don't know who to trust, and neither do I. That means I'm safer working on my own."

"Understood."

"The one thing that would be helpful right now is a new gun. And ammunition."

"I'm sure that can be arranged. I take it that means you're still going after them. You're going after Medusa."

"They're not done," Bourne replied. "A setback like this won't make them stop."

"So how will you track them down? Where do you think they're planning to strike next?"

Bourne said nothing. Nelly read his face and knew what he was thinking. "I see. You don't trust me, either. Well, I can't blame you for that."

"It's better if no one knows where I'm going."

"No, you're right. Tell me nothing. If you're correct that we have a spy, it could be anyone. I'll get everything ready and make sure you get off this island safely. Then it's up to you, Jason."

Nelly left him alone. The light of the candles played across his skin, and when he moved, he felt shocks of pain all over his body. He was already deep inside his head, planning what came next. These were the moments when his loss of memory became a kind of advantage. Having no past made it easier to leave himself behind and imagine the world through the eyes of his enemies.

He needed to get inside the head of someone he didn't know. Medusa was more than Miss Shirley. It had a leader. A strategist dictating every move, like a chess grand master. Whoever that leader was, he or she would already know that their plan had gone wrong. Medusa had aimed a body blow against the tech cabal, and they'd failed. But they wouldn't go away and lick their wounds. They'd strike again, hard and fast.

If you fail to kill your enemy with a body shot, then you cut off his head.

Treadstone.

Bourne already knew what Medusa would do next. They'd go after Miles Priest.

THE open door of the helicopter let a cold, driving wind into the passenger cabin. It was dark all around them, with no land in sight and nothing but miles of Atlantic water below. Miss Shirley sat on the cabin floor, dangling her bare feet out the open door. The fierce wind swirled her black hair and assaulted her skin, but she liked the bite of the cold. It kept her awake and alert. It kept her angry.

The Medusa operative named Dallas sat up front, monitoring the pilot. Only Gabriel Fox sat in back with Miss Shirley, and he was belted into the nearest leather seat, with his arms wrapped tightly around himself and his entire body shivering.

"Do we need to keep the door open?" Gabriel complained like a whining ten-year-old. "I'm shriveling up to nothing here."

"I like the chill," Miss Shirley replied calmly.

At high speed over the water, the helicopter jostled and bucked. Her body stayed in perfect balance, moving gracefully with the bumps of air. Gabriel, by contrast, clung to the straps of the seat belt as the turbulence threw him back and forth. His face was pale, and he had his mouth clamped tightly shut. She watched the bulge of his throat swell as he swallowed down bile.

"I hate choppers," he said. "They scare the shit out of me."

"You have to be one with the vibration," she told him.

"I don't know what the hell that means."

Miss Shirley got to her feet. She leaned as far as she could outside the helicopter, holding herself steady with nothing but the lightest touch on the door frame. She extended one bare leg straight out the door, level with her hip, then did the same with her left arm. Balanced on one foot, she finally let go of the door frame altogether and rode the waves of turbulence like an aerial surfer.

"Jesus Christ," Gabriel shouted. "Stop that! You're freaking me out!"

"You need to relax, my love. Here, let me help."

Slowly, Miss Shirley drew her body back inside the helicopter. She gave Gabriel a wicked smile. She spread her legs and mounted him with her knees on either side of his thighs. Underneath the thin silk of his robe, she felt him begin to grow hard against the fabric of her bikini bottom. She took his face roughly in her hands and kissed him, shoving her tongue inside his mouth.

"There's nothing to fear," she said.

"But we lost. We were supposed to take out the tech cabal. First them, then Medusa. You and I were supposed to take over everything. Now what happens?"

"You don't need to worry about that."

"Are you kidding? I was seen. People know it was me. They're going to arrest me for *murder*."

"That will never happen."

Gabriel shook his head. "I need protection! I need to talk to the head of Medusa. You know who he is, right? You know how to get hold of him?"

"Of course."

"Well, we need to set up a meeting. I've got what he wants. Prescix. All of my code. Medusa has wanted that from the beginning. But it's not free. He needs to get me out of this mess, pull strings, whatever the hell he does. Plus, I want a seat at the table. Influence. That's my price."

"I already informed him of our situation," Miss Shirley replied. "I told him what happened on the island. He anticipated your demands."

"Smart man. What did he say?"

"He said to assure you that Medusa has a place for you."

Gabriel sagged against the seat and let out a whistle of relief. "Hot damn. That's good news. You know what this means, don't you? Our plan is still good. We get me inside Medusa, and when the time is right, you and me push out the big man, and we take over instead. Then we can focus on the tech cabal again. The new legislation is moving forward in Congress. They'll be weak, distracted. We'll pick them off one by one."

"Yes, we will."

Gabriel let his hands roam over her body, his arousal returning. "This calls for a celebration."

"You're right, it does."

She stood up inside the helicopter, swaying with its side-to-side motion. She tugged on the strings of her bikini top to free her breasts and then did the same with the bikini bottoms and stood naked in front of Gabriel. With a seductive smirk, she flicked the bikini out the open door of the helicopter, where the wind whipped it away.

Miss Shirley sank to her knees in front of him. She pushed Gabriel's legs apart and clicked open the straps of the seat belt on his chest. With her fingernails scraping along his skin, she shoved the silk robe back off his shoulders and stripped it from his body until he, like her, was naked inside the helicopter. She leaned over and grabbed him by the waist, and then she bit his earlobe hard enough to draw blood. As he cringed with pain and pleasure, she whispered to him.

"Medusa has a *very* special place for you, Gabriel."

"Oh, yeah? Where's that?"

"The bottom of the sea."

He only had an instant for his eyes to widen in fear. In

one smooth motion, Miss Shirley hoisted Gabriel's body into the air and launched him through the helicopter's open door. The tumult of the wind drowned out his scream, and with a flash of white skin, he vanished, falling to the empty ocean below them.

Miss Shirley blew a kiss to the air and waved after him with the tips of her fingers. She slipped Gabriel's Chinese robe around her body and tied it, and then she slid the door shut. Humming softly to herself, she did a little dance in the bouncing cabin as the helicopter flew on through the night.

FORTY-TWO

THE stars spread across the Caribbean night sky, crystal clear over the dark ocean. Bourne lay on his back on the deck of the catamaran with his hands behind his head. Inside, at the boat's bridge, Teeling steered them north toward the Bahamian town of Freeport. From there, Bourne could charter a plane back to the U.S. and make arrangements to cross the Atlantic on his way to find Miles Priest.

His mind swirled with details. Maps. Money. Equipment. Transport. Scott had taught him long ago to break down a plan into a thousand steps, like a flowchart, with moves and countermoves that depended on how each component of the plan played out in real life.

A strategy is only as good as the steps you take to execute it.

Scott DeRay.

Bourne hadn't told Nelly what he was planning to do,

but it didn't matter. He was sure that Scott knew he was coming. Scott would have put himself inside the heads of the Medusa leadership and come to the same conclusion that Bourne did. The next attack would happen in Scotland. They would strike at Miles Priest directly. And if that was where Medusa was headed, then Bourne would be there, too.

The exhaustion of the day made him want to sleep, but he couldn't do that yet. He stared at the stars and felt the wind racing across his body and listened to the low throb of the motor. Normally, that was the perfect environment in which to separate himself from everything else and focus exclusively on the mission in front of him.

But he couldn't.

He kept finding his mind distracted. The more he thought about what he had to do, the more he found his thoughts interrupted by something else.

Someone else.

Abbey Laurent.

He'd left her behind, but he hadn't really left her behind at all. She was still with him. When he closed his eyes, he could picture her face, the spiky red bangs hanging over her eyes, the pale lips when she wiped her lipstick off, the smart dark eyes that didn't miss a thing. He could feel the softness of her skin and her fingertips running across his body. He remembered the catch in her breath as they coupled in bed.

Don't think about her! She's gone!

Marie had left him alone. Nova had left him alone. And now the only safe thing he could do was let Abbey go. He couldn't have anyone in his life. As soon as he did, they were both vulnerable. Both at risk.

But the desire to be close to her overwhelmed him. Teeling had given him a satellite phone, and all he needed to do was dial her number to hear her voice again.

Let her go!

Jason's fingers hesitated over the phone keypad. He tried to hold himself back the way an alcoholic stares at a glass full of whiskey and looks for willpower, but he couldn't stop himself. He punched in the numbers and waited through an interminable length of silence on the water as the satellites tried to connect him to Abbey Laurent.

The silence lasted so long that he thought the call had gone dead.

Then he heard her voice, curious, nervous, hopeful. "Hello?"

Jason took a long time to answer. He thought about hanging up. He'd found her; he knew she was alive. That was enough.

But it wasn't.

"It's me," he said.

Relief poured out of her across the miles between them. "Oh, Jason, thank God! Are you okay? What happened?"

"I'm fine," he replied.

"You don't sound fine. Are you hurt?"

"It's nothing serious."

"Did you get to the island? Did you stop them?"

"I stopped the worst of it. Medusa didn't get what they wanted."

"What does that mean? Is it over?"

Bourne hesitated. "No. It's not over yet."

"What about our twisted friend?" Abbey asked.

"She's still alive. She's still out there. That's one reason I have to keep going."

He heard Abbey breathing hard and fast. There was something strange in her voice when she spoke again. "Where are you now?"

"On the water, but not for long. I'm going after them."

Again the silence lasted forever and made him wonder if he'd lost her. Finally, she said, "Jason, it's not too late to quit. Come back to me."

He'd never felt so tempted by anything in his life. "I'm sorry. I can't."

"I know."

"I have to go," Bourne said.

"No. Wait. Stay with me a while longer."

"I wish I could, Abbey. What about you? Are you okay? Where are you now?"

"On the road," she told him. "Where else would I be?"

He thought that was an odd thing for her to say. "Is everything all right?"

"Fine. I'm fine. But do you want the truth? I miss you. I can't stop thinking about that night we spent in Oklahoma City."

Bourne tensed, because she'd made a deliberate mistake. They'd spent the night together in Amarillo, not Oklahoma City. She was telling him something. Sending him a message.

She wasn't alone.

"I remember that night, too," he told her, to make clear he understood.

"Good. When will I see you again, Jason?"

"Someday."

"That's not enough," she told him. "Tell me when."

He didn't want to make promises he couldn't keep, but he did it anyway. "It's April now. On June 1, if I haven't found you before then, go back to where we were supposed to meet the first time. Same time, same place."

"The last time you didn't show up," Abbey reminded him.

"This time I will. If I'm alive, I will."

"I'll be there."

"I have to go," he said again.

"Tell me where you're going next," Abbey pressed him. "Please, Jason. Tell me the truth. If all I do is find a headline in a newspaper about people being killed, I have to know if you were involved. If June 1 comes and goes and you're not there, I need to know where to start looking for you. Because I will."

He knew she wasn't the only one listening. He was sure it was Treadstone. She'd warned him; she'd given him a chance to lie. But he was tired of lying. It was time to face everyone who was hunting for him. Let them come.

"Miles Priest has a castle in Scotland," he said. "Medusa is going to bring everything they have against him. That's the endgame."

"Be careful, Jason." He heard the pleading in her voice. "I'll see you on June 1?"

"June 1."

Bourne hung up the phone and was left alone with the darkness of the ocean.

SCOTLAND," Abbey told Nash Rollins. "Are you satisfied? Jason is on his way to Scotland."

"Miles Priest?"

"Yes."

Rollins took a cell phone out of his pocket and dialed. "It's me. Get the jet ready. I need to leave immediately. Destination is Glasgow, but keep this off the books. I don't want any notice of the trip circulating on our computer systems. We don't know who's going to be watching for activity inside Treadstone."

He hung up the phone and began gathering up his things in the Denver safe house where they'd spent the last day. Abbey found that she could barely look at him.

"That was well done, Ms. Laurent," Rollins said. "Bourne wouldn't tell many people what he told you. Obviously, he trusts you."

Abbey said nothing. She wondered whether Jason trusting her would cost him his life. She'd hoped that he would lie when he realized she wasn't alone, that he would give her the wrong information and send Nash Rollins off on a fruitless chase to the other side of the world. But she could hear in his voice that Jason had told her the truth. He really was going to Scotland, and for some reason, he wanted Treadstone to know it.

"You did the right thing by helping me," Rollins added.

"Spare me your bullshit," Abbey snapped back. "Am I free to go now? Can I finally get the hell out of here and go home?"

Rollins shrugged. "Of course. One of my agents will accompany you and make sure you get back home to Quebec City. Obviously, she'll also be there in case you and Bourne make any further contact and you try to warn him away."

Abbey shook her head. "He won't contact me again."

"Well, I'm taking no chances."

Abbey got off the sofa, and her lip curled with disgust as she stared at the Treadstone agent. "I hate you people. All of you. You threaten, manipulate, plot, and kill, and somehow you convince yourself that none of this is wrong."

Rollins paused in the safe house with his briefcase in his hand. Slowly, he put his hat on his head and then leaned on his cane. "I'm well aware that we have to cross terrible lines, Ms. Laurent."

"Then why do you do it?"

"Theoretically? For a greater good."

Abbey shook her head. "You want the greater good, Mr. Rollins? Look at Jason. He seems to be the only one who hasn't forgotten what that is. Which is pretty ironic, isn't it, given his past. What does it take to convince you of the truth? He's *not* Medusa, and he never was. He's been trying to take them down from the beginning. He still is."

The Treadstone agent frowned. "Assuming you're right—assuming Bourne isn't simply lying to you, playing you—then what would you suggest I do?"

"You keep trying to kill him," Abbey replied. "Maybe, instead, you should try to *help* him."

FORTY-THREE

RAIN made the Highlands of Scotland green, and rain poured down in waves over Bourne's head. He stood at the fringe of a thick stand of fir trees a quarter mile from Miles Priest's castle outside the village of Glenfyrr. Manicured lawns and gardens surrounded the estate. Stony hills loomed in the distance, gray and ominous, swept by fog. The castle itself stood on a promontory high over the angry sea, built of old brown stone, with a single rounded tower facing the ocean. Turrets like the rooks of a chessboard lined the square wings that over-looked the gardens. Beyond the castle, he could see a cemetery and the decaying ruins of a chapel rising out of the green grass. The crumbling ramparts of the castle's stone wall clung to the sheer cliff face.

It was what he didn't see that worried him.

He didn't see Medusa. And yet he knew they had to be here. Somewhere in the trees around him and on the

beaches below the cliffs, a team of assassins waited for
darkness. Then they would strike. Medusa would have
no trouble penetrating the defenses here. No more than
half a dozen guards, widely spread out, patrolled the
grounds. He was surprised that Scott hadn't boosted security, but maybe Medusa had outthought him this time
with their plan.

Bourne waited until the next patrol passed out of
sight. Then he broke from the trees and ran at full speed
across the wet grass. The rain and twilight made him
mostly invisible, just a dark blur against the forest. He
reached the next stand of trees that hugged the high
cliffs, and he heard the thunder of waves breaking against
the jagged rocks a hundred feet below him. He surveyed
the area with his binoculars again, but from this new
angle, he still saw no evidence of the Medusa team ready-
ing their assault. He ducked through the trees to the very
edge of the cliff and studied the windswept water, but
there were no boats waiting offshore and no Zodiacs
dragged onto the rocky beach. Nothing looked amiss in
the rainy Scottish night.

Where are they?

He followed the coastline until the main tower of the
castle rose above the trees, four stories of old wet stone
staring toward the sea. Smoke from the chimneys stung
the air. Lights glowed inside a handful of windows. He'd
come prepared for a fortress, with a nylon rope and bow-
line knot hooked to his waist under his shirt for climbing; with a hacksaw blade if he needed to cut through
bars; and with smoke grenades if he needed a diversion.

But when he looked for a way inside, he realized that they'd left the door open for him.

Literally.

A thick, double-paneled oak door that led into the castle's round tower hung ajar. When he came closer, he saw cigarette butts littering the wet grass. Obviously, this was where the castle staff took their smoke breaks, and they didn't bother to lock up the doors each time they came and went.

Gun in hand, Bourne slipped inside the castle.

Too easy!

His instincts screamed that he was walking into a trap. But he was alone.

He found himself in a cramped circular hallway, with a stone floor that ran along the tower's rounded wall. The air had a musty smell, the product of constant dampness, and the interior was drafty and cold. He led the way with his gun, but no one challenged him. Halfway around the tower, he found a wrought-iron staircase that spiraled upward. He climbed the metal steps, which squealed with his footfalls. The entire frame shook, as loose bolts rattled under his weight.

Two stories up, Bourne found a landing with a small wooden door, barely wide enough for a man to get through. Slowly, he turned the brass knob and pushed the door open an inch. He listened inside and heard nothing, and he opened the door the rest of the way and found himself in a grand library, shaped like a half-moon, with a high ceiling and chambered windows facing toward the sea and the foggy Scottish hills. Bookshelves lined the walls, along with a series of Renaissance-style religious oil paintings. A huge fire crackled, giving heat to the cold castle. Persian rugs lay over the weathered wood floor, and a brass chandelier hung on chains from the high ceiling.

One man was inside. Scott DeRay.

"Hello, Jason," Scott told him. "Welcome. I've been expecting you."

His friend raised a crystal lowball glass that was half-filled with amber liquid. "Some scotch? It's Laphroaig. The good stuff."

"No."

Bourne felt disoriented, creeping into this medieval castle and finding nothing but an old friend in a business suit, drinking whisky.

"You really could have come in the front door," Scott added with a twinkle, "but where's the fun in that? You never could do things the easy way. I hope we won't have any medical bills for the guards you met along the way."

"They're fine," Bourne replied, distracted.

He checked out the windows. Through the rain-dotted glass, he studied the stone wall along the coastline that led out to the cemetery and the ruins of the chapel. Below the wall, the sea crashed against the rocks. No one was there. Not on the beach or the grounds, not in the forest. The assault he'd expected wasn't happening. Medusa wasn't here.

He shook his head. "This doesn't make sense."

"Medusa?"

"I was sure they'd come after you and Miles."

"I thought the same thing," Scott replied. "That's why I sent Miles away to keep him out of danger."

"Where did you send him?"

"A hotel he owns near Prestwick. He's been there since we got back. But I sent a limo to collect him. He should be arriving shortly. The fact is, it looks like we were both wrong, Jason. Believe me, the security in this castle is much more than it appears to be. We have electronics in place around the grounds and surveillance in a perimeter for several miles. No one gets in without our knowing about it. That includes you. I tracked you from the time you arrived. There's no one out there, Jason. Nobody's coming."

"They could still be on their way."

"Maybe so, but you know as well as I do that Medusa isn't about to walk in blind. They'd start with an advance team to scout the area. They haven't done that. No, I think your success in stopping them on the island forced a radical change in their plans."

Bourne frowned. He went over the flowchart he'd mapped out in his head of actions and reactions, moves and countermoves. He'd anticipated every possible plan of attack by Medusa, but he hadn't considered the possibility that they might do nothing at all.

"I don't like this," he said.

"Agreed. I don't like it, either, but if they move in, we'll have plenty of warning that they're coming. In the meantime, I'm glad you're here. For now, let's sit and relax until Miles gets back."

Bourne took another look through the castle windows. Below him, one of the guards patrolled the back of the estate, and somehow, he still expected to see the man crumple to the wet ground with a bullet in his head. He expected an assault team to appear from the trees on all sides, closing on the castle.

But no one did.

He turned away from the windows, but he didn't sit down.

"Nelly gave us a report from the island," Scott told him, sitting on the stone hearth, where the warmth of the fire made his tanned skin glow. "That was amazing work, Jason. And honestly, it's more than the cabal deserved, based on how we treated you. You saved a lot of lives. You also finally convinced Miles that he was wrong about you. He'll be reaching out to his contacts in Washington to see if we can restore your reputation. It won't be easy, given the evidence that Medusa mounted against you, but if anyone can get it done, it's Miles."

"I appreciate that."

"You validated my judgment, too," Scott added. "But of course, I'm not surprised. I know you better than anyone."

"You know me better than I know myself," Bourne replied.

"I suppose that's true. Someone has to remember everything you've forgotten. Like all those days we spent at the beach when we were kids. Thunder Mountain? Do you remember that? I guess not. We'd climb the trail up to the top of the hill through the trees and then race each other down the sand dunes on the other side. You always won."

"It's all gone," Bourne said.

"And that summer in Europe? I was at a private college in Switzerland, and you came over and we traveled around together. That was the best summer of my life. Italy. Germany. Turkey. Estonia. Russia. The Czech Republic. We went everywhere."

"You showed me pictures. It looked like we did it all."

"We did. Two twenty-year-olds who weren't afraid of anything. We were going to rule the world."

"I guess the plan worked out for you," Bourne said.

Scott shrugged. "It's a work in progress. You know, that summer was also the time we had our one big fight. We went a couple years without speaking to each other after that. I guess in some regard, I'm glad your memory loss wiped that away. I have a lot of regrets about that time."

Bourne was surprised. "You never told me about that."

"Like I said, I was just as happy to have you not remember it."

"What was the fight about?"

Scott got up from the hearth and refilled his glass from the bottle of Laphroaig. He wasn't a big man, and the size of the room under the high ceiling made him look even smaller. And yet his personality, his ego, and his charm always filled the space wherever he was. Bourne's skill was to disappear, whereas Scott's was to have everyone remember him.

"Oh, it started with an argument about politics," Scott said. "We'd been simmering about that all summer. You were always the government boy, particularly after 9/11. Me, I became pretty cynical about government after going to school in Europe."

"You joined the FBI," Bourne pointed out. "Doesn't that make you a government boy, too?"

"I thought I could change things from the inside. I was wrong. Some things need to be torn down before we can rebuild them. Back then, I already knew that technology would rule the world, but you had these naive notions about privacy."

"So was that what split us up? Government versus technology?"

Scott smiled and shook his head. "Oh, no. In the end, we argued over a girl. Isn't that always how it goes?"

"We both wanted the same girl?"

"Actually, no, you didn't like her at all. She was younger than me. Sixteen years old, but all grown up, believe me. You thought she was wrong for me. Funny thing is, I always had the suspicion that she wanted *you* even more than me. Anyway, it came down to a choice, and I was young and in lust, and I chose her. You went home. I kept traveling with her. You and I didn't talk again for a long time after that."

"Well, I'm sorry we let it come between us," Bourne told him.

"As am I. But it's been water under the bridge for a long, long time." Scott put down his glass as he heard the ringing of his phone. He grabbed it and listened to the call, and then he hung up with a smile. "The limo's on its way in. Miles is back."

"I'd like to meet the car," Bourne said.

"Whatever you want, but it's not really necessary. We have security on the grounds, and even a sharpshooter would struggle in this rain, if that's what you're worried about."

"Even so."

Scott nodded. "Of course, let's go. But we'll use the front door this time, if you don't mind."

His friend gestured at a larger doorway out of the library, and the two of them headed down a wide set of carpeted stairs past walls paneled in oak, featuring ornate carvings and medieval paintings that Bourne assumed could be valued in the millions of dollars. In the marble foyer, Scott retrieved a trench coat and secured a hat on his head. A security guard opened the heavy castle door for them, and they walked out under the covering of the stone porte cochere. In front of them, an entrance road crossed over a pond from the gardens and led into a circular driveway. Bourne could see a stretch limousine emerging between the trees, drawing closer to the castle.

He checked the area. There were no threats from the tree line. He spotted no aircraft over their heads, and Scott was right that there were no useful sightlines for a sniper. Four security guards converged on the car from both sides of the estate, and he saw that they had light weapons in their hands. The men looked capable and alert. Even so, Bourne left the cover of the porte cochere and walked into the driving rain to meet the limousine himself.

His gun was in his hand.

He wiped rain from his face and yanked open the back door of the limo. It took him a moment to see into the back seat, which was mostly in shadow. Miles Priest was there, his tall frame slumped down in the leather seat, his chin tucked on his neck. Bourne thought at first that he was asleep, but he wasn't.

He was dead.

A bullet in his forehead. Blood covering his face.

Bourne ducked out of the car to shout a warning, but as he spun around, the four security guards all pointed their weapons at him. He had nowhere to go. Meanwhile, the driver's door of the limousine opened, and a dark-haired woman climbed out into the rain and pierced him with her reptilian eyes. Her lips bent into a nasty smile.

Miss Shirley.

"Scott, *run!*" Bourne shouted.

But his old friend, his best friend, made no attempt to get away. He walked into the rain in his trench coat and headed for the limousine. There was no fear or surprise on his face. When he got to Miss Shirley, he grabbed her neck and their bodies slammed against each other like the horns of two rams as he pulled her into a violent kiss.

"Hello, Shirl," Scott said when they finally broke apart. "I've missed you."

FORTY-FOUR

"**M**EDUSA is *you*?" Bourne said to Scott.

His old friend slung his arm around Miss Shirley's waist, and the dominatrix assumed an unexpected new role and nuzzled him like a kitten, licking his face. "I'm sorry, Jason. There was never an assault team hiding in the woods. Medusa didn't need to storm the castle. We're already here."

Bourne shook his head in disbelief. "I don't know you at all. I never did."

"Actually, you knew me better than you think," Scott told him. "Right from the beginning. That political argument we had back in college? You accused me of believing the ends justified the means, and you were right. Profound change always requires disruption. I had the raw idea for Medusa even back then. It took a few years for the technology to catch up to what I wanted to achieve, but I knew it would eventually. When I saw what

Gabriel Fox was doing with Prescix, I knew it was time to move. Of course, I needed funding to make it happen, but that wasn't hard to arrange when I had the right bait to offer."

"Namely?"

"Social manipulation. Conflict. Western civilization divided and at each other's throats. Civil war. Don't worry, it's only temporary. Technology will be the greatest unifying force in human history, once we get rid of the obsolete nation states standing in the way. It will take a couple more generations, but we'll get there in the end."

"At the cost of how many lives?" Bourne asked.

Scott shrugged. "You never did see the big picture. Always too focused on the individual. By the way, gun on the ground, please, Jason." Scott gestured at two of the Medusa operatives. "Take away his weapons."

Bourne felt the guards take away his smoke grenades. His hacksaw blade. His knives. The backup pistol on his ankle. The only thing they didn't find was the length of slim nylon rope clipped under his shirt.

"I'm sorry you don't remember our time in Prague," Scott went on. "That visit changed my life. I met Shirl there. You didn't understand that she and I were two halves of the same soul. You thought she was amoral, ruthless, violent, and you're right, she was all of those things. She was only sixteen, but how many old men had you killed in bed by that point, lover?"

"Nine," Miss Shirley said with a smirk.

"Nine. I told you, she was all grown up. Anyway, the

thing you never understood, Jason, is that you weren't wrong about Shirley. You were wrong about *me*. I was just like her, but you didn't see it."

Bourne was tired of the game. "So what happens now, Scott?"

"Isn't it obvious? Miles takes the fall for everything. Miles and the rogue intelligence agent he recruited. The two of you are the perfect villains. Let everyone think Medusa has been crippled. I'm sure you remember the Treadstone lesson. When your enemy thinks he's winning, he's at his most vulnerable."

"People will know that's not true," Bourne said.

"A few. But they won't say a word. Nelly Lessard will be suspicious, but she's a loyal soldier, and if she gets out of line, well, she'll be dealt with. Of course, there's one other inevitable consequence, Jason. I can't have you around to get in the way of our plans again. Now that you've played your part, you have to die. I want you to know, I'm genuinely sorry about that. Growing up, you were like a brother to me. But those days are gone. After all, you don't remember any of it, do you?"

"For the first time, I'm actually glad about that."

Scott shrugged off the insult. He signaled to the men to drag the body of Miles Priest out of the limousine. "Make sure he's never found. It'll be to our advantage for people not to be sure if he's alive or dead. And Jason, it's time to say goodbye. I've got to get to Washington to get the next phase of our plans underway. Just so you know, I wanted to make the end quick for you. But Shirley decided to make it more interesting, and I really hate to say no to her. Like I told you, I always had the sneaking suspicion that she wanted *you* more than me."

Miss Shirley studied him with her snake eyes and gave him another smile that was colder than the rain.

"Goodbye, old friend," Scott told him.

He got into the back of the limousine, and two of the Medusa agents climbed into the front. The vehicle's engine roared to life, and the limo continued around the circular driveway and disappeared across the castle pond into the trees. The other two agents took hold of the body of Miles Priest and dragged it across the wet grass.

Bourne was alone with Miss Shirley.

She wore a black bodysuit that clung to her lithe frame. Her soaking-wet black hair was pasted to her face. They were the same height, staring at each other eye to eye. He tried to grasp a memory of her from his youth, when she was a depraved sixteen-year-old in Prague, seducing his best friend. Every now and then, images of his past came back like photographs, but the only memory he had of this woman was the look on her face outside the Lucky Nickel hotel.

It was as if she knew exactly what he was thinking.

"Yes, it was me, Bourne," she told him. "I'm the one who killed your precious Nova."

He shook his head in despair. "*Why?*"

"She found out about Hackman. She was trying to figure out how he fit into our plans. That was what gave her away, actually. We traced the online research she was doing on him, and so I knew she was still taking orders from Treadstone. We had to get rid of her before she put it all together. Hackman was our ultimate beta test, you see. He was our proof of everything we could do to manipulate people once we combined Prescix with the data hack. We couldn't let that be discovered."

"So you lured Nova to the car show," Bourne said. "And you killed her."

"That's right. I took the first shot. I couldn't rely on Hackman finding her in the crowd, but the truth is, I wanted to do it myself. Partly because she betrayed us and partly because she was with *you*. I'm very possessive when it comes to you, Jason. I always have been."

"But you didn't kill me," Bourne said.

"No. That would have been too easy. Scott is right. I've wanted you since I first met you as a girl. Not just for sex, of course. Sex is easy. I've wanted the *battle*. The battle is so much more satisfying. So yes, I could have killed you from the Lucky Nickel, but I had to be patient. Sooner or later, I knew I'd get my chance to deal with you up close. To end things in an appropriate way. And here we are."

"How do you know you'll win?" Bourne asked.

"Because I'm better than you. I always have been."

She slid her hands behind her back, and when they emerged again, she had a Glock in her left hand. In her right, she held the viciously sharp crescent-moon knife that she'd used to threaten Abbey.

"Piece by piece, Bourne," she told him, making a

threshing motion with the knife. "That's how this goes down for you. Piece. By. Piece. Now turn around and walk. Keep your hands up."

"Walk where?"

Miss Shirley gestured over his shoulder. "To the cliff."

Bourne had no choice. He walked. The rain poured down over both of them, filling the air with a ceaseless drumroll of water slapping against skin, earth, and stone. Black clouds massed overhead. The distant low hills disappeared into mist and fog. Still he walked, hearing her footsteps right behind him. Beyond the castle, they reached an old cemetery, where the carved names had been worn away by centuries of weather. Some of the tombstones had fallen; some sagged toward the wet ground. Mold and moss grew on the gray stones. The ruins of an old chapel stood watch from behind fallen walls and gaping window holes that had once housed gleaming stained glass. The wind howled, as if trying to wake up generations of ghosts.

"Keep going," Miss Shirley ordered him.

Ahead of him, Bourne saw the twelve-foot castle wall clinging to the cliff's edge. On the other side of that wall, a hundred feet below, he heard a storm of sea waves assaulting the rock and mud of the hillside. Stone steps led up to the top of the wall. When he stopped at the base of the steps, he felt the sharp point of Miss Shirley's knife. With the barest touch, it cut through his black shirt and made a bloody line across his back.

"Up."

He climbed the wet, slippery steps. Miss Shirley followed. At the top, he found himself on a walkway no more than three feet wide. A low stone parapet was built along the edge, but erosion had worn it down, and entire stretches had long since tumbled into the sea. He glanced down and saw black rocks jutting out of the water like broken teeth scattered at the base of the cliff. The waves made a nonstop crashing thunder.

"Turn around," Miss Shirley called loudly over the rain and the waves.

Bourne did. She stood no more than five feet away. They faced each other, both soaked to the skin. She had heels on, but she kicked them off and stood on the wall in her bare feet.

"Jump if you want," she said to him. "I won't stop you. Take the coward's way out."

"No thanks."

"Do you still think you can beat me? I told you, Bourne, I'm superior. Before we're done, I'll take off your clothes. I'll take off your skin. I'll take off your limbs. And then I'll fuck what's left while you're still alive. You'll wish you'd jumped."

"It's easy to say you're superior when you're holding a gun and a knife."

Her face had no expression. Like a poker player, she showed nothing. But he'd succeeded in inflaming her ego. With her eyes as hard as two aquamarine jewels, she flicked the pistol off the parapet and into the sea.

"No gun," she said.

"And the knife?" Bourne asked.

Miss Shirley squatted to place the crescent blade at her

feet, never taking her eyes off his face. "If you want the knife, you'll have to come and get it."

Bourne did. He took the first step toward her, but she struck back with insane speed. He never even saw her move. Her foot lashed out, hammering him under his ribs, driving the air from his lungs. He stuttered backward, barely keeping his balance on the rampart, and he doubled over, coughing and gasping for air.

"I'll make one last offer of mercy," Miss Shirley told him. "Crawl over here on your hands and knees and kiss my feet. If you do that, I'll make it quick. I'll just cut your heart out and we'll be done."

Bourne steadied himself on the wall. Oxygen slowly swelled his chest again. He felt the tiredness of the past days catching up to him. His headache throbbed. His wounds opened up and leaked blood. A part of him knew it would be easier to jump. A part of him knew he was going to lose. Then he stared through the driving rain at Miss Shirley, and instead of her face, he saw Nova. He could see Nova's body coming into focus through the scope of this woman's rifle. He could see Miss Shirley's finger, her sharp black fingernail, as she squeezed the trigger.

He charged. He threw himself at her across the walkway. She deflected his blow as if she were schooling a child and then drove a knee into his groin and hit him in the head three times, left right left. Pain split open his skull. His ears rang. Dizziness made the wall spin. She hit him once more, a jab square in the neck, and he fell backward, choking. His legs crumpled underneath him.

He collapsed to the stone, rain and sky spinning around his eyes like a kaleidoscope. Blood spat from his lips.

Miss Shirley picked up the knife and came for him.

Bourne tried to move, tried to scramble away, but her foot kicked across the bottom of his chin like it was a football, and his head crashed against the stone. He lay stretched out on the walkway over the sea, unable to fight back. Miss Shirley knelt on top of him. Her knees held his thighs down. With the point of the blade, she cut open his shirt and exposed his bare chest. The cool fingers of her other hand found his heart, which was beating wildly. She caressed him, stroking his skin. Then her fingers squeezed into a fist, and she thumped down hard on his torso with a single blow that made his entire body scream with agony. His heart, staggered by the impact, nearly stopped right there.

"Shall we begin?" Miss Shirley said.

Her right arm raised the crescent blade in the air. She swung it like a scythe, with lightning speed, and his left hand reacted by instinct. He grabbed her wrist and locked it in his fingers. He held her arm frozen in place, the blade inches from severing his shoulder. She pushed down; he pushed back, like a tug-of-war. But her strength was unbelievable. Millimeter by millimeter, she overpowered him. The knife drew closer.

Miss Shirley's other hand pinched his throat. She cut off his air. With his right hand, he tried to pry away her fingers, but her grip was like a tiger's jaws clamped around prey. His lungs boiled. His eyes began to roll up into his head. His left arm, the one keeping the knife at bay, began to weaken. In a few more seconds, he'd lose consciousness, and he'd awaken to find himself in the midst of a slow, torturous death.

She knew she was winning. She bent down close to his face, eye to eye, and kissed his lips like a lover.

"After we're done here, I think I'll take a little vacation, Bourne," she told him with a sadistic giggle in her voice. "I know just where to go. *Quebec City.*"

Bourne's muscles tightened with rage. He saw the threat in her eyes, and he believed every word of it. She'd go after Abbey next. She'd kill her, too, slowly and horribly. And he was the only one who could stop it.

His lungs, his limbs, his whole body wanted to give up. But his brain refused.

He let go of the wrist clamped around his throat. His right arm pawed on the wet stone for something, anything, he could use to fight back. That was when he felt the coils of the nylon climbing rope still clipped to his belt. Under his shirt, he found the loop that was knotted into the rope. With his eyes burning into hers, he jerked the loop over her head and around her neck before she understood what was happening. Then he wrenched the rope back hard, dragging her head with it, and her dark eyes widened with shock and fear as her own lungs were stripped of air.

Her hands weakened, just for an instant. The knife wobbled in her grasp. He used that second to let go and drive his left hand like a piston into her chest. She shuddered with the blow; the knife spilled from her fingers. Her other hand unlocked from his throat, letting in sweet air. Her body reared back, giving him a single moment of freedom, and he dug his fingernails under the calf pressing down on his thigh and upended her. She screamed as she flew. Her body landed against the parapet, then broke through the old stone and disappeared backward over the wall into the air.

As she fell, the rope uncoiled from his belt, slithering like a snake. It dragged him with her toward the edge of the cliff. He braced his feet against the worn outcropping, but the weight of her body yanked him forward and tumbled him over the edge. His fingers grasped for any handhold that would keep him from falling. Then, with a jolt, the pressure at the end of the rope vanished. He held on, clinging to the rock with the tips of his fingers. When he looked down into the voracious sea, he saw Miss Shirley falling the rest of the way to the bottom of the cliff.

She fell in two pieces.

The rope around her neck had cut off her head.

Her body landed in the white surf, which sucked it in and consumed it. Her head bounced like a soccer ball off the pointed sea rocks and became wedged in a furrow in the granite. Waves crashed over the head but failed to dislodge it. She landed faceup, and her eyes stayed open, staring grotesquely at Bourne as he dangled from the wall.

FORTY-FIVE

BOURNE made it down from the wall and back to the cemetery before he collapsed. He lost consciousness, his body yielding to a tidal wave of pain. When he opened his eyes again, he had no idea how much time had passed. The rain had stopped, but the daylight was almost gone, and thick dark clouds raced overhead. He pushed himself up slowly until he was sitting on the wet ground. A deep chill in his bones made him shiver. He rubbed his hands through his hair, blinked, and waited for the dizziness to pass.

Then he saw that he wasn't alone.

Nash Rollins loomed over him, a solitary figure in a hat and gray raincoat in the middle of the old graves. The Treadstone agent leaned on a cane and pointed a gun at Bourne's chest.

"You look like hell, Jason."

"Thanks."

"That must have been one hell of a fight."

"At least I kept my head," he replied.

"Yeah, I saw what you left at the bottom of the cliff. That's enough to give me nightmares."

"You and me both," Bourne said. He studied the empty grounds and the austere frame of the old castle set against the trees. "Is the area secure?"

"It is. MI5 gave us a hand."

"The Medusa guards?"

"We dealt with them."

"If you search the woods, you'll find the body of Miles Priest. They killed him."

"I'm sorry to hear that. I wouldn't say I liked Miles, but I had a grudging respect for him. We were a little bit alike. Both of us willing to make the hard choices and go it alone if we needed to. You're the same way."

Bourne stood up on unsteady legs. He didn't bother trying to run. He knew he wouldn't make it more than a few steps before collapsing again, and Nash was unlikely to miss at this range.

"I take it you're here to kill me," Bourne said.

"I'm sorry. That was always the plan. The director wants you dead."

"I'm not Medusa, Nash. I never was."

"Abbey Laurent told me the same thing. She said I should help you instead of killing you."

"Do you believe her?"

"Honestly, I don't know what to believe anymore."

"Then I guess you have a choice to make," Bourne said.

Rollins sighed loudly and sat down on top of one of the gravestones. He propped his chin on the end of his cane. "You and I go way back, Jason."

"Yes, we do."

"You were always one of my best men. I work with a lot of agents who are smart and tough, but you had something more. Somehow you managed to hang on to your soul long after the rest of us had lost ours. I respected that. But ever since what you went through, ever since the memory loss, I've had my doubts. Damaged men are a liability in our business."

"We're all damaged," Bourne said.

"Maybe so. Maybe you're right about that. I've sure as hell made my share of mistakes. The fact is, I was willing to believe the worst about you. I was absolutely certain you'd turned. What happened in New York just confirmed what I already believed. You needed to go, Jason. You needed to be taken out. I was willing to pull the trigger myself, regardless of our history."

"Well, here I am. If that's what you think, pull the trigger."

Rollins let out a humorless laugh and shoved his gun back in its holster. "I was wrong about all of it, wasn't I? Every last thing."

"Yes."

"Ortiz? Benoit? It wasn't you. It was that monster at the bottom of the cliff who killed them."

"And Nova, too," Bourne said.

"Christ. I'm sorry, Jason. Truly."

"Don't blame yourself, Nash. You made a judgment

based on the evidence you had. The evidence Medusa wanted you to see. Anyone looking at who I was, at what I'd done, would have come to the same conclusion. I didn't give you any reason to doubt yourself."

"Well, I've never been troubled by self-doubt," Rollins replied. "I always thought it was a sign of weakness."

"Since I lost my memory, I'm never without it."

Rollins's mouth wrinkled into a frown. "We still have a problem, you know. We haven't stopped Medusa. You dealt them a blow, but it's not fatal. Taking out the black widow leaves a lot of other spiders behind."

"Except we know who's spinning the web."

"Oh?"

"Scott DeRay," Bourne said. "Medusa was his brainchild from the very beginning."

Rollins whistled with surprise. "Seriously? You two were close. He was willing to set you up?"

"I made it easy for him."

The Treadstone agent shook his head. "Unfortunately, knowing that doesn't change anything, Jason. Even if you're right, we can't simply make a move against him. Scott has Medusa spies in place throughout the government. They'll cover for him if we try to do anything without evidence. No one will believe your story."

"A mentally deranged ex-agent suspected of shooting a congresswoman? No. They won't."

"Plus, Scott will never tip his hand if he knows you're still alive. As long as he thinks you're out there hunting him, he'll keep operating in the background, and we'll never be able to expose him or the network."

"You're right."

"I want to roll all of these bastards up, Jason, but right now, the biggest thing standing in the way of that is you."

Bourne didn't say anything at first, because everything Nash said was true. Scott needed to feel safe if they were going to take him down. He needed to believe that Cain was no longer a threat. It was the same lesson that Scott had quoted to him earlier.

When your enemy thinks he's winning, he's at his most vulnerable.

Treadstone.

"In that case, you know what you have to do," Bourne told him. "It's why you came here in the first place."

"What's that?" Rollins asked.

"You have to kill me."

DISAPPEARANCE OF CARILLON CEO EXPOSES A WIDE-RANGING CONSPIRACY

May 3, 2020
WASHINGTON (AP)

In the wake of the disappearance of former FBI director and Carillon CEO Miles Priest, federal officials are releasing details for the first time about a shadowy anarchist organization in which Priest is believed to have been involved.

Known by the nickname Medusa, the organization has operated in secrecy for several years, using technology and violence to foment divisions along political and cultural lines. Medusa is suspected of playing a role in the recent assassination of Congresswoman Sofia Ortiz and in the murders of several chief executives of worldwide technology companies on a private Caribbean island owned by Priest.

Long considered one of the most influential leaders in the technology community, Priest is now described by officials in the Department of Justice as the mastermind of Medusa and the architect of a strategy to undermine popular confidence in democratic government. His whereabouts remain unknown.

The shocking developments have raised questions about the future of Big Tech, with aggressive new legislation targeting the industry expected to pass Congress in the next few days. Analysts expect a wave of much tighter regulations governing how the largest tech companies handle data and interact with customers.

At Carillon Technology, where Priest served as CEO, the revelations have prompted a leadership shake-up. Carillon, which is a key provider of database infrastructure to a wide range of internet companies, announced yesterday that senior vice president and COO Scott DeRay would take over as the new chief executive.

DeRay, who claims to have no knowledge of Priest's activities with Medusa, promised a full internal investigation and cooperation with federal authorities.

In a prepared statement, DeRay said, "Now is the time for the tech giants of this country, including Carillon, to regain credibility with the government and the public, and I plan to lead that charge."

According to anonymous intelligence sources, the Medusa organization has been under investigation by officials in the United States and Europe for some time. The investigation recently culminated in a joint US-UK raid on the Priest compound in Scotland, in which several Medusa mercenaries were killed.

Among the dead was an ex–intelligence agent so far known only by the code name Cain, who was widely suspected of being the mastermind behind the Ortiz assassination. . . .

FORTY-SIX

SCOTT DeRay strolled along Rue de Vaugirard next to a wrought-iron fence outside the Jardin du Luxembourg. It was mid-morning under a blue sky, with May weather that was unseasonably warm for Paris. He wore a bespoke gray business suit he'd collected from his Savile Row tailor the previous week in London, and he used a hat and sunglasses to avoid being recognized. The media had featured him in its headlines recently, which meant that his photograph had been seen around the world. He didn't want to take chances.

Stopping on the sidewalk outside the park, Scott threw a casual glance back the way he'd come, looking for signs that he was being followed. With his intelligence training, he didn't think that anyone would be able to stay on his tail without him spotting it. It would take a skilled agent to do that. Even so, he had an instinct that he was being watched, and that instinct had dogged him for days.

Ahead of him, he heard a cacophony of voices. A crowd of Chinese tourists emerged through the park's northwest gate, following a petite raven-haired guide who waved a small flag over her head. The crush of visitors spilled into the street and took up all of the space on the sidewalk, squeezing Scott uncomfortably against the high railing. Just in front of him, a Chinese man in a suit took pictures with an expensive camera while walking backward. Scott shouted a warning as the man came closer, but the elderly Chinese man piled into him anyway and nearly knocked both of them down. As they untangled, Scott strained to keep a polite smile on his face, and the tourist apologized profusely in Chinese.

When the crowd had passed on the way back to their tour bus, Scott checked his surroundings again to confirm that he was alone. Then he walked two more blocks and crossed into a cobblestoned side street. He found a small bistro named Bergeron with red awnings, where two beefy bodyguards with radios stood watch outside. Russian security was always painfully obvious. The café typically didn't open until dinner, but Scott had arranged for a private breakfast to be served that morning. He nodded at the two bodyguards, allowed himself to be searched, then went inside.

A single table for two had been set in the café's corner, far from the windows. There, he saw Fyodor Mikhailov waiting for him. The chairs in the café were made of delicate braided metal, and Scott was surprised that they could stand up to the Russian's massive girth. Fyodor had a napkin stuffed into the collar of his shirt, and he was already halfway through breakfast, with a silver urn of coffee on the table in front of him, along with croissants, a crusty baguette, apricot pastries, macaron cookies in rainbow colors, and a selection of aromatic cheeses.

"Scott, my friend," Fyodor rumbled. "Sit, sit. Take a load off."

Scott sat down and wiped his brow. The interior of the café felt extremely warm, and he found himself sweating. "Good morning, Fyodor."

A waitress in a crisp white blouse and short black skirt appeared next to him with a double espresso. He shook his head when she asked if he wanted anything else. She fluffed the fresh flowers on the table, then disappeared with a flirty smile. She couldn't be more than twenty years old.

"The shit of getting old is that you still feel young," Fyodor said, his eyes following the girl back to the kitchen.

"You, Fyodor? You're not old, you're timeless."

The Russian snorted. "If I get any more timeless, I'll be dead. My doctor says I need to give up vodka, wine, and rich food."

"How's that going?"

"I gave up my doctor instead. Try the Epoisses. It smells like an infantryman's boot after a month at the front, but my God, it's delicious."

"Maybe later."

The Russian bit off half a croissant smeared with a vile-smelling paste and groaned with delight as he chewed. "The newspapers are painting you as the savior of the American tech industry. That made me laugh out loud, I'll tell you. The only thing better than fucking over your adversary is getting him to thank you for doing it."

Scott allowed himself a smile. "The U.S. media is even easier to manipulate than Congress. Give them an anonymous source, and they'll print whatever you want."

"Miles Priest a traitor to his country. I love that."

"I figured you would," Scott said.

"Still, I didn't like seeing the name Medusa out there so much, my friend. That's a hell of a risk. You exposed too much of what we're really doing. My colleagues in Moscow aren't happy."

"Tell them not to worry," Scott replied. "Putting out details about Medusa was part of the plan. The point is to convince most of the Western governments that Medusa is under control. A neutralized threat. We served up Miles as our sacrificial lamb, and we showed enough of our real hand to make them think they have us on the run. So while they waste time with their subpoenas and congressional investigations, we can proceed with our next step."

"You mean Prescix?"

Scott nodded. He took a lavender-colored macaron cookie from the tray in front of him, but when he ate it, he found it oddly difficult to swallow, as if an apricot pit had begun to swell in his windpipe. "Yes, my first major initiative as CEO of Carillon will be to announce that the Prescix board has agreed to a merger."

"Assuming your DOJ doesn't stop it," Fyodor pointed out.

"The feds? Please. They're salivating at the idea. I've already promised them that we'll adapt the Prescix code to help with their antiterrorism investigations. They'll identify a few white supremacists shouting '*Sieg Heil*' and look like heroes. For them, the merger can't come soon enough. That will also take all of their antitrust threats off the table. Meanwhile, we'll integrate the personal data from the hack and run all of it through the Prescix algorithms. That's tens of millions of people. We'll have them believing whatever we want them to believe. Left, right, it doesn't matter. The next election is going to be utter chaos. It's everything you want."

"Oh, we want much more than that," Fyodor reminded him. "This is only the beginning, my friend."

Scott sipped his espresso and wrung a hand through the fabric of his collar, which was now damp with his sweat. *Yes, you want civil war, you old fool. And I'll give it to you. People will be at each other's throats, but not just in New York, Portland, and San Francisco. The streets of Moscow and Beijing will erupt, too. We'll burn it all down and get ready to rebuild under a new master plan.*

The Medusa plan.

"It will take more money," Scott replied.

"Oh, don't worry about that. You'll have whatever you need. I'll make sure of it. Of course, I'll expect some favors of my own. I have a few names of people who may need special attention from the Prescix software. Political rivals. Some diplomats who have been uncooperative. My wife's brother. That sort of thing."

Scott chuckled. "I expected as much. Just give me a list."

"Good, fine, excellent," Fyodor announced, happily slapping the bistro table and making his coffee spill. "I've always liked doing business with you, Scott. Hard to believe it's been all these years, isn't it? I remember meeting you that summer in Prague, this cocky college kid with all these ridiculous plans to run the world. And that girl with you, oh my God. Even at sixteen, Miss Shirley was scarier than anyone in the FSB. But I saw something in you. You were different. I knew you'd make one of the best assets I ever recruited."

"Thank you, Fyodor," Scott replied.

Although the truth is, I *was the one who recruited* you.

Fyodor cut into another of the cheeses, and the wafting smell affected Scott with a wave of nausea. He had to hold on to the table to steady himself as the room spun. He felt a strange tingling in his lips, like the pricks of a hundred needles.

"You all right, my friend?" Fyodor asked, chewing loudly. "You're starting to look sick."

"I'm fine," Scott replied.

"I was sorry to hear the news about your Miss Shirley, by the way."

Scott said nothing at the mention of her name. He missed Shirl, but he hadn't cried for her. She would have detested any show of weakness like that from him. Even so, it was still hard to imagine his world without her.

She'd been a secret ally at his side for almost twenty years.

"I'd always assumed she was indestructible," Fyodor went on.

"So had I."

"Bourne killed her?"

"Yes."

"I would have liked to see that battle," Fyodor mused. "It must have been one for the ages. How did he do it?"

"He cut off her head," Scott murmured angrily.

"Just like Perseus and Medusa, eh? How ironic. What about Bourne himself?"

"Treadstone killed him."

"Are you sure? Bourne has proved to be a slippery adversary in the past."

Scott rubbed his temples with his fingers. A fierce headache had now taken root behind his eyes. "This time I'm sure. Treadstone tried hard to keep it quiet, but we intercepted an encrypted transmission of a classified report directly to the attorney general. It confirmed his death."

"Well, RIP Jason Bourne. I do like it when the American government does our work for us."

Scott nodded in agreement, but he'd begun to feel light-headed. He didn't understand what was happening to him. The flu? He found it hard to concentrate on their conversation. He needed to get back outside into the fresh air of Paris. "I told you Bourne wouldn't be a problem, Fyodor."

"Indeed you did."

"I'll let you know when we're moving ahead on Prescix. And how much more money we need."

"Do that." Fyodor reached across the table and wrapped up Scott's hand in his paw. "Anyway, congratulations, my friend. I appreciate a man who delivers on his promises. There's bound to be a bonus in it for you. Whatever you want."

Scott stood up from the chair. As he did, the inside of the café made somersaults in front of his eyes. "I don't care about anything like that."

"Ah yes, of course," Fyodor replied, with a cynical rasp in his voice. "You don't care about material things, says the man in the five-thousand-dollar Savile Row suit. You're an idealist. You know what we call idealists in Russia, don't you?"

"What?"

Fyodor leaned dangerously far back in the little café chair and laughed until his belly shook. "As soon as I find one, I'll let you know."

FYODOR was in no hurry to leave the café.

When he was done with the food, he signaled to the lovely little French waitress and ordered a bottle of Pouilly-Fuissé to wash it all down. She poured him the first glass, and while she did, his thick fingers explored her ass under the thin fabric of her skirt. She didn't slap his hand away. Instead, she gave him a grin and a wink that said: *Ask me how much.*

Ah, Paris. He loved this city.

An hour later, he'd finished the wine and had a buzz that would last him until lunch. He stripped the linen napkin out of his collar and crumpled it on the table. He pushed his huge frame out of the chair and took heavy, unsteady steps toward the café door. Outside, he paid no attention to his bodyguards standing on either side of the bistro entrance. His town car waited for him at the curb. He closed his eyes briefly to savor the sunshine, and then he bent down and yanked open the town car's rear door.

The car wasn't empty. Nash Rollins sat in the back seat.

"Fyodor Mikhailov," Rollins announced in a pleasant voice. "It's been a long time."

The Russian whirled around with surprising speed for a big man, but that was when he noticed for the first time that the two bodyguards outside the café were not his own men. They were strangers. Americans. With guns.

Fyodor gave a long, loud sigh of resignation. Life was what it was. You won until you lost, and then you dealt with the consequences. "Nash Rollins. I take it we're going for a drive, are we?"

"Yes, we are. Come, join me."

Rollins slid over to the opposite side of the town car and patted the leather seat next to him. Fyodor squeezed his bulk inside, and one of the American agents slammed the door shut behind him. No one outside could see through the smoked windows. The car headed off slowly into the Parisian streets.

"I'm a diplomat, Nash," Fyodor reminded him. "You're making a serious mistake by kidnapping me."

Rollins gave a friendly tap on the Russian's knee with his cane. "Kidnapping? Don't be so dramatic, Fyodor. You're free to go. In fact, we can drop you off at your embassy if you'd like. However, we both know that Moscow doesn't like the smell of failure. Agents who fail tend not to live very long. And that's what I'm smelling on your suit, Fyodor. Failure. It's even stronger than all of that French cheese."

Fyodor frowned with his many chins. "Explain."

"We have everything on tape. Your meeting with Scott DeRay. Medusa. Prescix. That waitress you were groping? She's mine. She could crack that thick neck of yours like a pretzel if she wanted, by the way. See, that civil war you want is officially over before it starts. Tomorrow, the American media will report that the Prescix software is being used as a front for Russian counterintelligence. Trading will be suspended. The company will be shut down and its code taken apart byte by byte to see what little games you and Medusa have been up to. So by all means, go back to Moscow if you want, but we both know the only thing waiting for you is an extra-large hole dug in the taiga forest."

The Russian spent a moment evaluating what Rollins had said. "I take it you're offering me an alternative."

"I am."

Fyodor was nothing if not practical. "What do you want, and what do I get?"

"What I want is information. You come back to the U.S. and tell us everything you know about the inner workings of Medusa. Names, locations, moles in the government and private industry, targets, plans. All the details about the data hack and how it was done and who was affected. You give us everything we need to take apart the entire Medusa infrastructure person by person. Do that, and we give you a free pass. You get a beachside Florida condominium with an all-new identity and plenty of money to spend on hookers, vodka, and caviar."

Fyodor stared out the window at Paris, knowing he was unlikely ever to see the city again. He lit a cigarette in the back of the town car and reflected on his options, which didn't take long, because he didn't have any. He wasted no time on patriotic sentiment. A living traitor was better than a dead patriot.

"Florida?" he asked. "You want to send me to Florida?"

"Or anywhere else you prefer," Rollins replied.

The Russian shrugged and blew out a cloud of smoke. "Florida is fine. Humidity and cockroaches don't bother me. But throw in a lifetime pass to Disney World, okay? I like to ride the teacups."

FORTY-SEVEN

BOURNE followed Scott DeRay from the Parisian bistro into the sprawling grounds of the Jardin du Luxembourg.

By the time his old friend reached the geometric gardens laid out in front of the palace, it was obvious that the poison was rapidly taking effect. He could see Scott's steps grow erratic. Getting closer, he saw sweat pouring down the man's face and tremors wracking his limbs. Scott staggered to a bench near the green waters of the pond, where children played with brightly colored toy sailboats. It reminded Bourne of the time they'd met in Central Park, not long ago.

The truth was written on Scott's face. He didn't know how, but he knew he was dying.

He watched Scott pull out a phone to call for help, but the phone slipped from his numb fingers and fell to the pavement. Bourne came over and picked up the phone and then sat down next to him.

"It says on your Prescix profile that you're going to die horribly today, Scott. It's scary how accurate that software is."

Scott turned his head slowly and tried to focus, and his eyes finally widened with recognition. "*You.*"

"Yes, I'm sorry to still be alive," Bourne replied. "I really didn't think you'd swallow the story about Nash killing me, but he said we just needed to make the information hard for you to find. I guess he was right."

If you want someone to believe a lie, cover it up like a secret you're desperate to keep.

Treadstone.

Scott struggled to fight back. He lifted a hand to reach into the pocket of his suit, where Bourne knew he kept a gun, but then his hand fell back to the bench and lay limply at his side. He had no strength. Even his voice sounded like an effort.

"What's the poison, Jason?" he asked. "Tetrodotoxin?"

"The symptoms fit," Bourne agreed. "Given how quickly it's working, I imagine it was a massive dose. You only have a few minutes left."

"Are you saying you didn't do this?" Scott asked.

Bourne watched the families playing in the park. Children ate ice cream cones. Lovers kissed. No one noticed the man dying on the bench in front of them. "No. Sorry, Scott, that wasn't me."

"*Who?*"

"You chose the wrong enemy," Bourne told him. "One of the CEOs that your team murdered in the Caribbean was Hon Xiu-Le from Shanghai. He wasn't among the bodies, so we didn't know where he was at first. Apparently, Miss Shirley tied him up in one of the Jeeps before she blew it up. Treadstone found what was left of him and was able to confirm his identity. Definitely a mistake. Hon had a lot of friends high up in the Chinese government. You don't make that kind of money over there unless you're connected to the party circle. They were very upset to find out that he'd been killed. When I called one of my counterparts in Beijing, he was extremely interested to learn that *you* were the one behind Hon's death. They were happy to work with us."

Scott closed his eyes. "The old Chinese tourist outside the park."

"Yes, he was good. I was watching for it, and I still didn't spot him giving you the injection. I've been following you for a couple of weeks now. Actually, Nash and I were getting nervous that the Chinese might go after you before you had a chance to lead us to whoever was funding Medusa. They told us they'd wait, but we weren't sure how long. But then you arranged the meeting with Fyodor this morning, so we gave them the green light. By the way, Fyodor is with Nash now. Telling him everything. Medusa is done, Scott. It's over."

Scott opened his eyes and spat the words at Bourne as he struggled for breath. "I could have killed you any time I wanted, Jason. I let you live because we were friends."

"You let me live because you could manipulate me. That's all."

Bourne dug into the back pocket of his slacks and pulled out a worn, wrinkled photograph. The picture showed two boys on an anonymous beach, with the whitecaps of the Atlantic behind them. They couldn't be more than eleven years old, both in baggy swim trunks. The boys had their arms around each other's shoulders and big grins on their faces. Looking at them, he found it hard to see himself in the taller boy on the left or Scott in the boy on the right. It had been another lifetime for both of them. They'd grown into completely different people.

"We stopped being friends years ago," Bourne said, dropping the photograph into the man's lap. He had no use for it anymore. "Goodbye, Scott."

He stood up from the bench, but Scott grabbed his wrist in a weak grip. "Wait."

Jason stared down at him and said nothing.

"You're not just killing me," Scott told him, as if it were a curse. "When I die, you die, too. Your whole childhood. Who you really were. Your past will be gone forever. I'm the only one who remembers it."

Bourne shook his head. "You're wrong about that. I have no past."

He slipped sunglasses over his face and walked away into the park.

———

IT was June 1 in Quebec City. Ten o'clock at night.

Darkness shrouded the boardwalk below the Château Frontenac. Abbey checked her watch to be sure of the time. It was the early summer season, and dozens of people strolled in and out of shadows in the glow of the fairy lights. A cool breeze blew across the cliff top, and the St. Lawrence River made a black ribbon between the hills below her. Her mind was tense with anticipation. She leaned on the railing under the gazebo canopy, in the exact place where she'd waited for a mystery man two months earlier.

A man who'd never appeared.

This time I will, Jason had promised her. *If I'm alive, I will.*

But weeks had passed, and she hadn't heard a word from him. He was a ghost. Even so, she wanted to believe that he would be here for their rendezvous, that he wouldn't leave her with nothing. Jason wouldn't be that cruel.

If he was still alive. If the media reports were wrong.

Life had gone on for Abbey since she'd come home. She'd quit *The Fort*; she'd given up her studio apartment. She'd decided that she couldn't go back to the person she was before all of this started, but she still had no idea what she was going to do next. Since then, she'd been in limbo, sleeping on a friend's sofa and wandering the streets of the upper and lower towns in a kind of fog.

Her relationship with Jason needed closure before she

could put away the past. All she could do was count off the days and nights until June 1.

Until now.

Would he show up?

Abbey pulled out her phone and keyed in a text. She'd texted the same number over and over for weeks, but all of her messages had gone into the ether, with no reply.

I'm here, mystery man.

Just like the first time. She waited, staring at her phone, biting her lip. But he didn't answer her. He was never going to answer her. The minutes crept on, just as they had in April, and she was alone. Ten-fifteen came and went. Then ten-thirty. She came to grips with the reality.

The papers were right. Jason Bourne was dead.

Or maybe that was what he wanted her to think. Maybe, like last time, he was watching her right now from somewhere close by, with no intention of coming to meet her. It was his way of saying: *Move on without me.* She got ready to do just that, because he'd given her no other choice. She had to go. She had to figure out her life. She stared down at the river in the grip of a deep depression, and that was when she heard a whisper behind her.

"What do you like most about Quebec?"

Abbey's hands flew to her mouth. She spun around, and there he was. Jason. Alive, unharmed, passion for her written all over his face. She stared back at him, the man who'd kidnapped her, the man who'd nearly gotten her killed, the man she was in love with.

"Those wonderful little maple candies," she replied, hardly able to get the words out.

He took a step toward her, and they wrapped their bodies together and kissed. She could feel the longing pouring out of him, the need for her, the pent-up desire to hold her in his arms. His kiss said all the things he'd never be able to say out loud. His kiss said he loved her, the way she loved him. But his kiss also said something else. She could feel it.

He'd come here for a reason.

He'd come to say goodbye.

The strange thing was, she'd come here to say the same thing. She couldn't stay with him. No matter what they felt for each other, they couldn't be together. Real life didn't work that way. They had to go on alone. Him to his world. Her to whatever came next.

But the hard part could wait.

For the next hour, they sat on a bench in the darkness of the boardwalk, with Jason's arm around her shoulders and her head in the crook of his neck. They talked, and kissed, and talked, and kissed. She thought about suggesting that they get a room at the Château Frontenac, where they could spend the night and make love again. One more time. Before the end. But she didn't do that. It was hard enough, knowing he was going to leave.

"I'm jobless and homeless," Abbey told him eventually, with a little laugh, when he asked about the last several weeks. "I quit all of it."

"I hope you didn't do that for me," he said with a note of concern.

"I didn't, Jason."

"Really?"

"Really. I won't deny that you changed me, but whatever I do next is for me. You were right. I need to figure myself out, and this is the first step. Actually, I guess going with you was the first step, but I didn't know it then. Now I do. Scary or not, I'm doing what you said. I'm jumping out of the plane."

He smiled. "So what are you going to do?"

"I don't know. I'm still thinking about it. But somehow I like not knowing. I like having to think about new choices."

They were both silent for a while. The crowds on the boardwalk grew thinner as the night wore on. The end was getting closer, and as it did, the silences between them got longer. Neither of them wanted to deal with the future.

"Everyone said you were dead," Abbey told him quietly when they ran out of other things to say. "I didn't know what to believe. I hoped they were wrong, but I didn't know. It's been hell."

"I'm sorry."

"Even if you weren't dead, I wasn't sure you'd come."

"I promised I would."

"I know. And I'm glad you did. I'm glad you didn't leave me to wonder."

"Because now you can move on?" Jason asked.

She squeezed his hand tightly. She didn't want to say it, but she said it anyway. "Yes. Now I can move on."

"Good. That's what I want you to do."

"What about you?" she asked.

"My world has no room for outsiders, Abbey. You know that."

This time, she didn't argue with him. "Medusa?"

"It's buried. So is Miss Shirley. You're safe. You're free."

"What about you?" she asked. "Are you free?"

"I'm dead, which is almost the same thing. Nash wants me to stay dead for a while. It's easier to work behind the scenes that way. In the shadows. If people don't expect me, they don't know I'm coming."

Abbey frowned. "Does that mean you're going back to that life?"

"For now. That's all I know. That's who I am."

"Who do you think you are?" she asked, hating what she knew he would say.

"A killer," Bourne replied without hesitation.

Abbey shook her head with regret. That word sounded so harsh from his lips. And so wrong.

"I need to go," Jason went on.

"I wish things were different."

"I do, too."

"But they're not," she said. "Are they?"

"No."

"I guess I should go, too," Abbey murmured. "It's time."

She took his face in her hands and kissed him goodbye, long and slow. She should have left it there, but she couldn't stop herself from asking the question that was in her heart. "Will I ever see you again?"

He didn't answer. She didn't expect him to answer. He simply stared into her eyes from a place she couldn't go.

She eased away from him, already feeling lonely. She got off the bench and went to the railing that overlooked the lights of the old town and the dark snake of the river. Somewhere in the night, she heard a distant echo of music. She took in a breath of sweet, cool air as the wind rustled her hair. She could still taste him on her lips.

"You're not a killer, Jason," she told him quietly, without looking back. "That's not who you really are. That's never been who you are. Someday, I hope you'll see that."

Abbey turned around for one last look.

Bourne was already gone.

Three years ago, Jason Bourne embarked on a
mission in Estonia with his partner Nova,
a fiery UK-based Treadstone agent. Their job was to
rescue a Russian scientist and activist.

They failed.

Three years later, everything has changed for
Bourne. Nova is gone, and Bourne is a lone operative
working for Treadstone. So when he finds out that
the Estonian mission was a set-up and their target is still
hiding, Bourne must find her first—before the
Russians do. And his race to correct the errors of the
past will lead him to one inevitable conclusion:
Some secrets should stay buried.

Tallinn, Estonia
THREE YEARS AGO

FROM the doorway of a shuttered antique shop in the alley, the man known as Jason Bourne observed the holiday market in Tallinn's Raekoja Plats. It was almost time to move. When the moment came, he would have only seconds to get the target safely away, but he already had the escape route visualized in his head. He and Nova had rehearsed it a dozen times in the past two hours. Separate the target, hustle him past the old town hall, and follow Kullasseppa out of the square. Then they'd cross the city's medieval wall to the rendezvous point near the Nevsky Cathedral.

That was the plan, but plans had a way of coming apart once the mission began. In the darkness, with people packed shoulder to shoulder, there were too many ways for an unseen assassin to kill.

His face felt the bite of the bitter cold December

night. An inch of powdery snow had already fallen, trampled into slippery slush by hundreds of footsteps. A church choir sang from the steps of the *raekoda*, their voices competing with the happy chatter of visitors in the rows of open-air shops. Strings of white lights dangled between the rooftops and swayed in the wind, and a fifty-foot brightly lit Christmas tree dominated the center of the huge square. He smelled cinnamon wafting from vats of hot mulled wine.

On his radio, Bourne heard the honey-smooth British accent of his Treadstone partner. "Any sign of Kotov?" Nova asked.

Bourne eyed the stone archway ahead of him. A tunnel led to the restaurant where several of the Baltic defense ministers were having dinner. "Not yet. It should be any minute now."

"You have company," Nova warned him.

"Long beard, fur collar, fleece hood?"

"That's him."

"How many others?" Bourne asked.

"At least four. Looks like Holly was right. The FSB wasted no time sending in a team to take out Kotov."

Bourne's eyes swept the town hall square again. He spotted Nova twenty yards away, browsing at a kiosk that sold German nutcrackers. She wore a beret over her long, lush black hair, and she was dressed in leggings and a zipped navy jacket. Her body was short and pencil-thin. Her green eyes passed over him, too, without showing any sign of recognition. No one in the plaza would have guessed that they knew each other, that they'd worked half a dozen Treadstone missions together in the past year, or that they'd been naked in each other's arms at a Stockholm hotel only seven hours ago, before they got the emergency summons to Tallinn.

"It's go time," Bourne said. "They're coming out."

From under the stone arch, men in business suits and a few women in long winter coats flowed into the square in groups of twos and threes. Bourne knew all of their names and recognized each face, although he'd never met any of them in person. They hailed from the snow-bound north, including countries such as Finland, Latvia, Lithuania, and Poland that bordered the spidery fingers of the Baltic Sea.

And Russia. The Russians were here, too.

"There he is," Bourne whispered.

Grigori Kotov emerged from the tunnel and lingered under the arch as he lit a cigarette. Casually, he blew smoke into the air and pretended to admire the Christmas lights, but his eyes examined the people in the plaza. He was in his fifties and long past his field days, but a spy was always a spy. Something made him nervous, and Bourne knew that the problem wasn't what he saw, but what he didn't see.

His official security was gone. No one was here to protect him. The man's face was as immobile as a mask, but behind that mask was fear. *Where are they?*

Kotov was average height with a meaty Russian build. He wore no hat, as if to prove his toughness in the cold, and his charcoal wool coat was unbuttoned. He had a round face with a salt-and-pepper beard, and his brown hair was trimmed very short, making a sharp *V* in the middle of his high forehead. His skin was pale, marked by a prominent vertical scar on his right cheek, and he had bottom-of-a-well dark eyes and thick lips pushed together in a permanent frown. He still looked like what he'd been thirty years ago. A KGB killer.

Now! Move now!

Bourne marched toward the Russian defense minister with long strides. He noted the killer with the long beard perusing stuffed bears at a kiosk—just a father looking for gifts for his child, not an assassin marking his victim. The man made no move toward Kotov. Not yet. However, Bourne saw his lips moving, and he spotted the edge of a microphone jutting out from under the fleece of the killer's winter cap.

Tick tick tick, went the clock in Bourne's head. *No time!*

"Minister Kotov," he announced loudly as he drew near to the Russian, who tensed with surprise at the stranger calling him by name. "I was hoping we'd run into each other during the conference. My name's Briggs. Charlie Briggs. We had drinks together after the telecom panel in Copenhagen last year. You, me, and Dr. Malenkov."

Kotov was a professional with honed survival instincts. Everyone in the Russian *siloviki*—the Putin political allies with roots in the old Soviet security services—knew a day like this might come. Especially one like Kotov who'd been a U.S. double agent for nearly a decade. The man took a long drag on his cigarette, as if he knew it might be his last one, but his voice remained calm. "Are you quite sure it was Dr. Malenkov? In Copenhagen?"

The Russian knew the CIA signal.

Malenkov. Copenhagen. *You're blown. Your life is in immediate danger.*

"Yes, we went to a bistro on the Nyhavn," Bourne replied. "I'm afraid Dr. Malenkov had a little too much *akvavit.*"

"Ah, yes, now I remember. A most pleasant evening, Mr. Briggs."

"I was hoping you might have ten minutes to talk with me. My company is releasing an upgrade to our security software, and I could give you a look at the latest features."

Kotov's eyes swept the market, and he now saw what Bourne saw. Killers. He crushed his cigarette under his leather shoe in the snow. "Yes, all right."

"My hotel's just off the plaza."

"Excellent."

The two men headed through the market side by side. Wind swirled the snow around them in clouds. The assassin with the long beard glanced their way, undoubtedly reporting that the rules of the game had changed. Kotov wasn't alone. Then the killer took up pursuit down the row of shops. Bourne steered the Russian with a hand on his elbow, and the two of them veered past a kiosk selling scented candles.

Nova reported on the radio. "He's ten steps behind you."

"I need a diversion."

"Understood," she replied. "When you hear the shot, he'll be exactly two steps back. Head for the cathedral."

"See you there."

Bourne kept his pace steady. He didn't accelerate or slow down, as if he wasn't worried about pursuers. He was just an American businessman trying to do a deal with a Russian politician. He pretended to shiver a little in the cold, and he slid his hands into his pockets, where he curled his fingers around the grip of his gun.

Next to him, Kotov walked casually, a man without a care in the world. "I assume we're being followed."

"Yes. There's going to be an incident in a few seconds. Stay close."

"How does Ms. Schultz plan to get me out of the country?"

"Our job is to get you to Holly. After that, the details of getting you out are up to her."

Bourne focused on the crunch of boots in the snow behind him, which got louder as the bearded killer narrowed the gap. Automatically, his brain made calculations, and he estimated that the man was now four paces away.

"Four steps," Nova confirmed on the radio. "He's moving fast."

"Ready."

Bourne slid his finger over the trigger of his gun. An instant later, the loud bangs of an unsuppressed pistol and the shattering of glass rocked the market. Immediately, Bourne drew his gun and spun, seeing the bearded man two steps behind him. Despite the distraction, the man was already lifting his gun, but he wasn't fast enough. Bourne fired into the man's forehead, and the bearded killer crumpled instantly.

Nova kept firing into the air. Screams rippled through the square as people panicked and ran. Bourne dragged Kotov through the crowd toward the south side of the plaza. As they neared the town hall, he checked every face, hunting for the next assassin, the next threat. Everywhere around them, people flooded into the tiny alleys surrounding the market.

It was chaos! *Madness!*

Except for one old woman. She was calm in the midst of the storm.

Too calm!

The woman, at least eighty years old and dressed in colorful peasant clothes, stirred roasted chestnuts in a copper basin near the town hall's stone steps. Her other arm hung stiffly at her side, as if stilled by a stroke. But the woman's bright eyes roamed the plaza like a hawk, and when her gaze landed on Bourne and Kotov, her stiff arm shot instantly upward.

She had a gun in her hand.

"Down! Down!" Bourne shouted. He piled into Kotov and took the Russian to the ground. Shots banged around them, ricocheting off the cobblestones with little explosions of snow. The old woman kept firing, emptying her magazine, and Bourne felt a hot sting in his hand as shrapnel bounced off the pavement. He rolled through the slush and fired back three times, the first shot kicking stone off the wall of the town hall, the next two landing in the old woman's chest. The basin of nuts toppled over as she collapsed forward.

Bourne helped Kotov to his feet. "*Go!*"

They plunged out of the Raekoja Plats into the south-bound street, staying close to the storefronts on Kul-lasseppa. Bourne kept his gun in his hand, level at his waist. He walked quickly, with the older Russian laboring to keep pace beside him. He checked over his shoulder and saw no one following. Ahead of them, he eyed the door-ways and windows in the apartments above them. The crowd of people thinned the farther they got from the square, and soon, they were alone in the darkness.

"Who are you?" Kotov asked, huffing with exertion.

"I'm called Cain."

Kotov stopped to catch his breath. "*Cain?* You're Cain? I've heard of you."

"Oh, yes?"

"Stories get told. The man with no memory. No past."

Bourne didn't react, but he felt a roaring in his head like the surge of an ocean wave breaking over him. The pressure built like that whenever someone mentioned his past. What Kotov said was true: Bourne had lost his memory on a Treadstone mission a few years earlier, when a gunshot to his head had nearly killed him. His entire life had been erased in an instant. Ever since, he'd struggled to start over, not knowing who he really was.

But he couldn't think about that now.

There was no time! The past was irrelevant! The past didn't *exist!*

"Come on," Bourne said, pushing Kotov along the street. "We need to keep going."

"Who betrayed me?" the Russian asked. "Who gave me up?"

"It doesn't matter. The only thing that matters is that Putin knows you've been plotting against him. You can never go home."

Kotov shrugged. "When you do what I've done, you know there will be a price to pay eventually."

"He'll stop at nothing to find you."

"Oh, believe me, I know his methods. When we were both in the KGB, he was my mentor. Later, I ran missions all over Europe that helped him build his power base. But now he stands in the way of change. He has to go."

"Not as long as the *siloviki* and the oligarchs support him," Bourne pointed out.

"They're creatures of self-interest. Many of them think as I do."

"Maybe, but they'll never say so openly. Anyone who knows you is at risk now. Do you have family?"

"My wife is dead. My daughter will disavow me. Denounce me."

"That may not be enough."

He saw the first and only glimmer of emotion on Kotov's face. "Trust me. As of this moment, I'm dead to her."

Bourne raised a hand to silence him. Where the street ended, they reached a walkway that led past the grounds of the medieval church called St. Nicholas and climbed the hill toward the city's medieval wall. The church tower rose above snow-covered trees. There were no signs of life around them, and he saw no footprints in the fresh powder. Even so, his instincts told him that a new threat was close by.

"Do you hear that?" he murmured.

Kotov stopped. "Music?"

"Yes."

Somewhere nearby, a radio broke the silence. A loud burst of pop music soared over the wind. Bourne tried to pinpoint the source, but the song echoed around the buildings before it stopped altogether. It didn't come back.

Oddly, he was sure it had been a Beatles song. "Nowhere Man."

"Let's go," he told Kotov impatiently. "We're almost there."

Two minutes. They were two minutes from the Nevsky Cathedral. They climbed steep steps into the Danish King's Garden near the wall. Up here, they were high enough to see the lights of the city skyscrapers, and beyond them, the dark stain of the Baltic Sea. Fierce wind howled across the garden, and Bourne saw several ghostly statues of monks stalking the wall, their cowls turning white as the snow fell.

His instincts screamed at him again. *Threat!*

This time he saw dents of footprints that the snowfall hadn't completely covered up. Someone was waiting for them.

One of the bent-over monks near the wall seemed to move. A man stepped from behind the statue and fired, but Bourne had already dropped to one knee, and the bullets whistled over his head. He raised his own gun arm and fired back. The man fell, but as Bourne stood up again, he realized that the assassins had merely sacrificed a pawn in order to position a knight right behind him.

The barrel of a gun pushed into the back of Jason's head.

"Cain," a voice said. "Drop your weapon, please."

Bourne let his gun fall into the snow. He raised his arms and turned around slowly. The man in front of him, whose gun was inches from Bourne's face, was young, probably no more than twenty-five. He had scraggly hair tied in a ponytail, and his face still suffered from acne. Despite his youth, the killer carried himself with smart maturity, the product of intelligence training. And yet he didn't look like a member of the FSB—the Russian security service—and he didn't even look or sound Russian. In fact, he didn't look like any covert operative Bourne had seen before. There was nothing governmental about him.

"Lenin," the man murmured into a microphone. "I have them. You were right, Cain is with Kotov. Orders?"

Bourne watched the man's face. He knew his own death warrant had just been signed. He stared into the barrel of the man's gun, but felt no heat from the weapon and smelled no smoke. This man hadn't been one of the FSB team waiting in the square. He was new to the party.

So who was he?

And who was Lenin?

There was no time for answers. In another second, Bourne would be dead.

He saw the young man's finger twitch on the trigger. Then the explosion of a gunshot rippled across the garden. The man's expression changed; it grew surprised, then blank, and his eyes closed. He slumped sideways to the ground, where the blood from the gunshot in his head made a bright red stain against the snow.

Nova joined them from the city steps. The wind threw her long black hair across her face. "Do I have to rescue you every time, Cain?"

"Apparently so."

"We need to move. Holly's waiting for us."

The three of them hurried through a gateway in the stone wall. They climbed a snowy sidewalk toward the white-lit towers and black onion domes of the Nevsky Cathedral. Beyond the church were the pink walls of the Estonian parliament building. Bourne stayed on one side of Kotov, and Nova stayed on the other, their guns moving constantly. He knew someone else was out there, and it worried him that he didn't know who it was.

Lenin. Who was Lenin?

But he saw no ambush at the rendezvous point.

Ahead of them, a woman in her forties sat on a bench across from the cathedral steps. It was night, but she wore dark glasses, and she had a white cane stretched across her lap. She had a bird-like frame and an Audrey Hepburn bob in her dark hair. A yellow lab stood at attention in the snow next to her. As the dog spotted them, it let out three short barks.

Three people approaching.

"Thank you, Sugar," the woman said. Her head

turned as they joined her at the bench. She heard them, but she couldn't see them. Holly Schultz, associate deputy director of the CIA's Russian analysis team, was blind.

"Ms. Schultz," Kotov said. "It's been a long time since our first meeting. St. Paul's Cathedral, wasn't it?"

"Yes, it was. Hello, Grigori. My apologies for the sudden intervention, but we couldn't afford a delay."

"So it would seem."

"You know what needs to happen now?" she asked.

Bourne saw an odd reluctance on Kotov's face, as if the reality of never returning to his homeland had begun to sink in. "Yes, of course."

The Russian turned to shake Bourne's hand in a crushing grip. He did the same with Nova, but his eyes lingered on her face with a long curiosity. Nova's beauty did that to men. "Thank you both for your help."

"Good luck," Bourne told him.

"Dixon will take care of the next steps," Holly continued from the bench. "Everything is ready."

As if on cue, two vehicles sped into view from the rear of the cathedral. The first was a dark sedan with smoked windows; the second was a white panel van with an advertisement for a Helsinki-based commercial painter. Ladders were mounted across the van's roof. The two vehicles drew to a stop in front of the bench where the CIA agent was sitting, and an athletic black man emerged from the passenger side of the sedan. He was thirty years old, with a handsome face that narrowed to a sharp point at his chin, and he was dressed in a dark suit. Bourne knew him. Wherever Holly Schultz and Sugar went, Dixon Lewis wasn't far behind.

"Minister," Dixon murmured to Kotov. He gestured at the back of the panel van. "Shall we go? We only have a few minutes. I'm afraid this part of the journey won't be very comfortable."

"It's fine. Lead the way."

The two men disappeared toward the rear compartment of the van. Bourne heard a scrape of metal and the sound of doors opening and slamming shut. A couple of minutes later, Dixon returned alone, smoothing the creases of his suit. He offered a polite salute to Bourne and Nova and then returned to the sedan.

The two vehicles peeled away again at high speed.

"The car ferry to Helsinki?" Bourne guessed. "Is that how you're getting him out?"

Holly smiled but didn't confirm or deny Bourne's suspicion. She stood up from the bench and stroked Sugar's head as she unfolded her cane. "I'm grateful to the two of you for your assistance tonight. I'll be sure to tell Nash Rollins that you did good work."

That was all. The mission was over.

Holly tapped the ground twice with her cane, and Sugar led her away toward the parliament building through the snow. Bourne watched the agent in her tan trench coat until she'd disappeared around the corner of the cathedral. He was alone with Nova again.

"So we're done," Bourne remarked with acid in his voice.

"Holly and Dixon play it close to the vest," Nova reminded him. "You know that."

Bourne took another look at the empty park. Amid the darkness and the quiet hiss of the snow, his instincts still warned him of danger. They were being watched. He and Nova headed down the walkway away from the church, but he stopped as he heard another pulse of music, loud at first, then fading away. He only caught a snippet before it was gone.

It was another Beatles song.

No, wait—he was wrong. This was a John Lennon solo. "Mind Games."

Automatically, his brain filled in the lyrics, and as he thought about the words, a strange thought flew through Bourne's head.

Not Lenin. *Lennon*.

HALF an hour later, Bourne stood at the windows of their hotel room, which overlooked the Tallinn harbor. From where they were, he could see a car ferry slouching out of Terminal D on its way across the Gulf of Finland toward Helsinki. Somewhere on the lower decks, he was sure, was a white panel van with Grigori Kotov hidden behind a false wall.

Nova came up beside him. She carried two wineglasses in her hands. She'd already undressed, and her naked body was a tapestry of wild tattoos, ranging from roses and feathers to Greek gods and South American tribal masks. A gold chain dangled into the hollow of her full breasts, with a pendant made from an ancient Greek coin encased in a round bezel. Jason knew the necklace had belonged to her mother. Nova never took it off. Not ever.

She stood on tiptoes and teasingly bit his ear and planted kisses on his neck. Her tongue traced circles on his skin. The woman who'd calmly put a bullet in a man's head a few minutes earlier was a coquette now, ready for sex.

That was one of the many things he found attractive about her. She traded identities so easily, a spy and killer one moment, a lover the next.

He was falling in love with her. That was dangerous for both of them.

Rule number one. Never get involved. Treadstone.

"Let it go, Jason," Nova murmured, because she knew he was still obsessing.

He shook his head. "We're missing something."

"The job's done. Kotov is safely away."

"Is he?"

Bourne's gaze followed the lights of the ferry into open water. A moment later, he got his answer. Night turned to day in a brilliant flash. The harbor lit up like the sun, an explosion of fire. A shock wave rippled from the sea, shattered the hotel windows, and made the ground liquid, throwing them off their feet. The noise of the bomb hit like a cannon, and he felt as if his ears were bleeding.

Long seconds of darkness passed.

Dizzy and deaf, he finally pushed himself to his knees. Beside him, Nova was unconscious, her tattooed skin sparkling with a rain of broken glass. Bourne checked to make sure she was alive, and then he stood up and stumbled to the window. Even at this distance, he felt heat on his face and smelled gasoline and char.

Out in Tallinn Bay, there was nothing left of the ferry but smoke and flame.